GENIE OF PASARGAD
(A BABYLON/PERSIA NOVEL)

KRISTIN SWENSON

PG
B

First published in the United States in 2025 by Pretty Good Books, Charlottesville, Virginia

Identifiers: ISBN 979-8-9989339-6-7 (ebook); 979-8-9989339-7-4 (trade paper)

"Amputation," the judge said. "It's a straightforward case with precedent."

Amytis tore her eyes from the prosecuting party and looked at the accused – a girl, her eyes puffy and red, who clutched her robe – not fine – tightly across her chest.

"One breast," the judge said.

Behind her, Atossa's gasp brought Amytis back to this place, the throne room in Babylonia's great palace.

When Amytis had taken her seat, the queen mother's throne in that vast audience hall, she had wondered how it was that a place could seem exactly the same after so much had changed. Mosaics stretched from floor to ceiling in colorful imitation of the palm plantations that dotted the city's environs. Tiles of blue, green, yellow, and orange ran against a white field the length and breadth of this great room just as they had in the days of Nebuchadnezzar... and in the days of their son.

Amytis had felt the carved wood of the throne familiar against her back, the lions' faces beneath her hands, and the down cushion of the seat. And suddenly she had wished for nothing more than to be back in the mountains of Media, galloping through the rich grass of its valleys, free from all of this. Well, some things stayed the same indeed, she thought with a wry smile.

Today, it was not her son who sat beside her in the crown prince's throne. Amel-Marduk was dead, assassinated years ago. Rather, next to her sat Cambyses, nearly twenty years old now, her stepson. And behind him, stood his sister Atossa ('Tossa to some), who could detect the prince's fits before they came. At thirteen years old, she was not a little girl anymore but still every bit Amytis's daughter... except by birth.

On Amytis's other side, the king's throne sat empty. For Cyrus was at this moment travelling, as desolate as the most forlorn of the miles between Babylon and Pasargad. A cart carried the corpse of his beloved Sanda back to the land of her youth, the place where Cyrus had finally found home. Never had he imagined that the promise he'd made to her – that their palace would be in the place of her birth, an idyll that they'd share forever – would only be realized with her death.

Amytis's eyes smarted. She had caused such grief between them. Now here, Amytis faced another woman she had wronged. Amytis's gut clenched.

Gobryas repeated the judge's verdict. "The accused, hired as wetnurse for the Egibi Nupta's infant son, did deceive the aggrieved by secretly taking on additional charges requiring more than the milk she had. She killed the Egibi infant by negligent malnutrition."

"Starved my baby, my only!" the mother – not a young woman – cried out.

Gobryas waited for the echo to die. He continued, "The punishment, amputation of one breast, shall be conducted in the palace prison." Gobryas shuffled his notes to the scribe, who was busy pressing the record into a fresh clay tablet, his stylus all but inaudible against the soft medium.

Amytis heard 'Tossa whisper into her brother's ear.

Cambyses cleared his throat. "A minor change: our physician shall perform the punishment. The girl will remain under observation in the palace after that."

Amytis hardly wondered at the strangeness of 'Tossa's request but heard Nupta sputter with rage while Qudashu, the older woman, kept her peace with the very same grace that had unnerved Amytis so many years before. The bereaved father (whom Amytis could hardly look at, so painfully similar was he to his own father) was silent. The Egibi family turned to go.

"Wait," Amytis said. She stepped down. "I will walk out with you," she said.

They crossed the public hall, busy with all manner of people – palace staff, Babylonians and foreigners alike coming or leaving from the business of the empire's management... – and entered the still bustling but relatively quiet public courtyard.

Qudashu stopped and turned to Amytis, her unlikely queen.

Amytis opened her mouth and shut it again. She glanced at the others.

"Go on," Qudashu said to the young couple. When they'd gone some distance, she turned back to Amytis.

Amytis inhaled, pursed her lips, and then said, "I'm sorry."

"For what?" Qudashu said sharply.

Amytis took a step back, her eyebrows raised.

Qudashu said, "For Khai's death?" Her tone softened. She shook her head lightly. "From the first day I met you, when you came to our house... when Iddina," she glanced over at the man, "was just a little boy," she looked back at Amytis, "I knew that you loved him."

Amytis said nothing.

Qudashu waved her hand lightly, dismissively. "Everyone loved him." But she gave Amytis a searching glance, then turned to go.

"I also hated him," Amytis said.

Qudashu turned back.

"The man who assassinated my son... Khai worked for him."

"Igliss?"

"Your husband once said to me that he aspired to become the king's agent. Igliss became king because he killed my son. Even given our... friendship, Khai served that snake."

Qudashu tilted her head. "He had no choice. Don't you see that? To be allied with you, a sympathetic foreigner, in those days was death. And you were gone. It was a peculiar kindness of yours that you left no friends here, not of any consequence." Qudashu began to leave, then stopped and turned again. "Yet look at you now, back again. And married to our new king, Cyrus... your sister's son." She shook her head. "Rumor was that you would do anything for that land of yours," and walked away.

"I would," Amytis said quietly. "And I will."

PART I

550 – 543 BCE

CHAPTER 1

$\mathcal{I}$n Ecbatana's crowded palace hall, the air thick with a heady combination of celebration, anticipation, anxiety, and ambition, the groom – a simple gold crown nestled in dark curls - looked past the bride. His eyes searched the crowd for that one, most beloved face: his wife's. As for the bride– her own crown pressed against an old, feathered hair clasp hidden on the gray-streaked head, Amytis stood resolute as a mountain, placid as a lake at dawn. She had married for love twice before – love for this wild land, not the man. What was one more?

The wedding was formal and huge. Anyone of any rank and representing every region across the far-flung empire was there. Merchants whose goods – and news and opinions – had international reach, extending even beyond the borders of the empire, also stood among the guests to witness this crucial binding of the former Media to a new Persia. It had been too long in coming, Amytis thought. But her nephew Cyrus had to come to understand for himself that the lands she had so ably managed with her father, the defeated King Astyages could not be protected - the empire would not hold - without the victor, Cyrus of Parsa, marrying her the surviving daughter of the defeated king. Never mind that she was his aunt. Never mind that he was already married. Never mind that Cyrus and Cassandane had wanted to rule a modest kingdom from the idyll of a new capital far south of here. Ecbatana was the capital of the Median empire. Cyrus was its new king. And Amytis would give her life – whatever that looked like – to preserve the wild integrity of this land that she loved.

So it was that hundreds of people witnessed that every step in the old Median tradition was observed, making Cyrus the undisputed monarch of the sprawling Median empire, with its princess Amytis – now queen – beside him. Indeed, since Harpagus had turned the Median army against Astyages to side with Cyrus's scrappy band of Parsans, none other would sit on Ecbatana's throne. By marrying the defeated king's daughter Amytis – to whom foreign delegations, disparate tribes, and the machine of trade that passed through Ecbatana, so crucial to any east-west land route had looked for leadership... by marrying Amytis the former queen of Babylonia, Cyrus would rule a unified empire. This would not be a reduced and weakened Media, vassal of Parsa. It would rather be part of one, greater Persia. In that unity was strength and security.

Despite all this, Cyrus's mood was bleak. Cassandane – Sanda – the one he loved was nowhere present. And it didn't escape his notice that in the gala that followed, his best friend Prexaspes got drunk -- something no one had seen before.

CHAPTER 2

*N*o one knew would know exactly what transpired between Amytis and Cyrus on their wedding night except the couple themselves. There had been no need to make a case for the bride's virginity, since she had already been married twice and had famously born a son whom Medians remembered fondly as their representative on the Babylonian throne, short as his tenure – and life - was. As for the traditional "proof" of intercourse (and whatever charade might satisfy expectations), Amytis laughed. "Preposterous." And no one argued. Not only did she have a formidable position and a reputation to match, it was no secret that she was hardly a model for doing things just because that's how they were done, as she had told the newcomer Cyrus. Yet with age she'd come to appreciate the power of maintaining traditions. Some. So, this one concession: She and Cyrus would spend one night, in her suite of rooms, alone. That, Amytis made clear, would have to suffice. "Do you think any of our allies or indeed anyone of the thousands of disparate peoples from Lake Van to Cyrus's own Anshan care about such details?" No one dared answer. "I didn't think so."

Besides, the rift between Cyrus and Cassandane was painful

for everyone. It cast a jagged edge into the palace atmosphere, threatening to lacerate any who dared to joke about the young king bedding his fifty-year-old aunt.

In truth, the night proved more intimate, some might say, than sex itself. And possibly more exhausting.

* * *

CYRUS AND AMYTIS left the feast side-by-side, when the hall grew rowdy with revel. Back in her suite, Amytis dismissed the attendants. They stood quietly a moment, the only sound the snap and crack of a fire gently burning. Awkward, Cyrus's eyes dropped. When he raised them, he flushed to see the bed, strewn with peach blossoms. Amytis took off her crown, shrugged off the ceremonial ermine cape and replaced it with a chunky woolen weave. Cyrus didn't move. Amytis led Cyrus to a mirror hanging on the wall and bade him look at his reflection there.

"Did anyone tell you that you have your mother's mouth?" Amytis laid a finger on his chin. "Her lower lip swept down just so in the middle like that."

Cyrus flushed a deeper red. "I --"

Amytis stepped away and with one gesture, swept the flowers to the floor.

"It was hardly the only thing that set us apart," she said. Amytis laughed ruefully. She ran her hands over the fine silk bed coverings, gazed up at the embroidery – gold and silver threads through gossamer bed curtains. "This finery was *her* world. And what a princess she was." Amytis laughed again. "And I – a bastard whom your grandfather acknowledged only insofar as I protected Mandane, kept her alive to marry Nebuchadnezzar." Amytis shook her head. "But you know all about that."

Amytis walked to a window, the moon outside casting blue light over the snow-topped turrets of a deck and a silver path across the floor. "Would you like to know more about your mother, about Mandane?"

"Yes," Cyrus said, clearly relieved.

Amytis sat in a chair, hard-backed but finely carved, low. It fit her perfectly. She gestured to another chair. "Sit. We've got all night." She poured them each a cup of wine.

Cyrus smiled.

Amytis told about the sister who had always seemed too precious for the world and their father Astyages who cared nothing about them except that Mandane hurry up, grow up, and clinch the treaty that would protect his throne. "My whole purpose was to keep Mandane alive long enough for her to marry Nebuchadnezzar of Babylon," Amytis said, "So, we were raised side-by-side, but while your mother was good and true, sweet and kind, I was... troublesome. She was perfect and so beautiful. Perfect but for one thing." And Amytis told how Mandane's mother had died giving birth – a condition that Mandane would spend the rest of her life trying to prevent in others, no matter the danger it might pose. "She felt guilty – as if she'd killed her mother herself," Amytis said. "There was no reasoning with her, no arguing otherwise."

"And that's how you know the best midwives," Cyrus said.

Amytis nodded. "I picked up some such skills of my own along the way," she said. Her eyes clouded briefly, remembering the crisis of her closest friend, Nebuchadnezzar's daughter... Igliss's wife. So many memories. Amytis tossed her head clear of them. She smiled at the young man before her. Mandane's son, what great grace that here he was, Amytis thought, alive and well. "Cassandane is in good hands," Amytis said.

Cyrus grinned to hear it, though she could see that his relief was shot through with the pain unique to hurting the very one you love.

"And your own mother?" Cyrus asked.

Amytis sighed. "I had had no idea... All her life..." Amytis shook her head, took a deep breath. "My mother was enslaved," she began. "I was born at the same time as Mandane and immediately removed in order to be raised alongside your mother, as Mandane's buffer to the world, her guard and protector. Shortly after that, when we were yet newborns, there was a fire. Everyone said that during the chaos, my mother ran – ran away, escaped her bondage... and abandoned me." Amytis shook her head. "Nothing could be further from the truth. The woman who nursed both Mandane and me, a woman badly disfigured... the woman who raised us was herself a slave. Kara, we called her – Karadara, itself a bastardization of something like the word for a bonded servant.

"She insisted on accompanying me to Babylon and so became mine, my property. She was with me through... everything. She didn't leave me even after I'd been stripped of title *and property*, imprisoned... and released. Kara died helping me to save my son Bushu (Amel-Marduk), the prince imprisoned by his own father Nebuchadnezzar." Amytis blotted away the tears that had gathered.

"Kara had set that fire," Amytis said. "She had burned herself unrecognizable to stay with me. I learned that truth only moments before she was killed. For me." Amytis inhaled deeply, gathering herself. Then, with a smile, "But. Your mother. Perfect, as I said but for one thing. As it happened, that very thing that she simply could not keep from doing – ensuring the health of birthing women at risk of dying from what had killed Mandane's own mother – would have gotten her into terrible trouble in Babylonia. They would have killed her for it. And *that* would have rendered void the treaty that would otherwise protect this place. When I learned that... and that the treaty itself hadn't been finalized..." Amytis hesitated a moment before telling Cyrus about the moment when everything changed, the moment when the woman who sat talking with him now switched identities with his mother. "So I became the daughter of King Astyages who ended up marrying Nebuchadnezzar.

"I did it without any thought. Protecting your mother had become an instinct, a reflex. On the day she was to leave, it suddenly became clear that Babylon could be a very dangerous place for her. Without thinking, I stepped in. I'd thought it would be temporary, just long enough for me to make sure that the treaty was secure, Media safe. But it wouldn't have been safe – not Media, not Mandane. There were many many times over the years that I wished for nothing but..." Amytis shook her head. "Ironies abounded. Anyway, after a little while, Astyages married your mother off to Cambyses of Parsa, your father.

"I was worried about her at first – moving to that rude and petty place, far to the south -- Anshan in Parsa. But I soon learned what I needed most to know: she was happy. She loved your father." Amytis raised her eyebrows in disbelief. "I couldn't imagine it. I didn't love Nebuchadnezzar. Love wasn't even relevant for marriages such as ours..." Seeing Cyrus grimace, she said gently, "You did the right thing with this," Amytis gestured between the two of them. Cassandane will come around. Anyway, the rest you know," Amytis said. "Almost, anyway."

They sat quietly, then, each wandering individual paths of memory, longing, and loss.

"Thank you," Cyrus said.

"For what?" Amytis asked, an edge in her voice.

"For telling me about my mother."

"She was better than me."

Cyrus smiled. "Time will tell."

Amytis shook her head. "I've done more bad in the time I've survived her than I have years to make it up."

Cyrus looked puzzled.

"I am forever causing problems even while I try to do what's best." Amytis took a deep breath and a sip of wine. "In Babylon, I tried to help other foreigners, people distrusted and resented, like me. I raised my son that way. But when he became king, something neither or us ever imagined would happen, that made Amel-Marduk even more unpopular. I had no love for Nebuchadnezzar; you know that. But I did fall in love in Babylon. And if that weren't bad enough, it cost my son, Amel-Marduk, his life and with that a throne sympathetic to Babylonian diversity."

Cyrus shook his head, his brow pulled tight. "I don't understand."

"You know that Nebuchadnezzar was unparalleled among leaders in his conquest of foreign lands."

Cyrus nodded.

"He was also without peer in his building projects throughout the empire and beyond."

"Yes."

"Well, all of those accomplishments took a tremendous work force – not only hands and feet but minds and skill – highly trained professionals for all kinds of sophisticated tasks. Nebuchadnezzar recognized those skills in the peoples he conquered. He selectively removed those individuals from their native lands to settle in Babylonia. The best craftsmen, the finest artists of all sorts from literary to architecture to music..."

"I see."

"Babylon itself was a cosmopolitan wonder. What you don't see is how threatening that diversity began to feel to many of Babylonia's oldest families. After all, with time, the exiles, many of whom held reputable positions and led comfortable lives had children of their own, children who had known only Babylonia. Resentment grew, ever more as Nebuchadnezzar declined, people who believed that the nation they loved, their home, was at risk of becoming unrecognizable to them, that what had made it great was dissolving into the languages, dress – and demands – of people they considered to be foreign. I saw it myself – a foreigner, and in the palace no less.

"So where was your fault?"

Amytis took a deep breath. "There was a man, Babylonian – but not of the citizenry, not the elite…"

Amytis told Cyrus about Khai – selectively, but enough she thought – her finding in him a Babylonian she could trust, someone with whom she even shared a kind of closeness, connection. Nabu-ahhe-iddin, Khai, the one who built a family fortune and reputation that had earned his family a rare place in the company of those privileged by birth. "Yes, it felt like love." And Amtyis told about Amel-Marduk's own ill-fated love, about the rise in anti-immigration sentiment among native Babylonians and long-time residents, and how she suspected Igliss in the assassination of her son. "The worst of it, though, is simply selfish," Amytis said, her eyes swimming. "Khai was Igliss's business agent through it all. The man that I loved, and who I believe loved me was my enemy's friend. He became the most trusted official in Igliss's entourage. Khai has served the throne ever since."

"To include King Igliss, I suppose," Cyrus said with a bitterness that surprised Amytis. Cyrus jumped up and began pacing the room. Amytis watched his jaw fix tight. The muscles in his neck tightened, and his hands at his sides clenched and unclenched. "This Khai, he betrayed you," Cyrus said.

Amytis said, "I shouldn't have told you."

"No. You should. I'm glad you did."

"But it's not your concern. It's past now. Igliss is long dead, and Babylonia's king Nabonidus is a good man. His son Belshazzar…" Amytis grimaced.

"What of him, the crown prince?"

"Let's just say he's more like Neriglissar – Belshazzar deeply admired Igliss," she explained, "than he is like his father. Always wanting more – for Babylonia, no matter the cost, long-term or to anyone else." Amytis shuddered. It was that threat – to wild Media's integrity – that was her greatest concern.

"And Khai?"

Amytis winced. He alone among the Babylonians had understood, had seen and felt the love Amytis had for this land. And
then to turn around and work for the man whose ambition and
greed spelled her son's death and threatened her land... Amytis
had tried to avoid thinking about Khai, tried to avoid thinking of
Babylonia at all. But his success had made that impossible. "I hear
from merchants passing through that the Egibis have become a
quite a force... "

"Egibi did you say?"

Amytis nodded.

"What kind of force?"

"Business, generally. Trade, banking, real estate, you name it."
Amytis shrugged. "He grew it from nothing. Now it's a family
empire."

"And that family is Egibi." Cyrus sat. It wasn't such a stretch –
merchants – that that man in the market, Anshan... "Does he
have a son?"

"Yes," Amytis said softly. She remembered, so long ago: that
little boy leaning against his mother's knee, Amytis awkward in
the modest house Khai had recently bought... Her eyes cleared.
"Probably several by now, daughters, too. Why?"

"I think I met him in Parsa some years back."

Amytis shrugged, pretending indifference. "It's possible. They
trade everywhere." And she thought about how desperately she'd
hoped that Khai would be in Susa when she and Spitamas with
Nathan had gone to visit.

"Here?"

Amytis snorted. "Not since I've been here." Then, seeing
Cyrus's anger, she said, "I hardly think of it now."

"But such betrayal --"

"Is done," Amytis said. "Have some wine." Amytis changed the
subject to Cyrus's childhood, a tale, which elicited flashes of the
same fury at betrayal that she'd just seen. Cyrus also told the

bittersweet trajectory of his relationship with Cam, the king whom Mandane left bereft and desperate when she took her life.

When Cyrus described the wicked groundsman, pacifying Cam with opium and manipulating the governance of Parsa and rendering many of its people destitute, Amytis recognized both the recent visitor to Media and the circumstances that led the woman Amel-Marduk loved to fall into slavery. Later, she thought, she would figure out how to tell him about these connections.

As it was, Cyrus had become transported by his memories, and Amytis simply listened. She felt like a stow-away traveling with him back to his childhood as a shepherd slave on the outskirts of Ecbatana, to his first days at Anshan, to the years he spent avoiding that palace, so as it was with its stress and despair, and then to Pasargad, the note of which lit his eyes with warmth.

Cyrus told about the mare he brought from Media, the falcon he found by the lakes. He told about his reunion with Mit and Spaco and learning the full extent of the groundsman's deceit. Cyrus talked about meeting Prexaspes, how fraught it was –

"He's the one always at your side, yes?"

Cyrus nodded.

Amytis raised her eyebrows. "Devoted."

"He hated me then." Cyrus shook his head in disbelief. "And now married. No one thought he would."

Cyrus's voice softened when he recalled first seeing Sanda, so tall and proud, confident, simply unashamed of her interest and intelligence. He had loved her from the beginning, he said, like he loved her land, the high plateau, the deep cut gorges... Amytis nodded. She knew something about the power of place.

Cyrus told of the Pasargadae's suspicion, how when he showed up after many days of living decamped from the palace and with the tortured body of their kin they didn't think he could possibly be a prince. He told of exiling the groundsman from

Anshan and nursing Cam back to a kind of health independent from the opium.

Cyrus laughed when he recalled the pregnant mare and returning to Pasargad to ask Sanda to marry him. He described the relief that made him weep when Sanda safely delivered a baby -- a boy they named Cambyses after the grandfather who died immediately afterward, making Cyrus King of Anshan. And he told of the horror of Cambyses' first epileptic fits.

Cyrus was suddenly quiet.

Amytis held her breath.

Then, Cyrus looked at her. "I wanted to move the palace from Anshan to Pasargad –"

"Cassandane's home," Amytis observed.

"And I hoped, mine. I never really knew home until I saw that place. Neither did I know family, not a real one, until I married her and gained a father and a brother, too... Cyrus grimaced. "I promised her. I thought we would live there for the rest of our lives -- I, a simple king for a simple land with the most wonderful woman in the world beside me. I would reacquaint Anshan in friendship with the kingdoms around and raise Parsa's next king to be decent and just, and daughters, besides..."

"And now you have one," Amytis said gently, "newborn, a daughter. 'Tossa."

But Cyrus didn't hear her. His eyes went flat remembering all that had dashed his idyll. "Then, Astyages attacked," he said.

Amytis's voice broke the silence that followed. "And the very thing my father – your grandfather – dreaded came to pass. You conquered Astyages –"

"It was Harpagus."

"In part," Amytis said. "Well, whether you wanted it or not, this is how things are. Listen. Media was never as unified as Astyages had wishfully assumed." Amytis set down her wine and took Cyrus's from him. She called him into the adjacent room, a room cluttered with documents and the stuff of a kingdom's administration. Amytis lifted a scroll from one of the wall cubbies and laid it on a table. While Cyrus held one side, she unrolled it to the other. A map.

"I have no doubt," Amytis said, "that immediately after Astyages's defeat, some of Media's tribes began making plans to rebel if not to actually to try to subject others. We need to tend the alliances we've made and be prepared to subdue aggression." She pointed to a region northwest of the place they stood, the palace at Ecbatana.

"We need to bring Urartu back in line."

Indeed, even while they talked on into that night of things personal and political, of beliefs their own and as puzzling as the Jews', as they talked of loyalty and the high cost of betrayal, their new Persian empire faced threats from all sides. The Urartian defection was serious enough. And meanwhile, Media's former ally, Croesus of Lydia was plotting to take it all.

CHAPTER 3

*A*mong the recommendations that Amytis had for managing former Media, the sprawling Persia, was to install capable leaders in each of its discrete territories. And she stepped into the shadows. So it happened that Cyrus granted the most prestigious post to his and Cassandane's closest friends. Vishtaspa and his wife Hutaosa (namesake of the baby 'Tossa) left for the east with their little boy Darius. They would begin the work of managing Parthia, a broad territory extending to the edge of the former Media's frontier. Cyrus missed Vishtaspa's wise counsel and the gentle intelligence of Hutaosa; but he was confident that they were the best choice to govern the proud Parthians. And maybe Cassandane would ease out of her self-imposed shell.

But, Cassandane's silence continued. She wouldn't speak to Cyrus or to anyone except to agree to a wetnurse for 'Tossa. With the trauma of Cyrus's marrying another woman, the daughter of the king who had attacked their little country no less, the once bold Cassandane, pride of Parsa's most noble tribe lost interest even in her own newborn baby.

Cassandane quit attending on the baby altogether. Cyrus took another suite in the palace. But their son, the young Cambyses was blessedly busy; and (by Cyrus's command) the clubfooted orphan Gobyras with him. At ten years old, the crown prince had a schedule of study and training that barely left him any time with his mother. Yet even when Cambyses had one of his fits, a wracking experience that rendered him bruised and bleeding, Cassandane would not be present. All she did was sit in the seat at the window of her bedroom and stare at the mountain behind. The man that she loved, the partner who had adopted her home and family as his own, the father of her children, had married someone else. And not just anyone, but someone who Cassandane believed attacked their home and stole the hope she'd had of settling there in peace forever. And now they lived in her home, in Ecbatana. Call it what you will, to Cassandane, it was Amytis's country. It didn't matter that Amytis made herself scarce, absented herself from the palace.

Truth was, it was no sacrifice to Amytis at all. The palace had never been her home, not in her heart, anyway. That belonged to the wild land all around. The great trees, the mountain meadows, clear rushing streams, hawks and shy golden jackals had always been more family to her than any human she had known. And the great Nisean horses, made strong on the region's rich alfalfa were simply an extension her legs, her body, and her spirit. So, exactly as she had done for as long as she could remember, when the palace – huge as its columned halls, and many paneled rooms were – felt claustrophobic for the stress of suspicion and unhappiness within, Amytis would ride. She remained studiously distant and ignorant of Cyrus's private life. Another thing she'd regret soon enough.

Nine months after the wedding, Prexaspes' wife (a title that seemed odd, since he virtually ignored the pretty girl after that first night) bore a son, a golden boy. Everyone in the palace was smitten by the sweet infant Aspacanah. Everyone, that is, except Prexaspes, who could not have cared less. Not for the baby, not for its mother. If anything, the baby engendered a kind of hostility from Prexaspes, and it couldn't be explained by any misplaced jealousy for his wife's attentions. Prexaspes distanced himself from them both.

* * *

Mid-March, and the land around Ecbatana was still almost as cold as the atmosphere inside the palace. The rift with Cassandane left Cyrus irritated and restless. The baby 'Tossa, who had cried incessantly for the first weeks after Cassandane rejected her, was now even more alarmingly quiet and listless – alarming to those tasked with her care. Cambyses whined that Gobryas was obnoxious; and Prexaspes kept needling Cyrus to travel -- away, Cyrus assumed, from the demands of Prexaspes' new wife and baby. The uprising in Urartu gave them a welcome excuse.

Cyrus rubbed his hands together and said to Harpagus, "We'll need the army, a good number of infantry for the mountains, I suppose; only a few chariots, but plenty of riders. Distances, how far are we talking?" But Cyrus wasn't looking for an answer. He had forgotten that Harpagus was even there. "We'll leave as soon as the roads permit."

Harpagus cleared his throat. "Would you like to know more? I'll get Amytis."

"No." Since the wedding, Cyrus had done all he could never to be in the same room as she, and never alone. "I'll learn what I need from the military men. Meanwhile, let's see, I want to put a Parsan in charge there; and --" He looked to the servant at the door. "Is Prexaspes around? And fetch the Sagartian from the hall."

Harpagus pursed his lips.

"It was her idea, in the first place," Cyrus said. "She warned about Urartu, their restlessness."

Seeing Cyrus occupied with a map of the area and looking happy for the first time since marrying Amytis and the falling out with Sanda, Harpagus left.

CHAPTER 4

"$\mathcal{S}$ome troubling news, sir." The messenger found Belshazzar still lingering over his morning meal. In the crown prince's quarters, as ostentatiously appointed as the man himself, Belshazzar nibbled another pastry – almond with honey, well fried. Still the messenger stood.

Belshazzar wiped a crumb from his lips, carefully combing the beard below with his fingers – a habit not necessity. Not by accident, it was as usual perfectly coiffed in the latest Babylonian style (not by no little effort, since only half of Belshazzar's genetic make-up was Babylonian). "Well?"

"To the north, sir, the peoples of Urartu have revolted –"

"They're not *ours*, are they?" Belshazzar asked, peeved.

"Well. No, sir. Part of the former Media, now this... Persian's territory. He's mobilizing troops. There could be trouble... and not far from our border, not far from Harran," the messenger added.

"If that's all..." Belshazzar scowled at the man. "Oh, wait."

* * *

PRIVATELY, the Babylonian crown prince was delighted with the news. Finally an opportunity, an excuse really, to bolster his image as a pure Babylonian, devoted to Marduk, to show that he'd only been acting on the king's controversial wishes for Harran, not his own. He'd already been rewriting – merely editing, really – the inscriptions that King Nabonidus had dictated in order that credit go to Marduk, Babylon's high god, not to Nanna-Suen. If his father was so determined to favor the god of his youth, he could damn well come back from the desert and do it himself. As it was, Belshazzar did enjoy playing the part of king in his father's absence; but he bristled at the charge to execute policies that might undermine his image in the eyes of blueblood Babylonians.

"I have decided to abandon our projects in Harran for the time being," Belshazzar said to Khai. "The Persian is taking up arms against Urartu. Who knows what's next – the west? It's too risky for us to remain there. We'd be right in his path. Besides, Media has controlled Harran since the Assyrians. We're only there because my father, on account of some misplaced sentimentality and pressure from his mother, wishes to rebuild the temple of Nanna-Suen. I dictated orders that we move out of Harran. Now."

Khai simply nodded. Belshazzar liked the man. And was slightly intimidated by him, too. The Egibi seemed to rise above politics altogether. He'd served every king since Nebuchadnezzar, weathering coups, assassinations... all while expanding his business(es). Everybody respected him. And he didn't seem to care one way or the other.

In truth, Khai was relieved. Yes he had, and if he were judicious about it, still would serve the kings of Babylonia in a powerful role. After the assassination of Amytis's son, he'd been even more determined to do what he could to remain it the role, business agent of the crown. He did it in no small part to shield what Amytis loved – wild Media – from Babylonian greed. If he managed well the affairs of the royal family and by extension the nation itself, he would have some control over what they did vis-à-vis Media. He missed her.

"Meanwhile, I trust that plans for the lion hunt are progressing."

Again Khai nodded.

"I want to gather the party in Gutium on the first full moon after the New Year – that place where the Zab meets the Tigris. It's not far from the military outpost of Dur Karushu," he said. And, Khai thought, in the most lucrative trade location after (a distant second) Ecbatana - a site suitable for the grand tastes of one such as Belshazzar.

"I and my entourage," Belshazzar said, "can be there. Make sure that the Gutian chief or his son join us."

Belshazzar knew that he couldn't very well argue that the threat from Cyrus was serious enough to require Babylonia's leaving Harran without also demonstrating some military commitment. His advisors told him that spending some time at Dur Karushu should be sufficient.

* * *

BELSHAZZAR MIGHT HAVE EXPECTED that it was Adad-guppi, his ancient grandmother, who put up the most resistance. She begged the crown prince, her son the king's proxy regent to continue in Harran.

"I know these things, Shazzi. I am more than one hundred years old. I have seen much, and I know that this is the time for Nanna-Suen. I felt the hands of God, the king of the gods Nanna-Suen, upon me. He said, 'With you, I will charge your son Nabonidus to return the habitation of Harran and to rebuild the Elhulhul, to restore and perfect it.'"

For as long as he would listen, Adad-guppi argued that it was divine will that they finish building. The moon god would reward them for the effort and protect not only his city but also the Babylonians who had rebuilt it so carefully.

It wasn't long before Belshazzar interrupted her. "We have to leave. But Dur Karushu is on the Euphrates only a little way south of Harran... It's near Sippar --"

"Near Sippar is not 'only a little way' from Harran."

"Well. That's where I've decided that we should set up." He tried to sound concerned – and responsible – adding, "I don't know what the Persian is planning to do next, but he has gained much and proved unafraid to attack. We need to be ready."

"Cyrus isn't attacking a different nation, Shazzi. Urartu was supposed to be within Median control. What makes you think he'd attack us in Harran? Besides, this is Amytis we're talking about."

"But *Cyrus* is king. Women don't decide."

Adad-guppi sighed. "Yet here you are, talking to me..."

"The Medes occupied Harran before us, remember."

"I was there, priestess to the great Nanna-Suen."

But Belshazzar wasn't listening. "Even if Cyrus isn't expanding westward," he said, "he probably thinks that Harran, like Urartu, should simply be part of his empire. This is not the time to start a war over Harran. Nor is it my place to do so. Father made it clear that I am not king, even while he's off smoking with those desert Arabs."

"Nanna-Suen will protect Harran. Rebuilding the great god's Elhulhul will bring divine favor, and a man cannot prevail against the gods."

"Then let's trust Nanna-Suen to keep the Elhulhul safe until we're sure that Cyrus won't move against us. We can return and finish what's left to be done on the temple later."

Adad-guppi's lower jaw shook but her eyes were unwavering. "You know as well as I that the gods may judge our retreat as a lack of trust and allow the city's defeat to this tent-dweller. Besides, I'm an old woman, Shazzi. I have dreamed all my life of seeing the Elhulhul shining like heaven again, with all the songs and the prayers filling its holy space and making Nanna-Suen smile. Please."

But Belshazzar was already at the door. "We leave within the week," he said.

Despite the sudden absence of his stout presence, the aura of his ambition lingered. Adad-guppi felt tiny, defeated. Her shoulders dropped as she took the arm of the eunuch who hurried forward to guide her out.

Within a matter of days, Belshazzar, his guards, friends, Adad-guppi, their slaves and servants began to make their way to Dur Karushu.

CHAPTER 5

*P*rexaspes answered Cyrus's summons before Cyrus even had a chance to finish his point with the Sagartian tribal chief's son. Cyrus gestured for Prexaspes to sit while he continued his conversation.

"We will bring the Urartians to heel," he said to the Sagartian, "and when we do, I want you to be our liaison there."

The man, thirty years old or so, quiet and composed, agreed. One of the noblemen who had accompanied Cyrus from Parsa with the army after Astyages' defeat, he had seen Cyrus's leadership in that context and was grateful that Cyrus had finally married the woman with whom the Sagartians had dealt far more effectively than with her father, the king. He thanked Cyrus for the honor and pledged to maintain the people's loyalty when it was done.

Cyrus turned to Prexaspes. "The Urartians have revolted. They claim that they should be as independent as in the days of the Manneans. But the world has changed. It is time," Cyrus said, "that the peoples learn that I am not another Astyages, and this is not the Median empire continued. We are creating a new thing. We are all Persians, now. Each of the territories, when they beg for new leadership as the Urartians are doing, shall find it in the Persian men that I appoint. He clapped his hand on the Sagartian's shoulder.

"Prexaspes, talk strategy with me." Cyrus dismissed the Sagartian nobleman and then threw himself down in a chair. "This place, Prex, is killing me."

"I'm as eager as you to leave."

"And your son? Everyone says he's a charming little thing, smart and affable."

Prexaspes was silent.

"Send the boy with 'Tossa, if you like."

"They're the same age and just weaned, I think. They should have play companions, now."

"Babies?"

Cyrus shrugged. "Friends. Why not each other?"

"And what of Otanes? Word has it that Zarin is miserable. Hates the cold and makes everyone around her suffer for it."

"He'll not want to leave her then," Cyrus said, recalling the way that his brother-in-law doted on this wife who seemed to everyone else to be nothing but grief. "No," Cyrus shook his head. "I'd rather he stay to help with things here, anyway."

The men turned to the business of military strategy, how best to subdue the Urartians should armed action be necessary. Each egged the other on until they could hardly bear the delay that preparations and the weather imposed.

* * *

AMYTIS WAITED a few days hoping that Cyrus's battle hunger would have waned. Then she went, mid-day to the strategy room. Cyrus was there standing at the middle of a long table and bent over charts. Two men that Amytis recognized as new military commanders sat on either side of Cyrus, their elbows forming an arc around the documents.

Cyrus looked up, startled.

The men stood and began to gather their things.

"They can stay," Amytis said, thinking of the pains Cyrus had taken since their wedding night never to be alone with her. She smiled at each of the men and nodded to them to sit back down.

They glanced at Cyrus and sat, each straight- backed on the edge of his chair.

"It concerns the Urartians," Amytis said. "I'll be brief. I believe the conflict can – and should – be resolved without force."

One of the men leaned forward, clearly about to speak.

"You'll let me finish," Amytis said.

The man sat back, chastened.

Amytis went on. "First, it's a large territory and quite wealthy. The timber is unparalleled. Like us they breed excellent horses raised on rich grasses of fertile soil. They make the best wine that you will probably ever taste and trade in exquisite bronze castings treasured throughout the world. They have several massive fortresses on the borders of the territory; and I've heard that their palace citadel, made of stone and erected by skilled craftsmen, is a mile long."

Again, Amytis anticipated interrupting protest from one of the men. "I'm not saying that the Medes -- excuse me, your, our... Persians cannot defeat them in battle. But there is another way. Consider: the country is now only Urartian in name. Some time ago, a group of people from the north around the Black Sea, who had long done business with the Urartians and lived peaceably in the area, took advantage of weaknesses in leadership and gained control."

The men looked at each other. They tilted their heads, raised their eyebrows, and nodded. Each sat back.

"They didn't push the Urartians out and most remained, intermarrying and generally getting along with the new power. But the king is not Urartian. He is Arminan. By the name of Tigran, I think."

"What do you suggest?" Cyrus asked.

"Two things: take advantage of what nationalism remains among the Urartians. In their time, they were an extraordinary people. Even as they have accommodated the Arminans, I'm sure that there are some who recall their history of independence with at least a little nostalgia. There is much to remind them. Rusa II, their last king, was one of the greatest builders of all time. Those people may be less willing to risk reprisal from you, from Media.

"The other: notice how the people have assimilated to each other. There was no great military take-over by the Arminans as far as I know. Rather, they learned a way to benefit from each other rather than constantly struggle for an upper hand. Urartu was a cooperative vassal of Media in years past. My grandfather Cyaxares, even though he was the stronger, respected the Urartians and accommodated strong Armenian leadership.

"It was with my father that things went bad. Astyages alienated a lot of people by his remote demands and failure to cultivate respectful relationships with them. I'd rather not see it happen again. Also, whether you like it or not, this will not be the last resistance we'll face. If we can spare our troops, we'll be stronger when force really is necessary."

Cyrus was quiet. He tilted his head first one way, then the other, as if letting the weight of what she said roll from one side to the other, then gave a quick nod. "Thank you. Aunt."

"Another thing," Amytis said. "In case anyone asks, I'll not be going with you. The Urartian matter is not our only concern. It's good for one of us to stay here at the capital. Besides," she looked at Cyrus, "It's best that we don't both go."

Amytis was surprised, then, when riding out from the palace, Cyrus cantered up beside her.

"Ride with me a while?" he asked.

After they'd loped past the palace walls and reined the horses to a walk, Cyrus asked Amytis more about the Urartians and their Armenian king, everything she could tell him about the landscape, the different peoples. She did.

"I'll go with an army," Cyrus said, "I want to fight."

"I know you do." Amytis reined her horse to a stop. The streams rushed high this time of year. At her urging, her heavy mount picked his way carefully across. "Their greatest god is Haldi," Amytis told Cyrus. "You might remember that."

Amytis rode on well after Cyrus had headed back.

The air off the melting snows felt good on Amytis's face as she cantered back to the palace. There were some things a person could do nothing about. She watched Cyrus, several lengths ahead, sitting easily the quick horse she knew had been a wedding gift – his to Sanda – ages ago. She hoped he still carried a shred of the desire for peace that he and Cassandane had wished for in Pasargad.

* * *

WHEN THE TROOPS were finally gathered, outfitted, and ready, it was April. The foothills were greening, the streams rushing with the drive of water loosed from ice, and pale blossoms on the fruit trees draped the landscape in lace. Even though Amytis was far from the palace when the Persian troops rode out of its gates, Sanda did not see Cyrus off. He had tried to reconcile with her before leaving but succeeded only in stirring up the children – Cambyses and Gobryas begging to go, while the baby 'Tossa toddled restless (no doubt picking up on all the nervous energy). Prexaspes, for his part, ignored his wife's efforts to elicit affection before he rode. Neither man spoke to the other all day, though they went side by side.

CHAPTER 6

"*T*he bread is delicious and with all of the herbs that you love," Adad-guppi's attendant said to her. "And the yogurt, fresh with golden honey... Can I help you with it?"

"I'm just not hungry, dear." Adad-guppi looked away. Her jaw shook all the time now.

The servants performed their tasks quickly, hushed and embarrassed by the change in their mistress. Instead of her cheerful recital of hardships and ordeals, taken captive as a young mother to a strange country, her perseverance in believing that Nanna-Suen had reasons for everything, her successes in the court before Nebuchadnezzar had ascended the throne – so many stories! – and bragging about Nabonidus her son now king, Adad-guppi now sat for long stretches without saying a word. It seemed she had left her vitality with the hopes she'd had for Harran all those miles away. Aides doted on her, their anxiety reflected in near constant attention.

Belshazzar stopped by.

Newly energized (only Belshazzar had such effect, and that because only he could revitalize the work in Harran), Adad-guppi shooed her attendants away. "Such worry! Don't you know I'm too old to die? Sit down, Shazzi."

Belshazzar, still standing, said, "I trust you're comfortable. The quarters are spare but should be sufficient." His words were clipped, perfunctory. "Let me know if you need anything." Another moment, and he was gone.

The old woman sighed. For a while, Adad-guppi sat unmoving, quiet, her head tipped back. When she opened her eyes again, her jaw was still. She reached for the bread and savored it slowly. Adad-guppi summoned a scribe. She smiled at his youth.

"Write these things for me," she said. "With the reverence which Nanna-Suen has placed in me, the king of the gods has made me flourish -- me, imagine! My eyes, both of them, see clearly. My mind has never failed me. My limbs are healthy, hands and feet. All my life, I have chosen my words with care, making friends easily. I get along with everyone. Food still gives me pleasure. I can eat everything, and my heart has been glad. I have seen descendants. I am satisfied. O Nanna-Suen, king of the gods, you have looked on me with favor and given me long life."

On April 6, 547 BC, Adad-guppi, the Aramean woman who had been taken captive, decades earlier, into Babylon's foreign court, who kept her native piety even while she rose in reputation and power to become the queen mother of Babylon, died at a military outpost on the Euphrates River. She was 104 years old.

* * *

BELSHAZZAR HAD PARTICIPATED in the Babylonian New Year festival of Marduk's *akitu* only a few weeks earlier and had been looking forward to the lion hunt-- not so much the hunt itself, such things unnerved him, but what it would do for his popularity. The event should clinch his image as crown prince committed to traditional Babylonian ways while currying the favor of the empire's elite.

But when Adad-guppi died, King Nabonidus returned from the desert immediately. The hunt was off. And Belshazzar was demoted as his father resumed his kingly duties in the capital to lead Babylonians in mourning the queen mother.

CHAPTER 7

*C*yrus took his time traveling from Ecbatana to Urartu. Sure, the roads were still muddy, making travel difficult for the supply carts and foot soldiers. In truth, there didn't seem to be any real hurry. The Urartian revolt had taken the form of withdrawal, not attack, so Cyrus felt they had time. Besides, he wanted to think.

Prexaspes kidded him about it. What was there to think about? All they needed to do was locate the power centers, give them a punishing treatment, threaten more of the same, and the rest of the region would be cowed enough to step in line. But many of Cyrus's own troops were new to his command -- soldiers from Ecbatana, from Luristan, and Patusharra, the Busae, Arizanti, and Struchates -- each of them and others, too, with their own customs, local histories, points of pride, and beliefs.

Mostly, Cyrus contemplated Amytis's warning. He had heard her indeed, and time and distance from the palace had cleared his mind. Some. He thought about her warning, about creating resentment among people who were actually part of the greater empire. Would they wonder if they're next... if Cyrus might turn on them and attack... should they insist on some form of self-definition?

They tracked north through the Zagros mountains. Cyrus had considered the easier route west out of the mountains to the Tigris and then following the river north where it became placid within a lush landscape – inspiration, the Jewish scribe Nathan had told him, for the Jews' stories of Eden, a garden at the beginning of everything. Cyrus would have loved to see the ancient Assyrian palaces; but there'd been too much Babylonian activity in the region, especially Harran, and he didn't want to risk yet another confrontation. So they followed familiar mountain valleys and passes up from Ecbatana, moving west across the range until a scout reported that from "that peak there" he saw the sun reflect the glittering waters of Lake Urmia.

* * *

THEY WERE in Urartian territory now, Cyrus's guides were certain of it. The change in energy was palpable – nervous now, wary. Cyrus looked up into the steep rocky hillsides at the yawning entrance to caves. Median soldiers told him that the caves went deep and dark and had natural pillars as tall as a man. They'd seen the old Assyrian door reliefs depicting Urartian battles from long ago. They approached a settlement at a slow walk. Crops were in the fields, the houses appeared neat and well-tended, and pastureland was webbed with the trails of cattle large and small. Yet no human being or animal could be seen. As they went, the same eerie scene repeated over and over again.

"Where is everyone?" Prexaspes asked in a low voice.

Cyrus shook his head. Their horses stepped high, anxious nickering the only sound.

They passed along an old fortification wall. Adobe that had once run high, was broken. Cyrus could hear the men behind him exchanging hushed words. Bricks lay heaped and scattered where they had fallen, and small shrubs poked out from the ruins.

Pock-marked cliffs rose up on their right. Cyrus could almost hear the breath of the people hiding inside. Cyrus halted and called up for Tigran, their king. Privately, quietly… in the miles and time between Ecbatana and here, now, Cyrus had finally come to believe what Amytis had said: that it would indeed be best to avoid an armed confrontation.

In a voice made clearer by the crystalline silence, Cyrus called out the invitation he had issued weeks before, to surrender now and the terms would be easy, they'd have liberties under his rule. They listened as the words echoed against the stone.

Still they waited. Prexaspes shushed the troops. In the silence, time seemed suspended. Cyrus's horse shifted his small hooves and threw up his head. Then, disturbing as an earthquake, was a scuffle at the mouth of a cave just above Cyrus's head. He glanced up just in time to see a man lunge for his companion, who had leaned too far. In that fraction of a moment, Cyrus saw that it had been an accident, understood - as if it all transpired in slow motion - that to grasp his friend, the man had to let go of the spear in his hand. The man did. Cyrus saw it all. His face upturned, Cyrus watched the spear sail out into the cold air, the new wood wobbling with its freedom, the bronze tip throwing sunlight this way and that straight toward Cyrus's head.

There was no time to warn, no time to explain. Prexaspes saw it then. And that was all he saw, all that existed in the world: a weapon – speeding directly toward Cyrus. In truth, it wouldn't have mattered if Cyrus had commanded them all to drop their weapons. Prexaspes would not be swayed from his single-minded concern.

When Prexaspes saw the spear, "Attack!" he shouted, even as he thrust his shield in front of the king, who was ready with his own. The spear glanced off, harmless. But their men were already shooting fast into the caves – bedlam – while another contingent rode into the village, flushing out of every house and barn people and animals, swinging and slaughtering without discrimination.

Before Cyrus had brought it all to a halt, the hillsides were bloody with fallen Urartians, the pastures spotted with the bodies of the dead, and more than one house was on fire. Cyrus couldn't say it was a mistake. Not now. Captive Urartians, bound wrist and ankle, were herded before Cyrus. And wasn't he was justified in the attack by this people's resistance to his rule, inheritor of Media and king of the whole? Part of Cyrus was glad, felt cleansed by the melee, exonerated; but a quiet part deep within spoke reproach. The captured males before him were either very old or just boys. There were women and girls, too, some weeping, some shaking. Others, their eyes hard and jaws set, steeled themselves anticipating the assault to come. Cyrus scanned the group again, looking differently this time.

"Where is your king?" Cyrus asked.

The people exchanged confused glances.

"Where is Tigran?" Cyrus asked again.

An old man, wisps of hair standing up in the wind, cleared his throat. "Tigran," he said, and then something Cyrus couldn't understand.

Cyrus lifted his hands, interrupting the old man. "I don't understand."

One of the commanders, a stocky man from Media, stepped up next to Cyrus. He says, "Tigran is their king, sir."

"I know that -- that Tigran is their king."

The commander spoke to the old Urartian.

The Urartian replied.

"He says that Tigran has taken an army north against the Scythians."

"After taunting us with refusal to vassalage?"

The commander and Urartian spoke again.

"He doesn't know anything about that, sir. Just that the

Scythians keep attacking from the north. Tigran called up their fighting men to confront the horde and shore up their defenses."

Cyrus looked around, sickened. He shut his eyes briefly and pursed his lips. "Tell them that Tigran offended me." He looked around. "But Haldi, who rides the mountain lion, has directed me to desist. So long as the people oblige."

At the name of their great god, the captors squirmed; but when the translator was done, they had visibly relaxed.

"Release them. And clean up the place. Help the women with the bodies. Do not under any circumstances hurt or humiliate them further. Whatever they want, do. And tell the youngsters to find their companions, whoever are left in the caves. They can come out now. Their animals need tending."

That evening, as the villagers mourned their dead, Cyrus dictated another message for Tigran. He sent it ahead with a small company of riders, two Urartian boys leading them.

After Cyrus and his Persians did what they could to repair amidst the grief, they followed. On Urmia's southeastern shore, they passed the man-made Hasanlu, in ruins for centuries but still exhibiting an earlier grandeur. Its artificial citadel and huge columned hall a picture that Cyrus tucked into his memory should he ever have a chance to build at Pasargad. Pasargad, with Cassandane – he would *make* the chance. One day. Meanwhile, right here, now were wonders indeed. Along the lake itself, flamingoes bobbed their swooping beaks from long necks and longer legs into the briny water, their pink feathers a shocking hue at dusk and dawn. The men ate well from the region -- deer and fish daily supplementing the staples they carried.

They had barely cleared the northern end of Lake Urmia when the riders whom Cyrus had sent ahead, returned. "You can't imagine," one said, "palaces and incredible ruins all along the way. And the castle sits on a lake so blue --"

His companion said, "It might be poured of molten gems."

"Lake Van," Cyrus said. "I've heard of it." He called to his troops to stop. "Wait for me here."

"No," Prexaspes said. "It's a trap."

"I asked for this," Cyrus said. "I asked Tigran to meet with me."

Prexaspes shook his head. "It's too risky."

"Everything worth doing is risky, Prex." Cyrus looked at his broad friend, a fresh bandage covering one eye, scab-crusted knuckles, shoulders that could pull an ox-cart, "And you take more than I. For me, I know it."

Prexaspes opened his mouth to speak.

"Come with me."

Prexaspes shut his mouth and grinned.

* * *

AFTER CYRUS with Prexaspes at his side crested the last range and began descending from forests and alpine meadows into orchards and fields, a troop of heavily armed riders met them. Urartian warriors would escort Cyrus and his small band the rest of the way to the fortress on the lake ahead. It was as the guide had said -- a lake so blue it seemed it couldn't possibly be filled with water; and all around were more old vine vineyards than Cyrus had ever seen before. The trunks, ages ago planted in tidy lines were gnarled and striated with years of clinging to rocky soil.

"They say that these hills produce the finest wine," Cyrus said to Prexaspes.

Across the lake, Mount Suphan rose, a great gentle mound, from green to steely brown striped with snow to a white peak that nestled up against the sky.

The city itself was a wonder. Adobe bricks and ashlar masonry formed terraces up the citadel's steep slope, and the palace itself had round towers and high turrets.

Tigran himself met them at the palace gate – on foot and

unarmed. Pale skin, almost as light as the limestone around, made the dark of Tigran's heavy eyebrows, neatly trimmed beard, and hair in curls just above his shoulders even more striking. His nose, straight and strong, flared out at his nostrils. Cyrus heard Prexaspes clear his throat and straighten in his saddle.

Tigran did not bow. He directed grooms forward to take the horses. So Cyrus dismounted. The men were the same height. As they walked, Tigran gestured to the citadel. "Rusa the Second, the greatest builder in the world. This is only one of his palaces. You've seen the terraced city. We have irrigation systems that never fail, horses to rival Media's -- yours, and the world's best wine. Go on," he said to Prexaspes, indicating he wait in an adjacent room. Spires of wooden beams supported its round roofs, under which heavy furniture of cast bronze with ivory inlay gave a sense of permanence. The rosy sunlight of dusk flooded the room from large windows along the outer wall.

"Bring him wine," Tigran directed to a silent Urartian. Prexaspes folded his arms across his chest, clearly determined not to leave Cyrus alone.

"Go," Cyrus said. It brooked no disagreement.

CHAPTER 8

That his mother might have the send-off she deserved, Nabonidus slaughtered fattened stock and summoned people from even the farthest provinces. Kings, princes, and governors from the borders of Egypt on the Mediterranean to the Arabian gulf answered his call to come and mourn Adad-guppi's death. In all the hubbub and grandiosity, the absence of those from farther north including Cyrus and Amytis registered only passing notice, and only for a few. Khai didn't expect Amytis to come, but he couldn't help watching for her either. For her part, Amytis was grateful for the additional tasks of management left to her while Cyrus was gone. Still, her mind wandered to Babylon and the man who'd colored her life there.

The funeral was a show as great as any had seen since Nebuchadnezzar's time. For a full week, day and night, it seemed that the whole world grieved. In a great show of mourning, no one bathed but threw dust on their heads and kept their eyes on the ground. Meanwhile, any questions that citizens might have had about Nabonidus's loyalties, his religious leanings, and judgment in politics and economy were set aside. Adad-guppi had been beloved by all. And Nabonidus, who had lived for nearly eight decades with the whirlwind of his mother's opinions, advice, and wisdom was comforted.

On the seventh day of mourning, exactly as tradition dictated, all the people of the country shaved and cleaned themselves. They threw off their mourning clothes. Nabonidus himself provided new clothes to those visiting from far away. He delivered beautiful garments, fine fragrances, and cosmetics to his guests' living quarters. He provided for their return journey and sent the visitors home in peace and gladness.

For generations to come, scribes told how "Nabonidus, king of Babylon, the son whom Adad-guppi bore, laid her body to rest wrapped in fine wool garments and shining white linen. He deposited her body in a hidden tomb with splendid ornaments of gold set with beautiful stones, precious stones, expensive stone beads, containers with scented oil, and other luxurious things."

King Nabonidus conducted it all to the letter of Babylonian expectation. But when it was done, he returned to the desert. Once again, he left his son the crown prince to manage in his stead. Belshazzar resumed his illustrious post. His first order of business: that royal lion hunt.

CHAPTER 9

Tigran and Cyrus stood alone, side by side, at the top of an open turret, overlooking the lake. Cyrus appreciated the man's silence. It felt good simply to stand in the peace of that place, to get his bearings again after the furor in the hills. He'd regret that for a long time. Below them, a green island rose up from a blue bay. Cultivated hillsides rolled out from its shores.

"We did not conquer Urartu," Tigran said. An eagle flew over, three black birds in harassing pursuit until it disappeared into the hills. "We simply became them and they became us -- Arminans of Urartu. One people." He turned his head to Cyrus. "We will no longer pay into a treasury other than our own or send our men to fight battles that are not our own." Tigran's tawny eyes never left Cyrus's, and he never raised his voice.

Cyrus nodded – neither accepting nor rejecting. "And the Scythians?"

Tigran snorted. He looked out over the water. "They're restless. It's nothing new. I expect they'll always harass our northern frontier. Nothing that we cannot handle. Come."

Cyrus followed Tigran back through the sunny palace and asked for horses.

The kings rode along the lake. The horses seemed tireless. Cyrus lost sight of the palace behind. Cyrus knew that Prexaspes would not approve, and a wave of wary concern passed through him. But Tigran was a steady presence, and Cyrus felt he owed the man – and his people – a demonstration of trust after what had just happened.

The kings rode until the shore grew rougher, the hills steeper and more immediate. They reigned in the horses, dismounted, and continued on foot. Cyrus followed Tigran scrambling over a boulder pile and stood. They looked down on a rushing stream. The water ran clear and fast, churning over rocks and eddying in tiny swirls only to hurry ahead again. White gulls stood plump and watchful on rocks all around. Small, dark birds, flashing in the sun, appeared and disappeared over the rapids. They stepped closer to the bank.

Cyrus's eyes widened. "Not birds," Cyrus said, his voice laced with wonder. "Fish."

Hundreds even thousands darting up over rapids and muscling against the stream. Under the surface, countless more dark bodies swarmed into the current. They threw themselves into the air, against rocks, jostling and shoving against each other over and over again.

"They do it for love," Tigran said, "struggling and suffering their way high into the river to reproduce, to get back home." He watched Cyrus's gaze go long, his thoughts suddenly far away. "Such effort. And they don't give up."

Cyrus studied them again.

"Every spring it's like this," Tigran said. "Hold out a net, and they jump right in. We do this, but only on one day. One day out of the whole year, we allow ourselves to catch them. Any more and we'd upset the balance. Without such restraint, one day they'd be gone. No more fish.

"Here," Tigran had leapt downstream. He knelt. "Feel the

water," he said, scooping it in his own hands, rubbing them together as the water poured out.

Cyrus joined him. But no sooner had he scooped the water than he jumped back in surprise, hastily stripping the water – in vain – off his fingers.

Tigran laughed. "It won't hurt you," he said. "The water is special, soft. Those fish, dareka, are the only fish that can live in this lake. We use deposits on the shore for soap."

* * *

THEIR DINNER that night was rich, and Cyrus had to admit that the wine was indeed the best he had ever had. Neither man drank much, while the rest of the hall grew louder and louder. An argument erupted at the table where Cyrus's companions sat. Prexaspes dragged the offending Persian away, while placating the Urartians with gestures for quiet and calm.

"My people are angry about your attack," Tigran said.

Cyrus sighed, nodded. "I told them that it wouldn't happen again," Cyrus said, "if Urartu obliged."

"And I told you that we won't."

"Things are different now. I am not Astyages."

Tigran's eyes were hard.

"We can help you with the Scythians," Cyrus reasoned.

Tigran shook his head.

"Look," Cyrus said. "I don't intend to change the way you govern -- you would still be in charge of all of this, just as you are now. As Haldi has determined things should be," Cyrus added. "But you are part of the new empire, Persia now, and must recognize that."

Tigran stood. Cyrus did, too; and the whole hall followed to the sound of scarping chairs and stumbling feet. "My servants will see you to your rooms. You'll leave tomorrow. Should you choose to return, you'll need a bigger army."

CHAPTER 10

F inally, after exhausting very other option, someone
came to Amytis.

"Is there anything you can do?" the woman asked. She toggled
the baby against her hip.

No one had thought it possible, but since Cyrus's departure,
Cassandane became even less engaged with anyone, her children
included. For the most part, Cambyses was fine – busy with a
rigorous curriculum of training. Crown prince of an empire such
as this, the boy had much to learn in both knowledge and skills.
But the baby 'Tossa had begun to lose interest even in eating.

Now, the nurse stood before their last hope... and the last
person the baby's mother would countenance caring for her
child. The young woman clucked to the infant, whose dark eyes
seemed to have grown larger against a gaunt face to no response.
The baby let the woman bob and sway. The chain of silver stars
the wetnurse waved before her could have been nothing more
than a puff of air as far as baby Atossa was concerned. Her eyes
were blank against a mop-topped skull.

"She's not sick, doesn't seem to have any other ailment than..."
The woman shifted 'Tossa to her other hip.

Despite herself – she guessed that Cassandane didn't know that the wetnurse had brought her baby there – Amytis walked up closer. Amytis knew that she should send the nurse away, continue to keep her distance from Cassandane's family. But. Looking into the baby's face – blank – Amytis tilted her own and smiled the tiniest of smiles. Sympathy. To the wetnurse's great surprise, the baby reached out a pale hand. She closed her fingers around Amytis's cheek. And with that, the wetnurse extended the baby and Amytis received her as if this were exactly what they'd been doing since birth.

With 'Tossa at her own hip, a lock of Amytis's hair firmly in the baby's grasp, Amytis turned back to the documents scattered around her desk. The wetnurse shifted nervously on her feet.

"Come back in an hour or so," Amytis said. She extricated her hair from the baby's hand, trading it for a wedge of cedar lightly carved into the rough shape of a horse. Atossa gurgled happily. "She'll be ready to eat then."

CHAPTER 11

"*A*nd you still want the hunt to take place in Gutium?" Khai asked Belshazzar.

In truth, Khai had been so preoccupied lately that if this idea of Belshazzar's, this wish for a grand lion hunt, had even crossed Khai's mind, he dismissed it. He hoped the crown prince had forgotten all about it. Planning for and executing the queen mother's funeral would have been more than enough to erase any other official matter from their minds, but in Khai's case concern for his one daughter – unabashedly his favorite child – was a chronic preoccupation. She, so sweet and long-suffering, was simply not well.

"Now more than ever," Belshazzar said.

The prince's advisors had proposed a site closer to home in land that would make the crown prince's success in combat with the king of beasts not only easier for Belshazzar (known more for drinking feats than athletic prowess) but also more public. There were great swaths of open land for miles around Babylon where the lions could be released for chase and slaughter. Even the hills and copses along the Tigris were more open and easy to manage for a hunt than the dense forests and wild lands of the Zagros foothills where the Gutian peoples lived a semi-feral existence.

But Belshazzar said, "Think about it. I mean, not only is it an honor to be invited, but to host the event itself, to have the hunt on their land... it'll clinch their affection for Babylon."

Khai doubted that. But this was not the time to say.

The Gutians had a reputation for independence and self-sufficiency that Babylonia grudgingly acknowledged even as it demanded allegiance. The only spur of roadway accessible to Babylonian merchant caravans between the northern land route that passed through Ecbatana and the southern route via the Arabian gulf followed the Diyala River right through the middle of Gutian land across the Zagros mountains to the east. The territory was strategically crucial to Babylonian interests. In truth, it seemed to Khai that the Gutians had the upper hand.

"The people deserve to see their king defeat danger and the forces of chaos in real life," Belshazzar went on, "just as they can see it chiseled in stone on the old palaces of Nineveh and Khorsabad. The tradition goes back further than Assyrian hege-mony and farther than Media's eastern mountains. What better place for such a symbolically significant event than the wildest region of greater Babylonia?"

"We won't be able to guarantee that only the animals we bring will be prowling the hills of the region."

"I am aware of that."

"We will of course make sure that you have well-trained armed escorts in addition to the noblemen participating... as is traditional."

"But they are firmly instructed, are they not, to raise arms only against a human who might take the opportunity to threaten me? They do know that it is to be me and me alone who kills any lion I happen upon."

"Yes, my lord." Khai looked at the portly prince with his fleshy cheeks and soft, round nose. Khai thought that King Nabonidus, even at nearly eighty years old would be a better bet for success in the woods than this pampered prince. Yet it was always Belshazzar, not Nabonidus, who insisted on upholding every traditional expectation of leadership, the symbols of rule, and of course religious rituals and belief. He would not be swayed, even in this. After years of managing the Babylonian royal estate, and under how many kings now? Khai knew this about the present crown prince.

As it was, having had to postpone the hunt for his grandmother's funeral and mourning period, Belshazzar made up for it by reissuing invitations, this time accompanied by gold-handled spears crafted by artisans from Syria. Each weapon, identical to the others, would be not only a keepsake for the youths of this exciting event but also proof of their status as chosen by the Babylonian crown to be companions of the empire's king-to-be.

Youths from Belshazzar's inner circle of palace courtiers and friends cultivated from the great city's elite citizenry were invited, of course. But Belshazzar also identified from the greater reaches of the Babylonian empire chiefs or the sons of chiefs whose loyalties he had determined were crucial to his future kingship.

It was a difficult decision for Belshazzar in the case of the Gutians, whose territory would be the event's hunting ground. Precisely who should ride with Belshazzar? The chief, Ugbaru, was about the same age as Belshazzar; but his son – about thirty years old – was an impressive hunter and already a popular successor to Ugbaru. Peoples neighboring Gutium deferred to the son's opinion and judgment along with Ugbaru's, or so Belshazzar had heard.

So, Belshazzar decided finally, that it would be Ugbaru's son and not the chief himself to whom Belshazzar would extend the most personal invitation.

Khai didn't care. He wanted only to be done with it – and without so compromising the throne's financial holdings that they might seek to whittle their way north from Gutium into Amytis's wild land. And he wanted to fix Davcina – as impossible to do as it was to forget.

CHAPTER 12

*I*t had occurred to Lydian king Croesus, as he replayed his conversation with the Spartan, that Croesus indeed might be seen to have an obligation to avenge his late brother-in-law. It worked. Now, the time of year was right for war, so Croesus called up his troops. "My brother Astyages to the east has been humiliated and debased, his land and home, his very life taken from him by an untrustworthy ruler from an inferior country -- a vassal, no less. It is time to regain Media for honor and home. There will be reward in it for you all, too." Croesus could not have been more confident of victory. After all, the outcome had already been predicted, secured by the gods. The Delphic oracle herself had said – directly to him – that Croesus he attacked Persia, he would "destroy a great empire." He could hardly wait to get on with it. Matter of fact, he'd already waited too long – almost too long. And he didn't want to have to wait another season… or more.

Croesus's army was composed of Greeks from towns along the Aegean, an infantry that Croesus had provided with high quality armor. The best troops, however, were mounted. The Lydian cavalry were numerous and formidable, particularly adept at wielding lances while charging into enemy ranks. These were professionals whose training was subsidized by the extraordinary resources at Croesus' command, allowing them to develop not just the skills of riding war mounts while brandishing weapons but also the strength required to raise, aim, turn, and thrust lances weighing as much as small trees and to do it over and over again.

CHAPTER 13

*D*espite Tigran's unwavering refusal to recognize the sovereignty of the new Median-Parsan empire and the conflict that might engender, Cyrus slept that last night remarkably well.

Cyrus woke early, before the sun, and went down to the lake. He knelt and ran his hands through the cool water. He rubbed them together. The water clung to his skin. He brought his palms to his cheeks, and let his beard rub the silky water from them. At the horizon, the sky was just beginning to soften with the coming dawn. Cyrus thought of the gods that populated the sky, the water, the land, that rode in on storms and called up the fish, the birds, lions, and bulls to cooperate in some magnificent dance. He stood and let the breath of the morning fill his lungs, root him in place and then exhaling, sail away. The sun crested the hill. Cyrus dipped his chin, a small bow to the new day. He let his eyes wander over the shore, the vineyards, the deer grazing across the hills. He was here, he thought, and should look for a means to conquer, for weaknesses to exploit, roads for his armies. But all he saw was beauty.

He glanced up. On the patio above, Tigran stood, his hands on the top of turret.

"The hunting is good here," Tigran said. He'd come down and met Cyrus at the palace gate. "Stay today and hunt with me."

Cyrus raised his eyebrows. "I'll need weapons for that. My men, too."

* * *

PREXASPES STEPPED in front of Cyrus as Cyrus was reaching for his boots.

"First you agree to come here unarmed and with just a few men," Prexaspes said. "Then, as soon as Tigran told you to expect war, you agree to go hunting with him?!"

Cyrus took his friend's shoulders and firmly set him aside. Cyrus pulled on first one boot, then the other, and began to lace them up.

"There's a chance, if I can talk with Tigran some more, that he'll see the advantage of staying with us. I also need to make clear that if we have to fight, we will. But Prex," Cyrus finished and stood, bending his knees to get the fit just right. "Tigran isn't itching for war. He might kill me on a battlefield but surely not on a hunt. Not where I am his guest."

"Accidents happen."

"With you nearby, they won't." Cyrus laid his panther robe over a shoulder, buckled a belt around. "He's arming us, you know."

Prexaspes followed Cyrus out, muttering, "With what kind of weapons? I wonder."

As it turned out, they were good weapons -- excellent, Prexaspes admitted reluctantly.

It wasn't only men who rode. A young woman with the same striking light-dark features as Tigran, honey skin, dark eyebrows, and lips like plums, sat a spirited horse with the ease of a weaver on her bench. Cyrus's men didn't notice their king's flushed stare since they too were transfixed. Only Prexaspes saw. He frowned.

"Tariria," Tigran said, his eyes warm. "My daughter." He spun his horse, and the others followed.

Prexaspes rode close, just behind Cyrus, one eye on the Arminan/Urartian king. Tigran gestured to the mountain -- "an old volcano," and explained the water works that kept orchards and fields well irrigated. Tariria kept back but Cyrus saw that she rode with a beauty that matched her person.

The hunt was exhilarating. Cyrus could see that Tigran was right – the country's people had stewarded a natural balance. The biodiversity was striking, the animals many, healthy, and strong.

As for Cyrus, Tigran watched him with interest.

"You let him take that shot, didn't you?" Tigran asked, after Cyrus congratulated one of his men on felling a stag. "And back there, you could have been the one to kill the bear."

Cyrus shrugged.

"Your companions," Tigran said, nodding to Cyrus's men. "Different accents, skin..."

"Different, yes. But all of them Persian now," Cyrus said.

After a late lunch on a particularly breathtaking outcropping of stone, they turned the horses toward the palace at Tushpa, every person and beast comfortably tired. With their horses at a walk, Cyrus and Tigran rode side-by-side, Prexaspes as always tight behind Cyrus's flank. They rode in companionable silence for a time.

"Have you heard?" Tigran asked, "In the west, Croesus is assembling an army, equipping and training them hard."

"Amytis has said this. But whom would he fight?"

"We don't know. The possibilities are all... implausible."

"Such as?"

"One is that he would go farther west, sail against Greece."

"But his army is mostly Greek."

"Exactly. Unlikely. A second possibility is that he wants to take control of more of Anatolia, the northernmost reaches of Babylonia -- Carmania, Syria."

"But the Babylonians just put down such efforts and strengthened their hold on precisely those regions."

"Yes. Then there's Egypt."

"Absolutely not," Cyrus said.

The Urartian pursed his lips.

"I see." Cyrus said. "That leaves us."

The Urartian nodded slightly, his mouth tight. "Perhaps you'll be happy that we've defected, after all. Urartu is a buffer of sorts for Media, Persia."

"No," Cyrus said. "You are part of this empire. We stay together." Cyrus ignored Tigran's silence, the way the Urartian shifted in his saddle, and passed the reins from one hand to the other. "There's a treaty, is there not," Cyrus asked, "Media with Lydia that limits expansion past the Halys River... ours and theirs, too?"

"Yes," the Urartian said. He tilted his head in thought. "And a great fortressed city built by the Medes at the river itself. It should give them pause." He pulled his shoulders back.

"Maybe," Cyrus said. "But we should be prepared. We'll set up a military garrison here."

Tigran sucked in his breath. "You still wish to subdue us, then, keep us vassals in your kingdom."

Cyrus recalled the brief tenure of his kingship in Parsa, his desire to settle in Pasargad, simply get along with the neighboring tribes, renew a kinship bond with Elam, and foster a discrete region's mutual prosperity. He contemplated the responsibility he now bore for a sprawling empire that he had neither chosen nor wanted. He thought about its cost already to the happiness of his family... And, with a deep breath, he thought about all the thousands of people whose happiness and prosperity depended on his rule. His, with Amytis.

"That's not the way I see it. Listen, you asked me to stay. You volunteered this information about Croesus."

"That we might be allies." Tigran paused. "If you agree, well, Tariria has already consented to marry you."

Cyrus swallowed, as if to calm the stirring he felt. His cheeks warmed at the image of the raven-haired woman bent over the neck of her galloping horse that afternoon, ahead of them now her hips rocking to the roll of its walk. Then he thought of Cassandane.

"I am honored," Cyrus said. "It's easy to see that you have made this land prosperous. You've protected its people and led them against threats without and within. To continue, you have to tax for central supplies and recruit young men for battles against the Scythians, if not others. You'll find another good match for Tariria. But reject us, and we *will* fight you. That can't be good with the Scythians to your north and now Croesus from the west."

Tigran maintained his silence.

Cyrus waved forward one of his men – older than most, from one of the formerly Median tribes near Ecbatana. Cyrus had seen he'd excelled not only in arms but in reason, too. "This man," Cyrus said, "will be my liaison with Urartu. You continue to govern as you think best; but a Persian representing and answering to me, has the final word."

Tigran looked at the Sagartian Persian, and he looked at Cyrus. Then he squinted into the distance where a shepherd ambled her flock across the green hillside.

Cyrus indicated the Persian drop back again. He did.

"The only real change for you is the military garrison," Cyrus said. "Not a foreign occupation but composed of Urartians themselves, simply headed by a Persian. A deterrent. Who knows, with the Babylonians so close in Harran, it might be they who cause trouble. A strong armed presence can keep the peace."

"I don't want war," Tigran said.

Cyrus thought of Amytis, her clarity of purpose, confidence in this. "Neither do we," he said, and heard Prexaspes cough lightly behind him. "Someone told me recently that *not* fighting takes greater courage, endurance, and strength than battle does."

Tigran heard him out. Then, he turned his horse. Cyrus stopped and watched the chief lead his horse in a tight circle, slow. Behind him and all around were the hills with their vine-yards, the wild copses, glittering lake, and tidy stone houses in quiet hamlets. When he returned to Cyrus's side and they had resumed their course, "All right," Tigran said, "We're with you."

CHAPTER 14

*N*o one in the palace except the girl's nurses knew how much time Atossa spent in Amytis's care. But Amytis frequently took little 'Tossa to the stables and even secured the infant to her back, a tidy cloth bundle warm between her shoulders when she rode. Atossa thrived.

Amytis treasured the time. She knew it couldn't last.

So Amytis was wistfully relieved to learn that Atossa, weaned now and starting to find her own legs enjoyed the company of Aspacanah, whose own mother was gentle and kind. It seemed to Amytis that only Prexaspes, her husband seemed not to like the woman. Well, maybe that had changed, Amytis thought. The men were on their way back, a runner reported. And distance could engender fondness, even desire.

Meanwhile, even before receiving the news that Cyrus's group was on their way back to Ecabatana – and successful in retaining the loyalty of the Urartians – Cassandane seemed to be improving. Rumor (the only way Amytis learned) had it that the cloud under which Cassandane had lived ever since Cyrus had married Amytis had begun to lift. She called for the baby now and took interest in Cambyses's training. Her love for Cyrus and for home, Pasargad, were as strong as ever – their intensity the source of her great grief. But she seemed to be finding a way forward.

Cyrus had told Amytis about the woman he'd married – his only true wife, Cassandane. Intelligent and resilient, he'd said. Strong. Independent-minded. It seemed to Amytis as though Cassandane was finding her feet again... and those very qualities continued to keep the women at a distance from each other.

CHAPTER 15

The morning that Belshazzar was to depart with the retinue from Babylon, the priests of Marduk and of Babylon's lesser temples assembled to pray for the welfare and success of the prince and his companions, for the gods' blessings on this effort fundamental to the business of gods and kings, symbolic as it was: to restore order, conquer chaos, and protect the empire from destructive forces.

The animals caught and cultivated for the royal hunt were various, but it was the lions who garnered the most attention when the hunting party moved out with much fanfare from Babylon to begin its journey up the Tigris to the mouth of Diyala. Great iron cages, hauled by huffing oxen on heavy carts brought up the rear of the parade of animals and keepers. Children squealed whenever a beast turned a golden head, tawny eyes fixing on the activity of the street. They leapt behind flinching mothers and slaves should a lion twist its head, open its mouth, and let loose a rumbling roar from a blood-red mouth with long white teeth. Horses danced against their lines, straining reins and jerking chariots, nervous to be so near the lions. Despite training to inure the mounts to the great cats, boars, wolves, and foxes, the natural fear of a prey animal couldn't be entirely excised. So, in the presence of the hungry predators, they tossed colorful headdresses and shivered nervously beneath embroidered saddles.

Belshazzar rode in a chariot as was customary, or at least had precedent. He stood in full hunting regalia, one hand on the high-sided bronze carriage, the other waving to the crowds until the party was well out of town. He would ride the rest of the way in a litter with the hunt's musician, a priest, and the elderly administrator of the hunt.

When they arrived in Gutium, the party set up camp where invitees from the outlying areas had already assembled. Others had come with their entourages days earlier. The mood was festive and the energy muscular. That night, from a temporary platform erected next to Belshazzar's tent, Ugbaru welcomed Babylon's crown prince and the hunt's illustrious participants to the region of Gutium. The Gutian chief extolled the wild nature of his land as befitting such a momentous event and noted the role such occasions have played throughout history in transcending differences and clarifying loyalties.

It was a gracious speech, but the eyes of participants were as much on the rugged man standing next to Ugbaru as on the chief himself. Ugbaru's son, Thaer, was indeed a striking presence, not only physically but also in some felt way. He stood nearly still, his expression polite but sober and reserved. Belshazzar hated him immediately.

His speech concluded and to raucous acclaim, Ugbaru left. He would travel back into the hills to rejoin his people, non-participants to ensure their and their animals' safety throughout the event. After his father had gone, Thaer walked slowly to the place reserved for him next to Belshazzar. He greeted individuals as he passed, eliciting the shy response of admiring and intimidated men. Thaer was clearly beloved. Belshazzar gritted his teeth and slapped him on the back when the Gutian sat down.

The hunt's musician took the platform. On lyre and with drumming accompaniment, he regaled participants with praise hymns to Marduk of creation out of chaos, and sagas of great kings in hand-to-hand combat with snarling lions with teeth like spears and swinging talons as long and sharp as scythes. Belshazzar got quite drunk.

CHAPTER 16

*C*ambyses leaned back in his saddle, sawing on the reins.
"Wait!" He called to Gobryas, whose own horse trotted, well in hand, ahead.

The boys had just finished their lessons, the last of which had involved basic equestrian skills. Unlike the crown prince, Gobryas had taken quickly to riding. For once, his clubfoot was irrelevant. That Cambyses was less comfortable than Gobryas was an understatement. Now, the little prince choked back tears of fury and frustration as he bounced along.

At first, Cyrus had allowed for Cassandane's refusal to let Cambyses ride. But finally he simply had to acknowledge that the crown prince, no matter his frailties, must learn. Thankfully, he didn't have to add that Amytis said she'd teach him herself if they didn't act soon. With his aunt, Cyrus now ruled the most famous horse region in the world. The Nisean chargers of Media, raised on the semi-mythical grass of the pastures around Ecbatana, had been for centuries the most highly sought after steeds for chariots, hunting, and war. And Cambyses was the crown prince.

Besides, Cyrus figured, Cassandane was already angry with him. It seemed like forever since they saw things together, dreamed and planned together. He sighed. What better time to defy this too, he thought ruefully. Cambyses was twelve years old, admittedly small for his age; but here in Media, boys far younger and smaller than he rode as well as any man. Maybe it would even be good for the boy, Cyrus reasoned, give him more confidence, a sense of power.

But Cambyses's horse had the bit in its teeth and was trotting hard when Gobryas finally stopped to let them catch up. The destination had been Gobryas's idea. A new group of merchants had recently arrived from the east. He was eager to see them, to learn what they brought, and simply to take in the air of adventure and entrepreneurship that Gobryas found so irresistible. The boy remained fascinated by the business of business. Add luxury items, exotic clothes, the lilt of a foreign tongue... he couldn't stay away.

"What, are you afraid?" Gobryas said to Cambyses when the prince balked at his plan.

"No," Cambyses said, his mouth turned down in a pout.

"Well? " Gobryas turned his horse's head in the direction of the plaza. "C'mon!" he called as he spurred the horse forward. Cambyses's horse took off after them, the prince simply hanging on.

"This is not a good idea," Cambyses said, when his horse stopped alongside Gobryas's. He looked around nervously. Muscled slaves unpacked wagons, voices cried greetings and directions. More than one argument was in full swing, and the dust churned where hundreds of feet -- men and beasts -- wheels and sleds had long ago pulverized any grass near the gate.

They walked the horses closer, the boys' eyes wide. Some of the merchants were ghostly pale and as blond as a hare in winter. Here and there they saw the blue-black tattoos they'd heard some northeasterners inflicted on themselves for magic or the gods. Cambyses shivered. Suddenly, as they walked past a row of goods-laden wagons, a beige heap on ground shifted, rolled and stood. A camel swung its head toward them.

In that instant, the horses shrieked. Careless of the boys astride, the terrified horses whirled and bolted. As they took off, Gobryas seized the mane of his mount with one hand, regained his seat, and pulled his horses' head to one side as he'd been taught. Unable to charge straight ahead, the horse slowed. It turned with the rein and huffing in protest, it stopped.

Cambyses's horse flew by, riderless.

CHAPTER 17

First thing in the morning, slaves pulled the caged animals as far into the mountains as the hunt leaders determined necessary to keep them from the camp. Then, with ropes, pulleys, and trembling hands, they opened the cages. Most animals leapt free immediately and disappeared into the woods. But some still crouched within, slit-eyed, and quivering until the men were clear before finding the door and dashing to freedom. One lioness slunk swiftly from her cage only to turn on the poor man who had released her. She tore his neck open and flung him aside before glancing at the other keepers – terrified – and loping away.

It was late morning before the crown prince had gathered himself together and the hunters assembled. Horses shifted eagerly under the weight of their riders. Belshazzar boarded the chariot that would take him some miles along the dirt road that followed the Diyala River. Grooms led two warhorses, equipped for the crown prince's use, whenever it was that Belshazzar chose to leave the main road to penetrate the woodlands in search of game. The leaders of hunting rode ahead. They would flush animals into the crown prince's path wherever possible.

It took some time for the party to quiet down after they set out. Spirits were high, and the horses eager. Some of the young men rode immediately into the woods, when the dogs picked up a scent. As per the invitation, Thaer accompanied Belshazzar.

"I know where we'll find some promising outcroppings. Rocks form shelters an animal would find inviting," Thaer said. "When you're ready to leave the main trail, we can go there."

"Is it far?" Belshazzar asked.

"We should be able to reach the valley within two hours. One of the outcroppings is very near that; the two others are one to three hours' ride beyond. It should be a good hunt, and we can still be back at the camp, with trophies to show, by nightfall."

True to Thaer's prediction, Belshazzar could see a jagged mass of dark stones hung improbably off the hillside ahead. Thaer signaled a few men to dismount and follow him. They walked quietly ahead with long staves. The men had hardly reached the outcropping when Thaer let out a whoop, swung his stave inside the deepest cave, and whooped again. The men with him followed suit, and within moments, three wolves tore out.

One spun on a man with Thaer, snarling and snapping on quivering haunches. A second man struck it in the side. The wolf gave a high cry as it fell and then died with the man's dagger in its heart. The other two bounded toward the path, toward the rest of the party. Belshazzar loosed an arrow just as the wolves darted away. Thaer had run back down, anticipating the wolves' dodge. He swung his arms, throwing them off course, and away from the riders. One turned, hesitating. Belshazzar shot again. His arrow caught the animal across its back, bringing it to the ground. The other escaped into the woods. Thaer stood over the partially paralyzed wolf until Belshazzar rode up.

"A dagger to his side, right at the heart, should do it, sir."

Belshazzar hesitated.

"Shall I?" Thaer asked.

"No." Belshazzar dismounted, seized his dagger, took a deep breath and plunged it below the wolf's shoulder.

"A good kill, my lord."

Belshazzar gave Thaer a wan smile and reached for his horse's reins. His foot shook as he lifted it into the hand of a companion, ready to boost the crown prince back onto his saddle.

"The copse is just ahead," Thaer said mounting his own horse, "a good place for lions."

Belshazzar mustered a look he hoped was appropriately enthusiastic.

CHAPTER 18

"We'll need the largest army we can muster," Amytis said. "And get them to Pteria as soon as possible. Croesus cannot pass that river." Amytis's grip tightened on the armrests.

Messengers delivered the news regularly now. There was no denying it. Croesus had mustered an enormous army with international backing – Egypt, Greece, even those monsters of war the Spartans had joined him. Croesus had twisted the treaty terms against them. What was designed to keep peace between Lydia and Media – the Halys River a boundary neither would cross with aggressive intent – had become a point of war. Word was that Croesus said Cyrus usurped Astyages's throne; the Lydians would rectify that with a punishing blow.

"He cannot pass." Amytis said again. She looked at Cyrus, and her expression softened with understanding. "Sanda has taken it hard."

Cyrus nodded, mute. The notion that he should leave Ecbatana again – not for Pasargad, but instead for the sake of this new, Persian empire and go west to battle was too much. Adding insult to injury, Cassandane's children were as distant from her as she felt Cyrus to be. And 'Tossa clung to Amytis.

Amytis tried to explain. When Cassandane turned her back on baby 'Tossa, Amytis had looked away. The wetnurse was there, not unlike her own when Amytis's mother was believed to have run away. Amytis figured it would be fine. The child would be fine. But even after the girl was weaned, Cassandane – deep in her own depression and feelings of abandonment – still ignored her. Amytis couldn't remember when it happened (she wasn't going to blame the nurse), if there had been some particular event or moment that led 'Tossa to her; but now it seemed the little girl was a regular part of Amytis's days. She was no trouble – a toddler content simply to be close. The eunuch Bagapates watched her – and Aspacanah – when Amytis couldn't. But Amytis was clearly her favorite.

Amytis said, "I think your little girl believes that *I* am her mother."

Cyrus bent over, put his head between his hands, and groaned.

"Take them with you," Amytis said.

Cyrus looked up at her.

"It's not unheard of. Many people, who have nothing to do with the battles, travel with armies. Bring her," Amytis said. "Take Cambyses and 'Tossa. Bagapates, too."

Cyrus sat up.

"I need to stay here," Amytis said brusquely. "And –" having observed another source of conflict within Cyrus's immediate family, she said, "why don't you leave Gobryas with me? He's more interested in the affairs of state and all the merchants' activity than in war, anyway."

Cyrus nodded, visibly relieved. He even smiled.

"Now, about the city," Amytis said. "It's on the far side of the Halys River, seven kilometers of wall interrupted only by seven strong gates. After my grandfather and the Lydians established

that truce, he built the stronghold, just in case. Pteria, Kerkenes --
by whatever name, it's impressive. Despite the fortifications, it
was not supposed to be a military garrison, but simply a town.
Most people there today have been there all their lives. They are
not warriors. You have to get there before Croesus does. He
cannot cross that river."

Just then, Cambyses burst in. And right behind him,
Cassandane.

* * *

SANDA, out examining peach orchards, had seen her son's mount
return, its tack in disarray and the saddle empty. When she ran
back to the palace, Cambyses was already there, dirty but unhurt.
He had found Cyrus. With Amytis.

Sanda rushed in on them and pulled herself to a halt. She
glared at Amytis but as quickly gathered Cambyses into a hug,
kissed him. "Are you all right? Are you all right?"

"Mother!" Cambyses pushed her away, his face red.

Cassandane frowned but kept her distance.

"Tell me again what happened?" Cyrus asked.

And while Cassandane listened, fury building, the little prince
told the story of the merchants, Gobryas's fault... the camel. "I
don't know," Cambyses said, "It all happened so fast. And I was
doing everything I'd been taught."

When he had finished, a moment of silence.

Then, "Camels," Amytis and Cyrus said simultaneously.

Cassandane huffed. She turned to Cambyses. "Go on. Get
cleaned up." When he was gone, she spun on Cyrus. "I told you he
shouldn't ride! I hate those beasts." She didn't look at Amytis.

"It wasn't the horses' fault," Cyrus said.

Trying to keep her voice level, Amytis said, "Camels. Unless
the horses have been trained, carefully conditioned, there's

nothing that can override their terror." She ignored Cassandane's glare and said instead, "You're right. It *can* be very dangerous."

"And that boy, Gobryas..."

Amytis gathered her robe and stood to go. At the door, "Croesus and his Lydians," Amytis said to Cyrus. "End this thing."

After she had gone, Sanda said, "Gobryas has to go. He's going to get our son killed."

"I made a promise."

"You and your promises! What about Pasargad? When? Will we ever?!"

"Oh, Sanda," Cyrus said. He reached out to draw her to him.

But Cassandane crossed her arms against her chest.

Cyrus stepped back. "The ruler of Lydia, Croesus, is marching toward the Halys River. They have a huge army. We have to stop them." Cyrus took ahold of Cassadane's hands. Only their warmth gave them life. "Will you come with me?"

"Against the Lydians?" Sanda pulled her hands away.

"Yes. We'll have the army, of course; but other people will be coming, too, you know -- magi, cooks, women. They mend, look after the wounded. Some tend horses..."

"I won't tend horses."

Cyrus smiled. A joke? He wouldn't presume. "We could take Cambyses and 'Tossa -- our family. There will be other children."

Cassandane knit her brow.

Cyrus watched her closely as he said, "I was thinking that we could leave Gobryas here. There's enough palace life... he loves all that administration, management..."

Cassandane nodded slowly.

"Amytis will stay, too."

Cyrus waited.

Finally, Cassandane nodded. "I'll go."

CHAPTER 19

Belshazzar followed Thaer into the woods. After riding a narrow path through tall trees that had shaded out the growth of most underbrush, the sky suddenly opened above them. A rockslide years earlier had leveled the old growth down a wide strip of hillside. Young trees and dense shrubs dominated instead.

"If there isn't a lion somewhere in here, I'd be very surprised," Thaer said, hopping down off his horse. The mounts were nervous, stepping quickly in place and snorting lightly. Thaer looked at Belshazzar's face. The crown prince was pale. "Are you ready, my lord?"

Belshazzar nodded and reached for an arrow to thread his bow.

"It's a spear you'll want, sir. There'll be little chance to shoot."

Belshazzar's eyes were wide. But he returned the bow to his attendant's quiver and held out his hand for the long spear.

"Whatever you do, don't drop it," Thaer said.

The horse that Belshazzar rode was a veteran of the lion hunts of years earlier. As for Belshazzar himself, this was the first time he'd attended as anything other than an accompanying courtier. Babylonia's crown prince shrugged off his outer robe and mustered a smile. He cleared his throat. "Let's go," he said thinly. Then, adding volume, "What are we waiting for?"

Thaer smiled and jogged into the thicket.

Belshazzar waited. He wiped his brow with his arm, holding tightly to the spear. It was terribly quiet. His horse bobbed its muzzle up and down, then whinnied as a roar shook the leaves on the underbrush ahead. Belshazzar held his horse still and strained to see. Suddenly the brush parted for a rust-colored mane. Huge paws padded lightly then pushed off in a run – away from Belshazzar. The crown prince urged his mount forward. Another man galloped ahead. The lion swerved back around and leapt onto the haunches of the second horse, bringing it squealing down. Its rider shouted as he jumped free. Belshazzar rode up, his spear high. The lion turned its bloody muzzle, gaping and roaring on the approaching prince.

Belshazzar froze. His mount reared. The prince's spear fell from his hands. Belshazzar gasped. The lion leaned back onto its hind legs. As the horse came down, the lion rose up. Belshazzar threw his empty arms in front of his face. Claws caught at his sleeve. The prince tumbled, his horse whirling. The lion reached out its paddle paw, cracked claws seeking angry purchase. It twisted its head in a roar, snarling as it lowered its fangs toward Belshazzar's quivering face. Cut short. Thaer's dagger sliced through the lion's throat, spilling blood all over the screaming prince.

Belshazzar's cries of fear turned to rants of rage as the full knowledge of his failure came to bear with all the violent energy he had intended for the lion.

"You, you!" he screamed at Thaer, "How dare you!"

Thaer shook his head, breathing hard, confused.

"But --"

"*I* should have been the one to kill that lion. That was mine, the prerogative --"

"*He* would have killed *you!*"

"But, but –" Belshazzar spluttered in rage.

Thaer looked around. No one else was there. "No one needs to know," Thaer said. "And they *do* know I hate killing lions. Actually..." His gaze went to the wolf's carcass slung across the back his own horse. His eyes shut and head moved with the hint of a shake.

Belshazzar squinted at him, measuring this curious man. Others rode up. They looked from Belshazzar to Thaer and back again.

"The prince's first lion," Thaer announced with a wide smile. He left Belshazzar to the congratulations of his companions.

And Belshazzar hated him more than ever.

OTHERS JOINED them throughout the afternoon, one party reporting sighting two more lions. Another party produced a small boar and a fox.

That night, the feasting was accompanied by a new song -- of Belshazzar's valor in the face of danger, of Babylon's king-to-be upholding Marduk's desire that chaos and the untamed wild not threaten their great civilization. Again, Belshazzar got quite drunk.

The next day, Belshazzar asked his Gutian guide to ride with him.

"Let the others go ahead to flush the game," he said.

"In these woods," Thaer said, after a long silence, "we probably won't see anything but deer for a while. String your bow, if you like."

Belshazzar did.

They rode on awhile.

"Ah!" Belshazzar exclaimed, his voice hushed. "I think I heard something. Off to the right there, maybe even behind us."

Thaer tilted his head.

"There it is again!"

"I don't hear anything.

"Maybe it's our companions," Belshazzar said.

"Couldn't be. You sent them far ahead."

Belshazzar craned over his horse's neck, then sat back and shrugged.

"I can look, though, if you like."

"Yes," Belshazzar said, "Do."

As the Gutian rode off, Belshazzar strung his bow.

The arrow that Belshazzar shot found its mark. That shot would change everything.

CHAPTER 20

"Amytis?" Prexaspes asked Cyrus. "This could be a long time."

"She knows this place, greater Media too, better than any of us," Cyrus said to Prexaspes. "Besides, she was married to Nebuchadnezzar, one of the greatest administrators of our time... and daughter to one of the worst. She is no stranger to matters of state. She handled things just fine alone, when we went to Urartu." Prexaspes tilted his head in reluctant agreement. "Vishtaspa has Parthia to the east, and Tigran is a strong leader to the west. Cassandane's father has Anshan in hand. I need Harpagus with us. He has more knowledge of Croesus and Lydia than anyone else. It'll be fine."

"Do you plan to leave Otanes in Ecbatana again?"

"No," Cyrus said. "We'll need him against the Lydians."

"Please don't tell me we have to put up with Zarin," Prexaspes groaned.

"At least she's beautiful."

"So they say."

But they didn't have to put up with Otanes's wife. Zarin revealed that she was pregnant and became insufferably determined to return to Parsa. Poor Otanes was deeply torn between loyalty and duty to Cyrus and his adoration of Zarin. Finally, he consented to send her – in a luxurious and heavily guarded caravan – back to Parsa. As for Prexaspes's wife and Aspacanah, the little boy almost 'Tossa's age, no one asked. Not publicly, anyway. Prexaspes insisted that they stay.

Amytis was alone when she received the news: Croesus's troops had ravaged Pteria. The message came not long after Cyrus's troops had left, not long enough for them to have arrived in time. She sank into a chair. All those people, the animals, the place. War, she thought. And we speak of 'winning'?!

CHAPTER 21

So swiftly had the Lydian forces come, and so shocking was their disregard for the old treaty that Croesus took the people of Pteria by surprise. It was a slaughter. Croesus's Lydians came on like the sea against reeds, inexorable and imperious. What population remained, the Lydians made their slaves.

Cyrus's army wasn't far, the great river only another ridge away, when he got the news. Cyrus learned of the attack from Tigran, as the Arminan/Urartian had promised. His stomach sank at the news. The Halys River, red before Lydians had ever decimated the Pterians, ran thicker with their blood. With Amytis's words ringing in his ears, Cyrus sent word to Croesus. "Surrender now, and we'll spare you. All the people with you, their families and lands, will be welcome in my kingdom. I'll even let you manage the region's administrative affairs."

Croesus listened as his messenger read aloud. With each word, the king's face grew redder. His cheeks blew out with the effort of containing his rage so that it seemed his eyes would pop from beneath their puffy lids.

"How dare he?!" the Lydian king shouted.

A general said, "He's bluffing."

Another added, "Maybe; but it doesn't matter. Even if he believes it, we all know that Media is fragmented and has been for decades. With all respect, sir," he said nodding to Croesus, "your brother-in-law wasn't much of a military man. There's comfort in that. The Medes – now Persians, but what's a name? – are hardly prepared to fight the likes of us. After all, look at what happened to them against that nothing, Anshan?"

Croesus narrowed his eyes. "But they're all his now."

"You really think so? Listen. Few of the peoples in Media, if any, would join Cyrus," the commander went on, "not *practically*, not effectively, anyway. After all, think about it. The Urartians rebelled. Luristan can't be far behind, and those barbarians in Parthia surely won't tolerate him long. The Anshanites, themselves, the only army he can rely on, are so few and poor that they're hardly worth counting. Besides, he's surely left some there in the south."

"He's right," the general said, tilting his head toward the commander. "If Cyrus dares to advance, he'll soon regret it."

Croesus nodded. His face resumed its normal color. "Tomorrow we begin. When it's done, I want him alive. I want to meet this Cyrus."

* * *

BUT THE RIVER resisted the coming fight. It was too high to cross. For a moment, it seemed that the river itself – "Anahita," Cyrus whispered standing at its rushing bank – would force the Lydians to keep the treaty, after all.

It wasn't to be. Or maybe the goddess had other plans.

As it happened, Croesus had among his thousands, the Greek scientist Thales of Miletus, a friend. Thales considered the current, observed the quality of the banks, the direction of flow.

"I've got it," he said.

Sure enough, Thales engineered a way to divert the river's

course, reducing its flow at a critical point for the Lydian army's passage. When it was done, the great waterway that had marked a profound line in the treaty between empires barely wet the stones at its bottom. Croesus rubbed his bejeweled hands together in happy anticipation.

When Croesus's army crossed the Halys River, Cyrus's troops met him. Arrows from each side collided in the air like flocks unswayed in flight. Otanes's archers, many bearing the duck-headed composite bow of Elam, were arrayed in the center, with regular infantry close by, holding short swords and spears, waiting like the flanking for their fight to come. After the archers, slingers sent stones and hunks of lead into the Lydian infantry, dropping some men and bruising others. The troops on foot gained sheltering defense from wicker shields, but it was not enough. The battle raged on. Croesus's cavalry mowed with their lances while Cyrus's troops took whatever advantage they could find. Both sides of foot soldiers fought hard and long, close enough to smell the sweat and hear the grunts and gasps the muffled screams... All of them fighting to the death.

When the sun went down on a ravaged field, Croesus from his golden chariot could hardly believe that Cyrus's troops remained. They fought until it was too dark to see.

CHAPTER 22

*L*eaving Ecbatana might have been a relief to Cassandane. There was danger in their destination. She knew that. But Cyrus was right: theirs was hardly the only family attending the troops. Bagapates was indeed a capable help with the children, and Cyrus included Cambyses in as many conversations about logistics and strategy and such as possible. She only wished they were heading south, instead, back to Pasargad.

When they arrived and the armies clashed, Cassandane couldn't help but remember. The drama of battle, the casualties and concern -- a future in the balance -- recalled to Cassandane when Astyages had brought his Medes, men in Cyrus's own army now, against them in Parsa. That was before everything. Before the victory that broke their lives. She and Cyrus were on the same side, then. Cassandane remembered how the women poured into the field, doing what they must to keep their men in the fight. Cambyses was a little boy with a quick laugh before this surly competitor, Gobryas, came along. Cassandane had been pregnant. They were happy then.

After the battle, the blood of the wounded and the urgency of care, the repair of weapons and armor and clothes, the practical logistics of provisions -- water and food... Cassandane felt guilty that these horrors drew up an odd contentment in her. The need to feed courage and to chase away fright. There was such clear purpose, for a woman as well as a man. She tucked a stray hair back into the tight knot at her nape and fixed her scarf before she waded among the injured again.

Cyrus was back from the battle but hadn't yet sought her out. Cassandane was told that he walked among his troops, seeing to all those needs, not minding his own. Well, Cassandane had done that today, too. But now she was back in their tent, and the toddler would not be comforted.

"Ahmi, Ahmi," the little girl called all day, crying for Amytis. It was easy to see, even at three years old, that 'Tossa had Cassandane's long limbs. The rest of her -- her face, that mouth, that nose, the curly hair -- was Cyrus. Sanda's heart pinged. What was handsome in a man was different for a girl. Skinny and tall with strong features. 'Tossa would be no beauty, Sanda thought. Cassandane held out her arms, gathered the child in. But 'Tossa wriggled free. "Ahmi!" she wailed.

Cassandane tried everything, but 'Tossa would not be comforted. Not, that is, until Cyrus came back. And then, his attention was only for this daughter wailing herself into hiccups. As she watched them, Cassandane wondered with a cutting remorse, when had the girl begun to walk? When did she talk? What were her first words? Had Amytis taught her? Cambyses? She turned away.

In the morning, Cassandane was still angry, hurt... and ashamed of all her feelings. She wanted nothing more than the husband she had married. Finally, she found a way to say it.

"I miss you," Cassandane said. And then it all rushed out. The candor with which she told Cyrus this simple fact and would he please stay, only a few hours, that they rest in the tent there together? went straight to his heart. He had hoped that this time away from Ecbatana, away from Amytis might soften this wife, his true wife. If this is how it could happen that Cassandane returned to him, well...

"The battle can wait," Cyrus said. "The men could use the rest."

Harpagus, Prexaspes, and Otanes had assembled to go over their battle plan.

"And look." Cyrus gestured to the open plain on which the army camped. "The Lydians can hardly effect an ambush. A few hours," he said. "It's enough."

* * *

WHEN CYRUS FAILED to bring out his troops on the following morning, Croesus was relieved It didn't feel like much of a victory, but – as he said to his generals – Cyrus's absence on the field spoke volumes. Preparation, travel, and the recent battles themselves (Pteria, a definitive victory) had taken time. A lot of time.

Privately, Croesus allowed that Cyrus's army was far stronger than he'd anticipated. The battle had been costly, and they'd already been gone too long. Despite his reach and riches, Croesus couldn't very well call out additional help now, not so late in the season. Croesus considered the situation – Cyrus's forces far more reduced than the young man's bluster would suggest. And look, Croesus thought to himself – he wasn't even on the field, the camp quiet.

The thing that clinched it for Croesus, though, and it brought a smile to his plump cheeks, was knowing he had the oracle on his side. The gods themselves said that he would win. So, he took his plan to the generals, reminding them of these things. The oracle had said he'd win. But she didn't say when. It could just as well be next season. Yes, Croesus thought. He would confront the Parsan again and take Media for his own... in the spring. For now, he would lead the Lydians home. Let them bring in their harvests. And while they did, he'd call again on the Babylonians – surely they saw now the danger this Persian posed – as well as the Egyptians and Spartans. What a force he'd have! Yes, he'd return and conquer Media, this Persia, in the next war season.

* * *

CYRUS HUNG HIS HEAD. Bickering again. He could see there'd be no easy reconciliation between him and Cassandane. If there would be any at all.

"And how do you know she's not plotting right now to undermine you, us," Cassandane said.

They'd risen in the spacious tent. The children played with a set of toy soldiers one of the Anshanites had carved for Cambyses. Their voices were high, animated.

"Amytis has known only force," Cassandane said, "aggression – look at Nebuchadnezzar's Babylonia – her husband. Her first."

'Tossa flung one of the soldiers and hit Cambyses in the face. He pushed her away, and she howled.

"Stop it!" Cassandane shouted to them.

"They were just wrestling," Cyrus said as Bagapates gathered them up and shooed them outside.

Cassandane shook her head. "A warrior's children." She stood and moved toward the doorway without touching Cyrus. He jumped up.

"Cassandane, wait –"

Just then, "They're leaving!" Cambyses bounded back into the tent. "That other army – they're going away!"

"The Lydians?" Cassandane asked. "Croesus's army?"

Just then, 'Tossa, laughing, burst through. Charging after her brother, she flung herself at him. Grabbing her big brother behind his knees the little girl, barely a toddler took him down.

"Not fair!" Cambyses, more humiliated than hurt, shouted. "You came at me from behind!"

"'Tossa!" Cassandane said sharply.

"I think he's fine," Bagapates said. After he'd helped Cambyses to his feet and brushed him off, "It's true – the camp is elated. The Lydians packed everything and have already begun heading west."

Cyrus heard Bagapates, and he heard the sounds of celebration in the camp. But he was staring at the children. Slowly, a grin transformed his face. Suddenly, he scooped up a bewildered 'Tossa. "That's it!" he said and swung her aloft until she laughed. "We'll tackle them from behind."

* * *

"WE PRESS FORWARD," Cyrus told the commanders' assembly later.

"What?" Otanes asked.

"We're going to tackle them from behind."

The others exchanged a look.

"Surely you don't mean to continue," Harpagus said.

"That's exactly what I mean," Cyrus said. "Don't you see? We surprised them once. They never thought we'd fight so well. We'll surprise them again."

"But our men are exhausted, many are horribly wounded, and even more will have to be buried here. The army cannot take a fresh assault. Plus, if we move forward, we expose our southern flank to the Babylonians. And if that's not enough, consider: if the men don't return to work the land they've planted and husband their animals, it will be a starving winter for their families. Croesus knows that you cannot fight so late in the year. No one fights now."

"That's the point. Look we have nothing to fear from Babylonia. Belshazzar has abandoned Harran. And the king is simply absent. As for Croesus, we have scared the old Greek-lover. He thought he could bully his way into our lands without any regard for an existing treaty. But all the gold in his coffers and all the numbers of men, fighting for love of nothing but pay, could not defeat us. Croesus sees what they all know. That's why he's running for home."

Again, the men exchanged a look. No one needed to point out how unrealistically optimistic was Cyrus's interpretation of recent events.

"Think of all there is for us to gain." Cyrus's eyes were bright. "Wealth beyond imagining…"

The men shifted in their seats. Who couldn't use a bit more gold?

"But most important of all…" Cyrus lowered his voice and leaned in. "We will have defended our land, *our* homes and the welfare of this land. This land that *our* people, formerly Medians now all of us Persians have for so long tended and kept. And –" He sat back and fixing each commander with fierce eyes said, "We will have punished an oath-breaker. An oath-breaker!" Cyrus said again, bringing his hand down hard on the table. "We can win, if we go forward."

In the silence that followed, each man looked straight ahead. Cyrus could see the men softening, some nodding. "Tonight, tend your men and rest," he said. We'll give the Lydian a good head start and follow him in a few days' time."

As the men filed out, Cyrus gestured to Harpagus to wait. "I appreciate your concern, and I share it. But don't you see? Our armies were equally matched. That is a situation we won't enjoy again any time soon. We have all of our allies fighting with us now, and people whom we've only recently won over. Croesus has more long-time forces and probably allies, too, to draw from. He will be back and stronger. Besides, if we retreat now, without a definitive victory, we jeopardize the faith that's fragile and new among these chieftains and even the Median forces. We have to do this, and we have to do it now."

"It's a huge risk."

"I know. But -" Cyrus thought of Amytis, what she'd told him that night, what she'd done for the good of her land, what she'd been willing to do. And against such odds. If they didn't prevail against Croesus now... "We have to finish this thing," Cyrus said. "Or die trying."

CHAPTER 23

*K*ing Nabonidus had settled into desert life as if he were born to it. Yes, he conducted official business from his base in Teima. He facilitated valuable trade routes, established relations with peoples no Babylonian had been able before to reach. But mostly he relished the simple severity of the landscape, the way the horizon stretched out long all around him. Many were the nights that Nabonidus ordered the tent's covering rolled away. Lying on his pallet, the dome of sky seemed close enough to touch. Many were the nights that the face of the moon, Nanna-Suen's benign presence, brought him to grateful tears. Awe and the company of like-minded people, spiritually sophisticated, humble in practice, made his days complete. The desert itself stripped all else away. And the veil between gods and humans seemed thin indeed.

So, news of Belshazzar's indiscretion came like the clang of iron against a helmet of war. A hunting trip gone awry. The Gutian chief's beloved son killed by Belshazzar's own arrow. Nabonidus had heard nothing of it from Belshazzar but rather from the Gutians themselves. Nabonidus sighed. Belshazzar, when through the slow exchange of messengers, Nabonidus confronted him, said it was an accident – a terrible accident. Belshazzar said he'd asked their pardon, but those uppity people wouldn't have anything to do with him.

After a great deal of thought, Nabonidus sent to the chief official condolences sensitive to the Gutians' own religious sensibilities, and he forgave their annual tithe that they might instead do with the goods in a manner honoring the deceased Thaer. When it was done, the missive sent, Nabonidus stepped outside. Not into a throng of sycophants or wheedling priests, not directing the countless palace staff in the countless ways expected of the monarch on the throne, not to the thrum of festival arrangements and public appearances. No, simply outside. And yet again, Nabonidus was grateful for the silence of the desert all around him.

CHAPTER 24

*T*hey didn't give chase right away. Cyrus's troops needed to rest, and the army to resupply and plan. While they did so, they'd live in the fortress and what was left of the settlement at Pteria. Those sections and buildings that had suffered most at the hands of the Lydians Cyrus determined would have to await repairs; but much of the city was still habitable. The reservoirs were clear and the undulating countryside with its rocky outcroppings and gray-green shrubs and trees still bore some of the fruit and crops its former inhabitants had tended. Cyrus moved his family into the big house which stood near the best-preserved public building in the settlement.

The day was cool, a harbinger of winter ahead, when Cassandane first stepped into the main hall of their new home. Despite herself, she smiled. A great round hearth blazed in the very center of the room. Cyrus stepped up behind her and put his arms around her waist. She stiffened but let him hold her.

"Do you like it?" he asked.

Cassandane nodded.

"I'm told it's a common style around here. And they have

those columned halls that you and I both liked so well at Ecbatana --"

Cassandane stepped free and walked toward the fire.

"But this is different." Cyrus went on speaking like he would to a skittery horse. "The Greeks call it a megaron -- this central hearth. Cozy in a place like this. But don't get too comfortable," he said lightly. "Soon we'll press even further east."

Cassandane could hear the conciliation in his voice. She knew that he was trying to draw them back together, that he hoped the farther they went from Ecbatana, the closer they might come to each other. She felt sorry for pushing him away. But something in her resisted. She simply couldn't come around.

It was as if some cold wind of furious strength kept intervening. She could as likely grab ahold of air as control it. Cassandane couldn't get Amytis out of her head. When she thought of the Median queen, that Amytis was also Cyrus's wife and all of it so public, and on top of it all, that Cassandane had to be not only far from Pasargad but in Amytis's home, indefinitely it seemed -- even the sparking fire before her wasn't warm enough to ease her chill.

But for all that, this alienation that Cassandane couldn't seem to change pained her most because she still loved Cyrus. She knew it and wanted to give him something for hope, something.

Finally, all she could say was, "And one day, Pasargad."

But there was no answer. When she turned, Cyrus had already gone.

* * *

OVER THE SUCCEEDING DAYS, Prexaspes made it a point to wander among the troops, echoing and adding to Cyrus's expression of confidence that they can and will defeat Croesus in his own country. Some still in doubt sought out Otanes, who simply said that the gods favor Cyrus. It would be all right -- he didn't know how but believed it to be so. Despite such reassurances, some of the men left in a night's darkness. Cyrus knew it but he let them go. Not all of the men who remained were convinced. A contingent from northwest grew more and more restless as they neared departure. Prexaspes saw it, and alerted Cyrus, who called them out.

"Croesus will surely have scouts not only ahead but also behind," their spokesman said, "watching for trailing assassins if not for a pursuing army."

"He cannot imagine that we'll pursue."

The man glanced uncertainly back at his companions. They urged him to hold his ground. "With all respect, sir," the man said to Cyrus, "how do you know that?"

Cyrus stroked his chin. "What do you suggest?"

"There is another route, one to the south."

"Can it bear the strain of the army, the wagons, the camels with baggage and packs?"

"We think so, sir."

Cyrus gestured for parchment and pens. "Map it out for me," he said.

And so they came up with a plan that – if it didn't convince everyone of success – at least gave them some hope that they'd make it all the way to Lydia, where many of Croesus's troops would have laid down their weapons and reintegrated into their rural and civilian lives.

The next morning, they left Pteria, following not Croesus's route, a well-traveled road through Cappadocian Ankara but south, past the silent sentinels of fairy chimneys, rock-cut caves and tunnels, and the ruins of civilizations long gone. The road was barely passable in places, and the going slow. Prexaspes watched closely the men who had suggested the way, quietly trailing each if he broke away from the company. But he would catch them merely relieving themselves, tracking a hare, or braving a hive for honey. Still, his suspicion was on alert the long miles through foothills, a plateau's monotonous flats... for any sign of betrayal.

* * *

ONE EVENING, after they had traveled for many days with many still to go, Cassandane left the children in Bagapates's care and wandered to the top of a distant mound. Stones, rounded by weather, still stood atop one another in what looked like the walls of a modest enclosure. No roof remained. Cassandane wandered in through the gap of a doorway. The silence inside had a softness, a calm that Cassandane breathed in like a surfacing swimmer too long underwater. She walked slowly around the perimeter. Weathered reliefs, carved hundreds of years before her portrayed deities in long procession. Every so often, a breeze blew through cracks with a low hum. A wisping curl worked itself loose from the tight knot at Cassandane's neck. She ran her finger along the ancient carving.

A hand on her shoulder made Cassandane jump. Cyrus stood behind her.

"Hittites," he said. "Long gone."

Cassandane stepped away.

Cyrus lifted his arm and swung it slowly. "Or not really gone at all."

Cassandane looked down at the ground.

"I'm interrupting." Defeated, Cyrus turned to go. He stepped back over the threshold.

"They were egalitarian," Cassandane said.

Cyrus stopped and turned. He smiled and stepped back inside. "Maybe that's why they left such beauty." He reached out to Cassandane's curling lock and wound it gently around his finger.

"Maybe that's why they all died."

Cyrus's smile evaporated.

* * *

FINALLY, Cyrus's scouts reported Lydia close ahead. It was clear to see, the scouts reported, that Cyrus's company had made the trip without Croesus being any the wiser. It was true: no one had imagined Cyrus would pursue. The surprise had worked. So far.

Croesus learned of their advance only when the Parsan company emerged into the outskirts of Sardis. Croesus leapt into action, hurriedly reassembling an army from those who'd thought the season of war was done. But he was on his home turf and had ways of quickly gaining soldiers to fight.

Meanwhile, Cyrus's troops were tired, diminished not only by the battle at Pteria on the Halys but also by the many who had quietly left, defected for home. So, even with the surprise of Cyrus's appearance, the Lydians army outnumbered the Parsan troops three to one. And Croesus grew it by the hour. A commander showed Cyrus what Croesus was offering to mercenaries -- gold and silver disks, stamped with images on each side.

"Coins," the man said, "worth specific amounts. They trade them for goods or services."

Cyrus turned the strange object over and over again in his hand.

So, when Cyrus issued his customary invitation to the Greeks along the coast: surrender now and Persia would spare them assault and grant them near independence for the future, it could not have sounded more preposterous. The Lydians took in the sight of Cyrus's band – travel-weary foreigners with armor and weapons far inferior to any that Croesus provided – and they laughed.

Croesus said, "We'll put an end to this Persia once and for all."

CHAPTER 25

a messenger from Ecbatana arrived in Cyrus's camp that evening. He had ridden hard, following the northern route. Word was, Vishtaspa was sending supplementary forces from Parthia along with camels. He had been successful in gaining the support of that region and hoped the reinforcements would arrive in time. They were on their way.

Cyrus shook his head. "Our advantage is timing. We must attack tomorrow." He looked out at his men, a disparate company. He could offer them so little by comparison with Croesus's great wealth. Yet another contingent had defected the night before. There was nothing to do about it now.

As Cyrus sat digesting the grim facts, "There's another thing, sir." The messenger said. "Your wife --"

Cyrus's mind snapped back. "What of her?"

"She reports that Ecbatana is behind you --"

Cyrus's face went blank, then relaxed in recognition. "Amytis."

"Yes," the messenger said. "And two more things she insisted I tell you."

Cyrus nodded for him to go on.

"The boy Gobryas has disappeared. She thinks he ran away, sir."

Cyrus sat heavily. Another loss. "Does Amytis have any idea where he is, where he's gone?"

"No, sir. She's still looking."

Cyrus brightened. "Did Vishtaspa's message come before or after Amytis's?"

"After, sir."

Cyrus's face fell again. "So Gobryas didn't go there. Vishtaspa didn't mention any visitors, did he?"

"No sir. Well, there is one; but he's an old man, a philosopher or prophet or something who wasn't accepted among his own people. Zarathustra they call him. Hutaosa was quite taken by him, by his teachings. He lives with them, now, I think."

Cyrus raised his eyebrows, then shook his head. "Not Gobryas, though."

"No, sir."

"And the other?" Cyrus asked. "You said there were two things."

"Rather cryptic, sir." The man took a breath. "Amytis said she knows about Vishtaspa's contribution. 'Camels,' she said. That was it: 'Camels.'"

Cyrus looked his question at the messenger. "Nothing else?"

The messenger grimaced, unable to interpret further. "She said you'd know, sir."

Cyrus groaned. Cryptic, indeed.

* * *

CYRUS STEPPED into his tent and banged his shin on the sharp edge of an overturned table. The place was in disarray. Bagapates knelt comforting a sniffling 'Tossa while Sanda sat on the floor cradling Cambyses, his head on her lap. Blood speckled the floor and covered her skirt. Cyrus rushed to her.

"His tongue," Sanda said. "He bit his tongue this time. It will heal."

Little 'Tossa, quiet now, watched Cyrus with wide eyes.

"'Tossa," the eunuch said, "Tell your father what you told us."

The little girl nodded and wiped her nose on her sleeve. "It was me," she said.

Cyrus looked puzzled.

Bagapates shook his head as if to say, "there's more."

"I pushed everything around, away," 'Tossa said. "I'm sorry."

Bagapates said gently, "Tell your father why."

"By-by was going to fall down again."

Bagapates looked up at Cyrus. "She anticipated it. They had been playing together over there," he gestured to a bright corner where they had kept a small wooden chest, a table, and a couple of chairs, "when all of sudden 'Tossa began shoving things out of the way. A minute or so later, Cambyses fell down, shaking like he does. He would have hit the furniture if hadn't been for her."

Cambyses clamored out from Cassandane's lap.

"She knew it was going to happen before I did," Cambyses said, his voice thick with the injury to his tongue, but excited. He took 'Tossa's hand, and looked down at her, his face soft. "Didn't you?" Cambyses looked up and suddenly angry, called toward the door, "Hey!" A little blond head disappeared from the flap. "Aspacanah. He's always spying."

Cyrus stooped down so that he was at eye level with his three-year-old daughter. "You did well," he said. She grinned shyly.

Cassandane stood and they began to reorder the room.

While they worked, "Gobryas is gone," Cyrus said, "disappeared from Ecbatana."

Sanda pursed her lips. "He's a smart boy, independent, resourceful. It's not too much to hope that he's all right." She gave a small smile. "Remember that time with horses, the camels...?"

"Yes!" Cyrus exclaimed, and before Sanda could stop him or

he could stop himself, he took her face in his hands and kissed her full on the lips. Sanda sputtered in protest, but Cyrus had already dashed out of the tent.

* * *

"WE WAIT," Cyrus said. He had called together his friends, the men who led each of the Persian armed forces, such as they were: Harpagus for the infantry, Prexaspes for the cavalry, and Otanes for the archers. "Vishtaspa is sending reinforcements, and they should be here soon."

Prexaspes paced, "We can't," he said.

"It's true," Harpagus added. "Your instincts this far have been good – we surprised Croesus. That was the whole point."

Prexaspes nodded vigorously. "We got all the way here without their knowing. But now – you've seen it yourself – with every passing day, every passing minute, Croesus expands his forces."

Otanes said, "But you know all this. So why wait now?"

Cyrus grinned, but the smile was tentative and gone as quickly as it had come. "It's a gamble. That's true. But – " And he told them his plan.

When he was done, Harpagus said, "It's dangerous – a risk, all right." He didn't need to say that he remembered a time when he'd come this close to using such a strategy to kill the young man before him now, when he'd set the boy Cyrus in a lethal path and only in the last moment swept him from it. He'd realized then the magnitude of his ambivalence toward Cyrus. Now, with Cyrus his king, the ambivalence was gone. And thankfully, Cyrus had a more recent, less damning example to share with these men unfamiliar to the phenomenon. "I'm in" Harpagus said. "I'll lead the men as you direct."

"I'm beside you. Always," Prexaspes said.

"I think it sounds good," Otanes said. "… But the men will not.

Depending – again – on surprise, this time you can't tell them, right?"

Cyrus sighed. "Right."

"I suppose we will lose some," Harpagus said.

"More," Prexaspes said.

And it was true. They did lose more men, more who defected. They knew that Cyrus was waiting for back-up. But meanwhile, they watched Croesus grow and hone his forces. Despite the confidence, the pride, the rousing words the generals employed to keep up morale, there was grumbling in the ranks. And for good reason. Their odds worsened with each passing day. Finally, a runner came with the news. Vishtaspa's forces would be here by nightfall.

"Tell them to camp where they are. Tomorrow, advance but still keep back."

"Yes, sir," the runner said and headed back the way that he'd come.

* * *

CYRUS CALLED a final meeting with the commanders. He had one more surprise for Croesus. Cyrus outlined the strategy. Cavalry were to be divided into two groups. He and Prexaspes would each lead one.

"Whatever else happens," Cyrus said to the cavalry officers, "whatever you think in the moment, the cavalry must follow us. You -" he pointed to several of the officers, "in a company following Prexaspes. And you –" he pointed to the remaining officers, "in a company following me. Is that clear?"

The men nodded.

"War chariots and riders shall assemble at the front lines. We have no reason to believe that Croesus will not do the same."

The men nodded again. This was the most practical.

"Infantry behind them, archers to the back. Now, listen carefully." Cyrus turned his attention to commanders of the ground troops. "It is crucial," Cyrus said, "that an aisle remain open through the middle of the army – infantry and archers – all the way from the rear to the front lines. Now, how you create that aisle, I leave to your leadership. But it should be at least as wide as three chariots abreast. And prepare your troops to widen it for their own safety as necessary." At his last sentence, Cyrus watched confusion cross the men's faces. "It will be clear in the moment. Do you understand."

The officers nodded. "Otanes will have archers at the ready to shoot at his discretion. Since they're behind the infantry, it'll be important for army officers to direct their troops drop down to one knee– out of harm's way – when the arrows fly. Finally," Cyrus leaned forward, his palms on the table, and looked around at each man gathered there. "Not a word of these details shall be spoken outside of this group." He straightened again. "Are there any last questions?" There were none.

That evening, Cyrus issued his invitation to Croesus, "Surrender now, and you'll be spared."

Croesus reply was quick in coming. "Haha. You will not, though yours will be a pretty face on the wall. I'll be sure to give it the highest of spikes."

* * *

THE NEXT DAY, the armies assembled exactly as Cyrus predicted. Croesus's war chariots shone in the morning light. Drivers and riders astride well-rested mounts wore plates of bronze and steel. Cyrus's men came as they'd arrived after weeks of wearying travel. Although Cyrus had assigned men from differing ethnic and tribal groups to the same companies in an effort to unify the diverse troops, the variety of clothing and armory made it easy to identify one from another. He couldn't worry about it now. It was clear from the assembling forces the advantage that Croesus enjoyed. Far fewer Persian horses had made the journey than the horses the Lydians held in place, rested and eager to fight.

Cyrus swung around in his saddle. The aisle was clear. He caught Prexaspes's eye and nodded. Suddenly, the Lydian horses surged forward. Cyrus's leapt to meet them. But no sooner had they charged than Cyrus gave the command to swing away. Prexaspes turned one way and Cyrus the other, drawing their companies of cavalry behind. The Lydians delighted to see such flight. Cyrus's troops peeled away and galloped back, away from the Lydians, away from the battle. Indeed, the Persian riders didn't hesitate to leave the field behind Cyrus and Prexaspes. Some thought like Croesus that Cyrus was finally running away.

But as the Persian horses disappeared around the perimeter, down the middle aisle that split the Persian troops a red cloud grew. By the time Croesus's mounted troops could see what thing had so stirred the dust, it was too late. Out of the cloud great animals came, their wide feet hammering the Lydian clay. Long muzzles, yellow teeth bared, strained forward on sinewy necks. Camels thundering toward them with awkward jockeys driving them on. The Lydian cavalry froze. They hardly had time to wonder at the strange matter than their mounts screamed with fright and would not be controlled. Croesus's cavalry broke its ranks as crazed horses crashed back into the Lydian infantry, pounding the men on foot without regard for anything but flight. The Lydian infantry, battered by its own army, fell into disarray against their archers who struggled to shoot and, in the chaos, shot many of their own. The Lydian forces struggled to recover in time to face the Persians, newly energized by this turn of events. They never did. And Croesus, thrown from his chariot, overturned in the melee, was brought before a victorious Cyrus.

* * *

Amytis read the message that Cyrus sent with a mix of emotions. He told her that while representatives from the Greek colonies sent appeals to Cyrus for clemency in their cities – he would grant it - his own troops built a pyre for the doomed Lydian king. Cyrus told her that as he strode toward the defeated king, a crippled boy broke through the crowd. For an instant, Cyrus thought it was Gobryas. It wasn't, of course. The boy threw himself at Cyrus's feet and begged for his father's life. "I thought of Mardonius," Cyrus wrote. "How could I not? This child to lose his father – because of a battle... because of me. I couldn't. When I looked on Croesus, all I saw was the dead Mardonius. Good Mardonius. 'Douse the flames,' I said. 'Life,' and watched as Croesus was led away, his son limping behind. It is finished. And thank you."

CHAPTER 26

They moved into the palace in Sardis, Cyrus, his family and their personal servants. It was a wonder -- everything new, everything different. Marble sculptures, mosaics of tiny tiles, lush parks filled with wildlife and all manner of blooming things. They drank from skyphos – beautifully decorated two-handled vessels that a person could set flat on a table. The bread was flat, baked with a crisp crust around its edges. And the olives. Such a wonderful fruit, vegetable, oil. They spread tapenade on bread, swirled olive oil into pureed chickpeas, savored salt from the sea. Cyrus sent another message to Amytis: He'd need to stay a while, stabilize the region and such. She read accurately between the words: The ice that had taken shape within Cassandane had begun to thaw.

Cyrus worked out the details of administration, changing little of the ways that Sardis and all Lydia had operated before. He put a Parsan in charge of final administrative decisions, answerable to Cyrus, but tried to keep Lydians in important positions as well. "The Lydian Pactyas will assume control of the treasury. He will answer to the Persian head of the garrison," Cyrus directed.

Life was good in Sardis. The days turned into weeks turned
into months. Sanda spent long hours on bluffs overlooking the
sea. She took the children to the coast to play in the waves and
bake in the sun. They didn't speak of Pasargad, didn't speak much
of the future at all. That would come. In the meantime, this was
enough. Time passed, and it was good. To his great delight, Cyrus
felt an ease with Cassandane that he'd forgotten was possible.
One day, after they had sent the children with Bagapates to ready
them for bed, Sanda laid her hand on Cyrus's arm.

"I'm pregnant," she said.

Cyrus returned her smile. He wrapped his arms around her.
And she wrapped her arms around him.

* * *

BARDIYA WAS BORN IN LYDIA, with the sea salt air to season his
first breath, the sun to brighten his spirit, and the gold-giving
river to whet his appetite for luxury. 'Tossa continued to prove
able to predict Cambyses's fits, which drew the adolescent
Cambyses even closer to his little sister. He resented, then, the
time she spent with Aspacanah, Prexaspes' boy. And truth was,
that where 'Tossa went, so went Aspacanah.

Aspacanah accepted his father's negligence with the same
pensive quietude that he brought to the world. He and 'Tossa,
companions since infancy, were inseparable. But they were as
different as their hair – light from dark. While Aspacanah was
contemplative and gentle, 'Tossa was eager and opinionated, even
at only eight years old. Aspacanah deferred to 'Tossa but watched
closely when he doubted her judgment, more than once catching
her just before she got hurt. Aspacanah struck no one as comedic,
but he could make 'Tossa laugh with a guileless lilt that brightened the face of anyone who might overhear. Anyone but
Cambyses. 'Tossa's brother was quite simply jealous.

"They shouldn't play together like that," Cambyses said to

Sanda, when 'Tossa's rough-housing brought her and Aspacanah to the floor in a tickling fit. "It's not right." Cambyses's voice broke in its register.

Sanda looked at her eldest son, his chin sprouting the beginnings of a beard, his eyes sober. He had never grown like boys his age but was undeniably a young man. Sanda sighed.

"It's okay for now, By. Let her have fun. There are so few friends someone like 'Tossa can have."

* * *

ONE DAY, Cyrus took Sanda to the sea. Hand-in-hand, they walked along old paths, long silences interrupted by anecdotes about the baby, Bardiya, already walking, chasing his older sister and brother, mimicking Cambyses and always on the lookout for ways to best him. Sanda laid her head on Cyrus's shoulder as they watched the shore birds dip and flit, catching prey unseen. They walked on and talked about the wonder of the Lydian parks, the value of a system of coinage, and about the olive oil so ubiquitous here that they couldn't imagine having lived without it. They laughed at 'Tossa's fearlessness, a poignant counterpoint to the steady shadow that was Aspacanah.

Cyrus drew Sanda down to sit beside him on a broad rock overlooking the Aegean. He opened his mouth, shut it, opened it again, and shut it again.

"We have to go back, don't we?" Sanda said. "To Ecbatana."

A fishing boat bobbed on light waves, its oarsman pulling steady to bring it back to the docks.

Cyrus looked at his wife, her dark eyes flanked by tiny lines, her mouth straight but relaxed. "Yes," he said. Cyrus reached out and ran a hand over her dark hair and replaced a flyaway lock behind her ear. "But here's what I plan to do. Bring craftsmen back with us. I'll settle things in Ecbatana. But then, Pasargad."

Cassandane's eyes shone.

"There, you and I together will build a palace that marries the best of all that we've seen -- the columned halls of old Media, the open and airy stonework of Lydia, and gardens such as no one has ever seen before. We will arrange them as the gods have ordered the universe and irrigate them for green, for life. There'll be no place for chaos, no place for conflict. Your home and mine, it will be a place of peace. With the right people in place to manage the territories, we can live in Pasargad. We'll live even better than before. And there we will stay for the rest of our lives."

Sanda's eyes were swimming when she took Cyrus's hand. She smiled a soft, small smile into his broad face. Cyrus stood and took Sanda's hand to lift her beside him. And like that, side-by-side again, they began to walk back to the palace.

"My brother will be happy." Sanda gave a little laugh. "I can't imagine why, but Otanes misses Zarin more than he would ever say."

"And now he has a child of his own, I hear."

"A daughter."

"Do you know her name?" Cyrus asked.

"Phaideme, I think."

Neither spoke of Amytis.

PART II

542 – 540 BCE

*N*abonidus reluctantly removed the linen turban he had grown so accustomed to wearing, its fabric easy to manipulate against the blowing sand, and accepted instead the ornate crown that his steward held out to him. So heavy. Never mind that it had been an accident, years ago now, Belshazzar killing the Gutian chief's son during that fateful lion hunt. But try as Nabonidus might – and he had tried everything – the Gutians would not be consoled. On the contrary. Finally, in the face of what they, like others, perceived to be a rift in the halls of Babylonian power, they defected.

Nabonidus felt the dread of the throne settle cold on his shoulders. It wasn't so much the business of leadership that weighed on him as the expectations of a circumscribed piety dictated by Marduk's priests; all the social expectations – the unwritten expectations of appearance, stroking the egos of Babylon's elite citizenry…; and the great grand city itself – busy, loud, constantly in motion.

Nabonidus had been in Teima for almost ten years when it became clear: he had to go back. With Cyrus's acquisition of

Media, which Nabonidus observed that he'd managed to hold; his successful conquest of Lydia; and now this – the loss of Gutium, Nabonidus concluded that it was time to return to Babylon. The empire needed its king at its heart. Nabonidus might yet be able to bring the Gutians back. More honey than a stick he hoped would convince the geographically critical tribe to return to the empire. If force were required, he was prepared to call out the army, of course; but the Gutians were ostensibly Babylon's own people. Such a threatening course of action seemed not just foolish but perverse.

Nabonidus looked up at the roiling sky, searching for the pale sliver of Nanna-Suen, but he couldn't see even that tiny hint of the moon for the gathering clouds. He knew his god was there, nonetheless, high in the firmament, serene and constant, and it strengthened his resolve finally after all these years of kingship to elevate the rightful head of Babylonia's pantheon. Marduk had had his time, imposter for centuries. It was Nanna-Suen's time to lead, and Nabonidus would see that it happened no matter what hurdles he faced, his own son Belshazzar included.

Nabonidus had planned his return to Babylon to coincide with Nanna-Suen's great annual festival. He hoped to go directly from Babylon to Harran, to witness the moon god's temple renovations. He knew that Belshazzar had slowed the progress – how much, he couldn't have guessed . But he hoped to celebrate there. It would be the first time in decades that this monumental recognition had happened. He sighed. As usual, Belshazzar had complicated that. Years in the desert had indeed reinforced Nabonidus's devotion to the moon god... and confirmed to him why the gods had made him king of Babylonia.

But, as his caravan began to close the gap between desert and rivers, between the sea of sand and the bustle of buildings and bridges and streets... Well, it had seemed clearer under the wide sky with people of like mind what he had to do, and how. Anticipating his homecoming and his son's inevitable resistance, Nabonidus felt a tremor in his resolve. He looked up again. Nothing.

CHAPTER 28

"From Khai Egibi," the man said. A messenger from Babylon stood before Amytis in her audience room, a papyrus roll extended in his hand. Nothing about the man or the matter of receiving a message, even one from another empire, was unusual. Yet Amytis looked at the man as though she'd been struck immobile and the words he used incomprehensible to her. Another moment, then still speechless, she simply took the note. The man still stood.

"Take him to the kitchens," Amytis said to the eunuch who had escorted the messenger there. "See that he's fed."

Amytis did not open the note right away. Instead, she held it in her hand – a message that Khai's own hands had held, that he had composed while thinking of her. Amytis let herself soak a moment in memories she'd worked all these years to bury – memories sweet and tender and rich with heart and yes, passion.

Her hands trembled as she broke the seal. It was brief. Too brief. Khai apologized for interrupting her peace, sure she didn't want to hear from him, from Babylon. Amytis gritted her teeth to keep from crying out, "No, I want more, always more from you, of you." She took a deep breath and forced herself to attend to the contents of the note.

"There's a young man here," Khai wrote, "bears the brand of a Babylonian slave but says he lived with you, as a member of your household before that – Gobryas, son of Mardonius. My son leased him from his owner to work on repairs in preparation for Nabonidus's return. Has a clubfoot, admittedly good at managing a big project. I wouldn't disturb you with this, or anything, except that it concerns my daughter. Do you know this man?"

Amytis lowered the note and let her eyes go as they often did – to the window, the window, the one that faced southwest. Gobryas, she thought. Found, and in Babylon. With Khai, no less. And what of this daughter? Amytis looked again at the note – this simple papyrus, so flimsy and fragile, so fleeting – it would crumple to dust in no great time, it could be burned in an instant. She ran her hands back over its surface. To think that Khai had held this, written it in his own hand. What would she say in reply? She brought a hand to her lips. It would take a forest of reeds to hold the words she wanted to write.

CHAPTER 29

Belshazzar had been preparing – tributes to Marduk upon his father's return. After a spectacular sacrifice of prize oxen, horses, and lambs in Marduk's temple precinct, and a show of gifts to the god (appreciated by Marduk's priesthood on every level), Belshazzar repaired to an open-air courtyard. It had been transformed into a grand dining room for the big event. The night was clear, the air welcoming and fresh.

Drink flowed fast and full in the court, rhytons drained one after another by an increasingly rowdy crowd.

"Will your father resume the throne?" came a voice from somewhere in the middle.

"Of course," Belshazzar called in reply, though it had been a sore spot. "And I remain your crown prince." He'd become accustomed to acting the king.

"Word has it that your father intends to depose Marduk in favor of Nanna-Suen."

Belshazzar's already ruddy face flushed a deeper red. He peered into the crowd in the direction of the speaker. "Who says?"

"I've heard it, too," a voice called from his left. "And I," the voices came from all sides.

"Nonsense!" Belshazzar stood, stumbling against his chair. "Marduk established the universe and this city as the center of world. Marduk!" He raised his cup and with wine splashing the table over roasted meats, fruit, and bread torn and scattered, "To Babylon!" he called.

"To Babylon!" the crowd responded.

"Babylon, Gate of the Gods!" Belshazzar called.

"Gate of the Gods!"

"Babylon, city of Marduk, king of the gods, god of gods," Belshazzar thrust his rhyton higher with each slurred word. "Marduk the greatest and the highest."

"Marduk be praised!" someone cried.

Still raising his rhyton in salute, Belshazzar more fell than sat back into his chair.

"Praise Marduk! Praise Marduk!" the chant went up.

Belshazzar nodded to the chant as his face resumed its normal hue.

But when the din died down, "But what about your father, what about King Nabonidus?" someone called.

Belshazzar glowered as a strained silence fell.

"What indeed?" a voice intoned with strength from the doorway.

Everyone turned, then in a great crashing and scraping of chairs, got to their feet again. There stood Nabonidus, still wearing his traveling robe and sandals; but on his head, his gray hair long and loose, lay the crown of Babylon. In his right hand, Nabonidus held the staff of kingship. He leaned on it lightly.

Belshazzar hurried down from the high table. Nabonidus strode forward to meet him.

"What is this?" Nabonidus asked, frowning as he looked around at the tables strewn with food and drink.

"Welcome, father," Belshazzar said. He embraced Nabonidus, swaying a little as he released him.

Nabonidus looked around the room, nodding occasionally in recognition of one or another of the guests, then under his breath, Nabonidus repeated, "What is this, Shazzi?" He needn't have worried. The guests – too drunk to be discreet whispered loudly to one another.

"Just a bit of dinner, father." Belshazzar coughed. He caught the edge of a table for balance. "I wanted you to get off on the right foot again here in Babylon."

Nabonidus gestured for the guests to sit, resume their evening.

"Come," Belshazzar said. He tried to pull his father to his own high table. "Sit. Eat."

Nabonidus slipped his grasp. "No. I'm going to bed."

The crowd stood, sloppily again as Nabonidus turned back toward the door. Suddenly, above them, the moon broke through the clouds. Nabonidus stopped. His golden crown glinting white in the silvery light, the king lifted his face. "Nanna-Suen," he said, his voice strong and clear, "Lord of the gods, king of all the gods – above and below…"

As the courtyard behind him went quiet, Nabonidus continued to pray. "Nanna-Suen, god of the gods who dwell in the highest heaven and in the darkest places of the underworld, when you joyfully enter the temple may you bless each of your temples – here in Babylon, in Ur and Uruk, too -- temples of your great divinity."

Hushed exclamations, shushing, and astounded whispers rushed the air like a sandstorm in the desert.

"Give to my people faith in you, great Nanna-Suen. Give them reverence and honor that they might not sin against your great divinity. Make us firm forever."

With that, and in the stunned silence that followed, Nabonidus left.

Back inside, a drunken Belshazzar tried to manage the outrage. "Just as we thought," he overheard someone say, "The king lost his mind in Teima."

"You'll see," Belshazzar called out, his voice seeking purchase in the commotion. "The king will walk with Marduk the greatest of the gods in our – Babylon's – Akitu. You'll see!" Belshazzar's voice rose with each word seeking in vain to dampen the roar of protest.

CHAPTER 30

*A*mytis looked again at the note to her lap. How long had she sat there, how long replaying the moments, the years, how long crafting and recrafting the things she wanted so much for Khai to hear, to know...? The sun was long gone from the window, the stars already emerging in the sky. She tried to still her hands. She'd verify Gobryas's identity, for certain; but how else to respond? She had so many questions. Threading through them all was the image of Khai on the afternoon when they were finally, and only then, together – a love that endangered not only their own lives but also her son's. And after, she'd told Khai never again to come to her. Yes, she had saved wild Media – for now – but not her son. And that Khai worked for the man responsible for Bushu's assassination... The familiar ache of betrayal finally quieted her hands.

She knew what she'd say. She'd simply answer his question. Any more was to loose a dam with waters that had no end. She'd verify Gobryas's identity. That's all. With the decision - the clarity and simplicity of it – came tremendous relief.

"My lady?" Nathan said, poking his head in the door. "Am I interrupting?"

Amytis smiled and waved in this Jewish scribe – a friend – who had been with her through so much, with her since Babylon.

"It's all right. I'm just thinking. What is it?"

"Cyrus's household is on their way back to Ecbatana."

Amytis exhaled. "Yes, of course."

He shifted on his feet.

"Is there something else?"

"No." Then seeing the note on her desk, "Let me know if you need any help?"

"Thank you, Nathan. I will."

He hesitated a moment, then went back out the door.

Amytis looked out the window at her snowy mountains. Yes, a simple reply would be just right.

The door opened again. Nathan.

"What is it?" Amytis asked.

"I met a woman," he said.

Amytis smiled. "Just now?"

"No. I've known her for some time now."

Amytis looked at Khai's letter on her desk. She pushed it aside. "How did you meet?"

Nathan lifted a shoulder and let it drop again. "At the meeting house."

"So she's Jewish, like you."

Nathan nodded. "The daughter of a woman whose ancestry is Israelite. Her father is Median."

Amytis raised her eyebrows, pursed her lips, and said, "You've lost me."

"May I sit down?" Nathan asked.

Amytis smiled. "For certain." She took a chair across from his.

"You know that I was born in Babylonia, in Nippur where my father was a respected teacher, a rabbi."

"Yes. I remember meeting him, meeting your whole family."

"And that family is from Judah."

Amytis nodded. "Conquered by Nebuchadnezzar and taken from there to Babylonia."

"Right. Well, Sarah's family came from lands north of Judah that had been conquered decades earlier by the Assyrians. Our tribes are related. But their histories diverged after the king who had built the temple in Jerusalem died. Anyway, I guess the point is that not only was she born in Media, but so were her mother and her mother's mother. And her father is Median. Plus, whatever Israelite she is, is northern. They're different."

"She is special to you?"

"Yes."

"What is your hesitation?"

"We're just so different."

Amytis thought again of Khai, of the young man with no standing or means, who had taken on the project of making the gardens of Babylon something that truly hinted of home for her, Babylonia's queen.

"She doesn't even know about Ezekiel -" Nathan said, "-God give him peace – though his students collected his teachings, his prophecies. He had these amazing visions and a message that makes sense only if you know everything we Judeans went through."

"Have you asked if she thinks the same?"

"About how different we are?"

"Yes."

"I haven't."

"Ask her. And ask her again what she wants."

In the course of his work for palace, his work on the great gardens, Khai had come to know – and understand – what Nebuchadnezzar's new wife missed in her marrow about Media… and how crucial its protection from human assault.

"Then ask yourself, Amytis said, "if it's anything like you." She dropped her head, shook it. "Who am I to give advice on love?"

"You've lived a lot," Nathan said.

Amytis looked up at him, straight into his eyes, kind and true. She nodded. "You're not a young man yourself," she said with a smile.

Nathan tilted his head. "Maybe for some things, the best ones," Nathan said, "we must wait a lifetime." He shrugged. "Or more."

Amytis fingered Khai's note in her hands.

"Some missive?" Nathan asked, professional again. "Are you sure I can't help?"

"You already have."

CHAPTER 31

*N*itocris received Belshazzar's most recent notice while she was in a holding pen, coaching a young woman how to handle the goddess's panthers when they reached adolescence. She stepped back to the edge of the fence.

"Read it to me," she commanded the messenger, her eyes on then novice handler as the girl approach a particularly savvy but historically placid cat. Nitocris had taken a certain pleasure in hearing from this son she'd hardly known. That he an adult and successful by all accounts would appeal to her, an estranged bastard – never mind she was Nebuchadnezzar's bastard, tickled her in her advanced age. She had to admit there was also some satisfaction in hearing that her husband was finally facing some resistance to his promotion of Nanna-Suen. The desert tribes had been an easy sell. She knew that they held a similar god in the highest place. And Babylonia's rural residents and those from cities a long way from Babylon were less invested in Marduk's primacy than in worshiping their local deities, raising animals, crops, and families. But Belshazzar loved Babylon and all things great and powerful.

"He writes," the messenger said, nerves lending his voice a

whispery quality, "'Father returned from the festival in Harran, angry at how little work had been done on the Elhulhul, yet even more determined to make Nanna-Suen the high god of all Babylonia.'"

Nitocris rolled her eyes. Then serious, she took a quick step forward. "Watch his tail. It's in the tail. And the ears." She stepped back again. "I assume there's more," she said to the scribe without taking her eyes off the girl.

"Yes." The young man read again, "'He prayed in front of hundreds of people, the most important and powerful in Babylon, that Nanna-Suen would take over Marduk's temple here.'"

"What?!" Nitocris exclaimed, startling the girl, who looked at her. "The cat!"

The panther swiped at the girl, who ducked just in time. The messenger ran for the door.

"This way," Nitocris said to the novice. "Walk backward to me slowly."

When they were out of the pen, Nitocris dismissed the girl.

"Give me that," she said to the scribe and took the papyrus from his startled grip.

Nitocris read on silently, her face reddening in anger. The scribe stood perfectly still, watching her, his eyes wide, anxious.

"How dare he? It's a sacrilege and stupid, besides. He can't possibly be planning to turn all Babylonia over to Nanna-Suen. Come. The governor must know this and the temple's shatammu, too."

Nitocris dragged the anxious scribe away. Within the afternoon she had made her case that Uruk should stand against Nabonidus's plan. They would not participate in such a travesty of tradition. "And this, from a man who claims to love history," Nitocris said.

"Remind the king that Uruk suffers already. The drought has caused widespread famine. Even the temple is running low on food. You've got that young widow's letter?"

The scribe nodded. He withdrew a scrap of papyrus and read, "Even the famine is hungry. I branded my two little boys with the star and gave them as slaves to the Lady of Uruk, hoping that there at least they may eat."

"Send that, too. And make sure it gets to Rimut. The king's highest official of religious affairs will surely impress on Nabonidus how dire the situation is. This is no time for games."

* * *

WHEN BELSHAZZAR TRIED to berate Nabonidus for further alienating the Marduk priesthood and the Babylonian elite, Nabonidus cut him off.

"We lost Gutium because of your foolishness."

Belshazzar scowled.

The king's expression softened. He understood. Belshazzar had grown up in a court suspicious of foreigners, suspicious even of people such as he: only half-Babylonian. So Belshazzar had ingratiated himself or otherwise become a trusted advisor to the most outspoken nationalist – the anti-immigration, traditionalist and late king Igliss. Belshazzar had worked all his life to gain powerful friends and to fit in to a dynamic Babylon. And here was Nabonidus, Belshazzar's father and king, from the former Assyria, from a defeated Harran.

"I don't know if I can get them back," Nabonidus said, his voice weary.

"Who cares?" Belshazzar saw anger flush his father's face again and added, "I mean, the empire is strong and you did open trading opportunities through the desert, right?"

"Our relationship with the Arabs is better, yes; but the Gutians offered unparalleled access to east-west routes in the north. You know that."

Belshazzar shrugged. "Then it's even more important not to alienate people here. My dinner guests questioned your commitment to Marduk. And when they heard your prayer to Nanna-Suen, 'god of gods'..." Belshazzar rolled his eyes. "Well, you're lucky I had given them wine. They might have killed you otherwise."

"Lucky that you and everyone was drunk? As you say. But Shazzi, I *will* give Nanna-Suen his due. It is time to elevate the moon god beyond Harran."

"Doing so will be fatal to you."

"You wouldn't mind that." Nabonidus waved away the beginning of Belshazzar's protest. "No, it bothers you mainly because it could be the end of you, too, my son."

Belshazzar shook his head. "First, I don't wish for your death."

"But you would like to be king."

"Second, I have been in touch with Mother."

Nabonidus started. "Nitocris?"

"I only have the one, don't I?"

Nabonidus smiled wryly.

"As the daughter of Nebuchadnezzar, she links us both to Babylon in ways none can deny."

"She is hardly the model you make her out to be."

"Babylonian princess?"

"Do you forget that she was born to a slave woman before Nebuchadnezzar was ever king? She was a bastard, Shazzi. That's why they let me marry her."

"She is coming to Babylon for the Akitu."

Nabonidus raised his eyebrows in surprise. "She's been in Uruk nearly her entire adult life, where incidentally, a terrible drought has demanded leadership from Ishtar's temple. She has her hands full."

"You *are* going to perform Marduk's Akitu, aren't you, Father?"

"It is *Babylon*'s akitu, and Babylon, the entire land, belongs to Nanna-Suen. A case could be made that it is time, past time, to give the temples over to their rightful occupant, Nanna-Suen."

"You can't be serious. Babylon and the Esagil have been Marduk's forever."

"Six hundred years, Shazzi, that's how long. Not forever. And consider: can't the crescent on the Esagil be symbolic of Nanna-Suen, not Marduk?"

"Perform the Akitu, Father. *Marduk*'s. Here. I beg you."

CHAPTER 32

*E*ven if he'd known it, even if he liked Gobryas, Khai could hardly have told Amytis the whole of what had happened since Gobryas had snuck away from Ecbatana. Fed up with playing second place to Cambyses the crown prince, fed up with nearly everything – believing that the world had wronged him in every way – Gobryas had slipped out of the palace and gone to the merchants' plaza in Ecbatana. There, he'd awaited his chance. It came soon enough. When he learned of a merchant caravan headed for Babylon, he hid himself in one of their wagons and settled in for the ride. It didn't take long before he was discovered. In that moment, Gobryas was mistaken for an escaped slave. And there was no one to vouch otherwise.

"One man's loss is another man's gain," the merchant had said. "Fire up the irons."

So it was that Gobryas entered Babylon as the slave of a middle-grade merchant and began a life measured by beatings and humiliation.

His merchant master worked occasionally for the Egibis, but Gobryas was never allowed out of the small rented warehouse for fear he would run (again, they thought). The work was hard –

shifting the burdens of merchandise from one place to another --
constant and mindless, and Gobryas was so frequently berated
and beaten (his clubfoot a liability in every way) that he hardly
thought at all anymore. He woke, he worked, he hurt, he ate what
he got, pissed, shat, slept, and did it all over again until that
became the sum of his action, the sum of his thoughts, the sum of
his self.

Then one day, Gobryas was led out to join a half dozen other
slaves. The Egibis had won a contract to renovate the palace
gardens in preparation for King Nabonidus' return from the
desert. Gobryas was leased out and quickly proved himself
capable of managing the irrigation works. It was there that he
met Khai's daughter Davcina.

* * *

AS IT HAD HAPPENED, she had been reclining on one of the
garden's benches. Gobryas almost tripped over her in his focus
on the machines. He caught himself and looked down. Her eyes
were closed. Gobryas caught his breath. He thought he'd never
seen someone so lovely before. Her skin was almost translucent.
Tiny blue veins ran along a slender forearm pulled tight against a
flat chest. Not exactly beautiful... definitely not pretty... simply
lovely. She opened her eyes.

Gobryas jumped back. The girl pulled her eyes tightly shut
again, winced, and with her hands behind her, eased up slowly.

"What are you doing here?" Gobryas asked.

"I might ask you the same thing."

Gobryas pursed his lips.

The girl frowned. "You are my father's slave."

Gobryas kicked at the ground.

"What's wrong with your foot?" the girl asked, pointing at
Gobryas' club.

Gobryas flushed. "Nothing, " he said, and stormed away, grimacing with every limping step.

The girl watched him go, then gingerly lay back again, her arm over her eyes. She returned the next day and again the day after that, each time watching Gobryas work. But when he caught sight of her, she moved on.

Gobryas told the overseer that he had figure out how to repair the system and requested materials and men for the task. Without hesitating, the overseer put him in charge of workers, both slave and free. Within a week, it was clear that they were making progress.

This time when the girl came back, she caught Gobryas in the midst of an operation just after he'd told two men to position a set of gears while Gobryas held the wooden tubing perfectly still.

"You asked who I am," the girl said. "I'm Khai's youngest daughter." Her voice was flat. "A waste, who should never have been born."

Gobryas struggled to keep the piece in place while he searched the girl's eyes. "How can you say that?"

"I hurt everywhere, all the time -- in my joints, in my head -- and I make everyone miserable."

"Not me," Gobryas said, then squinted his eyes closed. "I mean, I like seeing you."

Finally, the task done, Gobryas called a man to take the tubing from him and secure it to a pivot near the gears.

"You're Khai's daughter? Not my, my –" Gobryas choked on the word, "master's?"

"You work for Khai, don't you? Or Iddina. It's all the same."

Gobryas told her that he belonged to a middling merchant but had been lent to Iddina for special work. "I shouldn't be a slave at all," he said, then flinched.

She didn't laugh. "No one should," she said. "Yet we all are. If only we could be like Maddu."

"Who?"

"You don't know?"

Gobryas shook his head.

"Madanu-bela-utsur is probably the most famous slave in Babylon. He belongs to Iddina's father-in-law, if you could say that he belongs to anyone. Maddu is wealthier than most free Babylonians. He actually lends money to elite citizens, with interest, of course. He's really quite striking, physically, I mean." She said this without blushing as though it were common knowledge, a simple fact, "But also always perfectly dressed, dignified, powerful. He's married and has six children, can you believe? He bought his own house, a large canal-side building near his master's. Maddu has as much to do with the Nur-Sin family's prosperity as anyone, and no one would deny it. Word has it that the patriarch has determined that Nupta, my brother's wife, should inherit Maddu along with his entire family when the old man dies."

Gobryas shook his head again, this time in wonderment. "Such a thing, a slave with such authority and wealth, would never happen where I came from."

"Where --"

The overseer happened by just then and sent Gobryas away with a harsh reprimand for troubling Davcina, the Egibi girl.

Davcina, Gobryas thought, Davcina – the most lovely name for the most lovey girl. Gobryas thought about Davcina the rest of the afternoon and all that night. He thought about pale skin over the finest hands knit with veins, of cherry red lips... and those eyes.

The next morning, she was back. Gobryas tried not to look at her; but Davcina came directly to him, to a bench near where Gobryas was working. She motioned him to join her. Gobryas looked – the overseer was distracted -- and sat down beside her.

Gobryas waited for the girl to speak. But she simply laid her head back on the bench and closed her eyes. Gobryas saw the overseer walking toward them, his face the picture of disapproval. Still, Gobryas didn't stand. Before the overseer had a chance to speak, Davcina said, without getting up, indeed without moving at all, "I asked him to join me. You can have him back now."

* * *

GOBRYAS THREW himself into the remaining work with a hint of the passion he used to have. They'd seen that he was worth more than a laborer. He was intelligent and could even manage other people on a large-scale project. If he didn't escape (the only future that had given him any hope before), maybe he could be a slave like this "Maddu" or one of the skilled and integrated exiles like some of the Jews. Maybe he could even work for Khai. He imagined the pleasure of working with numbers again, ordering and planning, coordinating this and that, perhaps managing other people to build things or simply business prospects. And of course, being near the girl who had so captured his heart. Davcina.

One day, the irrigation system almost done, the overseer told Gobryas that the boss wanted to see him. His heart pounding, Gobryas turned the final details over to another slave, rubbed his palms along the side of his old tunic to clean them as best he could, rubbed the sweat that had sprung to his hands, and limped over in the direction the overseer had pointed. There stood Khai, Davcina beside him. Khai looked hard at the clubfoot then up at Gobryas's face.

Reflexively, Gobryas slapped his hand over the rough brand on his arm to hide it.

"You should have seen this place at the beginning," Khai said without introduction. "One of Nebuchadnezzar's many grand plans. It was all for his young wife." Gobryas saw a cloud pass quickly over Khai's face. And then it was gone. "I volunteered to fetch plants from Media, the country of her youth. I had never been outside of Babylon before. Media stunned me. A mountainous land. Wild and beautiful. You've never seen anything like it. And if you saw Amytis, Nebuchadnezzar's wife, you'd know why she missed it so much. Like some extension of each other they were – that land, the woman."

Gobryas bit his tongue.

Davcina said, "Tell about figuring out how to irrigate, Father." She glanced quickly at Gobryas then back to her father. "Gobryas has been in charge of fixing everything."

They wandered through the gardens, slow and halting, on account of Davcina's pain, Gobryas's clubfoot, and Khai's reminiscences. Something about the way Khai's face changed when he spoke of Amytis and Media made Gobryas think it best not to reveal his own connection to them. He needn't have worried. Between the two of them – Khai and Davcina – Gobryas was speechless. Gobryas was dumbstruck in the presence of his idol. He had heard of Nabu-ahhe-iddin, knew the respect he held among the elite and lower classes alike. He had heard of Khai even while he was in Ecbatana – the family's businesses and trade... And when Davcina smiled, Gobryas had to tear his eyes away. He walked carefully, as if trying not to jostle out of the dream.

They came to the gate. Davcina walked through. Khai, behind her, turned back to Gobryas. Khai's expression when his eyes landed on Gobryas tore away any happiness the young man may have felt. In a voice too low for anyone to hear, Khai said, "Speak to my daughter once more, and you will never see the sun again."

* * *

"But," Khai explained in a note to Amytis, "he did see her again, speak to her, and more."

One day, when Gobryas was directing two slaves in how to replant a specimen that had grown too large for its space, he heard a cry. He recognized the voice, and it rent his heart. He directed the men to keep digging and dashed away as fast as his clubfoot would allow.

Davcina lay in the path, her foot twisted awkwardly behind her. Gobryas ran to her. He crouched down, put her arm over his shoulder and one under her knees and stood slowly. As he rose, he felt her hair warm against his cheek. The skin behind her thighs was soft on his arm. She moaned and turned her face toward his shoulder, and something within Gobryas burst into flower. Fierce and tender, he knew with sudden certainty that he would do anything for her. Gobryas would never have been able to explain, never knew exactly how it happened himself. But his mouth found Davcina's lips. She kissed him back with passion.

Gobryas lowered Davcina back down to the ground, slid his hand between her knees as she drew him down to her. Minutes or hours, neither could say. But when their bodies parted again, they found that they were still alone. Gobryas smiled into Davcina's pale eyes, caressed her cheek, and she smiled back up at him.

"Your ankle?" Gobryas asked. "Is it hurt?"

"Nothing hurts right now," Davcina said. But when she stood, she winced. Davcina gave a half-smile. "It's not bad," she said. Gobryas watched as she adjusted her dress. "I'll be fine."

Gobryas scrambled to his feet.

"But I should go."

"Wait," Gobryas said.

"I'll be back."

Gobryas cleared his throat, his surety gone. "You can't."

When she turned back, Gobryas said softly, " I can't see you again."

Davcina's face fell then hardened with anger. "I should have known."

"No." He reached out. Too quickly - he stumbled. She swerved away. "It's not like that. It's just –"

But she was gone.

. . .

GOBRYAS DIDN'T SEE DAVCINA. Agonizing days turned into weeks. He struggled to accept it: he was a slave and she the daughter of Babylon's most widely respected and successful entrepreneur. It was true. She shouldn't have anything to do with him. He kept his head down and worked like the slave he was, with each day growing more weary and depressed.

Then one day, there she was.

"I just have to know one thing," Davcina said. "How did you become a slave?"

"You believe me?"

"I don't know. But you said you weren't born a slave. I want to hear, then, how you explain that you became so."

Gobryas pursed his lips. He saw the overseer join the work crew. Sweat sparkled on his brow, and he clenched his hands together.

"So it was a lie," she said.

"No, no." Gobryas caught her arm as she turned away. He released it gently. "I'll tell you. But it's a secret. No one would believe me. It only makes things worse. Please don't tell anyone, least of all your father."

Davcina turned her mouth to the side in distrust.

Gobryas glanced at the overseer still talking to the workmen.

Davcina followed him reluctantly behind a thick shrub. "Go on."

Gobryas took a deep breath. "I was born in Susa, the son of a nobleman, Mardonius." He choked on the memory of his father's name, recovered again. "My mother didn't survive my birth. My father, too decent for his own good, gave up everything to raise me." Gobryas looked down at his misshapen foot. "We lived in the palace, he a servant and I - charity... One day, my father learned that a neighboring land, long ago our ally and once again a friend, was under attack by the Medes, a far more powerful force than they could ever confront alone. My father took me to join that fight. He died."

Davcina's eyes pooled.

"I was ten years old. Turns out, the king of the tiny country that my father had gone to help had made a promise that he would look after me should something happen to my father. That king is Cyrus of Anshan. He won that war and gained all of Media. I guess you know that already. And you probably know that he took his household to Ecbatana and married the daughter of the late king. I was in that household. Cyrus married Amytis, whom you know as the wife of Nebuchadnezzar for whom he built these very gardens.

"What?"

"See, it's too much."

"No," Davcina said. "Go on."

"When Cyrus traveled west to confront Croesus of Lydia, he left me behind with Queen Amytis at the palace in Ecbatana. I don't expect you to believe any of this, but I swear that it's the truth. I wanted nothing more than to become a great businessman like your father. So, when the opportunity seemed to come, I slipped away and hid in a merchant's caravan. When they discovered me, they made me a slave. The rest you know well enough.

"I am a slave now, and for that reason, I cannot be with you." Gobryas looked up to see the overseer walking toward them.

"I will talk to my father."

"No! Absolutely not. Promise me that you won't."

Davcina tilted her head to the side. "If that's what you wish. But I must see you."

"You have to go." Gobryas said, catching the overseer's disapproving expression.

"Maybe one day," Davcina said.

"Maybe." Gobryas gave her a small smile. "Go. Promise me, not a word to your father."

"I promise."

The next day, without warning or explanation, Gobryas was not returned to the field. Without explanation, two men seized him from the warehouse and threw him into a dark cell in the basement of someone's mansion. When they released him, Gobryas, too weary and depressed even to drag his clubfoot under him, simply fell to the ground. He rolled over, put his head into his hands, and wept.

CHAPTER 33

*A*mytis rode out to meet the returning company in time to see Sanda close the curtains of her litter. Amytis scanned the riders in front. She rightly surmised that 'Tossa and little Bardiya rode with Cassandane. Cambyses, who'd managed to avoid riding a horse ever since they'd left Ecbatana, had a chariot of his own. Not much grown, but a young man – Amytis noticed – he stood at its front, next to the driver.

Amytis cantered up beside Cyrus. Her hair, almost completely gray now, flowed back in silvery streams behind her. Her green eyes flashed back to the litter, then to Cyrus who stared staunchly ahead.

"Welcome back," she said simply.

"We've brought a lot," Cyrus said, gesturing to the swaying carts behind them.

"Another son, I understand."

Cyrus dropped his eyes to his horse's withers. When he lifted his face, there was no smile in it. "We were happy there."

Amytis pursed her lips.

Cambyses's chariot caught up with them. The prince stood, his hands on the edge behind its driver.

"Where is Harpagus?" Amytis asked, craning her neck for the old steward.

Cambyses said, "He stopped in Urartu to stay awhile with Tigran."

Amytis smiled at the new depth in the prince's voice.

Cyrus said, "He wanted to be certain that they'll continue to make good on their promise to remain within the empire. He's leading a band of reinforcements against the Scythians, too."

"What a place!" Cambyses said. "You should see the lake, so blue, and the palace. Round turrets. huge fireplaces..." Cambyses rocked back then forward again. "I hear Gobryas is gone."

"Actually," Amytis brightened. "I recently learned –"

"What?" Cyrus looked at her, momentarily distracted from his focus on Cassandane's carriage.

"He's… fine." Amytis nodded. "A young man, now."

"Where?" Cyrus asked.

"In Babylon."

Cambyses rolled his eyes. "Of course, he is," he said. "I hope he stays." And with that, Cambyses urged his chariot on.

"How did you learn?" Cyrus asked. As they pulled into the courtyard, Amytis and Cyrus riding side-by-side, it was easy to see that as eagerly as Cyrus wanted news of Gobryas, he was eager to feel again the intimacy he and Cassandane had shared in Sardis. Amytis watched Cyrus's eyes track toward the palace and glanced at Sanda's litter – empty without a word.

"It doesn't matter," Amytis said.

Instead, Amytis told Cyrus what she knew of the prophet, a certain Zarathustra by name, living with Vishtaspa in Parthia. And she said that she'd heard of another prophet even farther to the east – also from a wealthy background, who had given up everything for a personal quest and yet another who spoke of the harmony of the harmony of opposites within an animate universe. But Cyrus, distracted and preoccupied by Cassandane's unhappiness, didn't hear.

CHAPTER 34

*N*o windows, no light, the only way Gobryas marked the passing time in the mansion's dungeon was by the foul food he got occasionally and the increasingly fetid conditions of his cell.

Then finally, one day, the door slid open. A man's shadow fell across the inside his cell. Gobryas sat up and squinted into a torch's dancing glow. The flame bowed and bounced tricking Gobryas into thinking that it was Khai who stood before him.

The figure spoke. "I cannot begin to tell you how much I hate you." It was indeed Khai. "When Davcina learned where you are, she begged me to release you. I wouldn't. She was inconsolable. She's pregnant."

Gobryas inhaled sharply.

"She insists that the child is yours. Do you have any idea what you have done?"

"Sir?"

"The baby will kill her. Her condition makes it impossible for her to bear a child and survive."

"No!"

"Yes," Khai said, the calm in his voice saturated with menace. "You." His voice rose. "You have as good as killed her."

Gobryas groaned.

"Groans are mine. As are you. I bought you."

Gobryas sat up.

"I checked your story – seems true… enough. Amytis –" Khai stumbled on the word, cleared his throat, "…confirmed your identity. For her – and for my daughter, I bought your release."

Gobryas hurried to his feet, awkwardly catching himself – weak and clubfooted – to stand as tall as he could.

"But understand this." Khai's face was granite. "I hate you more than ever. So, think hard about that before you make the choice that I'm about to offer to you."

CHAPTER 35

A crowd had gathered to welcome the victorious king and his household back to Ecbatana.

"We're not staying," Cyrus said to Amytis as they turned the horses over to grooms.

"I know. Pasargad."

Cyrus nodded.

"And I'm not going," Amytis said.

Cyrus exhaled. They both smiled.

It wouldn't be that easy.

They'd barely begun to walk toward the palace, when "Sir!" a breathless messenger pushed his mount forward through the crowd. "Revolt! The Lydian in charge of the treasury, Pactyes, murdered the Persian head of the garrison. He is distributing money and luxury goods to anyone who will join him against you. Much of the coast has already defected."

"Betrayal!" Cyrus's face flushed a deep red. "Kill them all, every one!" he shouted.

The crowd shrank back, silenced by Cyrus's rage.

"Mazares!" he called.

The Persian rushed forward.

"Put it down. Spare no one. And make it as public as you can. Make them suffer."

Amytis laid a hand on Cyrus's arm, hoping to quiet him. "Tell them to take up trade," she said, "rather than weapons."

"Make them suffer!" Cyrus roared.

"Remind them," Amytis said, keeping her voice level, "that they are part of a new system, which can be just and profitable." As Cyrus growled next to her, Amytis said. "And if they don't –" she glanced at Cyrus, "they'll see how we handled the rebels."

Cyrus's dreams of leaving, with a happier Cassandane, finally to build their home in Pasargad were dashed. If they weren't to risk further defections and unrest throughout the new empire, he'd have to stay – and with Amytis, a united front, long enough to bring the former Lydia back into Persia's control.

* * *

IN THE MANSION'S DUNGEON, Gobryas struggled to stand. Before him stood the man who once represented all that Gobryas had hoped to become. Now, Khai was simply the man who stood between Gobryas and all that Gobryas wanted.

"On my daughter's urging and as Amytis has allowed, I offer you a choice," Khai said. "You may return to Cyrus's household – I would gladly provide safe passage myself. Or..." Khai hesitated. He ground his teeth as if to reduce this other option to dust, "You may stay."

So, there really was no choice at all.

* * *

MAZARES FAVORED VIOLENCE. His response was brutal and swift. To those who'd participated in the plot, the punishment was merciless. Once Mazares had settled things in Sardis, he went up and down the coast, doling out horrible deaths to all conspirators. Mazares' men captured a number of the Lydian ring-leaders. Residents who had joined Pactyas were sold into slavery. Occasionally, he introduced the message of trade but used terror freely.

CHAPTER 36

So it was that Gobryas came to live within the Egibi household. Technically free, he worked like a slave. He worked for Khai and Iddina while Davcina grew bigger and bigger with the baby she should never have carried. Khai endured Gobryas's presence and made use of what talents the young man had for the sake of his daughter Davcina and for Amytis too, the two women he loved most in the world. But every discomfort his daughter showed, every hint of the threat pregnancy posed to her life refreshed his anger toward Gobryas.

Meanwhile, the rift between Belshazzar and Nabonidus grew. With every effort of Nabonidus's to elevate Nanna-Suen in the Babylonian pantheon, Belshazzar entrenched himself further with an opposing elite. Belshazzar's appeal to Nitocris further complicated the family's relationships. She had never fully forgiven King Nabonidus for taking their daughter to Ur to be Nanna-Suen's high priestess there, and she shared Belshazzar's concerns about what this revolution in Babylonian theology would do to the social and economic fabric of the empire.

Nabonidus's management of the crisis in Uruk went some way to demonstrate his fitness as king. The altercation unsettled

Nabonidus, though. He left more troops in the south than he had first intended and left instructions to their commander that his daughter in Ur be included in all correspondence and decisions. Ennigaldi-Nanna, as high priestess would mediate with the great god Nanna-Suen, and if that moon god was so pleased, he would protect the region. Then, as expeditiously as possible, Nabonidus returned to Babylon.

As soon as he could, Nabonidus returned to the business of rebuilding Nanna-Suen's temple in Harran. Little had been accomplished under Belshazzar's direction. What's more, he learned from the foreman that Belshazzar had commissioned an inscription declaring that all work on Nanna Suen's temple was done "at the command of Marduk," "leader of the gods." With contained fury, Nabonidus made sure to revise it.

"Can you finish by fall? In time for Nanna-Suen's akitu?" Nabonidus asked the foreman.

"At this pace, yes."

In the midst of the bustle of workers and conferences with temple staff to ensure the temple be returned to its original glory, Nabonidus also found time to walk the streets of Harran. He didn't remember much from the few years of his boyhood spent there before being taken captive to Babylon, but it was easy to imagine his mother a young woman there. He also had heard from among Jews in Babylon that an ancestor by the name of Abraham that they claimed to have been selected by their particular god had once lived in Harran. Nabonidus wondered at the competing theologies that could so complicate relationships.

For his part, he was confident in the supremacy of the moon god but like others he didn't discount the existence and even necessity of other gods. Babylonia's own gods were a pantheon, and with care for their temples and personnel, he paid special attention to Ishtar and Shamash whom he believed formed a complementary trinity with Nanna-Suen. As a matter of fact, after he'd finished overseeing the renovation of the Elhulhul in

Harran, he took care that the temples of Shamash and Anunitum in Sippar received the maintenance that they required.

Such tasks were the work of a Babylonian king, he knew, work he was happy to undertake. Plus, he'd rather be in almost any other city than Babylon these days. He could handle the disapproval and even hatred of the conservative elite, but it pained him to be so at odds with his own son.

Finally, it was completed. The Elhulhul restored. The nights had begun to cool, though the fall days were still hot. Belshazzar refused to join Nabonidus in Harran for the temple's dedication, claiming that he should remain in Babylon, if the king were to be so far away. Nitocris also refused to come.

Yet nothing could dampen Nabonidus' spirit on the day that the statue of the moon god traveled north from his shrine in Babylon to the moon god's temple in Harran. Late October. The trees themselves in red and gold seemed to cheer the day. Nanna-Suen's akitu that year, a festival that Nabinodus orchestrated to coincide with the temple's dedication, was the grandest any had ever seen. Still, it was not Babylon, as Nabonidus was acutely aware. As he traveled south again, back to the empire's capital city, his resolve deepened. In the heavens, Nanna-Suen was waxing.

CHAPTER 37

*N*early winter in Ecbatana, and the air there at the foot of Mount Alvand had teeth. Things in the palace between Cyrus and Sanda were as frosty as they had been before they ever went to Lydia. Unlike the disinterest she'd shown the baby Atossa those years before, Cassandane retained her attention and care for Bardiya. A cheerful toddler and growing as fast as 'Tossa had, little Bardiya was a constant reminder of better, sunnier times. Though Pasargad seemed a distant memory, privately, Cyrus determined to leave just as soon as they could.

As it happened, 'Tossa was consistently able to anticipate Cambyses's epileptic fits. She explained that there was "a kind of buzzing" she felt or heard - she couldn't explain exactly. It gained them a few minutes to prepare. Because of this, unless the prince were in otherwise specially controlled surroundings, 'Tossa needed to be close to Cambyses. So, she became a fixture in his tutoring and training, inevitably learning everything he learned.

Seeing it reminded Amytis of her own childhood, always looking out for her sister, Mandane, always so aware of Mandane's safety above her own. But it was different, too: for 'Tossa, Aspacanah was also there, a faithful shadow. The boy was

growing strong like his father and even at eight showed an aptitude for working with the lance and spear. Consequently, when
Cambyses's training required a sparring partner, Aspacanah was
a natural choice. No one protested. And Aspacanah quietly
became not only quite skilled but indispensable to the prince.

FOR HER PART, Amytis loved having the children back again.
'Tossa, now eight years old, was as leggy as a colt and just as spirited. But it had been a long time, a lifetime to a small child, since
they had seen each other, years since Amytis had fallen into the
role of 'Tossa's primary caretaker. So, one day, when Amytis
knew that Sanda was shuttered in her suite, Amytis invited 'Tossa
to come with her to the stables.

"See if you can pick out the two-year-old bred from your
father's stock," Amytis said to the shy girl who had consented to
join the aunt-like step-mother whom she could hardly
remember.

They walked slowly side-by-side through the paddocks,
Amytis gesturing to the grooms to continue their business, to
ignore the woman and child.

'Tossa looked up from the ground.

"Take your time," Amytis said.

'Tossa peered into one stable and then another, her lips rolled
in on each other, her hands clasped in front of her. Suddenly she
grinned, a chestnut with a white star on its forehead thrust its
muzzle into their path and flicked its tidy triangles of ears
toward them. 'Tossa put one hand to her mouth and with the
other, she reached out to stroke the soft nose and rub its star. The
horse leaned into her touch.

"This one," she said.

"You're right." Amytis smiled. "You can see its desert blood-
lines in the dish of its nose, the lift of its tail when it steps out.
See how much smaller it is than the Nisean warhorses?"

'Tossa nodded.

"But don't be fooled. It is no less fearless or intelligent. Maybe more."

'Tossa gazed at the horse's face, its red-brown neck and shoulders.

"Would you like to ride?"

'Tossa looked behind them, searching the shadows.

Amytis's eyes followed hers and settled on a golden-haired boy standing off to the side, his face sober but watchful.

"Aspacanah," 'Tossa said. "Amytis says we can ride!"

Amytis began to correct the girl but checked herself.

The boy said, "You should ask your mother."

'Tossa looked up at Amytis. Amytis looked from one to the other – the girl dark and quick, the boy light and sweet. She knew enough to see that Prexaspes would as soon not have a child at all. It wasn't about Aspacanah; but Cyrus was everything to him. When it came to riding, Prexaspes wouldn't care one way or another what his son did. As for the girl 'Tossa, Amytis let a smile play on her lips. Amytis bent to the child.

"It's important that you're able to be near your brother, Cambyses, isn't it?"

'Tossa nodded soberly.

"Well, there might be times when Cambyses, as crown prince of Persia, will have to ride..."

'Tossa's face broke into a grin. She looked at Aspacanah. "So I have to know how, too!"

"Your mother will understand," Amytis said, suspecting that it wouldn't be quite that simple. Yet the logic made sense.

"If she rides, I ride," Aspacanah said.

Amytis grinned. "Of course," she said.

"First," Amytis said, "you must learn some things about them, how to put on a saddle and bridle, how to listen and to give clear signals that will talk to them. And you need to learn how to manage their fears..."

Aspacanah stood calmly next to 'Tossa.

BAGAPATES FOUND THEM LATER, the children on either side of a heavy old gelding. 'Tossa leaned on the horse's shoulder while Amytis demonstrated how to check its hooves for stones.

The eunuch looked from the children to the horse to the children and back to Amytis again. Then he said simply, "An urgent matter at the palace – about Babylon, some Egibi family?" he said.

Amytis flushed. She directed Atossa to lower the hoof, "We'd better get back."

Before they reached the gate, Aspacanah tugged 'Tossa to a halt. Amytis hurried on. The little boy brushed the horse hair off 'Tossa's robe, looked her over again carefully head to toe, nodded, and they went on.

* * *

AMYTIS TRIED to quiet her heartbeat as she entered the room. "Something from Babylon?" she asked Cyrus. She glanced, puzzled, at the others present -- men they'd commissioned to improve roads in the greater empire. She waited for them to leave. They did not.

"Oh, not *from* Babylon –" Cyrus said. He jumped up. "I found a way to get back at the man who betrayed you." He looked at her, eagerly.

Again, Amytis glanced at the others present. She knit her brows.

"The Egibi!" He studied her expression. "I thought you'd be more excited."

Amytis shook off her disappointment and the concern that was quickly replacing it.

Cyrus stepped around the table toward her. "We'll cut them out of trade throughout Parsa. It would ruin them." He laughed.

"They'd better hope that Nabonidus hurries up in the Arabian desert. That'll be their only route when we're done."

Amytis took hold of the back of a chair, drew it out, and sat down slowly. "I see," she said. "But that seems awfully hard to enforce, logistically."

"It *would* take a lot..." Cyrus sat down. He waved to the others. "We were just discussing that."

One of the men said, "I'm still not sure how we could do it, actually."

Cyrus's face reddened. "I just hate," his voice trembled with energy, "betrayal. And of you." He slapped the table top. "You said he was a friend, someone you trusted." Cyrus shook his head.

Amytis gave him a small smile. "I appreciate it. But finally, I believe that it would cost us too much to put in place, much less enforce. You agree, I'm sure, that it's worse to set rules we cannot enforce than not to have them at all. Besides," she waved her hand in the air, "it was a long time ago. I never even think about it, never think about him, anymore." Amytis figured it didn't make sense to try to explain. She couldn't have, anyway, even if she'd tried.

* * *

ONE DAY, from western Lydia the news came: Mazares was dead – heart attack, it seemed. Harpagus – until then, still in Urartu – offered to resume the work. By spring, sympathetic to a more enduring answer than violence, he succeeded in bringing the Lydians to heel.

When Harpagus had completed his work to the west, he surprised everyone by returning to Urartu, where he married Tigran's daughter. Within the year, Tariria was pregnant.

CHAPTER 38

Finally, it seemed that Cyrus's household could return to Anshan in Parsa, finally begin building their dream – the Persian palace at Pasargad. With Lydia secure, and Amytis managing things from the now Persian palace at Ecbatana (having demonstrated that she and Cyrus promoted a unified empire even while he'd been in Lydia and she in Ecbatana), they could leave.

Otanes was in Parsa already, of course, having returned just as soon as Cyrus and Amytis had released him from military service. No one could understand how he put up with Zarin and Phaideme, a miniature of her high-maintenance mother; but he was as devoted as a man could be. And Pharnaspes was thrilled to be able to welcome this family home again. An old man now, Cyrus's father-in-law had handled things in the southern provinces well; but he was eager to have his daughter and the grandchildren he had yet to meet settle again at home.

The only one who elected to stay in Ecbatana was Prexaspes's wife. No one asked. Prexaspes had continued to ignore her, as he had ignored their son, ever since Cyrus had married Amytis. And the former Media was her home. Her one great grief was in sending her son. Yet it was no surprise to anyone that Aspacanah would not stay in Ecbatana. There was no question. If 'Tossa was going, Aspacanah would go, too.

* * *

FINALLY, they were off. With each mile that passed as Cyrus's household traveled south from Ecbatana toward Parsa, Sanda grew lighter and brighter. After a couple of days, Cyrus saw her smile when 'Tossa mimicked the song of a strange bird, and in the evening when they camped, Sanda leaned on her elbows and hummed hymns to the heavens. One day, Sanda asked Cyrus to ride with her in the carriage for a while. Sanda drew back to curtains to watch the landscape roll by, threaded her hand into Cyrus's, and leaned her head against his shoulder.

That night, Sanda slipped onto Cyrus's bedroll next to him. He sat up and put his arm around her shoulder.

"Don't ever keep anything from me again," Sanda said quietly.

"I won't."

"Not even if you think it might make me unhappy."

"I promise," Cyrus said, pulling her close. "Only the truth."

They slept together each night for the rest of the journey. And when they arrived back into Parsa, when Cyrus drew Sanda to him, kissed her hair, her cheeks, her lips, she didn't resist. When he pulled back, holding Cassandane's shoulders to look into her deep brown eyes, she smiled.

CHAPTER 39

They stopped first at the palace in Anshan. To Cyrus, everything looked better on this arrival than it did when he first came as boy of ten to live with his father, the ailing king. But it was a poor comparison to Ecbatana much less, Lydia. And even quieter, since they'd sent the palace staff on to Pasargad to assess needs for building there.

While Cassandane was preoccupied in the carriage with Bagapates readying Bardiya, the others walked in. Cyrus watched 'Tossa's face as they stepped through the city gate. Her shoulders slumped, and the sparking excitement in her eyes disappeared. Cyrus saw her whisper to Aspacanah, who nodded soberly.

Cambyses said, "It's not exactly like I remember." Cambyses's voice drew Cyrus's attention away from his daughter.

"You remember it?"

"Yes. But everything seems so much smaller."

The enthusiasm of Pharnaspes in greeting his daughter, Cyrus, and the little ones too, injected a happy welcome into an atmosphere otherwise thick with memory and melancholy.

They left the horses with a team of grooms – none of them Upadarma, Cyrus noticed with a pang of sadness. Well, Cyrus had been a mere ten years old when Upadarma was Anshan's only groom. And Upadarma, an old man even then.

Then they walked back into the palace's domestic quarters. Just a few steps ahead of Cyrus and Sanda, 'Tossa, a slip of a girl, nevertheless walked with a customary confidence next to her grandfather Pharnaspes.

"Do you know Amytis?" 'Tossa asked her grandfather.

Next to him, Cyrus felt Cassandane stiffen.

"I haven't met her."

"She's my aunt, actually my father's aunt."

Cyrus glanced at Sanda. Her expression was unreadable.

"She taught me how to ride. My favorite horse is still in Ecbatana. I miss him. But Amytis said she'd take care of him for me, for when I come back. We would ride all day, sometimes, into the mountains behind the palace, and when we came to big fields, we would race. She has a friend, a scribe who came from Babylon and doesn't ever work on Saturdays. She is very beautiful. And old, like you. You should meet her."

Sanda broke away from Cyrus. "'Tossa," she said sharply.

'Tossa looked back and seeing Sanda's expression, set her jaw.

"Don't bother your grandfather with silly stories." Sanda caught up with them and leaned down to speak into 'Tossa's ear.

"I'm not. He asked how I like it here." 'Tossa glared at her and then dropped back, scuffing her sandals in the dirt.

"Don't be too hard on her," Pharnaspes said.

"She's too bold. She says things she shouldn't, and –"

"You forget I that I raised a strong-minded daughter, too."

Sanda smiled at him then. "I just don't know how to talk to her, how to be with her. It was different when I was little. I adored you."

"Not so different," Pharnaspes said. "Ah, here's Cook!" He directed Cyrus's attention to the stout, red-cheeked woman, hurrying stiffly toward them with a grin that scrunched her eyes nearly shut. "She wouldn't go to Pasargad," Pharnaspes said under his breath, "not knowing you might be hungry."

When she grew closer, Cyrus saw her suddenly hesitate. He stepped forward and embraced her with a strong hug. "What's for dinner?"

She crossed her arms over an ample bosom and said, with a mischievous grin, "I was thinking worm soup."

Cyrus laughed. He caught the look on 'Tossa's face and said, "The first dinner Cook ever made for me was full of surprises – one was a soup with special wheat-flour threads that I thought were worms." 'Tossa giggled. "I was as horrified. It turned out to be delicious… and utterly worm-free." He turned back to Cook, "Enjoy the kitchen while you can. We won't be staying here long." He felt Sanda take his hand. "We are moving to Parsargad. And you, dear Cook, are coming with us."

"I'm too old."

"You can have the very best kitchen –"

"I like this one."

"And sit in a chair in the middle, just ordering people around."

Cook smiled and nodded.

CHAPTER 40

*I*n the palace at Ecbatana, Amytis closed her eyes and imagined distant Babylon, preparing for the akitu. So many logistics. Khai had written to her that his firm managed nearly all of it now. Their correspondence was regular, though few besides Nathan knew that.

Amytis had also written to Cyrus telling that Gobryas had decided to stay in Babylon. After many drafts of the letter, she reported simply that he was now part of the greater Egibi household and seemed to be doing well.

Khai had told her about Gobryas and Davcina, that for all Khai's simmering fury at Gobryas's part in what Khai believed would kill the girl, Davcina was happy and hopeful about the baby. She wrote that she hoped Khai wasn't being too hard on the boy. He was difficult but very smart and didn't really mean to be such a pain. Khai wrote that he grudgingly admired Gobryas's ability to repair the gardens' irrigation system, to grasp the finer points of lending with interest, and to understand when to subcontract and to whom. Amytis wrote that spring was late in Ecbatana, that she almost envied him the soft air but would ride that afternoon along the edge of snowmelt that signaled warmer days ahead. Khai did not write that he wished he could see her ride. And Amytis did not write that she wished she could see him.

CHAPTER 41

*C*yrus let his memory wend with the stream they followed through the pass before Pasargad, the days of escaping the brutal treatment of the groundsman and the helplessness he felt in the face of Cam's addiction and decline. He remembered the surprise of his reunion with Mit and Spaco, the glimpse of Sanda that tore his heart away, the energy of Prexaspes's hatred and later with equal energy his friend's loyalty and love. Cyrus remembered the first morning he woke at Pasargad and how he wished he would never have to leave that place. And now, to be returning with more than he could have dreamed... He breathed in, long and deep, smelling the herbs in the valley, feeling the softness of the air.

Sanda also savored the approach, the anticipation of coming home. She felt her belly jump -- a little flutter as if in answer to her heart ,and she treated herself to a secret smile. Pregnant again. This would be the first of her babies to be born in the dearest of places – Pasargad.

Even before they came through the last of the pass, a breeze from Pasargad's high plain met them with a cool caress. Then, there it was. 'Tossa grinned and pointed – a leggy fox darted past in pursuit of a hare with feet and ears bigger than she had ever seen.

"And look there," Sanda said, nodding toward a herd of deer-like creatures, who raised their heads in unison and bounded into the hills. When 'Tossa yelped with delight, Sanda resisted the urge to hug her daughter fiercely, relieved that maybe Pasargad would give them something to share. Like Lydia, but better: home.

'Tossa looked all around, her eyes bright with delight. The plain was almost entirely bounded by mountains and hills, and there at the far end, she squinted to see, was a shimmering lake. Parcels of cultivated land in the varying greens of diverse crops in spring shared the plain with great trees and flowering shrubs. A few horses and cattle, too, specks ahead, grazed near the settlement's large, circular tents. A constant rushing roar to their left signaled a deep gorge. Dense trees grew along its rocky edge.

Aspacanah rode up alongside the carriage. 'Tossa leaned out and said, "It's almost as good as Media. Aunt Ami should see this!"

"This is our home, not hers," Sanda said sharply.

'Tossa pursed her lips, sat back, and crossed her arms over her chest.

Sanda shut her eyes, then turned her head away from 'Tossa to let the landscape of her girlhood draw her mind away, back before children, before Amytis...

CHAPTER 42

"*Y*our feet!" Khai said, horrified, to Davcina. He had come home early, surprising his daughter at their mansion on Prosperity Canal. She stood in a loose-fitting shift, her belly round beneath its sheer fabric, barefoot on the limestone floor of the entry hall.

Davcina bent her knees then straightened them again. She could no more hide her feet with her sleeping gown than she could hide the baby in her belly. And Khai had already seen: they were not only swollen but cruelly twisted, too. Khai's heart broke all over again. His daughter's face was tense all the time. He hated that the only time she smiled was when Gobryas walked into the room.

"It's the pain, Father," Davcina said. "It's twisted them a bit. But it'll pass. They'll straighten out again soon."

"Agh, that deform-footed boy!" Khai's face was a storm of anger and concern. If possible, he hated Gobryas almost as much as he loved this girl.

"It's not his fault." Davcina held out her hands, imploring. "It just happened, Papa."

But Khai didn't hear her. "Your hands, too!" he exclaimed, staring horrified.

She slipped them behind her back. "That's enough," she said. "He is the father of this baby, just as you are mine."

Khai sank onto a deeply carved bench. Its ivory inlay and golden arms might just as well have been clay for the pleasure he took in it. He put his head in his hands. Davcina sat next to him, shifting her thin legs to make room for her belly, and put her arm around his shoulder.

"When the baby is born, you'll see. Everything will be fine. I will be well again, and he will shower your grandbaby with love and good things. Then you two will have something dear to agree upon."

Khai lifted his head. He cupped Davcina's face with his hands, her skin so soft and fair in his work-worn and sun-darkened hands. His eyes were like those of the sacrificial beasts of Nanna-Suen, heifers held still, awaiting the blade. He stared and stared at Davcina, dropped his hands, and said, "Now why are you up?"

"It feels better to stand on the stone than to lie in bed. And this way I could watch for you," she added with a little smile.

Khai knew the only one she would be waiting for this time of day was Gobryas, but he let the gentle lie stand.

"I'm glad you were."

CHAPTER 43

*I*t was always busy for Amytis these days in Ecbatana, not (she was happy to report to Cyrus) that there seemed to be trouble within the provinces or from outside, but probably because of what she did to prevent such problems and to keep things running smoothly from the former Median capital. Cyrus had made few changes to the administration and if anything took less from the population than Astyages had before him. Amytis should have been content. She was in the place she would have given anything in her Babylonian years to have again. And she had the power to define it.

But she was lonely. For all the tension between her and Cassandane, she missed the family. Most of all, she missed 'Tossa. She saw her younger self in the awkward girl, full of bravado while anxiously measuring her effect on others. 'Tossa could be stubborn and single-minded, which Amytis knew from her own experience could get her in a lot of trouble. Maybe Cassandane showed 'Tossa more concern than when they were in Ecbatana. The girl needed a sensitive eye and a confident hand, not unlike the horses she loved so much.

Amytis tried not to think too much about Khai. But sometimes before she fell asleep at night and again before she fully woke in the morning, her mind wandered back to Babylon, to his smile at her wedding feast, his earnest work building the tiered gardens for her to make mountains in Babylon, the afternoon they shared. Sometimes, when she received his letters, she dismissed everything else and indulged in imagining what he was like today. She wondered what Khai looked like now. Did he dress better, now that he was among Babylon's wealthiest? Had he grown soft around the middle? Was his hair white? Gone? And she couldn't help but look for him among the merchant caravans, hoping that one day he would come.

A gentle knock interrupted Amytis's thoughts.

"Nathan," she smiled. "Come in."

The scribe brought the news regularly – bits and pieces he gathered from Jews scattered throughout the territories. It was valuable information to have alongside the official reports. On balance, they continued to enjoy a relative peace.

"Have you spoken again with Sarah?"

Nathan brightened. "Turns out, she is even more devoted to Jerusalem than I."

"Though she's never seen it?"

"That's right. But neither have I."

"And *her* ancestors aren't even from there, are they?"

"Actually, they are. But you have to go further back. Her tribe and mine were part of a single nation that at its greatest was led from Jerusalem. Our people, all together, are connected to that place as the site where our God, Yahweh, established an earthly rule through David of the tribe of Judah (my tribe) and promised to be present to us from the house that David's son Solomon built. Jerusalem, my lady –"

"You miss it, don't you?" Amytis interrupted. She knew he'd go on and on. "Like I missed this wild place."

"If it's possible, even more."

CHAPTER 44

"*P*eople are talking, Father, about what you did for Nanna-Suen's akitu in Harran," Belshazzar said sternly.

"And?"

"They're saying that next year you plan to hold it in Babylon, that you're not even going to follow through with Marduk's akitu this spring."

"How many times..." Nabonidus began, exasperated at the intractable division between them, at the efforts he's made – the proof he shown in the archives right there. "It is not Marduk's but Babylon's akitu, Belshazzar."

"All that doesn't matter. Babylon is Marduk's city. Babylon's akitu should be on *Marduk*'s day. In the spring."

"It was first Nanna-Suen's. And his day is in the fall."

"Blasphemy."

"I will not forsake the god of gods, even though Babylonians have been doing so for decades."

Belshazzar swept out of the room. "You *are* crazy, father," he tossed back as he left.

* * *

PREPARATIONS for the annual Akitu proceeded just as they had for centuries. To any outside observer, it would seem that nothing was amiss. Yet Belshazzar sent alarming messages again to his mother in Uruk. Finally, Nitocris told him that old as she was she would nevertheless come with Ishtar's entourage for the annual festival. "But don't expect me to dictate his beliefs," she said.

The likenesses of the gods (believed to be in some way the gods themselves) filtered into Babylon, with great fuss and fanfare. Citizens crowded the river quays to witness their arrival and slaves hustled to ready the docks and land transport. The gods of Marad, Kish, and Chursagkalamma arrived first. Then, the gods of Akkad, from Babylonian points north. Some of the statues, clothed and accessorized with the garb particular to both the day and travel, were too heavy for human beings to transport, even by litters hoisted on the shoulders of half a dozen paired men. Oxen snorting heavily drew carts that took up the entire width of secondary roadways as they pulled Babylonia's deities to their particular shrines.

Nathan's eldest brother, who had moved his family from Nippur to Babylon said, "Look at them come. The gods dip and bow, sway and rock, burdensome for the weary who carry them. By contrast, our God says, 'I carry you. I always have and always will. I have carried since you were born. And even to your old age and gray hairs I will sustain you. And I will rescue you.'"

Temple officials rented boats by the month. "Bazuzu has brought a boat from Babylon to lease it for a sum to be negotiated; and he said, 'I will take the barley for the regular offerings of the Lady of Uruk to Babylon.'" That boat, which departed from the Nanaya family's quay in Uruk was just one of many to make the trip accompanying the goddess to the capital of the empire.

To the two new highest officials of the Ishtar temple (Eanna) in Uruk, Rimut wrote, "May Nabu and Marduk bless my brothers! Send me one leather mat and five (inflated) goatskins for the boat concerning the Lady of the Eanna via the soldiers who will bring the boat parts to me, so that the goddess may go to Babylon on the Euphrates." Officials in Uruk were none too happy about the arrangement, having to provide boat-building materials and then to lease the boats from private enterprises in Babylon. Only certain boatmen could be used, as agreed by the temples. Even the craftsmen tasked with building the vessels had to be approved. Given the number of cultic personnel and goods for the goddess's regular offerings of food and drink, several boats were necessary and not simply for a single use. So it was that after months of preparation, the fleet bearing Ishtar and her entourage set off for Babylon to the north.

* * *

NITOCRIS WAS 73 YEARS OLD. No one had expected her to leave Ishtar's city again except by funeral barge. So, the court was surprised to learn that she was coming and to find Nabonidus eager to take extra care that all be to her liking when she arrived. He himself wore his customarily simple monarchal attire. Belshazzar, by contrast, bore more weight in the form of a highly wrought breastplate, jewelry, ceremonial weaponry and decorative bracteates than an ordinary foot soldier wore in battle.

A grin spread across the old king's face when Nitocris disembarked at the royal quay behind the goddess and Ishtar's immediate attendants. Nitocris shushed away the slaves who held out their arms to bear her on the waiting litter, and with a grace that belied her age, swung up the docks to the waiting crowd. Her gray hair caught a breeze from the off the river, and she brushed it impatiently back from her face. Nabonidus and she stood staring at one another for a moment before Belshazzar swooped in. "Mother!" he exclaimed and kissed her cheeks. Then tucking her hand under his arm. Belshazzar led Nitocris to the waiting carriage. She smiled back at Nabonidus who caught her arm on the other side.

Nitocris settled into the palace and despite her reputation for trouble-making, assumed the office of queen mother with dignity if not restraint. Over the next several days, Nitocris spent many hours in conversation with her son and husband but seldom all together. Within a week, Belshazzar was on task with a team of Phoenician craftsmen, Jewish scribes, and Babylonian masons to renovate some Babylon's lesser temples and shrines that had fallen into disrepair. And after two weeks, Nabonidus had inaugurated preparations for the traditional akituof Marduk. All of Babylon seemed to breathe more easily.

"What Belshazzar says is true," Nitocris said to Nabonidus as they sat beneath old almond trees in the revived hanging gardens.

Nabonidus leaned his head back and looked up at the sky.

"People are talking. Many are upset with your attention to Nanna-Suen and concerned that you'll go ahead with demoting Marduk."

"Let them talk," Nabonidus said. "I know what's in my heart. I know what I must do."

"But that's just the problem. You may be wrong. Have you listened to the Jews? They are absolutely certain that their god is king of the universe; yet look at them – conquered by us, their god nowhere to be seen, and Jerusalem in ruins. What makes you different from them?"

Nabonidus brought his head forward and looked at Nitocris. "I am the king, of course."

They sat silently for a while, companionably.

"Would you do it?" Nitocris asked.

"Do what?"

"Replace Marduk's role with Nanna-Suen in the akitu? Would you take Nanna-Suen's hand in the great procession?"

Nabonidus was silent.

"It's a rumor, you know."

Nabonidus's smile was resigned to the conflict he engendered. "It is already Nanna-Suen who walks with me, who guides me, and who made me king."

A messenger interrupted them with a breathless bow. "Iddina Egibi to see you, sir. Something about arrangements for Nabu's barge. Ninurta's flotillas won't anchor upstream like the others. And there's not enough room on the quay, my lord."

Nabonidus raised his eyebrows and shrugged, put his hands underneath him, and lifted himself up from the bench. "Enjoy the birds for me," he said to Nitocris.

CHAPTER 45

On the first day of the month of Nisan, just as the sun was beginning to show its light, the head chef of Marduk's temple rose, took up the wooden key, and went to the temple courtyard. There, he opened the door of Exalted Gate, approached the cistern, performed the water rites and prepared the precinct. The old year was coming to an end. Babylon's spring *akitu* had begun.

In the Egibi household, the atmosphere was bright and joyful. Mere days before, Davcina had given birth to a baby girl, perfect in every way. And to everyone's great relief and delight both mother and daughter were well. As Davcina had predicted, Gobryas adored their tiny daughter.

On one of the rare occasions when they were alone with their baby, "I want to tell her every day," Davcina said to Gobryas, "that I love her."

"And you will," Gobryas said. "Until she is grown with children of her own, you will tell her. *We* will tell her."

In those first days, Khai watched Davcina constantly, anxious that the doctors' warning that having a baby would be her death. When she seemed instead to thrive, Khai let himself relax into her happiness. He even began to feel that he might be able finally accept Gobryas as a decent husband and father.

So, when Davcina begged that Gobryas be allowed to attend the great New Year's festival with her, Khai agreed to it, yes. After all, there was all sorts of talk that King Nabonidus might not do it, might – in those crucial moments – elevate *not* Marduk but rather Nanna-Suen of his native Harran, adding the festival's intrinsic drama.

And that night, exactly as they had been doing every night before, Davcina and Gobryas told the little girl they loved her.

* * *

THE NEXT MORNING, while it was still dark, people gathered at the banks of the river. Davcina took Gobryas by the hand to witness the priest's customary bathing. Through the early morning darkness, they watched the shatammu of the temple step into the water and let the river wash over him. Onlookers nodded reverently as he recited the "secret of the Esagila."

The shatammu prayed to Marduk "who crosses the heavens and collects the earth into dry land, ... Before the people of Babylon, let there be light!" and to Marduk's wife "whose garment is light... who saves the captives and grasps the hands of the fallen."

Davcina squeezed Gobryas's hand.

Still at the shores of the river, the priest prayed, "Grant mercy to the slave who speaks good things of you. In difficulty and trouble, grasp his hand. Grant him life when he is in sickness and pain. Let him walk constantly in happiness and joy."

Gobryas smiled back at his frail wife – happy tears catching the first morning light.

The people disbanded while the priest returned to perform the daily rites.

"Today," Davcina explained to Gobryas, "three craftsmen begin to fashion two effigies, made of tamarisk and cedar, one holding a scorpion and the other a snake, both coated in gold and precious gems. The images will be very important in the days to come. Now, I will rest. I want to be able to hear the recital of 'When on High.'"

Reluctantly Gobryas let one of the servants lead Davcina back to the house. He had to meet Iddina to go over plans for the god's banquet in a few days.

They returned later, many in their finest dress for the moment when Marduk was asked to affirm the god's covenant with Babylon's privileged citizen class. Khai insisted that the Egibis attend, even though they were not born into such status. Davcina and the infant girl were there. Gobryas remained behind.

When it was time for the temple reading, "Are you sure you want to go?" Gobryas asked.

"Yes," Davcina said.

But she leaned heavily on him during the priest's dramatic recitation of Babylon's national epic, a lengthy poem that begins with the beginning of creation. She regained her strength during the part about Marduk's battling the chaos monster and her demons, but asked to sit when the victorious Marduk founds Babylon, lays the Esagila's foundations, and receives from the grateful gods the Tablets of Destiny. Her eyes were shut by the end, when Marduk takes his place as the highest of all the gods, who praise him by all fifty of his wonderous names.

As they approached the Egibi mansion, Davcina smiled under Gobryas's worried gaze. "Did you hear," Davcina asked Gobryas, "that during the part where Marduk blesses the community leaders, Belshazzar was there - at the temple - with his mother Nitocris through the whole thing. But King Nabonidus left before the end?"

"But isn't he supposed to be gone?" Gobryas asked, "to Borsippa to fetch Nabu?"

"That's not until tomorrow."

In truth, Gobryas couldn't have cared less. The only thing he cared about was right next to him – this young woman and the mother of his newborn daughter. Gobryas looked closely at Davcina. Under her eyes, pale blue moons shone through translucent skin. "Do you feel alright?"

"I am tired, I guess." She walked toward their suite without looking back at the nurse holding their daughter. "So tired," Davcina said. Their awkward gaits bumped their bodies down the hall.

* * *

DESPITE THE RUMORS, King Nabonidus did go the following day first to Nabu's Babylonian shrine and then on to Borsippa. At the shrine, he took up the scepter of kingship as expected. And in all the magnificent regalia of a traditional Babylonian monarch, he went down to the quay. Nitocris and Belshazzar were at the head of the great group gathered to see him off. As per the festival's order of events, Nabonidus would travel to Borsippa to retrieve the statue of his namesake, the god of writing and wisdom from Nabu's home city. With a great crowd to witness it, he left. As expected.

Still, Belshazzar could not contain his anxiety. That evening, after the palace staff had escorted a resplendent queen mother and the crown prince back to the palace from the recital of the epic, Belshazzar asked to speak with Nitocris alone.

"Just because Father is going to Borsippa as expected doesn't mean that he'll follow through with the rest." Belshazzar removed his gold studded belt and chest piece with a relieved sigh.

"You know you don't need to wear all that," Nitocris said.

"I like it," Belshazzar replied. "I've always dressed well."

"And lived well, too."

"We're not talking about me."

Nitocris sat at the end of an ornate table and rested her arm on it. "There's not much we can do about how your father will act in the festival days to come."

"But we can be ready. We don't have long before he returns, but..." Belshazzar's eyes were bright with anxious zeal. "What if he changes the liturgy, what if he doesn't take Marduk's hand in the parade, what if he refuses to submit to the ritual humiliation?" substitutes Nanna-Suen for Marduk?!"

"What indeed?" Nitocris said evenly.

"We have to do something, interrupt it somehow, or get him out of there."

Nitocris unpinned her hair and shook it out. "For all your father's fanaticism, he is not deranged. He saved Uruk, he has repaired Babylon's quays, he rebuilt and rededicated the temple in Harran, --"

"There!" Belshazzar interrupted her. "That's just it. He's got everything all set for Nanna-Suen to take over."

"You forget that these are the gods you're talking about. Surely Marduk will defend his hold on Babylon, direct Nabonidus to perform as expected, and hopefully grant our empire success for yet another year."

Belshazzar nodded a concession.

"And really, there's little we can do or plan for. Your father will do what he does. And the gods will what they will."

* * *

BEFORE SLEEP, Davcina took Gobryas's hand. "If one day I am too tired... If I fall asleep before I have told our sweet child that I love her, will you tell her for me?"

"Yes," Gobryas managed to say.

"Promise?"

"I promise."

But Davcina never recovered her strength. And in the space of a night, in the short duration of time that it took – a single change from Shamash's setting to the god's rise again – Davcina was dead.

Alone with her in the night, Gobryas fell across his wife's cool body. He took one last look at her. For once, she bore the unlined face of an ordinary teenage girl. Then, he couldn't bear to stay. In his grief, Gobryas ran, his clubfoot dragging like clinging death. Gobryas limped through Babylon's sleepy streets. He hobbled down to the quay, untied one of the Egibis's small transport skiffs, and let the river take him away. He had no destination in mind, no route – simply the animal need to get away from what hurt.

Gobryas was nowhere present in Babylon, then, when a sorcerer exorcized malevolent spirits and demons from the temple. Like the high priest himself, Gobryas would not look on the temple that day. While the sorcerer sprinkled the temple with river water to chase away evil, Gobryas watched the tiny wake behind his finger as his small raft drifted along. Gobryas could just hear the great drums. He caught the scent of burning juniper. Soon they would slaughter a flawless sheep and cleanse the area with its blood. Gobryas groaned. Upstream, temple staff hoisted the sheep's headless body into the Euphrates while the sorcerer and slaughterer left for open country where they were to remain, unclean, for the remainder of the festival.

Gobryas was gone. And Khai wasn't present to oversee the Egibi team, who were at that moment preparing the meal that would greet the god, who should at that moment be coming down the river escorted by King Nabonidus himself. Because in the morning, Khai learned what he had dreaded from the first. And he'd been denied the one outlet for his anger. While Khai wept and raged through the house, in Nabu's shrine the men put up the "Golden heaven" canopy for Marduk's meal -- twelve loaves of bread, roasted meat, salt, and honey, to be served to king and god that afternoon on a golden tray.

"Where is he, the coward!" Khai shouted. "Bring him to me!"

* * *

GOBRYAS FLOATED on the broad river without aim or purpose. He lay on his back and watched the sky. When the sun grew too bright, Gobryas closed his eyes. Water stroked the boat, turning it this way and that. It rolled from time to time with the wake of passing craft. Gobryas imagined toppling off and sinking into the rivers silty depths. But the boat always righted itself again, and he was too tired to die.

It was the forerunners of Nabu's barge, securing the god's way, who retrieved Gobryas to the city. He didn't resist. They had pulled up alongside, recognizing an Egibi vessel. When Gobryas opened his eyes, he saw the crew jump back in alarm. He was a wreck. He said nothing to their questions. They soon gave up trying to communicate with the unarmed, mute cripple.

They had far more important concerns: to escort the Babylonian king and the god Nabu into the city, the center of the world whose order depended on each ritual step proceeding as dictated by the gods themselves.

Iddina was at the quay. Gobryas let the Egibi hurry him back to the family mansion, where Khai roared through the house, thundering his rage. And when Gobryas appeared, he unleashed it all again – his target, this clubfooted oaf.

"How dare you leave, murderer and thief!"

Gobryas stood, his hands at his sides.

"You are mine! I bought you for the kindness of my daughter, the girl you killed."

Gobryas's foot twisted in on itself. He made no move to straighten it.

"You had no right. You have no right."

Gobryas hung his head.

"And the baby, that baby is not yours."

At this, Gobryas started.

"She is Egibi. Like her mother. You are trash."

"But - my daughter," Gobryas coughed. "She is all I have."

"You have nothing, deserve nothing. Yet I have given you everything! You have taken everything. I want you gone, *this day!*"

"No!" Gobryas his clothing dirty and torn, his ankle purple and bloody, his face haggard with grief, fell to his knees. He clung to the hem of Khai's robe, tears streaming down his face. "Let me stay," he said. "I would sooner be the lowest of your slaves than leave my baby daughter."

"When you took mine from me?!"

"Every night... we told her we loved her," Gobryas said. "I made a promise!"

"Take him," Khai said to a servant. "Out of my sight." And he stormed away.

The servant looked at Gobryas, his clothing dirty and torn, his ankle beginning to show the bruising of his effort, his face haggard with grief, and took pity on him. He offered Gobryas his arm.

* * *

NITOCRIS COULD FEEL Belshazzar fidgeting next to her under the fringed umbrella as they waited on the quay. She tried to ignore his anxiety and pushed from her mind what she imagined to be his worries -- that Nabonidus wouldn't show. The day was warm, but in the shade perfectly comfortable. Nitocris deafened herself to the whispered doubts of the few elite citizenry that Belshazzar had invited to join them on the docks.

She put aside her own concerns and replaced them with an image of Nabonidus, decades earlier, the man in her father's court who was not like the others. Nabonidus was earnest and in no way plain, though his dress was simple and his hair cut for practical care. He was well-built, she had noticed right away, and knew from his bearing that he was nothing if not honest. So, startled out of her reverie, she alone was unsurprised when the cry went up that his barge had been sighted. Nabonidus and his namesake god would arrive on time.

"He could still mess this up," Belshazzar said into her ear while the crowd cheered Nabu's approach.

"By honoring the god of his youth?"

Belshazzar took a step backward. "By putting that god in the position of Marduk."

"Let's just watch, Shazzi." But Nitocris felt her chest tighten in anticipation of the days to come.

* * *

GOBRYAS RETURNED to the rooms he had shared with Davcina and let the servant replace his clothes with clean ones. When he was alone again, he climbed onto Davcina's bed and put his face into her pillow. Every pain she had suffered, every wince and cry, he felt as if they were his own. And he remembered the last promise he'd given to her. Every day to tell their daughter that Davcina loved her. That both of them did. Suddenly, the door flew open. Two heavy servants threw shackles on Gobryas's arms and led him away. They gave no explanation. Gobryas needed none.

* * *

MEANWHILE, across town, from the quay on the river, the high priest escorted Nabonidus back to Marduk's temple, the royal family and a great crowd behind.

Inside, despite the sanctuary's cool space, Nitocris could hardly catch her breath. She saw Nabonidus glance her way as he was led to Nabu's shrine in the midst of the great Esagila. This was a crucial moment. Would he or would he not submit to the ritual humiliation at the hands of Marduk's proxy? Beside her, Belshazzar, too, barely drew breath.

The moment had arrived. Nabonidus lifted neither hand nor

voice, as Marduk's sheshgallu stripped him of the insignia of kingship. Nitocris exhaled. Nabonidus held Belshazzar's eye as the priest lifted his arm and brought it down hard across Nabonidus's cheek. He pulled the king's ears and slapped him again, harder this time. Nabonidus's eyes smarted with tears. Belshazzar exhaled. It was a good omen. The crowd cheered.

As Nabonidus recited exactly the words of Marduk's liturgy, words of confession, which the priest followed with Marduk's words of forgiveness, Nitocris felt Belshazzar next to her relax. To their great relief, Nabonidus did not protest when the shatammu gave back to Nabonidus the signs of kingship and said that Marduk in his mercy would support and guide the king in the year to come.

King and priest led the crowd back into the temple courtyard. There, a beautiful white bull, imported from the east and held tightly by strong men, stood shuffling on its hooves at the edge of a pit. Reeds now soaked with honey, ghee, and precious oils lay in the bottom. Nabonidus joined the priest in singing the "O Bull who burns in the heavens" hymn while he watched the slaughterer dispatch the animal with a single stroke. It fell dead into the pit. Nabonidus was given the honor of lighting the fire that would send the savory sacrifice to heaven.

* * *

GOBRYAS'S BONDAGE WAS SHORT-LIVED. He had been instrumental in the Egibi's planning for this most spectacular and logistically complex days of the akitu. (Gobryas – enslaved after all – had no choice but to fulfill them.) So, he was released to work. And as per his decision, he could stay. But Khai directed that under no circumstances was Gobryas ever to have contact with his infant daughter.

So the next day, while the rest of all Babylon had gathered in excitement for the carnival that was the arrival of the gods – each deity with an entourage, each requiring a fleet of boats that would dock this day on the quay, and once there keep moving through the crowds and up to their shrines and temples in the old city - Gobryas stood with them. But he scowled. And under his breath, he muttered ceaselessly, "I hate him, I hate him, I hate him," his voice lost in tumult of the crowd.

In the afternoon, the two effigies, gorgeous in their gold plate and jewels, would be humiliated like the king before and then cast into a fire to burn until the sweet wood of their centers could be smelled all around. In Gobryas's nostrils, nothing stank worse.

The next day's most exciting event – the grand parade of gods - Gobryas watched with empty eyes.

To everyone else, it was dazzling indeed to see the gods in their most resplendent garments -- blue-violet linens and wool, a red sash at the hip, headbands ornamented in gold -- tiaras fashioned specially for each, and dazzling accoutrements of precious metals and gems. The gems that covered Enlil's chariot shone out against the vehicle's dark wood "like the light of day and the crescent of the new moon." Nabu's chariot dazzled in shining bronze. Goddesses processed in a delicious atmosphere scented with pleasing aromatics and pungent juniper.

On this day, the invisible was made visible. Ordinarily, people weren't allowed access to the statue of the great god; but on this day, Marduk rode into their midst magnificently.

The beer brewers had been awarded this year the prestigious honor of pulling his chariot, which they did with proud chests. The king rode alongside the golden Marduk, who was "clothed in splendor, suited to lordliness… He is surrounded with radiance, endowed with awesome radiance, he shines out splendidly, appears brilliantly." Weavers, cleaners, gold- and silver-smiths, cooks, and all those who by birth and training became specialized craftsmen for the gods proudly attended each statue, the deity made immanent. Also in procession, the city's officials and privileged citizens, confirming the hierarchical order of society.

Gobryas barely noticed when the deities came down Procession Way atop their floats, attendants and accoutrements on full display.

From there, the gods would continue on to the Akitu House, "the house of Joy and Gladness."

Gobryas knew that for three days in this country house, the gods would enjoy banquets and music, the adoration of worshipers, and preside over rituals demonstrating the people's hope for a prosperous year. When on the eleventh day the deities returned to Marduk's temple complex, they were prepared to issue their final decree of destinies. Along the road to and from the Akitu House, the ways the gods moved -- bobbing, leaning, and stooping -- and the expressions on their faces signified their dispositions and intents. People watched closely for such auspicious gestures, interpreting and discussing them for days to come. At the end of the day, Babylonians indulged in the most lavish of the banquets. People brought gifts and tributes, confirming loyalties and communicating good will. The twelfth and final day was a day of goodbyes. The gods and their companies loaded again onto boats to begin journeys of return to their individual city homes.

GOBRYAS DIDN'T CARE that Nabonidus performed exactly as the traditionalist Babylonians had hoped, exactly as they believed the gods dictated. He alone barely noticed that King Nabonidus had taken Marduk's hand and led the way.

CHAPTER 46

a bright day in spring, the hills just greening... flocks of migrating birds passed through the sky above Pasargad calling to each other like messengers of promise and hope.

"Aspacanah," Cassandane said, tearing herself away from the happy reunion. "Go, on." Well on in her pregnancy, she bent awkwardly, and gave the boy's back a gentle push. "Tell your father that Vishtaspa's family has arrived." She nodded at him encouragingly.

Aspacanah glanced at 'Tossa then dashed away.

They'd been looking forward to this for months: Cyrus and Cassandane's dearest friends visiting Anshan and to see what they were doing at Pasargad. Ever since the Elamites had come over the hill and joined Cyrus's small band against Astyages's tremendous army years ago, Vishtaspa and Hutaosa had been as good as family. While Vishtaspa set himself apart in that fight not only as an astonishing warrior but even more a man of principle and integrity, Hutaosa nine months pregnant had joined the other Anshanite women – including Cassandane, barely beginning to show the baby she carried – to prove as fierce a defender of their land as any other in a heroic gesture that got their men to fight on. But now, with Vishtaspa and Hutaosa stationed in Parthia since Astyages's defeat...

"Too long!" Cyrus said with a grin.

'Tossa stared at the new boy in his felt boots and soft cap. The boy stood next to his father, whom Cyrus had just released from an enthusiastic embrace. The boy assumed a stance relaxed, even bored, while the adults exclaimed happy greetings. The boy's mother, whom 'Tossa had been told was her namesake, shifted a baby – Zarin's most recent; Otanes had brought him – from one arm to the other. She smiled at 'Tossa.

"What a fine girl," the woman said looking at 'Tossa with a smile.

'Tossa put her hands behind her back.

Cambyses leaned over and whispered, "Go to her."

'Tossa walked up to the woman.

"My name is like yours," the woman said. "Hutaosa. And this," she stepped around her husband, who was talking animatedly to Cyrus, and put her hand on the boy's head, "is Darius."

The boy shook his head as if her hand were a fly. Proud. Hutaosa returned her hand to the infant's back and bounced the baby lightly up and down on her hip.

"Do you know that Darius was born on the very day that your father became king of Media as well as Parsa?"

'Tossa watched the woman's mouth as she talked. The woman smiled the entire time.

"And you were born only a few short months after that."

"Your name is not the same as my name," 'Tossa said in a low voice.

"Different versions, that's all."

"Why?'

Darius stepped in front of 'Tossa. "Why what. Why are they different? Language. Or why are you named after my mother? She and my father won the battle that got your father Media."

"Darius, that's not quite right," Hutaosa said gently.

He shrugged.

"Your mother, Cassandane, was very brave during that time," Hutaosa said to the serious, dark-haired girl before her, taller by several inches than Darius. "And your father was such a great man that the whole army of Media decided they would rather fight for him than for the old king."

"Where we live, they call *my* father 'king,'" Darius said, throwing his nose into the air. "And he is, too. Everybody obeys him."

"Shush, Darius," Hutaosa said.

'Tossa looked away.

Cassandane broke away from the men. She took Hutaosa's arm and led her toward the great tents, talking warmly about the baby and how good it was to be back in Pasargad.

"Is that your brother, the one who will be king when your father dies?" Darius asked, pointing to Cambyses.

'Tossa stepped back, scowling. "My father isn't going to die," 'Tossa said.

"Not now. But when he does -"

'Tossa suddenly became pale. Her eyes glazed, and she clenched her hands. "It's happening," she whispered.

As Aspacanah darted forward to her side, Darius jumped away, startled out of his nonchalance.

Aspacanah took one look at 'Tossa, laid a hand on her shoulder, then dashed to Cyrus. "It's Cambyses, sir. 'Tossa feels it coming."

Cyrus stopped in the middle of telling the story of Lydia's defeat. Sure enough, Cambyses had frozen, struck with fear in anticipation.

"Vishtaspa," Cyrus said calm but urgent. "Go ahead with your family into the palace. Prexaspes will show you the way."

As they went, Darius craned his head to look behind, fascinated by the scene of Cambyses suddenly overcome. As usual,

'Tossa helped to get her brother into safe surroundings before the fit overtook his arms and legs. But this time, her attention was divided. Atossa kept looking over at the boy walking away.

CHAPTER 47

*B*elshazzar was elated.

The crown prince congratulated his father for performing Babylon's great new year festival with dignity, most of all for confirming Marduk's place as the highest in the order of the gods. Belshazzar, not a young man, felt the freshness of Spring, and the promise of great things ahead more joyfully than he had in a very long time.

"I won't do it again," Nabonidus said.

Belshazzar's face paled. "What?"

"Nanna-Suen's akitu should take place here in Babylon. And one day, the great moon god will unseat Marduk to re-claim his rightful place. I aim to see it happen, Shazzi. Go ahead, tell your friends."

CHAPTER 48

*V*ishtaspa's family settled in at Pasargad, urged by Cyrus to stay at least until the first big feast to the lands' many gods and until the hunting lodges along the river were built and operable. Cyrus delighted in sharing with Vishtaspa and anyone who would listen, his plans for Pasargad. It would include elements of Assyrian palace work, Ionian temple complexes, Sardinian parks, and elegant columned halls such as he'd seen throughout the central Zagros. He would direct engineers to manage the Pulvar River for predictable irrigation to the area he intended to develop and have masons from the north teach locals how to build with mortar and stone. The river ran from about 2 kilometers to the north of the site. A series of dams and canals to run on either side would provide water enough for the plain to make of it a lush park.

But instead of containing everything within a heavily fortified edifice like Nineveh, Cyrus said that this would be open. Audience hall, apadana, even the fine sculptured images of royal power and mythical heroic encounters would be outward-looking, much of it simply open to the outside. When he sat on his throne, he said, he wanted to look out on gardens and breathe air perfumed by the plants that grew in it rather than the static walls and stale atmosphere of some enclosed room.

Yes, there would be a gate; but not a heavily fortified affair designed to keep troublers out. It would be open and inviting. The place would communicate welcome and peace. Besides, he assured the skeptical crew, no one can have entered the plain of Pasargadae unnoticed or unannounced.

But the palace was still far from done when Cassandane delivered their fourth child. So she gave birth inside an elegant tent like the one in which she herself was born. "A girl, tiny but healthy," the midwife announced. They named her Irtashduna, "Truth's pillar." The Greeks in residence at Pasargadae called her Artystone.

* * *

CAMBYSES'S RIDING had improved in 'Tossa's company, but he was never as eager as his sister to gallop across the meadows or pick their way down the river gorge, exploring the wilderness around Pasargad. Aspacana provided a measure of restraint, but if 'Tossa was absolutely determined, he didn't resist her.

Darius, on the other hand, did resist her. He was opinionated, and 'Tossa begrudgingly admitted, smart. When it came to horses, he was even more daring than 'Tossa. Darius had learned to ride with the people of the northern steppes, so very little frightened him or even gave him pause. He could swing at a full gallop from his horse's mane, one side then other with the grace of a falcon on the wing. Somehow, 'Tossa noticed, Darius could ride wildly but still maintain all the bearing and dignity of a nobleman.

"Why do you stare at him all the time?" Aspacana asked 'Tossa.

"I do not."

"Yes, you do. Like right there. You were watching him, again."

'Tossa hesitated. "I don't know. He's different, I guess. And annoying. He bothers me."

"Me, too."

* * *

CYRUS HAD WANTED to take Cambyses several kilometers north of the palace site to observe a series of dams they were building along the Pulvar River. Like the palace, the dam structures he had in mind involved cutting stones just so, something that had never been done in Parsa before. Ionian workmen that Cyrus had brought from Lydia taught the skill to local craftsmen. While the experts worked on the palace and pavilions, amateurs cut stones for things like the dams. Like everyone, Cyrus had assumed that 'Tossa would come, too. Long rides on horseback were dangerous for the epileptic prince.

When the eunuch Bagapates came to fetch him, Cambyses happened to be in the middle of an argument with Darius about the nature of a conquering king – should he adopt the traits of the people he conquered (Cambyses) or not (Darius)? -- and Darius seemed to be winning. Cambyses, the older – a teen – sputtered in frustration at the indignity of it all. Darius at ten was already nearly as tall as Cambyses and at this moment far more composed. So, when Cambyses was told to fetch his little sister so that he could accompany Cyrus, the young prince exploded in anger.

"'Tossa should stay, stay here, with the other children." Cambyses glared at Darius, who smiled back.

Bagapates looked from Cambyses to Darius and back again.

'Tossa arrived just then, her hair wind-blown, her cheeks ruddy. "There you are!" she said to Darius. "You should come see." Her eyes were eager. "Mother's horse, the one Father gave to her but that she never rides, that is the offspring of – never mind. It is turning colors! Its parents did the same, but everyone was wondering. Maybe he'll be white!"

Darius said, "I know the horse."

"Of course you do," Cambyses muttered under his breath, looking at Bagapates for support.

The eunuch did not return Cambyses's look.

'Tossa noticed Bagapates for the first time and took in Cambyses's sullen glare. "What's going on?"

"You're to come with your brother," Bagapates said. "A trek to the dams, I think."

"Riding?"

"For certain."

'Tossa dropped her voice, glanced at Darius, and asked, uncharacteristically shy, "Can he come, too?"

"No!" Cambyses's face was red.

"I find the qanats more interesting, anyway," Darius said.

Cambyses shook his head in angry wonderment at the insufferably precocious boy and stormed out. Bagapates hurried after the prince, then turned and flapped his hand, waving 'Tossa forward. She shrugged and went after them.

Cambyses took the opportunity as they rode to ask Cyrus how long Vishtaspa's family would be staying in Pasargad. 'Tossa, who had been watching a wild falcon circle overhead, rode closer to listen.

"Not much longer. They'll stay until Hutaosa has had the baby, though. She's in no condition to travel."

"How long do you think that will be?" 'Tossa asked, trotting up alongside Cyrus.

Cyrus smiled. "Excited to have another baby around, are you? Your sister's getting too big, I guess?"

'Tossa's face was blank, uncomprehending for a moment. She thought of Darius, how she had grown accustomed to his confidence, his nonchalance, his spontaneous daring.

"I just hope she doesn't have the baby too early," 'Tossa said.

Cyrus laughed. "A budding midwife in our midst."

'Tossa dropped back to hide her disgust.

* * *

WHEN HUTAOSA and Vishtaspa took their family north again to Parthia, 'Tossa became sullen. Not even Aspacanah seemed able to boost her spirits.

Cyrus reached out to Gobryas: "It's overdue, my invitation," he wrote, "to join us here."

Gobryas's reply was brief: "I cannot leave my daughter," he wrote.

Cyrus summoned a messenger to send the obvious question: Wouldn't you bring her with you?, when it occurred to him that things might not be as good for Gobryas in Babylon as Cyrus had assumed. And if not, Gobryas could hardly be expected to send an honest reply. Cyrus sent the messenger away again. "Never mind," he said. "It's nothing after all." But the matter stuck in his mind.

CHAPTER 49

"*A* band of men -- three, my lady, with heads as black as night." A runner dispatched by the guards at the gate stood catching his breath.

"Bring them to me," she said.

When they arrived, Amytis could tell by the cut of the trousers, the boots, their honeyed complexion, black hair, and square cheeks that the men were Gutian. She knew that their land was technically a territory of Babylon, though they'd never fully adopted a Babylonian identity. And like Amytis's wild land, the Gutians dwelt farther south along the same Zagros mountain range in a rugged country of deeply wooded forests and streams. Like Ecbatana, their land between mountains was a natural route for trade. She'd heard they'd defected.

The leader introduced himself as Ugbaru, chief of the Gutians.

"I have come to you to pledge my people to yours," Ugbaru said.

When Amytis's son was king of Babylon, like Nebuchad-nezzar before him, he had respected the Gutians' fiercely independent nature, never forcing more than nominal official allegiance.

Amytis raised her eyebrows.

"The Gutians to Persia." Ugbaru repeated. He glanced briefly at the empty throne next to Amytis's.

"Cyrus is in Pasargad," Amytis said to answer his question. "But yes, this is now Persia, too."

"I have discussed it at length with the elders of our country, some of whom are here," he added as he gestured to the black-headed men waiting, impassive. "There is increasing unrest throughout Babylonia. But our defection was also personal for me."

Amytis nodded for Ugbaru and the others to sit.

"As you probably know," Ugbaru said, "King Nabonidus was in Arabia for years. During that time, he left his son Belshazzar in charge of Babylon. Some time ago, Belshazzar had a hunting party. My son had the honor of hosting the expedition in our own area." His voice broke. He coughed lightly and went on. "Thaer, my son, went out in the morning, happy to be riding with the crown prince. He came home dead, shot by that very prince."

Despite herself, Amytis's face paled. Her own son's murder thrummed in her ears. And Belshazzar, again. Always she had wondered what role he, such an obsequious friend of Igliss's, had had in her own grief. Amytis took a deep breath and tried to concentrate on this man's story rather than relive Amel-Marduk's assassination.

"I've never believed the official story of what happened." Ugbaru stood and began pacing. "They say that it was an accident, that the king was shooting at a lion and my son happened to dash directly into the path of the arrow. But I know that's wrong. The day before – years ago but if feels like yesterday – a lion had leapt toward Belshazzar before the prince had time to ready a shot. The beast would have torn the prince from his horse if it hadn't been for my son's quick wit and steady hand.

Thaer threw his dagger straight and true, right between the lion's eyes."

Ugbaru stopped and wiped his brow with a long gesture, his hand pausing over his eyes. "Belshazzar, who should have been grateful beyond measure to my son, was furious. He cursorily thanked my son but must have been seething. We all know, my son as well as anyone, that slaying a lion is the king's prerogative. But the conditions in this case would have prohibited that man from ever becoming the king he pretended to be. Belshazzar would have been a lion's toy but for my son's quick action. I think that the prince's tender pride couldn't take it. At the next opportunity, he shot my son and explained it away as I've explained to you."

Ugbaru looked at Amytis, "I cannot stop thinking about it. I could tolerate our vassal status as long as the Babylonians kept to their side of the Tigris and left us to our foothills and mountains. But those sissified men of the Babylonian court feel entitled to everything they can get their fat hands on. They even use the sacred vessels of peoples they'd conquered to swill their wine until the beautiful cups fall from their drunken hands. Now this: They've demanded a tithe of lumber. I can't take it."

Amytis consciously loosed her grip on the chair's arms. "So, you would rather align with Persia than with Babylonia. I understand. But there are consequences – alliances commit to mutual aid. It's not my decision alone to make. I'll take it to Cyrus."

Ugbaru sat forward. "And..." He bit his lower lip.

"I am sympathetic to your position." Amytis nodded reassuringly. "I'll give you our answer soon."

CHAPTER 50

*I*t would take more than one correspondence with Gobryas for Cyrus to learn what had happened. Although privately Cyrus sympathized with Khai's anger – the fault that Khai believed Gobryas bore for Davcina's death – he could understand too the depth of Gobryas's antipathy for the man who held him responsible for killing the woman Gobryas loved. But when Cyrus learned that Khai now served as Belshazzar's business agent (Belshazzar, friend of Igliss, Amytis had told him), any sympathy Cyrus had for Khai was far bested by angry indignation.

So, when Amytis presented Cyrus with the idea that they embrace Gutium within great Persia, honoring their independence and appreciating the buffer their territory provided against Babylonia, especially in the soft belly of the strip between Pasargad and Ecbatana, he agreed. It relieved some of the resentment he held for this Egibi to the west, limiting access to wealth as it did.

* * *

CASSANDANE LOOKED AT THE BABY, asleep. From the moment of her birth, Irtashduna's whole being was brightness and light. The baby's hair was soft, her skin rosy, and her eyes had a blue-green cast that deepened with time. Her personality was easy, happy and relaxed, as if the whole world were, too. And indeed that was the air in Pasargad.

Even Phaideme, Otanes's daughter and a mini version of her high-maintenance mother, was captivated. Sanda nursed Irtadushna herself, just like she had nursed Cambyses in this place years ago – when she and Cyrus were young and confident and happy in the modest kingdom they led. They'd been through the furnace since but emerged with a new happiness and peace.

Cassandane laid Irtashduna on the cushion-covered stone bench and inhaled the perfume of garden air sailing through the pavilion on a cool breeze. Walls on three sides afforded privacy, but from this spot, nothing obstructed the view across the garden's quadrants to the rim of mountains beyond. Before she adjusted her dress and pulled the soft robe back over her shoulders, Cassandane examined her breast. Earlier, when she had tugged it free to nurse, she had thought she felt a tiny pea-like spot deep inside. She couldn't find it again and had already forgotten about it when 'Tossa ambled in, head low, dragging her feet.

Cassandane felt the familiar tension rise, tight at the back of her neck. She made an effort to relax her face, her jaw. "Something wrong?"

"No," 'Tossa said, but expression said otherwise.

Cassandane exhaled. "Come, sit down."

"I don't want to sit down."

"What do you want then?" Cassandane could hear the edge in her tone and was helpless to soften it.

"Ahmi." 'Tossa kicked the ground. "I want Amytis. Why can't she be here."

Cassandane closed her eyes, took a deep breath, and said, "It's not that she can't be here. She is managing things up north." Sanda thought about how 'Tossa, born in Ecbatana, knew that place better than any other. And with a painful twinge, Sanda thought about she had ignored this child, pushed her away in those first tender years. Is it any wonder that 'Tossa developed such affection for Amytis? "I'm sorry that you miss her," Cassandane said.

* * *

THE NEXT DAY, 'Tossa returned. Cassandane looked up, over the nursing baby's head.

"Can Amytis come visit?"

Cassandane stiffened briefly. She took a deep breath. "Of course," she said. "Some day." Cassandane looked at 'Tossa and forced herself to smile. "That would be nice."

'Tossa sat soberly watching while Cassandane finished feeding Irtashduna. As Cassandane eased the infant from her breast, she startled. Her fingers went back to the spot. There. "Tossa," Cassandane said, her voice gentle. "Will you look at this for me?"

'Tossa tilted her chin, put her hands under her seat, and stood up.

"I felt something just here." Cassandane pinched the skin on the underside of her breast. "Like there's a tiny bump in there."

'Tossa leaned over, tipped her head and looked. It made her uncomfortable, but she was curious, too. The skin was so smooth, red where Cassandane had pushed and pinched it. 'Tossa looked carefully. "I don't see anything."

Cassandane covered herself again. "I hear that you and Aspacanah rode out to the dams."

'Tossa scowled guiltily.

"What did you think?" Cassandane asked with a smile.

'Tossa's scowl faded as she leaned forward.

"Are they everything your father has been bragging about? Tell me all about it."

'Tossa began gingerly, watching her mother's face for disapproval. When all she saw was open interest, 'Tossa loosened up and soon became animated with the excitement of relating discoveries in the gorge, the marvel of the qanats. Neither one noticed when Aspacanah joined them, and neither was surprised. Gradually, he added to 'Tossa's report and made them both laugh with a story of how he and 'Tossa had imagined a huge beast rustling in leaves only to flush a small rabbit, its big feet stirring up as much noise as the horses, so spooked by the tiny creature that he and 'Tossa had trouble keeping them under control.

"Aspacanah got down and held the horses' heads until they were calm again," 'Tossa said.

Sanda swallowed her anxiety and smiled.

* * *

CYRUS CONTINUED TO BUILD PASARGADAE. He sent workmen north to study again the monuments at Nineveh and Khorsabad, wanting to incorporate not only images of the king but supernatural beings at freestanding gates, like the bird-footed lion demons that strode behind smiting gods. He told the sculptors, however, to smooth the musculature of these beings at Pasargadae. Their associated ferocity was enough. When a visitor entered, he'd know that this place was no back-water but had the same strength as the Assyrians in their heyday.

The same divine creatures attended at Pasargadae as at the formidable capitals of Assyria. But their orientation and style was to have Cyrus's own unique stamp. Not only would the beings be softer in their lines but he would mix them in ways that hadn't been seen before. So, he told the sculptors to set a fish-garbed man in front of a bull-man, striding in the same frame at Pasargadae's most pronounced entryway. In the doorway of a royal not religious structure, this magical being would guard the king.

Elegant canals divided a large rectangular plot into a formal garden of four distinct squares. The image of running water and its burbling would contribute to the serenity of the space while providing a supplementary source of irrigation. At strategic intervals throughout the five-kilometer area, Cyrus commissioned master masons from Lydia and locals under their direction as well as men trained in fine sculpture to erect open-air pavilions with lofty columns.

He had seen in a site not far from Susa, how busts of bulls – their heads and shoulders, front knees tucked under, placid but formidable could serve as pedestals or simply decorate the tops of columns and asked workers to fashion such massive images to line the public ways.

"Water courses of cut stone and open to the eye will run straight there and there and there."

Cyrus and Cassandane – alone with their newborn, a rare thing – walked through the land, a great square in front of the palace, that workmen had leveled, showing Cassandane what he had in mind. He pinched the baby's cheek and said to her plump and grinning face, "With basins at exact intervals, you can sit and dip your pretty feet, if you like." Cyrus swung his arm and followed it, turning. "From any place, Sanda, a person would see both lushness and order. We'll plant the trees and flowering shrubs in exact rows. Visitors won't need to be told but will see for themselves that this is place of peace, and their noses will tell of pleasure and delight."

"It's lovely," Cassandane said. She turned to face Cyrus. He stopped, too. Cyrus waited for her to speak. But instead Cassandane simply smiled. He relaxed and returned the smile. Silently they stood, the baby quiet at Cassadane's shoulder. And they nodded to each other, grinning and nodding. Neither needed to say what each of them thought: Home. Forever.

CHAPTER 51

When Amytis relayed their acceptance – Persia's of Gutium, more alliance than vassalage, Ugbaru met it with qualified enthusiasm.

Amytis looked long into the aggrieved chief's eyes. "But that's not all, is it?"

Ugbaru nodded. "I want to kill Belshazzar," he said. "Myself."

Ugbaru's companions suddenly shuffled, startled. But Amytis exhaled and nodded.

"Forgive me," Ugbaru dropped his head. "I didn't mean to say that… not right away." He looked up again. "I think it's possible to defeat Babylonia altogether."

Amytis sat forward. "Babylonia is the greatest empire in the world," she said. What she didn't say is often over the years, she had imagined punishing Babylonia for killing her son.

"Has been," Ugbaru said. "Divisions in Babylonia have grown worse. With our support, this greater Persia could defeat Babylonia, take it over. Both Media and Gutium would be safe from their constant resource-hunger…" He ground his teeth.

"I'm listening," Amytis said.

"And I," Ugbaru said, his voice clear and strong, "I want to be at the front of the troops. I want to kill Belshazzar."

Amytis took a deep breath. "I understand," she said. She hated Babylon for all it had taken from her, but what was dear to her there had also been so recently laid bare -- Khai's face, his broad shoulders, his mouth always on the verge of a grin... And there were all those people, people whose foreign extraction like hers made them suspect, lesser... people such as her dear scribe Nathan's Jews, who wanted -- more even than the prosperity that Babylon promised – to return to their land, the place where their god's temple had lain. They didn't deserve more violence, more pain. Yes, for what Babylonia did to her son, she would like to take it down. But.

Ugbaru watched thoughts play over her face.

"My first priority is to this place," Amytis said, "Wild Media. Babylonia's trouble could soon become our own. Discord has a way of spreading its damage. That would be reason enough to get involved... But also, my son, when he was the king of Babylonia, died for something that *I* believed in. I would like the chance to make that right, to give Amel-Marduk a legacy worthy of his goodness."

"But --?"

"But I don't think war is the answer."

Ugbaru's face flushed. "Belshazzar must die."

Amytis nodded. "And you believe that you should deliver that death. I understand. But - "

"There's another thing," Ugbaru said.

"What is that?"

"The Babylonians long relied on our resources – the forests in particular – for their fancy things."

Amytis sat forward.

"Nabonidus doesn't have much taste for it, I hear. All those years in the desert... But his son certainly does."

Amytis nodded. This she'd seen first-hand.

"And one day, that son will be king."

Amytis inhaled sharply.

"If he can't get it from us – tribute and all that…"

Belshazzar, Amytis thought. The zeal of a convert: more "Babylonian" than the pure Babylonians themselves, if such a thing could be possible.

"I'll think about it," she said.

CHAPTER 52

*T*he lump in Cassandane's breast grew, and one day, the skin itself broke. Cassandane winced with pain as she lifted the breast.

"It looks sore," Tossa said.

"It is. Go. Ask for the healer." Pasargad's healer was a skilled herbalist who had helped as many as ailed and died in his care. "But don't tell your father, all right?"

The man prescribed a bitter drink and packed the area with a green paste. He instructed Cassandane to pray each morning at the river to Anahita while dipping fresh yarrow to reapply. "Find a wetnurse, and wean the baby, my lady," he added before he left.

"It's just a small thing," Cassandane explained to Cyrus that evening. "Gone again soon."

Cyrus knit his brow. He had heard of women dying after breast wounds that began on the inside didn't heal. He knew that Cassandane had heard such things, too.

When the wound worsened despite Cassandane's care to follow the healer's instructions, Cyrus suggested that they consult other doctors. Maybe there was someone in Susa, even Egypt, who could help. Cassandane objected, certain that it would get better soon. But it didn't. The man from Susa prescribed a different kind of treatment – stones as hot as she could stand, and more prayers.

'Tossa pursed her lips as she examined the spot. She lifted her head. "Worse. It's worse."

Sanda's face fell, and 'Tossa's eyes filled with tears. Suddenly 'Tossa jumped up. "Stop spying!" she yelled toward the door. Sanda closed her robe and tied it quickly. "I hate you!" 'Tossa said and ran out.

* * *

"ASPACANAH, WHERE'S 'TOSSA?" Cyrus asked.

The boy shifted his weight, then clasped his hands behind his back, his square jaw set. "I don't know, sir."

Prexaspes hissed something into his son's ear, but Aspacanah's expression didn't change.

"Find her, please."

From the gorge to the north, where the river cut a pass through the mountains, a pair of dark eyes followed a solitary rider slowly picking his way closer. 'Tossa sat back in the lonely silence of the rocky wood. She pushed her hands under a pile of leaves, lifted them, and watched the dried sheets fall back again. Aspacanah found her there. He sat down beside her. They watched a hawk circle on eddies of wind. The shadows lengthened.

"I didn't really see her," Aspacanah said.

"She's sick."

"I know." 'Tossa rested her chin on her knees.

Aspacanah pulled a sack of dried fruit from his belt and held it out to 'Tossa. She shook her head, and he put it away.

"I'm going to ask Aunt Ahmi to come. Maybe she can fix it."

Aspacanah nodded. The hawk was gone. The light's

increasing softness threw the edges of things into deep relief. "Want to ride back with me?"

'Tossa looked at the boy next to her.

His gray-blue eyes were cloudy with concern. "We can go really fast, if you want."

"Okay."

* * *

CASSANDANE WAS pale when Cyrus sat down next to her. The second floor of the palace was done. Their bedroom, on a corner, had views of the mountains to the east as they flattened toward the south. Trellised flower vines would twine a corner column to the low rails of their balcony. Cassandane sat inside, propped up against a plush roll, embroidery in her lap. "It's just a bad day," Cassandane said. "You know that I'll be better tomorrow. I want to talk to the orchardist about planting olive trees, like those in Lydia."

It had been another good year in Pasargad aided further by the advanced irrigation Cyrus had installed across the plateau. A series of underground channels with outlets at strategic locations brought water to the land's dry areas. Crops grew where none had before, and the animals grew fat on rich grasses. The palace complex was still under construction, but the main palace was complete as were the central gardens, Cyrus's favorite development of all. They covered a huge expanse but were in every way ordered and tended. Cassandane spent long hours with Bardiya and Irtashduna at the pavilions. He could see her whole body relax in the orderly space. Her face brightened as soon as she stepped onto its paths, and she delighted in the ever-changing variety of plants within. It was a true *paradis*. Cyrus had hoped it would heal her. It had not.

Cyrus pursed his lips and stood up. He put his hand on her

shoulder, began to speak, and then turned away. He sat down again, his face earnest and anxious.

"Tell me," Cassandane said.

Cyrus stood up again.

"What is it?"

Cyrus looked at her with eyes already begging her forgiveness. "I've asked Amytis to come, to help."

"'Tossa put you up to it, didn't she."

"I don't know what else to do."

Cassandane turned her face away.

"The woman has some age in her, experience too. She told me that she learned some healing from my mother; she's seen a lot – in Babylonia, Media..." Cyrus said, sitting down again beside Cassandane. "Maybe she can cure you. And then she'll go back to Ecbatana. Right away. She won't stay." Cyrus put his hand on Cassandane's back. "She'll only look, do what she can. And when you're better, she'll leave again. Please don't be angry."

Cassandane slowly lay down and rolled onto her side, her back to Cyrus.

Cyrus put his head in his hands. "I cannot lose you," he said, his voice muffled and broken.

CHAPTER 53

$\mathcal{A}$mytis looked out from the porch of her bedroom at Ecbatana's palace. The peach blossoms that everyone worried had been killed in a late frost emerged from millions of tiny ice sheaths bright and pink, remarkably alive. Hope isn't always fruitless, she thought and looked again at the message from Pasargad. She thought of 'Tossa, almost ten years old, now, old enough to know... and young enough to hunger for certainty. Amytis missed her. Cyrus sounded desperate. Would she come? Could she help? Amytis watched a blossom loose from its branch dip and float in the air and fell gently to the ground. The wet dragged it down, erasing its color, leaving it limp against the dark.

She had considered the Gutians' request. Or rather, it kept bubbling up in her mind, in her heart – Babylon – and always with a seesaw of emotion.

* * *

IT SEEMED TO 'TOSSA, as she watched the caravan from Ecbatana wind its way into the plateau of Pasargad that she would explode with happiness. Oh, the things she wanted to show her Amytis, the things they would do, and ('Tossa was careful with this hope) that Amytis might know how to heal 'Tossa's mother.

"We should get back, if we're going to be there and ready when they arrive," Aspacanah said. "We'll want to wash and dress."

There was little about Prexaspes that Aspacanah imitated, but his father's fastidious ways he did. Cyrus, too, was insistent on regular bathing, clean clothes, good grooming, and even the subtle application of scents.

'Tossa nodded a concession. They cantered back and dropped the horses at the stable. Aspacanah headed for the company tents while 'Tossa disappeared into the columned hall.

* * *

THE ENDS of 'Tossa's hair were still wet and gave off the fresh smell of lemon verbena that she'd put into the water when the Median caravan arrived. Next to her brother Cambyses, 'Tossa shivered with excitement when she saw Amytis, the woman's silver head encircled with gold and blue beads on a heavy horse at the head of the caravan. At its rear, the Gutian contingent was a silent entourage.

Cassandane stood stiffly on the flagstone patio in front of the palace, Bardiya on one side of her, Cyrus on the other. Irtash-duna fretted lightly in her arms. Trees planted in uniform wells cast shade in the same direction as the columns behind, as if instructing the stone how it should behave.

Cyrus threaded a hand through Cassandane's arm and called out, "Welcome, Aunt!"

Amytis raised her arm against the sun. A servant hurried over with shade as she walked the horse forward. When she dismounted, long trousers billowed around her legs. 'Tossa burst forward. Amytis laughed and took the hand that 'Tossa gave to her. Amytis caught Cassandane's stony glare. With a gentle shake, Amytis released the girl's hand while she said to her, "Show me now where is the baby sister I heard about?" 'Tossa dashed to Cassandane, scooped up a giggling Irtashduna, and stood beside their mother. Amytis walked forward.

Cassandane said, "Cyrus will want to show you around. The servants will show you where you'll be staying." She disentangled her arm from Cyrus's as if he were nothing but a pesky vine, took Irtashduna from 'Tossa, and walked into the palace.

Amytis watched her go. She gave her head a little shake, inhaled briskly and said, "You remember Nathan," Amytis gestured the bright-eyed scribe forward, a small paunch at the belly his only sign of age. "And these," she said pointing to the three Gutians, "are our neighbors, Persia's newest allies --- men with an important issue to discuss. In time."

They dismounted behind her. At Cyrus's direction, Nahhunte led them toward the palace to get settled.

Amytis looked at Cambyses. "Ah, the prince," Amytis said with added resonance in her tone. She extended a hand to Cambyses, who took it carefully, nodded, and returned it again. "You are looking fine."

Cambyses stood as tall as his small frame allowed.

'Tossa hopped on the balls of her feet next to him. "The horse is almost white now!" she said. "Come to the stables, and I'll show you."

"Amytis has been traveling a long while, 'Tossa," Cyrus said, "Let's give her --"

"Nonsense. I'd love to see the horse," Amytis brushed her trousers. "Are there others, too? Have you got a favorite? I hope you'll show me all the best places to ride."

'Tossa clapped her hands against her sides. "Yes!"

To Cyrus, Amytis said, "Hear out the Gutians. I'll join you later."

Amytis took a few steps after 'Tossa and then stopped. "And

this is Aspacanah, I presume," Amytis said, nodding to the boy staring quietly at her.

"Her boyfriend," Cambyses said under his breath.

"Is not!" 'Tossa said furiously.

Aspacanah blushed.

"Well, it's nice to see you, too," Amytis said to the golden-haired boy.

* * *

UGBARU PACED in front of Cyrus. "The people feel oppressed, beaten down by Nabonidus's policies. You are the king they need and seek. And if you take Babylon, you gain the world to the edge of the Mediterranean. You gain the many peoples (and riches) that the Babylonians have confiscated over the past decades. Have you seen the city?"

"No."

"It is the most marvelous on earth. If you seek artists and intellectuals, they are there. If you wish to study the past and gain from its advances, Babylon will show you the way. And this, Cyrus, is the time to make it happen. The place needs a ruler such as you."

"I seek nothing, I wish for nothing more than I have here. Peace. Cassandane, Amytis too – we want peace. And look, I haven't sought the conflicts I've won. Finally, I'm here. I'm just beginning to build a heaven on earth. Paradise all around. I have plans for this place, a capital unlike any you've seen before."

Ugbaru heard him out. Then he spoke. "I've pledged my people to yours. All Gutium. I have discussed this at length with the elders of our country, some of whom are here," he added as he gestured to men waiting, impassive. "They agreed that there is a future in your leadership. Besides, you already control much of the area around our eastern border. It isn't any distance from territory that you already hold and would provide a valuable buffer and defense against aggressors from the west. It could be an even better peace," Ugbaru said. "As for the business of battle itself, if you would give me the honor, I could lead the attacking troops myself. Under your command, of course, I could head up and deliver the army to its gates. I ask only one thing..."

* * *

AMYTIS HAD BEEN grateful to have a little time to become reacquainted with 'Tossa – and quiet Aspacanah, too. And she was curious if the girl could tell her any more about Cassandane's history with the condition that had so alarmed them. She wasn't sure what – if anything – Cassandane would say. But now, it was time to rejoin the men.

"What is it, the one thing you ask?" Amytis from the doorway heard Cyrus ask Ugbaru.

She knew the answer. She stepped into the room without either man noticing.

"That I be allowed to kill Belshazzar and so avenge the death of my son. I want to tell see the terror in his eyes before I drive my dagger into his shriveled heart." Cyrus had watched the sadness of Ugbaru's eyes transform into a fiery anger, his face redden with the desire for revenge. Cyrus almost pitied the man who was its object.

"Amytis told me of this, the so-called accident. I'm sorry for your loss, Ugbaru." Cyrus stood and laid a hand on the grieving man's shoulder. "And I'm glad you've joined with us. The reputation of the Gutians is good. Your independence and rugged lifestyle are widely admired. We promise what defense you might need in the future as a part of Persia."

Amytis stepped forward and took a seat opposite Cyrus.

To the others, Cyrus said, "Will you excuse a moment?"

Ugbaru sighed. He nodded and followed his men out into the hall – a columned portico. Sunshine fell through high slats in orderly bands of light. A cool breeze washed the lingering resentment, this familiar pain and anger from Ugbaru's lined face.

Inside, the discussion was brief.

"I've thought it over, long and long," Amytis said. "I've searched my heart – why would I want one thing or another... what are my motivations?"

"And?" Cyrus asked, his face open and curious.

"And I've concluded that a greater good is possible with either course. And great damage, too." Amytis took a deep breath and released it. "I'm prepared to accept whichever you choose." Amytis walked out as the Gutians walked in.

Cyrus welcomed them back with a half-smile.

Ugbaru sat quickly, desperately. "They say that you have the *kitin*," Ugbaru said, "that the gods love you. Do you know Babylon means 'gate of the gods'? So you see, the heavens have ordained that it become yours. They are on your side."

"I don't know whose side the gods take, Ugbaru, or if they take sides at all. For my part, I prefer to let the gods at their business. Meanwhile, I'll take care of my own. I'm sorry that I can't do what you wish. You have my sympathy. But the answer is 'No.'"

When Ugbaru stood, he did so with great effort, as though lifting a tremendous weight. He didn't protest Cyrus's decision, though, but rather thanked Cyrus for listening to his case. They would leave in the morning.

* * *

CASSANDANE LET Amytis examine her breast. The atmosphere was strained, the two of them alone. But Amytis was single-minded in her attention to Cassandane's condition; and Cassandane was too proud to say anything except to answer Amytis's pointed questions. Amytis had brought her own herbs, salves, and charms. "I put my greatest confidence, though," Amytis said, "in simply cleansing. I've noticed your Pasargad appreciate that, too."

Cassandane straightened with pride, gave a quick nod. It was true.

Amytis advised that Cassandane leave the spot open to the air for a while each day. Then Amytis spread a cooling salve over the lesion, wrapped it gently, and returned to meet with the men. She didn't expect thanks. And got none.

* * *

"Can you heal her?" Cyrus asked.

"I don't know."

"Have you seen it before?"

"Maybe, or something similar."

"And?"

Amytis shook her head, her lips pressed tight.

Cyrus clutched his belly then straightened again, his face stricken.

"But every body is different. She is happy here, isn't she?"

"Yes. It's her home," Cyrus said. "And mine," he added softly.

"Or happy until I came, I suppose." Amytis lifted her chin sharply.

"You were good to come. And 'Tossa misses you so badly."

"I can teach a servant how to do what I would," Amytis said, "and leave you with the ointments and instructions. I should go."

"Not yet."

Amytis smiled gently. She put her hand on Cyrus's arm. "Sadness is one thing, even fear need not be bad; but bitterness, betrayal by those you love (even just the feeling of it, whether real or not), those can be hurtful indeed."

Cyrus grimaced. "I thought it was better, that she understood why I had to marry you.

Amytis removed her hand and brushed the sides of her robe.

"She may understand, but The mind has only so much control over the heart. It will be easier this way."

Cyrus paced slowly, but the energy in every step seemed only to coil tighter. He stopped, his face lit with hope. "I am going to make a great sacrifice to the gods. Bigger than has ever been seen here before. It will be a feast in the old Elamite tradition, a redistribution of goods among all the people; but especially a feast for the gods. I will give them a banquet such as has never been seen in this place. Then, if in their immortality and infinite wisdom they are capable of anything at all, they will heal Cassandane."

Amytis nodded, the corners of her mouth turned down thoughtfully as she watched Cyrus's transformation to hope.

"Stay for that. It will be as wonderful, more wonderful, than you have ever seen, than anything in Media or even in Babylon. Stay. Next week. Then you can go."

"All right."

CHAPTER 54

*I*n the coming weeks, Cyrus talked of nothing but the feast. Everyone was invited; nothing was in order. Cyrus turned the attention and energy of his staff to building up the platform he had earmarked for a sacred space on the central grounds of the broad palace complex. "Make it high and firm," he directed. Workmen from Media, skilled in wood, built a series of tables encircling the platform. There is where Cyrus, his family and friends would sit. Another, wider ring around the inner one would be for officers, administrators, leaders in the military, and the most illustrious of Parsa's citizens. Beyond that, and around the perimeter, space for common people, laborers and servants. On this night, everyone would eat like the king; and everyone would go home with gifts – precious things, gold and beautiful jewelry for people in the first two circles. Fruit, grain, and even meat for everyone else. No one would be hungry in the months to come.

Cyrus convened a small number of people in the new administrative building – Prexaspes, Pharnaspes, Otanes, Cook and the steward who had managed palace affairs in his absence, as well as two pious elders from Parsa and two magi from Media. With columned porticoes on all four sides, the building, some distance from the greater palace, was a most pleasant space to conduct the business of the empire.

"I will call on every god," Cyrus told the planning group, his voice ringing against the carved stone. "Leave none out. The gods of Parsa and of Elam, for certain, but also of everyone who gathers with us here. We will call on Zizkurra, Humban, Mazda, the River Anahita, Mount Ariaramnes, Pinigir, and ... Nathan, what is the name of your god, again? Yahweh, yes, Yahweh. To that one, too."

"No," Nathan said.

The hall fell silent. Only Amytis looked unsurprised.

"With all respect, sir. Not in that way," Nathan said.

"But doesn't your god appreciate a pleasing odor like all the others?"

"Such sacrifices belong only in the temple in Jerusalem."

"The temple is gone, though, isn't it?"

Nathan squinted his eyes tightly shut. "The sacrifice Yahweh desires is a pure heart, sir. To do justice, incline toward mercy, and live life humbly with one's god. Only that."

Cyrus leaned forward and narrowed his eyes. "If I do that, will your Yahweh cure my Cassandane?"

"Better to speak of healing, sir."

Cyrus leaned back again. He snorted with disgust.

"Yahweh is the God of all that is, was, and ever will be," Nathan said, ignoring the incredulous gasps. "Yahweh is Being itself. No one can presume to know, much less manipulate our God." He looked directly at Cyrus now. "But I do believe that healing -- the repair of a person spirit to body to mind to heart, of a person to others and those to others still, of people to place and beauty and all beings -- is what our God is always in the business of doing."

But Cyrus was no longer listening. "We'll not include Yahweh, then." Planning recommenced, and over the next few days, working all day every day, they were able to organize a magnificent event.

* * *

WHEN IT WAS TIME, Cyrus himself carried the wood to a broad central platform in the middle of the central grounds. Wearing the Elamite robe of kingship, he laid the first of what would be a great pyre.

He called on the gods of Parsa, of Elam, of Media, Lydia, and Susa to join him the King of Anshan that he and all his subject could give praise and thanks. Then Cyrus took the torch offered him, ignited the pile, extinguished the torch, and stepped back to join his family and friends. Then, while the flames leapt, the oil sizzled and the barley popped, while the blue-clear air gave way to swirling veils infused with the aroma of wine-soaked meat and baking grains, sweet fruits, and complex herbs, veils that rose languid and dissolving up to the heavens, officiating priests and magi prayed praise and thanks to each and every of the peoples' many gods.

At the inner table, Cyrus sat, Cambyses to his right, Cassandane to his left. With lifted head and eyes closed, he was to all appearances the reigning king in pious attention. More than one person leaned to her neighbor and said, "He has the *kitin* indeed." Yet with one hand clasped tightly around Cassandane's, Cyrus prayed silently and fervently his own prayer, his most heartfelt petition: that Cassandane be made well.

When the prayers were done, the feasting began. The afternoon was perfect, the first hints of autumn threw off the lethargy of heat. Spirits were high as everyone had a place and every plate was filled. For the great sacrifice would not be merely of flour or even also beer and wine, but involved all kinds of fruits including figs, mulberries, *kazla*, apples, and more; twenty ducks and geese; forty-seven head of sheep and goats; and even two head of cattle.

On this day, the royal table shared its poultry and large cattle richly and widely with the lowest of Parsa's laborers – meat as well as barley, fruits, and oil. All were invited. Cyrus intended that they would eat until their stomachs were tight, sing with the musicians, and drink until the stars blurred together.

On this one night, the normally abstinent Cyrus drank. He lifted wine to the gods and drank at least as much as any other man there. And he danced. In the midst of the people and in the presence of the gods, Cyrus directed the musicians with their lyres, cymbals, and drums to strike up a lengthy epic ballad. Then, Cyrus lifted the fringes of his robe and danced a dance that he had choreographed himself. The crowd cheered at the energy and grace that took Cyrus all around the wide festival grounds, in and out the tables, and they hushed when he nodded in time deeply toward the pyre, toward the mountains, toward the rivers. They gasped as Cyrus leapt from the platform, when he parried with his staff, and somersaulted over fire.

"Watch closely," Prexaspes said to Cambyses, leaning over to speak into the prince's ear. "This a Parsan king should do at least once a year."

When the song finally closed and Cyrus dropped back into his seat, sweat-soaked and panting, his eyes were wild with hope possessed. Cassandane took his face in her hands, kissed him deeply, and smiled.

CHAPTER 55

"Not better?!" Cyrus shouted into Amytis's room, his voice breaking in on her dreams like searing iron through flesh. Amytis pulled on a robe and hurried to him.

"She's not better." Cyrus's fists and jaw clenched and unclenched.

Amytis stepped out. She dismissed her ladies, their sleepy faces frozen with shock. "Give it some time, man."

"But the gods –"

"Will what they will and do what they do," she said gently, steering him to a chair. "Perhaps they have already begun the cure."

Cyrus jumped up. "Then it should have improved."

Amytis sighed and shook her head. "I don't know. I'm sorry. I will look in on her again this afternoon, but then I should get ready to leave."

Cyrus threw his arms up over his head, shouted frustration without words, and dragged his nails down his cheeks. His eyes were bloodshot, his lips still stained from wine.

"You should rest, too. Lie with her and rest. Both of you."

"I can't possibly rest. I have to do something."

"There is noth—Then go. Take your men. Go hunting, lose yourself in the river gorge. Maybe when you return, Cassandane will be better."

Cyrus fled, then. Amytis found Prexaspes. He would follow Cyrus. As always.

Cyrus was gone for three days. Another week, and Cassandane was no better.

Amytis had just finished training two women to replace her when they returned.

She was already gone, heading back to Ecbatana only days before the Gutian chief Ugbaru returned to Pasargad.

CYRUS DIDN'T ASK the Gutian why he had returned and so soon. To Ugbaru's eye, Cyrus simply didn't seem interested. He didn't seem interested in anything.

As they walked toward the palace, Ugbaru filled in the silence. "Even since I was last here," Ugbaru said, his eyes warm with admiration, "the gardens, a wonder; and this style of hall, lofty yet inviting; and just look at the fields, green and growing clear across the plateau..." He continued a running commentary of compliments on the beauty of the home that Cyrus and Cassandane had made in order to cover up his shock at Cyrus's appearance.

The king of Persia had aged a decade in the past weeks. Cyrus had lost entirely the easy buoyancy of a prosperous monarch at home in a peaceful land. His energy seemed either lost to lethargy or consumed with agitation.

"You may have guessed," Ugbaru said when they sat again at the table where they'd met before, "that my primary reason to visit is as before."

Cyrus didn't reply, one way or other. Beside him, Prexaspes remained equally silent. But he nodded for Ugbaru to go on.

"Well, things have changed. The displeasure of a powerful contingent in Babylon has only grown. Divisions reach to the highest level: the king and crown prince are on opposing sides. While Belshazzar has firmly sided with the traditionalists, Nabonidus is determined to promote the god Nanna-Suen above Marduk, even against his own son's counsel.

"Now, I don't presume to guess at your beliefs; but you are wise enough to know how powerful any beliefs can be. Belshazzar, who wants only to have the throne for himself, knows this well enough to betray his father and grandmother. People will die for such beliefs."

"How many? Cyrus said.

"Excuse me?"

"How many must die?"

Ugbaru sat back, tried to find words, gave up.

"Forget it." Cyrus ran his hands through his hair. "I'm distracted. Rambling." He looked up at Ugbaru with haunted eyes. "Have I told you that I wish to die and be buried here?"

Ugbaru heard Prexaspes inhale sharply. He shook his head.

"Already, workmen are hauling huge stones for the foundation of my tomb. When it's done, the base will be like a ziggurat. But it won't be high, only a few steps then a stone room just large enough for my sarcophagus and Cassandane's, too. Simple, Ugbaru, and so surrounded by trees that it will be hard to see." His voice rose in strength. "Cassandane will make sure of it. And then," he dropped each word like a precious stone, "when she is very old, and dies herself, she will be buried with me."

Ugbaru waited until Cyrus looked up again at him. "I'm sure it will be grand. But why this talk of death? Now about Babylon..." he said gently.

"I don't want to be grand," Cyrus interrupted, "only to live and to die in peace. This," he gestured to the land around, "is where I met my wife, Cassandane. She was the most beautiful woman I had ever seen and her people the most noble." Cyrus grew agitated in his chair, bouncing his heels against the ground. "Cassandane isn't well." He gripped the seat of his chair, his knuckles whitening. "And I don't know what to do," he said, his voice rising. "I have summoned the best doctors. Some do terrible things but none has helped. And I pray." Cyrus laughed bitterly. "You should see the sacrifices I've made and to every deity known to humankind." Cyrus stood. His face contorted, with anger or sadness, it was difficult to judge. "The magi... I'm accustomed to fixing things, Ugbaru. I can make right out of wrong." Cyrus's face went slack. His shoulders crumpled as he sank down again. "This escapes me."

Ugbaru, taking his cues from Prexaspes – a calm and quiet presence – let the silence settle. Then he said softly, "The Babylonians excel in science and medicine."

"I know." Then furiously, Cyrus added, "I brought Amytis from Media to cure her."

"They've learned more since then."

Cyrus was quiet. But Ugbaru could tell that finally he had the king's attention. And interest.

"Join with me and they will be yours."

Cyrus looked at him. "And what if their doctors can do nothing, like all the others?"

"You love her."

"Yes."

"Isn't it worth a try? You can hope."

"You're trapping me. Attacking Babylon to gain access to their physicians."

"Babylonians want change, they want a new king. The most powerful old families hate Nabonidus. Others, too, long for change. Belshazzar isn't at all popular with the imported populations. You could right that wrong, Cyrus. And think about it, if you take that city, you gain the whole empire."

Ugbaru continued to argue his case long after Cyrus had quit paying attention.

The anger, hurt, helplessness, ignorance, and frustration that Cyrus felt in the face of Cassandane's condition all channeled into energy for a new purpose. So, when Ugbaru had finished, and there was silence again, "I'm in," Cyrus said. He slapped the arms of his chair. "To Babylon."

PART III

542-538 BCE

CHAPTER 56

*I*t was agreed that Amytis would join the others as late as possible – after the Persian troops had been to Gutium, gathered elite forces there, and were ready to finalize their approach against Babylonia. It was clear even to Cassandane that Amytis's experience was indispensable to Persian success against Babylonia. Access to the world's best doctors was part of that success.

For now, there was a lot to do. In Ecbatana, Amytis needed to ensure that the tribes of her former Media understood the stakes – and how crucial to protect the wild land they all loved. Privately, Amytis welcomed, even relished, the goal of bringing old Babylonia to its knees. But if it went bad, if Babylonia prevailed, she knew that her land would suffer greatly. So, she hurried to prepare for its protection as much as she possibly could. At the same time as she went about those things, images of Khai flashed like sparks in her days – his quiet kindness on her first journey to Babylon, his taking on the job as foreman in building the hanging gardens; his carrying the great, heavy body of Gulash her loyal mastiff felled by Igliss's spear (meant for her little boy); and that one afternoon... Yes, the scrappy Babylonian entrepreneur was much in her mind as she wracked her brain and mined her experience for how to accomplish this thing with as little violence as possible.

* * *

THEY STOOD side-by-side on a palace parapet in the velvet dark before dawn, Amytis and the son-of-a-rabbi scribe she'd commissioned for Babylon decades earlier, at the height of a different time of discord.

"You and I..." Amytis said to Nathan, her voice warm with a natural fondness, "and the stars."

To the south, Mount Alvand's snowy peak shone silver-white in the half moon. In the east, as the sky's pastels heralded the coming sun, the bright star of dawn twinkled through the atmosphere.

"You know it's really a trinity he favors," Nathan said, "not only Nanna-Suen."

"Is that so?" Amytis studied the placid profile of her Jewish friend.

Nathan nodded. "Shamash and Ishtar alongside Nanna-Suen."

"Not Marduk, though."

"Not Marduk," Nathan confirmed. "That's the word from my cousins, anyway."

"Are they in Babylon?"

"Some are. But these are just north of the capital." He sighed. "It's easier to damn another when nuance is stripped away, don't you think? Recognizing complexity disembowels righteous indignation."

Amytis laughed despite herself. "That's a mouthful. Complexity, indeed." Serious again, she nodded. "Black and white turns red."

Nathan nodded. "That's another way to put it."

CHAPTER 57

*T*here was no question of Cassandane's coming along. So again, Cyrus's household joined the army as they traveled - first along the easier western edge of the Zagros Mountains, before angling into the steep valleys and rugged hills of Gutian territory. Cyrus rode his favorite mount, the horse that he had given as a newborn foal, to Cassandane on their wedding day. Its offspring, those that turned white, had become all but sacred to the Persians. Some horses they led, riderless – for backup. And for luck. Cyrus doted on them each night. The road was broad and smooth. Merchants from lands far to the east and in regions stretching as far west as the Mediterranean Sea had been using it for countless years. The company made good time.

When they reached the great Diyala River, they were in Gutian territory and would continue in the company of the river's rushing water. To reach Ugbaru's base, where Amytis's caravan would later join them, they would have to cross. But the river was wide and the current strong.

"This is as good a place as any for us to ford," Ugbaru said.

Cyrus looked down at the river. He was as still as the boulders around which the water frothed and spun.

Suddenly, one of the horses burst loose behind them and rushed headlong into the river. Time stood still as the company watched in horror. The magnificent animal plunged in over its head.

"No!" Cyrus shouted.

The horse struggled against the current, snorting and shrieking. The water drove it against a boulder, and when the horse turned, they could see its white shoulder streaked with blood. As its handlers shouted and Cyrus dashed down the shore, the horse went under. It thrashed back to the surface before slamming into another stone. The horse's neck snapped back and it looked for an instant over its flank back toward the helpless company, its eyes rolling white. Its rump swung downstream til its head was loose from the rock, waggling with the current. Dead. The river took the horse under again and quieted.

Cyrus screamed and screamed again. Over and over he screamed until the horse that he rode reared up, threatening to follow the first into the rushing water. Still, Cyrus shouted. He yelled out over the river as though he were all alone, just one man, his horse, and a relentlessly rushing stream. "I will not allow it! As every worthless god is my witnesses, I will bring this river to justice. I will make of its proud torrents nothing more than a little boy's piss."

People looked at each other, not saying a word.

Cyrus's face flushed even redder. He turned to the company and said, "You saw it. I did not give that horse in sacrifice. This water stole it from me. I will not rest until the river is unrecognizable – broken and bleeding into a thousand pieces all around." No one dared protest when Cyrus commanded them to dig. Canals would divert the Diyala into as many channels running as far into the countryside as necessary to reduce the original river to a trickle.

"I don't care how long it takes."

That night, after Cyrus had retired to his tent with Cassandane and they lay side by side in bed, she asked him, "Do you really think that Anahita is to blame for the horse's death?"

"Who else? What else?" Cyrus asked.

When Cassandane said nothing, Cyrus added with a sigh, "I suppose I'm a fool committing blasphemy. I'm just so angry. If I thought it would help, I would bring back that river's strength for you. The gods are idiots, Cassandane. Or we are for worshiping them. The magi have performed countless incantations, read sheep livers, and thrown bones trying to figure out what god wants what to relieve you of this wound, this pain. But what? Nothing. And now this, Anahita spits in my face, drowning one of our most precious horses. The gods are inscrutable, capricious, or just plain impotent."

"Shhh, Cyrus."

"I should be damned for saying it, for thinking it. Yet the gods let me live, while you..." Cyrus couldn't finish. He simply seized Cassandane in his arms and held her tight.

CHAPTER 58

*C*yrus's move with a full-scale army into Gutium was not lost on the Babylonians.

"Surely they wouldn't attack us," Belshazzar said.

King Nabonidus slowly shook his gray head, trying to puzzle out the Persians' next move.

"They had that trouble in Lydia. Maybe they're heading back there."

Nabonidus nodded slowly then said, "Yet the old Greek region's been quiet, as far as I know. Maybe they'll go east, visit that Parthian territory that Astyages had such trouble maintaining. I hear there's a prophet spreading a teaching that's become popular with the region's ruling class." He looked at Belshazzar, "Such conflict at the highest levels can be devastating for a country."

Belshazzar sat down heavily. His loud huff was nearly lost in the bustle of luxurious fabrics that he wore even though the early fall weather was still hot. "They would be foolish even to approach our border."

Nabonidus scrutinized his son's face. "The border, you recall, used to be on the other side of Gutium."

Belshazzar shrugged. "Good riddance to those barbaric rebels. They can go back to their subsistence mountain living for all I care."

"Mountains that we used to be able to cross easily for trade and diplomacy on the other side."

"Father, the Egibis will always find a way to trade. And others will follow soon after. You know that. They already are."

Nabonidus had called Belshazzar in to consult on the Parsans' move for two reasons, neither of which was actually to seek advice. Rather, Nabonidus wanted to remind his son that the loss of Gutium, Belshazzar's doing, was a true loss to Babylonia. So, while the crown prince grew ever more confident of a separate following among the Babylonians, King Nabonidus thought that his son's grave error in affairs with Gutium might give the man pause. The other reason was that Nabonidus hoped a common concern would bring them together, if not reconcile Belshazzar to him, then at least give them a purpose they could agree on.

Still, the king asked, "What if Cyrus *were* to move against us?"

Belshazzar squinted, in genuine thought or frustration at his father's obtuseness, it was hard to tell. "They've been in Gutium for a long time. If Cyrus wanted to, they would have attacked us by now."

"But if he did attack?"

Belshazzar rolled his eyes at what seemed like a drill from old schoolroom days. "Call on the gods to fight him off but have the army ready just in case."

Nabonidus raised his brows. He stroked his short-cut beard, his lower lip turned out. "The gods, yes."

Belshazzar leapt forward, his eyes blazing. "This is just what you wanted, isn't it? An excuse to bring the gods to Babylon. You want them here for Nanna-Suen's big feast. I can't believe you are going ahead with that."

"The gods should be protected."

The conversation was not going at all as Nabonidus had

hoped. Belshazzar was right, Nabonidus did intend to gather the gods for Nanna-Suen's akitu exactly as they gathered for Marduk's. And he did intend to hold the festival here in Babylon, center of the universe. Most of the people from outlying districts and from some of the rural areas weren't opposed. Some went along with the king, even Zeriya the *shatammu* of Marduk's temple, maybe only because it seemed opportune. Whatever the reason, it wasn't opposition. Other Babylonians actually shared Nabonidus's revolutionary desire.

But that was not at all what Nabonidus had wanted to talk about. He had hoped to find common ground with his son. He was failing.

CHAPTER 59

*W*hile Amytis prepared Persia's northern capital Ecbatana, in Gutium on the Diyala River Cyrus's people readied for the great engineering task before them. On the banks of the river craftsmen established temporary work spaces to produce what tools they could to aid the project, and the men set to work moving stones and soil that the river would be tricked into running away from its source. The effort took the better part of the summer.

The Gutians, for their part, were pleased. Just as Ugbaru had told them, by diverting the river as they did, peoples who had lived a tenuous existence through hunting and herding were able to settle and turn some of what had been uncultivable land into productive farms. Cyrus's reputation as a gardener grew.

When they were done, Cyrus had his wish. The Diyala had no strength left at all. Yet he wasn't satisfied. While the river's strength drained away, Cassandane's seemed to, too.

* * *

CYRUS HEARD 'Tossa shouting obscenities and nearly collided with Aspacanah, both of them rushing toward the sound.

"Sorry, sir," Aspacanah said, halting briefly in his tracks.

"Come on." Cyrus grabbed his arm and ran on.

They found 'Tossa in Cassandane's section of the tent. Cassandane, seated on a low bench, held her robe awkwardly off one arm. With the other, she tried to reach to soothe 'Tossa. But the girl would not be comforted. Aspacanah ran forward. Cyrus swept up 'Tossa, swearing and slapping at a woman kneeling on the floor in front of Cassadane. The woman, one of those whom Amytis had trained to treat the queen held her arm over her head against 'Tossa's tirade.

"You stupid idiot!" 'Tossa screamed, arms still flailing as Cyrus removed her. "You can't do anything right!"

Aspacanah turned his head from Cassandane's bare breast but not quickly enough. The flesh was ravaged. He slipped into an empty spot against the tent wall and looked back at 'Tossa, still screaming where Cyrus had deposited her. He winced. Tears ran down the girl's cheeks.

Cyrus raised the nurse to her feet and directed her out the door.

"Stupid, stupid, awful woman!" 'Tossa crumpled to the floor, weeping.

Cyrus helped Sanda cover her breast.

'Tossa lifted her head and spat as the woman scurried around the partition and out the door.

Aspacanah looked at Cyrus who nodded him forward. The golden-haired boy went to 'Tossa and sat on knobby knees beside her. He folded his hands in his lap and said nothing.

Cassandane looked up at Cyrus, her face drawn and weary. She shook her head. "It's not improving. 'Tossa blames the nurse, who is doing her best."

"She is not." 'Tossa's harsh tone was shot through with sadness. She muttered, "Ahmi was the best."

Cassandane adjusted her robe again and ran a finger slowly over one of her eyebrows. She looked at her daughter, who glared back, and at the sober boy on his knees next to her. And Cassandane looked up at Cyrus. But if she'd hoped for de-escalation, she was disappointed. It was as if 'Tossa's fury had fueled his own. His jaw clenched and unclenched. Helpless, his hands, in fists, dug into thick palms with a fury that she feared would soon draw blood.

Cassandane sighed. "Bring her back - Amytis, if you think it would help."

CHAPTER 60

The eclipse clinched it. Nabonidus would not back down.

The calendar neared a full moon, and the priests readied themselves for the eclipse ritual. Normally, Nabonidus welcomed this moment when Nanna-Suen was most lucidly visible to the world. And lately the sages and scientists had been blessedly wrong in their eclipse predictions. Nabonidus's chief of religious affairs, Rimut, made sure that musicians at the great temple complex had their copper kettledrums at the ready to beat long into the night, in order that evil forces be kept at bay. Nabonidus didn't go to bed that evening but walked down to the temple to witness the ritual for himself.

After Shamash's fiery chariot had dipped past the horizon, the drumming began. The moon rose, and Nabonidus joined the priests in prayers of praise and thanksgiving. Suddenly, a collective gasp broke the reverent celebration. A shadow had passed – brief but undeniable - across Nanna-Suen's splendid face. The drumming picked up in tempo and volume, the better to ward off whatever evil lurked, but Nabonidus was devastated. Surely, this didn't mean that Nanna-Suen was displeased or intended harm to Babylonia, he thought, not after finally finishing the temple in Harran, renovating the ziggurat in Ur, and – most controversial of all – commandeering Babylon's own Esagil no longer for Marduk but rather for the great and magnificent moon god. Yet an eclipse always only meant catastrophe of some sort.

"Gather the gods," Nabonidus said to Rimut. "You saw the eclipse. Parsans are at our border, and we must keep the gods safe from capture."

"But this time of year? It's unprecedented," Rimut said. "Hundreds, no thousands, of personnel will have to accompany the visiting gods. Managing them, with all their particular needs for sacrifice and oblations outside the period of the New Year festival will be chaotic. They'll clog the rivers and make roads impassable for anyone else."

"Such inconveniences mean nothing in the face of the alternative. If enemy forces seize the gods, we'll suffer cosmic consequences." Nabonidus shook his head. "This is a sign from Nanna-Suen. Marduk's akitu may be past, but Nanna-Suen's is approaching. As for its effects on travel, I'll worry about that. Just get the gods to Babylon. And I want to be sure that Ishtar is safely here by the next supposed Day of the Eclipse."

Rimut sent for the gods. To the two new highest officials of the Ishtar temple in Uruk, Rimut wrote, "May Nabu and Marduk bless my brothers! Send one leather mat and five (inflated) goatskins with these soldiers to properly construct the goddess' barge to bring The Lady of the Eanna safely to Babylon."

Still, some of the gods, including those from Borsippa, Kutha, and Sippar did not come to Babylon.

* * *

THE GATHERING of gods was indeed chaotic in a capital city already edgy with the increasing certainty that the Parsan forces meant to attack. And to keep the gods satisfied required enormous effort. Ishtar's three primary caretakers wrote to Uruk, "The Telmun dates which are offered on the first day of the month are in short supply. What's more, if we're to be here through the month of Uliilu, please send the following things immediately as there are none available here."

A small group of Jewish scribes watched the spectacle and agreed, "They hire a craftsman to make their gold into a god, and they bow down and worship it. Yet it cannot move. When someone cries out to it, that thing cannot answer. It cannot save them from their troubles."

CHAPTER 61

*A*mytis didn't need to ask. She had no sooner than dismounted than 'Tossa ran to her and wept. Even Bardiya was sullen. Only the baby, blissfully ignorant chittered a happy babble in the midst.

As Cassandane weakened, Cyrus's resolve to attack strengthened.

Pacing, "What Babylonia did to you," Cyrus said to Amytis, "to Amel-Marduk…"

Amytis's first evening with the company. Cyrus's mood was lacerating. People left the dining hall as soon as they could. At his table Cyrus sat hunched, agitating, over the remnants of a hunted dinner. Carcasses of rabbit and duck, venison, fish, and young mountain goat lay scattered in pools of blood and congealed fat. A candle sputtered. Only Prexaspes and Amytis remained with him.

"… and that Egibi," Cyrus growled in answer to nothing.

Amytis started.

"How he went behind your back, taking up for your son's murderer…" Cyrus bared his teeth and swilled more wine. "Just thinking about it makes me angry."

"Everything makes you angry these days," Prexaspes said, shooting Amytis a quick glance.

"And never held to account." Cyrus slammed his rhyton, sending the wine splashing over his hands, the bone-littered plate, the cloth stained beyond repair.

"It's over," Amytis said. "I hardly think of it now," she said. It was a reflex: appease. With a father such as Astyages, she had learned it well, the defense of a child, a dog, a woman in an angry man's world. Appease.

Prexaspes studied her then. And something in his look made Amytis suspect he understood. But Prexaspes let out a great sigh, slapped Cyrus on the shoulder, and swung a leg over the bench. "Off, man. To rest. We'll need it." He hoisted Cyrus by the elbow, and Cyrus let him.

Amytis thought the matter was done.

She wasn't there the next day when Ugbaru reported to Cyrus that the last of the irrigation works was completed. It was time, Ugbaru said, to set their sights on Babylon. "If only we knew someone on the inside, someone already in the city unbiased..."

Cyrus narrowed his eyes. He nodded slowly. "I may know someone. He's there, all right." Cyrus's jaws clenched. "And not on Babylon's side."

CHAPTER 62

$\mathcal{N}$itocris trusted that her entourage had settled the goddess and her panthers comfortably in their Babylonian shrine and had just dismissed an anxious Ishtar oblate when a eunuch announced Belshazzar at the door.

She heard him out, this son – himself full gray now – then said, "If your father insists on going ahead with Nanna-suen's akitu in Babylon, there is simply nothing you can do."

"But all of my friends, the temple staff – from chief officials to laundry ladies, Babylon's oldest great families, the judges, and... I don't know... everyone opposes this."

"I do too, but he is the king. And this is the *time* of Nanna-Suen's festival. He performed Marduk's as expected, you'll recall."

"But this reinforces his elevating another god. Can't you do something?"

"The festival will proceed, only partially attended, I presume. Listen. The more I protest, the more deeply your father is committed to seeing it through. He believes completely in Nanna-Suen's primacy, that this is what's best for Babylon."

"It's the worst for Babylon. Marduk will punish us terribly."

Belshazzar had been furiously wringing his hands. "There's only one thing to do."

"What's that?"

"Hold a rival feast." Belshazzar grinned at the brilliance of his idea. He grew more animated with each detail. "On the night before Nanna-Suen's akitu, when Father would have everyone *giving up* food and drink in preparation for his god's great festival, we will hold a *feast* of protest, a show of support for Marduk. I'll invite all the most important people, people who oppose Father's plans and people undecided. Besides," he blew his ruddy nose into an embroidered cloth, "who doesn't love a good feast?"

He was gone before Nitocris could reply.

* * *

GOBRYAS RECEIVED Cyrus's missive directly from the messenger, a Mede by birth. So, no one in the Egibi household suspected anything. Besides, they were terribly busy. Trouble indeed seemed to be mounting. Executing the logistics of Nabonidus's recent decision to gather the gods at this time of year, and so urgently, would have been enough. But add the stress, the unknowns and anxiety of watching the Parsan army clearly massing in Gutium just across the Tigris... No one was particularly focused on the black-sheep in-law's correspondences. In the midst of it all, Khai, Iddina, indeed the entire Egibi corporation were so busy trying to manage both the contracts and the chaos that no one vetted the message Gobryas received: it had come directly from the king of Parsa.

And no one noticed when Gobryas sent a missive in return.

"We rented boats to the temple in Uruk," Gobryas wrote in reply, "to transport Ishtar along with her entourage and supplies and have provided similar transportation to the gods from Akkad, Marad and Kish. The crown prince is furious, having publicly interpreted the act as another affront to Marduk. He says that Nabonidus is more interested in having the gods in Babylon for a festival to definitively elevate Nanna-Suen above all the other gods than he is in traditional protocol. Borsippa and Sippar have already refused to send their gods. The partial lunar eclipse evoked near panic. It is very tense here. King Nabonidus claims that the unusual summer rains showed divine favor. Others say that he has mistreated the land, that his *shedu*, the divine spirit inside him, has turned against him.

"As for the other matter," Gobryas wrote, "I share your rage at such a betrayal. In truth..." Gobryas hesitated in the writing. " I hate the man myself. And he hates me. Still, what you ask is not easy." Gobryas considered adding a more explicit counter-request but decided against it. Too much like a bribe, he thought. Cyrus knew what he was asking. Gobryas didn't need to get any dirtier.

CHAPTER 63

The plan was loose. Cyrus and Ugbaru would move their troops – a great number of extraordinary warriors – forward, into Babylonian territory. Across the Diyala River they'd head for Babylonia's city Opis, on the east bank of the Tigris River.

Late September, but despite a crisp autumn breeze through the tent's open flap, the air inside was thick, tight.

"Do we know that they got the message?" Amytis asked Nathan.

The scribe nodded. He knew the stakes; it was crucial that the people of Opis understood. "From Cyrus himself, "Surrender, and they'll be spared attack.' It's clear," Nathan said, "and I know personally the channels for its delivery. They've received it."

Amytis took a deep breath, released it. "Well, no reply doesn't mean that they won't."

As they reviewed the approach, Ugbaru said, "… and pull back, if the target isn't clear."

Cyrus nodded absently.

"Otherwise," Amytis said, "Remember: a lightning strike –

leave Belshazzar for Ugbaru to handle. And spare the king. Taken alive –"

"We've as good as taken Babylonia," Cyrus said, finishing her sentence.

He stood, the chair toppling behind him.

They'd been over it before, and Cyrus was eager to get on with it. His mood hadn't improved. Because Cassandane hadn't.

They watched Cyrus leave.

For her part, Amytis would stay behind, continue to care for Cassandane, and bring the household to meet them when things had settled down again. At worst, it would be a skirmish. That was the plan.

* * *

THAT'S NOT how it went.

On the Babylonian side, Nabonidus himself was at the front of the advancing troops, marching to repulse the Persian (an "insolent offer," Belshazzar observed) and gathering supporters from rural populations along the way. Belshazzar stayed home.

When the armies clashed at Opis, it was as though Amytis's warning was as substantial as smoke. Cyrus embraced the fight like liberation. On the banks of the Tigris, with Prexaspes at his side as weapons-bearer and guard, Cyrus leapt into the fray. The Persians were merciless, the battle a rout.

While Ugbaru looked in vain for Belshazzar; Nabonidus ordered his troops to retreat – west to the military garrison at Sippar on the Euphrates. The Babylonian king was gone when Opis fell. And Amytis was still miles to the east when Cyrus's troops plundered the city and massacred what inhabitants remained.

When she reached Cyrus, he was already preparing to move on Sippar. Ugbaru's palms itched for Belshazzar's dying pulse, and Cassandane was in nearly constant pain. With the blood of victory still dripping from his sword, a jubilant Cyrus had sent to Sippar the same "offer": Surrender now and be spared.

CHAPTER 64

"We had a plan!" Amytis shouted at Cyrus. The vehemence of her reaction startled even their battle-hardened generals. "What were you thinking?!" No one needed to answer. Cyrus's helplessness in the face of Cassandane's illness had strung him tight as the bows of Otanes, bows that flung death-dealing arrows at dizzying speed.

Amytis's heart pounded in her chest. She recognized that her own reaction was overblown – they'd acted in a moment; unfortunate the casualties, but it was war. Yes, now it was war. For her part, she knew it was the fantasy she had let herself entertain: seeing Khai when this was all over, sharing time, space. Finally, she'd be able to ask him about his motivations, his life and everything after that moment he'd agreed to leave the palace, leave her life. And again after Amel-Marduk's assassination. She'd been so looking forward to seeing Khai in person again – Gobryas gave them reason, excuse enough – to talk, even simply to talk would be enough that she'd been blind to the turn these events might take. Well, the violence was done.

And, when word arrived of Nabonidus's next move – his

retreat to Sippar – she grudgingly admitted that its effect worked in their favor. That, and the alliance of friendship that Cyrus had long ago fostered with Parsa's neighbor Elam. So, when Cyrus issued his "offer" of surrender, Amytis insisted that he wait for the word to sink in.

CHAPTER 65

*N*abonidus had reason to be hopeful that things would be better in Sippar. Not only had he commissioned a new fortress but also he had uncovered the most ancient temple foundation and rebuilt the structure, thereby pleasing the gods and honoring the past. Many years ago, when Nabonidus was still new to Babylon, Nebuchadnezzar had built a wall between Opis and Sippar, twenty-five miles east to west, to dissuade the Medes from attacking from the north. It ran between the Tigris and Euphrates at just the fertile point where those great rivers ran closest to each other. Nabonidus's troops followed that wall now. Their enemy had come from the east.

* * *

IN SIPPAR, Nabonidus heard the opinions of his generals and consulted the priestesses of Shamash whose residence Nabonidus had renovated a few short years before. He also learned that lightning had struck the temple in Uruk. "Thanks to divine protection, nothing in the temple was damaged," Rimut reported, "But the gods' personnel fled. We've dispatched magi and priests to fill in. Do you want guards to prosecute the offenders?" Nabonidus lowered the letter to his lap. Outside, the town was eerily quiet.

There was another thing, a complication. Nabonidus had heard, now he saw for himself: there were Elamites in Sippar. Long-time inhabitants of Babylonian Sippar, they were nonetheless kin of the king of Parsa. And Cyrus himself had reminded them of that with gestures of friendship and alliance that bound even more tightly by their rebuff of Astyages years earlier. Now, with the devastation Opis had suffered, those people, a sizable part of Sippar's population, were even less eager to join against Cyrus.

So, when Cyrus sent his public invitation, the same "offer," to surrender and spare themselves attack – the Persians were coming – Nabonidus considered it. And not only he. The Persian's message inviting capitulation wasn't for Nabonidus alone but circulated orally among Sippar's populace... all of them, no matter their origins. Nabonidus saw this. He didn't need his advisors, messengers, and spies to tell him.

When the king emerged from prayer and consultation, he commanded his troops to stand down.

"One massacre on the rivers is enough," Nabonidus said from the temple courtyard. "Any who wish to stay for Cyrus's arrival are welcome, even encouraged, to do so and without punishment when we regain possession this town, the wall, and Opis, too. And any who choose to join us, are welcome in Babylon. We will hold the empire from its heart and center."

So that was it. The Babylonians retreated to Babylon. And the Persians moved into Sippar as if it had always belonged to them.

* * *

IN BABYLON, preparations for war were already underway. Temple personnel directed their prebendary farmers and slaves to bring whatever of the harvest could be gathered within the city walls as well as flocks and herds in preparation for what might be a long siege. The Egibis advised lesser firms in managing their produce and livestock. Such practical measures were only part of Nabonidus' defensive plan, however. Nabonidus believed in his heart that he knew what would save them.

CHAPTER 66

$\mathcal{I}$n Sippar, Cassandane submitted to Amytis's ministrations without complaint. Something had shifted – something subtle but soft, a softening in them both as Amytis undressed, cleaned, and dressed the wounds again. Maybe it was 'Tossa, whose hostility toward her mother evaporated when Amytis rejoined their company. Or maybe it was simply that everyone had set their sights on Babylonian doctors – without much saying it – the hope that there might be one among them who could do more than offer this palliative care. Or maybe it was that here they were, thrown close together, facing a common enemy, and far from either place each woman called home.

Amytis was with Cassandane – sleeping – when Cyrus sought her out with Gobyras's reply. She stepped into the hall.

When Cyrus had told her gist of it – the part she needed to know – she smiled.

"That makes our course of action quite clear" and explained precisely why. "Introduce it to the commanders," she said. "I'll join you when I'm done here."

Cyrus turned to go.

"Another thing..." Amytis had been trying to think how to frame this. "Gobryas," she said.

Cyrus snapped his head around.

"I know that he has refused to leave – the daughter... the family..." Khai, she didn't say. "But it's important we do something to ensure their safety."

Cyrus laughed – a bit quickly, she thought. But he said, "This plan shouldn't endanger residents like them."

Amytis furrowed her brow. "I suppose you're right."

* * *

To THE MEN, "Our insider in Babylon," Cyrus said, "sent some valuable news. Nabonidus is determined to go ahead with a festival exalting his god. It's highly controversial. On the very day – two days from now – when the king's festival requires *fasting*, none other than the crown prince has planned for *feasting*."

Otanes let out a low whistle.

Cyrus nodded. "Yes, Babylon will never be – could never be – more divided. Just as Ugbaru said. Conflicting ideologies will be at combustion levels; and to top it all off, many of the most influential Babylonians will be drunk."

Prexaspes grinned. "At one end of the palace, Belshazzar will be partying; at the other end Nabonidus will be praying."

"That's about the sum of it," Cyrus said.

"Our two targets," one of commanders said.

Ugbaru, who had sat quietly while the others digested Cyrus's news, laid his hands on the table. The thing that he had been wanting, had been urging, pushing, and praying for all of the years since Thaer's death, had arrived.

"So that's it," Ugbaru said. "We have a date."

Cyrus saw in the old chief a resignation to the purpose that had been driving him on. As if it were inevitable. His expression was hard to read – as if he were already sorry for what he so deeply wanted to come next.

Seeing this, Cyrus said, "Prexaspes can lead the troops, if you have changed your mind."

"No. I want to do it." Ugbaru added quietly, "And now I know where to find him, that snake."

As she made her way to the commanders' meeting, Amytis thought of Khai. Like her, he'd never seemed to care much for stuff of power, of privilege. And yet like her, deeper passions landed him there. Deeper passions... It was war indeed now, but there was still reason to hope they could minimize the violence, that casualties might be few. They had a strategy, after all. If Cyrus and his Persians would just keep their heads.

"All right, then." Cyrus rubbed his palms together and looked around the table. "With Amytis's help, we'll work out a strategy for approach."

And he thought about the other part of Gobryas's note.

"It is done," the young man had said.

Done, Cyrus thought. He smiled grimly to himself. If he couldn't help one wife; at least he could help the other.

CHAPTER 67

*W*hen Amytis walked into the room, only the dying echo of the voices could be heard. She, too, had a focus that transformed her. Each man turned to watch her approach. Amytis moved with a sinuous grace. Her face seemed to shine.

'Perhaps more beautiful than your Zarin,' the man sitting next to Otanes said.

Otanes cocked his head and smiled. "Never."

Amytis took a seat at the broad table. "Babylon," she said, and let the word hang in the air. She looked around at each man. "It means 'Gate of the Gods.' As you have heard, many of those gods are indeed back in the city, each in his or her shrine or temple. Some are in the sacred precinct of the main temple complex, some are in the contested temple itself. Some lie in an ancient section of town, just west of the Euphrates, across a wide bridge from the rest of the city. Shrines and temples are also scattered throughout the rest of the city. Should you get into the city, it is absolutely crucial that you protect those spaces from your soldiers' pillage and even from any citizen who may try to hide the gods' images from us. The gods must remain in place, unmolested and undisturbed.

"Babylon is huge. At 850 hectares, no city rivals it for size. There is not only one wall encircling the city but a whole system. The first you'll encounter are the outer walls – three lines of them. The innermost, composed of mudbrick seven meters wide, is punctuated every forty-four meters by towers. A twelve-meter gap separates it from the next layer of wall (almost eight meters wide), which is connected to the final outermost layer (over three meters wide) by a twelve meter wide infill of rubble.

"One side rises straight up from the Euphrates. They will probably run chariots along that wall, supplying archers in the towers. Nebuchadnezzar diverted the river so that water runs around the entire urban area. And through it.

"The urban center is protected by yet another system of walls – two, laid out in a rough rectangle, with four clear corners to reflect the totality of the world, the four quarters of the universe. There is a seven-meter gap between the outer, Imgur-Enlil, Bulwark of Enlil wall, and the inner called 'Enlil showed favor.' Get inside of that and you have indeed gained favor. These walls require constant maintenance.

"Word has it," Cyrus said, "that Nabonidus himself has kept them up."

Amytis nodded. "It's a sacred duty. Then you'll need to know the gates well. There are eight. The tall palace gardens, 'hanging,' if you will –" Amytis hesitated, suddenly caught in memory, and as suddenly regained her focus. "... connect to acres of a public garden just outside the city wall. There is a passage – but it would be heavily guarded, if it's anything like I remember – from the public gardens outside to the hanging gardens within, and another private passage to the hanging gardens from the palace. That would be one of the least easy or attractive ways to access the city.

"We've got to find another way," Cyrus said.

"There are indeed other options," Amytis said. "But better?" She inhaled through her teeth. "The Ishtar Gate is *not* one, wide and inviting as it may seem. Its road, called Procession Way, is flanked by walls seven meters thick. Archers would make a quick end of you funneled into that street."

"What about that river? "You said it dissects the city. Where does it enter? Where does it leave?" Cyrus asked.

At Cyrus's mention of the river, Amytis's memory unbidden recalled that morning on the quay, Amytis mute with the grief of Mandane's death, homesick and forlorn. And Khai. His easy admission, his challenge to her... She knew what had troubled her then. Now, she could hardly wait to see him again. They had to get this right.

"Northeast of the main urban area," Amytis said. "The river runs past the summer palace, near the Akitu house. Both will be empty now. Though with Nabonidus planning to hold the moon god's New Year celebration in Babylon, there might be crews cleaning and tending last minute renovations there... Anyway, after that, the river skirts the eastern wall of the Northern fortress and south citadel at which point it does indeed enter and dissect the city. It runs straight between the western city crammed tight with houses, palm plantations and temples so ancient they go back to the days of Hammurabi. The great Esagila temple complex is there, to the east."

Ugbaru said, "From what I understand, Nabonidus built a fortification wall along the river's eastern bank, where defenses had been weakest."

"What about the western bank?" Cyrus asked.

"None that I know of," Ugbaru said.

Amytis said, "The eastern side, where the palace and Marduk's temple complex lie, is heavily developed with brick masonry and now this wall. Steps lead down to the water at intervals to reach the quay." She stopped another moment, cleared her throat. "It's very well ordered and controlled. The other bank is quite differ-

ent. It's a natural river edge, easily accessible to ordinary Babylonians, has docks and such, but no significant development. There
is a single, fine stone bridge, running along Adad Street, that
connects these two parts of the city. Word has it that Nitocris
was the force behind its construction, replacing the old ferry
system. The bridge ends in the middle of the great temple
complex.

"Wait a minute," Amytis said. "I mentioned that Nebuchadnezzar diverted the river to run around the urban areaa... but
also through it. The river flows out between the Nabu and
Shamash gates." She grew more animated as she spoke. "Nebuchadnezzar installed an iron gate where the river enters and
exits the city, precisely to keep invaders from taking that course.
This year's summer rains were significant. But. The river will be
at its lowest now." Amytis looked from man to man. "If you could
manage the river's flow –"

"To get around or under the iron gates you mentioned?"
Cyrus asked.

Amytis nodded.

There was silence as the men considered this. Then, Ugbaru
grinned.

"Just north of where we are now," he said, "there is a deep and
wide depression. In the spring, it fills with water as the Euphrates
widens with rushing spring melt from the north. If we could
divert the river into that depression, reduce its flow into
Babylon..."

They looked at Amytis. She raised her eyebrows and
shrugged. "It's possible," she said. "If you could do that, you'd be
inside Babylon immediately. *And* you would have numerous
access points through the center of the city."

Prexaspes laughed. "We know how to move a river," he said.

"If you did that," Amytis said, "a contingent could follow the
main city canal from a point south of the southern palace,
through the fashionable Merkes neighborhood, into the Kullab

and Te-eki neighborhoods. Houses spill out of the inner city into a suburban area where the canal meets the southeast gate, the Zababa, and runs out into less dense housing, fields and date palm groves. And one contingent would be right there, right within the palace itself."

"But move a river in two days?" One of the commanders asked.

"It's the best option," Otanes said.

"The only option," Amytis said.

"We start now," Cyrus said. "The cavalry will work to divert the Euphrates up north while the infantry begin moving toward Babylon. The plan depends on precise timing. Ideally, the river will slow and draw back just as the foot soldiers approach the city and the cavalry catch up. We'll enter at dusk while there is still some daylight but presuming that Belshazzar's feast is well underway. We'll run a loud and large contingent up against the Ishtar Gate as a distraction while the majority of the troops clear the iron grills at the river north and south."

"Precise timing, indeed." Amytis said, "The troops must enter Babylon on the 16th day of Tashritu. It bears repeating. The date could hardly be more significant. It is the eve of the beginning of the moon god Nanna-Suen's most important annual festival. That Nabonidus plans to celebrate in *Babylon*, the empire's capital and the city that has been – for the past *centuries* – Marduk's is revolutionary. It is inflammatory, as demonstrated by the crown prince Belshazzar's response. To the conservative traditionalists of Babylon, the Esagil has always and ever should be the temple of Marduk. Nabonidus might already have appro-priated that temple for Nanna-Suen. And Belshazzar has taken the traditionalists' side, favoring Marduk as Babylon's high god. *If* you do this right... " Amytis grilled each man with her eyes, "exercise restraint and not only that but actively protect the sacred sites, all of them, you could be hailed by the conservative elite as liberators from the tyranny of Nabonidus.

"If you don't, it will be a bloodbath and sure defeat."

Amytis held Cyrus's eyes until he nodded and the others followed suit.

"Remember," Amytis said, "not everyone in Babylon will fight for it." She pressed her palms against the table to steady them. "Merchants... spare them." She exhaled. "Also not everyone is native to that place. Babylonia has become great in part because of its foreigners – peoples and their descendants whom Nebuchadnezzar captured years ago. Honor the capitulation of individuals and their families. Keep in mind that if we're successful, these people will become our people. Just as both I and Nathan here," Amytis waved the scribe forward, "are now Persian so 'they' will be 'us.'

"Now. Nathan has some news of his own. Turns out, there's a gathering house in Kuneise-safyatib, only a few miles from here that's populated by Jews."

"Going there was for me a kind of pilgrimage," Nathan said. "The town has a reputation going back to the earliest exiles. I'd heard that in that town were actual stones and earth brought from the temple at Jerusalem. " He grinned, then sobered again. "There's talk among the rabbis there that in the future they will say, 'From the east, our God has summoned a bird of prey, from a far-off land, a man to fulfill Yahweh-God's purpose. Hold fast to that faith. Trust in Yahweh, who has summoned Cyrus."

"You see," Amytis said, "that there are peoples within Babylon and greater Babylonia who are ready for change. If we do this right..." Amytis said. "In order to do this right..." She looked at Cyrus. "You must stay here."

"What?!" Cyrus wasn't alone in the exclamation. "In Sippar?!"

"Assuming that we are successful in this," Amytis talked over the hubbub of surprise, "if we are to be successful in the times that follow..." She had their attention again. "Cyrus must be prepared to meet immediately with civic leaders. This would not be the first time Babylon has been overtaken. They have systems in place to arrest the chaos and reduce bloodshed. There is a time-honored and well-respected citizenry who control Babylon – its administrative operations and institutions including those of the temples – as much as the king himself. As you know, it's the present conflict between them, the king and the upper-class citizenry, that has created this moment for us. There are certain expectations in place for a conquering king to ensure a smooth transition of power. Cyrus should be ready to meet those people. And he must be seen as a man willing to listen, a man of peace."

From the doorway behind, a thin voice called out, "Yes."

Cyrus rushed to Cassandane's side. She let him take her elbow, let him lead her to a chair. But she did not sit. When she spoke, it was to Cyrus alone.

"It's what we wanted," she said, her eyes shining, "for Pasargad. It's why we've built it that way... and how we want it to be when we go home again."

She patted the hand on her elbow, kissed Cyrus's cheek, and walked back out again.

CHAPTER 68

$\mathcal{A}$s they marched, infantry and archers following the Euphrates toward Babylon, it was indeed Ugbaru who led the way. Commander of all the troops and responsible for the mission's smooth operation, Ugbaru watched the river like Babylonian priests watched the sky. So wide and deep, he thought. Yet everything depended on its reduction. Ugbaru was grateful for Otanes's calm confidence. Cassandane's brother seemed to take everything in his long, graceful stride. Otanes had insisted on walking with the infantry, to keep a sense of their fitness for what conflict may lay ahead. As the miles ticked by, and the river rolled on, what eagerness to avenge his son's death had so forcefully driven Ugbaru thus far began to fade. Closer and closer they marched with no sign of change in the river's width or depth. It was the same when they made camp that night.

CHAPTER 69

"*P*ersians are on the move, sir."

Nabonidus turned away from the window through which so many of his predecessors had looked, hoped their hopes and made their plans, watched Shamash drive his chariot over the horizon to the west, saw the sky darken toward night, and contemplated what signs the gods might give against the vault of sky before Ishtar herself heralded a new day.

"Only a small contingent," the messenger said. "Both Cyrus and Amytis remain in Sippar."

Nabonidus nodded. It was as he'd expected: a preliminary band would set up outside the gates followed by the rest of the forces and the king. They'd prepare their forces on the outskirts and settle in for a siege. So, there was time indeed to hold Nanna-Suen's akitu, time to right the heavens that the gods would look with favor and defend. Nabonidus exhaled.

Statues of the gods who had come were safely installed in their shrines, safe from external attack and present for the great celebration. Nabonidus could expect that the gods indeed favored his intent to elevate the moon god within them. He'd done well by them all – each one over the long years of his rule, renovating temples as expected by a monarch, repairing the walls, humbling himself to their needs. All that was left was to conduct himself with dedication and piety through the festival's events, beginning with tomorrow's pre-festival fast.

Nabonidus only wished that more among Babylonia's leadership class could see it this way and not as some sacrilegious affront. Ironic. He sighed. If only Belshazzar could see it this way. It pained him. What must it be like, Nabonidus thought – he could only imagine what pleasure the satisfaction of having an heir take up with him the responsibilities of leadership – yoked together and pulling toward the same goals. So many decades it had been like this, father and son at odds. Still Nabonidus could not stop hoping.

CHAPTER 70

*T*he morning dawned gray, muted with clouds that spoke more of the winter to come than of the summer past. Ugbaru stared at the river. If they were going to be able to take Belshazzar at his feast and Nabonidus in prayer, they had to go now. But the river was unchanged. Still it rushed high as ever.

* * *

IN THE GRAND HALL, Belshazzar oversaw the final details. Sturdy tables but grand. At each place, a silver rhyton with handles in the shape of Marduk's spade. Back in his room, a eunuch oiled the prince's beard, curled his hair in precisely the Babylonian fashion. The eunuch draped Belshazzar in clothes richly dyed. Golden bracteates cascaded down his shoulders and chest. Even from this distance, the scent of long-roasted boar, onions, garlic, and bread already wafted – harbingers of so much more to come.

* * *

IN THE QUIET of the stone cella, Nabonidus pored over the prayers. He cleaned his face, his beard, his chest and groin, his arms and legs. He put on the robes of kingship. In the temple, he knelt before the priest of Nanna-Suen who raised a silver chalice and intoned the liturgical words. Nabonidus bowed his head, closed his eyes, and felt, sifting down over his crown-ringed, age-thinned hair, the dust of the fast. It had begun.

* * *

UGBARU WATCHED Otanes prepare to travel, envying the man his confidence, his calm. Ugbaru's heart was heavy. Soon it would be necessary to apprise the others of their plan. He had a poor second plan: to surround the city at every gate except the main Ishtar and try to bully their way in. At best, it would be a very long siege. Only Otanes's assurance and the desire to find Belshazzar kept Ugbaru moving forward. They were within an hour or two of the city. The late afternoon sky brightened. As the clouds thinned and lifted away, Marduk's ziggurat came into view, its blue top lost in the clear sky. Even at this distance, they could see the walls. Massive. Ugbaru's heart sank. Dusk was coming on, and the river hadn't changed. That iron gate would still be underwater.

Still, they marched forward.

* * *

BABYLONIAN SCOUTS ALERTED Nabonidus to the Persians' proximity. He had already ordered troops to guard each gate. Over the years, he had maintained the sacred walls, conducted all the ritual dedications and upheld the expectations of a king responsible for this great city. Babylon was virtually impregnable. There was only one thing to do now: precisely what he had planned.

The king recalled the words of Nanna-Suen's prophet. "Put your faith in the god of gods," the man had said. In his spare chamber, the growl of Nabonidus's stomach was the only sound. He would do just that, keep the faith. Tomorrow's akitu would proceed, must proceed.

Meanwhile, across the palace, the din of revelers anticipating the night's excess shook the hall's rafters. Belshazzar, their host and prince, took to his feet and swung a jewel-studded chalice high into the air.

To Belshazzar's mind, it was precisely that conviction of his father's that now threatened the state (and his own standing within it). It was absolutely crucial that this feast proceed, a sign to Marduk that the most important of Babylon's citizenry, its officials and elders, its historic families and those who controlled the mechanisms of the state understood that Marduk's akitu was the only one that the city – Marduk' city – should see. Belshazzar looked toward the door. His mother had said she'd come. But not when.

"To Babylon!" Belshazzar roared as the servers rushed forward and wine flowed like the Tigris in spring. "Marduk's city!"

They would raise the cups of the defeated gods and feast to demonstrate their refusal to supplant Marduk with Nanna-Suen. Marduk would protect the city, if that greatest of the gods saw the citizens' support. The feast was resistance itself, and they threw themselves into it with warriors' zeal.

* * *

"Sir? The plan?" One of the commanding officers stepped up next to Ugbaru.

Ugbaru stared at the river, hating its muddy depth, its careless meandering.

"Sir?"

Ugbaru's eyes followed the wide path of water north from where they came. He put his hand up against its glare. Ugbaru squinted into the distance, then froze. For an instant, his breath caught in his throat.

* * *

BELSHAZZAR WAS WELL into his cups, and the great throng with him - a feast and revelry the likes of which no one in attendance had ever seen before – when slowly, he lowered his glass... He stared at the far wall. Squinting to focus as the room spun around, Belshazzar stumbled to his feet.

"What," he said, raising a bejeweled finger to the wall, "Is that?" He raised his voice, "What," shouting now, "Is that?!" Spittle flew from his lips as he roared.

The laughter, the singing, the shouting quieted to a rumbling murmur as his guests stared at the writing on the wall.

"A Jew can decipher it." A woman spoke. Nitocris.

Belshazzar didn't know when she had come in.

"Fetch that scholar, dan-El," she said.

* * *

UGBARU DROPPED TO HIS KNEES, Otanes beside him. A line along the bank revealed wetness where the water normally ran. The men grinned at one another. The river's surface was dropping. And under their hands, the ground trembled with the hooves of an approaching cavalry.

* * *

IN THE HALL, an uneven kind of quiet settled as the man studied the writing. It took him only a moment to decipher, though to the people gathered, it felt like forever.

Pointing to each word in its turn, dan-El read aloud, his voice clear, decisive. "Your kingdom is divided, given to the Gutian-Medes and to the Persians."

The revelers fell into a tense silence as a cloud passed over Belshazzar's face. He looked down at his drink, the ornate chalice that held it. It was the sacred vessel of the Jews, confiscated from their temple nearly fifty years earlier. The people gathered collectively held their breath. What would the crown prince do?

Finally, a grin spread across Belshazzar's face. He lifted his rhyton, raised it to dan-El with a smirk, and said to the hall, "the word of God."

Laughter shook the rafters. "The word of God!" they shouted in return.

The noise of their cheer drowned out even the clash of arms at Ishtar's Gate as Ugbaru's men slipped under dripping iron bars straight into the northern fortress. They were in – not merely the city but the palace itself.

It was from Nitocris, breathless and disheveled that Nabonidus learned, "There are Persians heading for the banquet hall."

Nabonidus didn't wait to ask how she knew. He already knew enough: Belshazzar, their son was there. The old king leapt from his knees, where he'd been praying.

"Go, protect the prince!" Nabonidus shouted to the guards at his door. "When they kill me, he shall be your king."

Clothed in a plain hooded mantel, Nabonidus rushed out behind them. In that moment, Belshazzar – clear across the monumental palace – was his only concern.

"If only," Nabonidus lamented under his breath, "we weren't so far apart."

CHAPTER 71

*N*abonidus ran through the minor corridors used by palace slaves and servants. In his plain robe and absent a cadre of royal attendants, he went unnoticed.

Meanwhile, Ugbaru's forces reached the doors of the banquet hall. There, Ugbaru among them and fighting with single-minded attention, engaged a cohort of Belshazzar's guards. The battle was intense but quick. The guards, not merely surprised, were outnumbered.

When the doors flew open to reveal the bloody warriors, Belshazzar's guests screamed in terror. But they weren't the target. In an instant, Ugbaru became as still, almost languorous, as he'd been furious before. His eyes on the prince, Ugbaru waved away the other Babylonians, openly weeping as they pleaded for their lives.

"Let them go. The one I want is there." Ugbaru pointed the red tip of his sword at Belshazzar's face.

The prince's drunken companions stumbled away. Belshazzar, swaying from drink, failed to rise from his grand chair. He fell back into it as he squinted in vain to focus on the sober man in front of him. Familiar somehow.

"Guard the entryways to this hall," Ugbaru said.

Slowly, he approached Belshazzar. The Gutian general was perfectly still now, staring at the prince with a gaze that burned everything except the two of them away.

Nabonidus ran into the kitchen, redolent with food from the recent feast. Breathing hard, heedless of the pain in his joints and the ache in belly, Nabonidus ran on.

"Do you know who I am?" Ugbaru asked, his voice steady and low.

"Some nobody," Belshazzar slurred. "Guards!" He coughed.

From one scabbard on his hip, Ugbaru withdrew not another sword but rather arrows – four. He held them up to Belshazzar's face.

Out of the kitchen, Nabonidus ran through the passageways so recently occupied with servers carrying platters of meats, birds, cheeses, fruits, bread, and all manner of delicacies.

In Ugbaru's grip, the prince jerked his head back, his eyes rolling down at the arrows' pointed ends.

"This," Ugbaru said, "is from the lion you failed to kill."

Belshazzar screamed as with one hand Ugbaru dragged the arrows down Belshazzar's cheek. Four lines ran red with blood.

Under the king's feet, the floor was slick with grease and wine spilt from plates and vessels. Despite his age, Nabonidus never slipped.

"And this," Ugbaru said, "is for the man who saved you from it."

Sliding to a stop, "Nooooo!" Nabonidus cried as Ugbaru drove his dagger into Belshazzar's heart.

Nabonidus's guards, arriving at the same time as their king, collided with the Persians at the door. Ugbaru's voice inside rose above it all.

"I am the father of Thaer, prince of the Gutians, the man who saved your life and whose life I now avenge!"

Belshazzar fell forward, his face crashing into the littered silver plate. Dead.

"My son!" Nabonidus cried. As he ran forward, the king's hood fell back, revealing a face deeply creased. Under the gold band of kingship, thin gray hair hung like a veil all around.

In the hush of the Persian troops' surprise, an arrow – flung from some Babylonian bow – winged its way directly into Ugbaru's neck. Another caught him in the side as a dagger found his back. The Gutian crumpled to the ground. As his men rushed forward, Ugbaru smiled.

"It's done," he said. And then he lost consciousness.

The general didn't see, then, King Nabonidus, weeping over the spent corpse of Belshazzar. He didn't see the king remove his crown and lay it on the spoiled table next to his son's lifeless head. But everyone else in that room did see it, Babylonian and Persian alike.

Ugbaru's deputy called, "Cease fire!" He shouted to the troops, "Tell Otanes at the gate! Pull back and protect the sacred sites!"

In the melee that followed – the haste to halt all fighting and to move Persian forces into defense to ensure the sanctity of Babylon's holy places, precisely as Amytis and Cyrus had directed them to do – no one noticed when Nabonidus walked out of the room. After all, having left his crown behind and no heir to succeed him, Nabonidus was simply an old man grieving his son's death.

CHAPTER 72

"*A*lready they're saying," Nathan reported, "among the Jewish faithful in Babylon that before Nanna-Suen had taken Nabonidus's hand in ritual recognition of kingship, *Marduk* had taken *Cyrus's* hand to rid the land of the heretic. They're saying 'Yahweh loves Cyrus. He shall perform his purpose in Babylon, and his arm shall be against the Chaldeans.' They say our god has decreed it: that Yahweh brought Cyrus, and he will prosper in his way."

After Nathan had left, "Any word from Gobryas?" Amytis asked. She looked at Cyrus. "Oh, no! Was he hurt?" she exclaimed.

Cyrus's expression had gone from elated, sharing congratulations all around, to stricken. He recovered quickly. "I haven't. For a moment I thought… maybe you had – that he got caught in the midst…" Cyrus grinned again. "But if anyone in Babylon is fine – and most are! - It would be Gobryas. He knew what was coming."

The answer hardly relieved Amytis. But she didn't know how to ask her real question.

CHAPTER 73

"Get him on the table," Ugbaru's lieutenant said and with a sweep of one arm sent rinds, carcasses, and hunks of torn bread to the floor. Gently they lifted their commander, still unconscious.

"Brace yourself," the man said. To another, "have the cloth ready."

While one soldier held Ugbaru's shoulder in place, the deputy yanked the arrow, straight and sure, from the wound. When it plucked free with a slurp, he slapped a wad of linen over the wound and leaned into it.

"Hold this here. Press hard." As another took over, he stepped back. "Let's hope the bleeding stops soon. Then we'll see how bad it is."

Ugbaru opened his eyes and then closed them again with a moaning sigh.

"He got lucky with the arrow – just missed the main vein in his throat and doesn't seem to have nicked his breathing tube. The blasted dagger looks like a bigger problem," the lieutenant said, as he examined the spot where the weapon stabbed, apparently puncturing through to his kidneys." He stood up and said, "Grab that chalice there. The prince was drunk enough, all right. It should have been good."

But the beer was cloudy, and when he swirled the remaining liquid it left a residue along the sides of the cup. The lieutenant frowned.

"There's wine here, too, sir," one of the men called, peering into a cup a few feet away. "Bring it; it'll have to do."

Leaning over Ugbaru, the lieutenant put his hand on the dagger's hilt and said, "Easy now," as Ugbaru gasped. The lieutenant sloshed the wine over the skin at the blade's puncture and slowly drew the dagger out. A strong gush of blood followed, mixing with the red of the wine in a viscous stream. At the lieutenant's command, another soldier pressed a cloth over the wound, and they looked up at each other, exhaled.

"The streets are clear, sir," a soldier reported. "Seems the peace is holding."

"See if you can find a quiet place here, where the general can rest. "Better we don't try to move him right now."

They needn't have worried. Word had spread like fire over oil. With the crown prince dead and the king forfeited his throne, palace staff had found other places to be.

* * *

WHEN UGBARU CAME TO, it was in a great wooden bed on top of a down-stuffed mattress. His wounds had quit bleeding but the site of the dagger's stab was ragged and deep.

"Where is the king?" Ugbaru asked his weapons-bearer, who hadn't left his side.

"In Sippar, sir, as planned," the man replied.

Ugbaru grimaced with pain. "No, I mean the Babylonian king. Where is Nabonidus, the old man?"

"I haven't heard. We were worried about you, and he seemed no threat."

"Find out."

"Yes, sir." The man stood and walked to the door where he spoke in animated whispers the guards there. Returning to Ugbaru, he said, "We'll know soon."

CHAPTER 74

*P*ersian troops had the city under control by dusk. A rotating contingent of armed guards was stood, shields up, at the gates of the Esagil, to defend the great sanctuary as Persian soldiers for temples throughout the city. Under such circumstances, all normal religious proceedings took place without disruption to people or place.

Still, Amytis waited in vain for word from Gobryas.

* * *

WITHIN A DAY of Ugbaru's troops taking control of the city, a contingent of Babylonia's most prestigious citizens traveled, As Amytis had predicted, to meet Cyrus in Sippar to negotiate the terms of his kingship. Cyrus asked Amytis to be present.

"You don't mind?"

Actually, Amytis did. She dreaded this meeting with Babylon's senior power-brokers. The only one other than Khai that she'd been thinking was about Bushu, Amel-Marduk, her son. But this was a crucial moment, and she had unique experience to lend. A former queen of Babylon – now among its conquerors. She gritted her teeth and went. To her great relief, senior though these people were, the individuals weren't the same men as had been in that role during her time. After all, so many years ago, those people had been senior themselves.

The eldest Babylonian spoke. "We don't assume that you are necessarily familiar with our customs, despite your wife's history with Babylon."

"My wife?"

Confused, he looked at Amytis. It gave her just enough time to recover herself.

"Right. My wife Amytis knows them well."

"Then you are aware that it is customary for the king to ally himself with Marduk."

"I am."

Amytis relaxed again. And she let herself savor this moment. Here she sat in one of Sippar's most prestigious residences – surely one that Igliss would have been happy to visit if he didn't actually own it at the time. And not only that but witness to great Babylonia's submission. In her earliest memories, Babylonia was everything – her father's fear, her sister's aspiration. Defeated? A little smile teased the corners of her mouth.

"You admit that it was Marduk who made your victory possible?"

"Marduk 'took me by hand,' as I believe you are accustomed to putting it."

The men nodded, a couple audibly exhaled, clearly relieved to hear Cyrus's allowance of that god's priority – and respect for the victory dealt.

"That's the most important thing," their spokesman said. "With that are some other expectations, demands of the gods on the king." He continued on without pause. Indeed, the rest was simple logistics, a recital of uncontroversial norms. "The king is responsible for maintaining the temple structures within the city and throughout –"

"I have a demand of my own." Cyrus's interruption froze the air.

The Babylonian elders exchanged a look of surprise. "Ah... Which is...?" their spokesman asked.

"My wife is ill."

Again, the men looked at Amytis.

"My other wife. My first wife. The mother of my children." Cyrus leaned forward, more eager than they'd seen. "Send your best physicians immediately."

"With all respect," one of the elders said, "the city is in chaos. It's true that the temples haven't been assaulted –"

"Yet," another said.

They nodded. "But troops are in the palace, the marketplace, the streets and even some homes. It's terrifying to the people."

"Send the doctors," Cyrus said. "I'll manage the troops. Send them, and I'll accept your demands."

Again, the men exchanged a look and with a shrug and some nods, "We will," the spokesman said.

"A Babylonian king carries bricks for renovations and promises to uphold the order of the empire established and supported by the gods... " the man resumed.

"Now," Cyrus said.

Amytis coughed into her sleeve. She couldn't help but relish the discomfort these traditionalists demonstrated. Finally, the spokesman waved a eunuch forward and spoke into his ear.

"All of them, sir?" the eunuch said.

"All of them. Immediately," the man confirmed. And when the eunuch had left, departing the hall at a fast clip, he said, "They will be here – the finest physicians Babylonia has ever trained, the best in the world – as soon as is humanly possible."

Cyrus exhaled. His neck and shoulders softened as if relieved of a great burden. "I'll hear your gods' demands and, with the gods' help, fulfill every one."

The men smiled.

"A king liberates the people from oppression and tyranny," the man resumed again. "Because Marduk has, as you yourself admitted, enabled you to defeat Nabonidus, it is clear that Nabonidus was sinful. The gods have identified you as our liberator. You will restore the gods to their places and do everything to ensure the welfare of greater Babylonia."

"Babylonia is part of Persia now," Cyrus said.

The man inhaled loudly through his nose, narrowed his eyes. "So it is."

"I will participate in the local rituals and publicly declare my allegiance to the gods of this land and intention for the welfare of its people. I will do these things, but Persia will not become Babylonia."

The men exchanged glances. "That's your prerogative, of course. As long as you honor our customs and traditions, you can expect allegiance and our wishes for your long life."

"We can then offer you goods," another added, "from the gods' table -- a royal prerogative, you understand."

Cyrus nodded.

"We have learned scribes, who can work with yours to develop such a statement."

Amytis glanced at Nathan and turned back to the men. "It should be written in literary Akkadian, not Aramaic, with the old-fashioned style. A foundation document for renovation in the city."

They nodded to each other, to Cyrus and Amytis, too. "It's settled, then."

There was scraping and shuffling as they began to push their chairs back from the table.

It had gone smoothly, this moment that could have exploded their world. Such sensitive diplomacy. Accomplished. Yet at no point in the exchange did Amytis feel she could ask the one thing that *she* wanted to know, needed to know: Khai. She hadn't heard from Gobryas – it's chaotic in the city, she understood. But that did not ease her concern.

So, she accompanied the men to Sippar's gates, thinking all the while how best to ask. Nothing seemed right. So, "The city," Amytis said as they mounted their horses, "chaotic, I understand. But the people…?"

"For the most part all right. The violence has been mostly armed – among soldiers."

"So, people… or businesses…?"

"Operating as normal."

"Their executives…?

The man looked at his companion, who shrugged. "Probably fine."

"Well." Amytis smoothed her palms down the sides of her robe. "That's good."

They were gone before Amytis could figure out a way to ask just where she might find Khai these days. She doubted he and Qudashu still lived anywhere near the modest home he'd already been talking years ago of renting out. She had a chance the following day.

CHAPTER 75

*W*ithin twenty-four hours, a cadre of doctor-priests had arrived from Babylon. The men carried with them their fish cloaks, divining instruments, talismans, and bitter concoctions. Amytis met them at the door. As she led them to the rooms appointed especially for Cassandane, Amytis said, "I was sorry to hear that Khai of the Egibis lost a daughter recently. Did you attend on them?"

Several of the men nodded. One spoke. "Long illness, a shame. She wanted a family of her own."

"Can you tell me where I might find the Egibis, offer my condolences?"

They gave her the address of a mansion on the best of the inner city's streets – along the tree-lined canal. She had loved to walk it when she'd lived in Babylon.

"And Khai... ?" Amytis looked from one to another as they looked to each other, eyebrows raised.

Finally, one said, "You're aware, of course, that he's dead."

"Nothing to do with the conflict," another added.

She barely heard him. Amytis felt the blood drain from her head. Her knees buckled. "But –" Amytis shook her head.

"It was a surprise – that morning, playing with the new granddaughter… Wife called us in – trouble breathing, vomiting… dead by afternoon. Qudashu has assumed control of the holdings, of course. Iddina runs the business," the man shrugged. "Then again, he had been for years."

Speechless, Amytis gave a quick nod. They shut the door. Alone, Amytis leaned against the wall and let it catch her as she crumpled to the ground. When she could rise again, she went directly to the stables. Amytis rode that afternoon into the shallow hills along the Euphrates, the dry air cutting at her throat. Despite Babylon's soft autumn air, Amytis's throat ached like winter on Mount Alvand.

* * *

So, Cyrus was alone with the physicians when they delivered their diagnosis.

Cyrus said, "You're telling me that Cassandane is ill because of some spiritual malevolence – a demon, a curse?"

Zerija replied, "It has been known to happen, Sir. Healers have been trying to figure out the source, yes. You heard what they said, '…."If a needling pain continually hurts a person intensely in his breast and something like suffusions of dirt suffuse him, when he burps he vomits bile and when he talks, he is continually short of breath, that person is sick inside his abdomen. He cannot keep down fish, garlic, meat, or kurunnu-beer but releases it…'"

"Healers, you say." Cyrus turned on the men, stepping close. "Healers! And yet she worsens by the day. What kind of healers are these?!"

Rimut cringed but held his ground. "The evil is powerful, my lord."

"And Ugbaru? I suppose that he, too, has been taken by some demon-force, has become the plaything of a perverse sorcerer?"

The men looked at each other again, their eyebrows raised in alarm. "Er, no sir," Rimut said.

"Speak up. I can hardly hear you!"

"No, sir," Rimut said again.

"No, what? No demon for the general?"

"Sir, Ugbaru's wounds are the cause of his ailments. Perhaps the gods determined that he should be so wounded. But his ailments do not appear to be the product of sorcery, my lord. No."

"Ah, so some are. Some aren't. Is that it?"

"Yes, sir," Rimut went on, speaking more confidently now. "Cassandane's illness is different." Rimut paused, waiting for another interjection from Cyrus. When none came, he added, "We fear that the evil may be due to a witch, my lord, some person with special powers."

Cyrus threw up his hands. "Ah! You know because you don't know. You suspect evil when there is no other obvious cause. I understand now."

"It's true that we don't know, for certain," Zerija said, "But we do have special priests who can try to exorcise the demon, or otherwise thwart the evil even turn it back against the perpetrator."

"And how do you do that?" Cyrus asked, sitting down.

"We'll need an *āšipu* priest, who knows the incantations and can perform the necessary rituals and sacrifices."

"So what are we waiting for? Let's get this done. Call this *āšipu*. I'll tell Cassandane."

"Actually, I trained in that," one of the doctors said.

"What do you need?" Cyrus asked.

The man sprinkled flour encircling each door to Cassandane's room. "Since the demonic force has taken root in her body," the man explained to Cyrus and Cassandane, "What we need is an internal rebellion, a revolt if you will, to displace the evil. I will call upon the great One who judges all and invoke the particular gods Nuska and Girra to summon and witness the arrival of a powerful rebellion to transplant the wickedness that resides in Cassandane. Then, taking hold of the witch, represented by this figurine, I will pray that the witch instead be judged and punished. Afterward, we'll burn this image and let Girra, divine fire, transport the witch to the underworld. May her words turn back against her! Are you ready?"

Cassandane looked at Cyrus and nodded.

The *āšipu* closed his eyes and lifted his hands. "Mighty One, Mighty One, who renders our judgment; before Nuska and Girra my charge is established. Come rebellion! Rage rebellion! In uprooting the feet of my warlock and witch, place your feet! May a fool lead the witch to her judge; may her judge roar against her like a lion; May he strike her cheek, may he return her curse unto her own self." When he was done, the ashipu said, "It may take some time to work."

"How long?" Cyrus asked.

"Days, a week."

Cyrus looked at Cassandane, who smiled weakly. He walked out of the room with the ashipu.

"In particularly dire cases," the ashipu said to Cyrus, "it is necessary to confirm the identity of the perpetrator. Our initial investigation and evaluation *has* yielded a likely offender."

It was Cyrus who told Amytis that the doctors diagnosed Cassandane's illness as a witch's curse. Cyrus delivered the rest of the diagnosis with a grimace: Amytis was the chief suspect.

Her one consolation: Cyrus was certain she'd be exonerated. In the meantime, he said that they hadn't told the children. 'Tossa in particular would be devastated.

CHAPTER 76

*I*n the noise and turmoil following Ugbaru's carefully orchestrated attack, the grief-stricken Nabonidus had pulled the rough hood of his robe – the humble clothes of his fasting – and simply walked out, away from the throne on which he'd spent so little of the past seventeen years. He passed over the inner city's stone bridge spanning the great Euphrates and for irony's sake went through the western-most gate, the "King's Gate," heading for Borsippa, southwest about twelve miles. Nabonidus didn't intend to flee -- no, he'd done that from Sippar, when there was still something to fight for... when Belshazzar was still breathing his ambitious fire.

But with Belshazzar dead, there wasn't anything in the king-ship left for Nabonidus. He had no ambition to raise a rebel force, though some were willing. There were those who remembered his conscientious leadership, care in tending the sacred places, and keen management of the economy - opening those trade routes in Arabia, for example. They would have been happy to see him on the throne again. But he was an old man, and a reluc-tant king, at that. Nabonidus looked up at the sky. Nanna-Suen was a pale outline against the bright October sky. Nabonidus knew it was too much to imagine that he might take solace in the countryside and live out his days among whatever old friends were still alive... or make his way back to Teima. Nabonidus's decade in the desert taught him the deep and simple pleasures of a wide sky and the quiet of wild things in open spaces.

No. He knew better. No conqueror would let a defeated king go, especially the deposed monarch of so illustrious a nation as the Babylonian empire. Rather, a defeated king such as he should better expect a public torture, flayed alive, dismemberment perhaps, maybe the hope only of amputation -- nose, ears... thumbs for certain -- eventually residing in the court, captive and shamed but alive. He sighed. For now, he would walk. They'd catch him soon enough.

With Amytis subject to her own house arrest, she wasn't present for the moment when Nabonidus, Babylonia's defeated king, was brought before Cyrus, its next. But Cyrus would not be "King of Babylonia," by his own choosing, neither would he call himself "King of Persia." That was for others to do. For his part, for the sake of the only place he called home, he would always be simply King of Anshan, that territory where he finally found love, peace, and home.

"Amytis has told me much about you," Cyrus said, when Nabonidus stood before him.

They didn't speak of Belshazzar. Nabonidus didn't speak at all. The meeting itself was brief. Finally, Cyrus assigned the old king a quiet territory in the existing empire, immediately southeast of Cyrus's native region, to govern as its leader on Cyrus's behalf. A younger king might have taken offense at this demotion and exile, may have taken it as bitter punishment, maybe even preferred a public death. But Nabonidus was an old man, around 87 years old. He would spend the rest of his days in Carmania. There the Persian Gulf meets the Arabian Sea in a conciliatory bend of the waters as though Carmania itself had negotiated a truce between them.

* * *

Cyrus told Amytis about it.

"I see what you mean about Nabonidus. The old man met it all with equanimity."

"He never even wanted to be king," she said and thought of Nabonidus's mother, how resourceful she had been, taken as a young woman to Babylon to rise and serve within the court, indispensable to its kings... Amytis had met Adad-guppi at the wedding feast...Amytis to Nebuchadnezzar. With a pang, she remembered Khai, lowest of the guests. He had been seated clear at the back of the hall. Even now, Amytis flushed to remember his salute.

"What's that?"

"Oh." Amytis looked down at the papyrus in her lap. "I finally heard from Gobryas."

Cyrus started.

"He's fine," Amytis said. "You were right. I'd wondered if he might want to come back and rejoin us." She shook her head. "Says that he wants to stay in the Egibi household... with his daughter. And he wrote this." Amytis's voice was soft as she read. "'Qudashu' – That's Khai's wife... widow," Amytis explained. She swallowed hard. Then reading again, "'Qudashu tells me that since Davcina's death, every night before our little girl fell asleep'..." Amytis ran her hand over the note, smoothing it. "'Khai told the baby that her mother loved her... and her father, too.'" Amytis smoothed the papyrus again. "It's wrinkled there at the bottom. I figure it must have gotten wet."

CHAPTER 77

'Tossa could hardly contain her excitement. "I'll have to ride next to Cambyses, of course…" She rolled her eyes – not everyone knew that her constant presence with Cambyses was to predict and protect him from the fits, protect him from physical harm but also from suspicions that could undermine confidence in him as Cyrus's natural born successor. "But ride on my other side? Please? All the way into the city. Will you?" 'Tossa asked, her eyes shining with eager hope.

"I'll have my own carriage," Amytis said.

'Tossa's face dropped.

"It's better that way."

* * *

AND SO IT was that Amytis rode with Cyrus's household out of Sippar toward Babylon not astride a charger of her own breeding. But accused by Babylon's most respected physicians of a devastating witchcraft, she was consigned to a closed carriage all alone, at the end of the caravan.

Cassandane's carriage on the other hand would be first. And

directly behind the crown prince. If 'Tossa signaled an oncoming fit, they could move Cambyses directly into the carriage, away from the eyes of the Persians' new subjects.

Aspacanah bristled when Prexaspes ordered the boy to ride in a third carriage with Zarin and Phaideme. Prexaspes would ride next to Cyrus, as usual, and carry the king's arms. Cyrus had invited a contingent of Babylonian noblemen, including those who had come to speak with him at their surrender, to escort the household.

Otanes rode up from the city to meet them.

"Ugbaru has arranged every detail of your entry."

"Where is he?"

Despite wounds wide and festering, Ugbaru had been determined to orchestrate every moment until Cyrus was installed as king. He had made Otanes swear not to tell Cyrus about the extent of his injuries.

Otanes cleared his throat. "He says that if you wish to be seen as a liberating king of peace and order, then the man who led the attack should not be present. This day should be yours alone."

Cyrus sat relaxed and tall. "How is Ugbaru?"

Otanes paused. "He'll be glad to see you later."

It was a clear day under a quiet late October sky when they left Sippar. Amytis had told 'Tossa all about Babylon but nothing of the accusations against her. The little girl relished her knowledge of the city as they approached, telling Cambyses everything that she had learned. "It's the largest city in the world and so amazing that the god Ishum called it 'a gemstone seal on the neck of the sky.'"

"I know," he said in a bored tone, but he rocked forward and back as if to quicken their pace.

'Tossa peered ahead and blinked hard. Had her eyes conjured

some shimmering mirage off the ribbon of the river? No, it was real. She pointed, eyes wide and grinning. "You can just make out the walls. They run for miles, all around."

Cambyses squinted.

"And there," she pointed to a towering structure. "That's where they say the world began. It's huge. Marduk's temple, 'the foundation platform of heaven and earth.' It has seven gates each protected by a pair of copper dragons.' Can you see its top?"

Looking where she pointed, Cambyses was silent.

"The top tier is painted blue. Melts right into the sky."

* * *

THAT MORNING, when Amytis woke alone, she had been surprised to find that if she could let go any worries about the future, her fate in light of this recent accusation – her isolation – was no punishment at all but rather exactly what she would have chosen. Cyrus's entry into Babylon, and in a moment the rituals of recognizing his kingship (including the visit to Nabu's shrine, …) were all so huge, so public, so grand and theatrical... Amytis had simply never gone in for such things. Realizing that – she put a fist to her chest – Amytis remembered her conversation with Khai, there at the river, when he'd confessed to the same. What was it he'd said? "palace life was not for him..." And there it was that he had challenged her to live into her circumstances – whatever they were – with integrity. Khai. As she rode in the carriage, hidden from every eye, through Babylonia's streets, no one could watch her, judge her, Amytis thought, here, she could indulge the extraordinary pleasure of seeing Babylonia – the Babylonia that had raised her son, a prince, and killed him for it – defeated. What's more, her own wild Media, whose protection had driven Amytis to this place in the very beginning, would not be subject to its greed or whim. And here, with the roar of the crowd outside, Amytis could raise her own voice to weep in grief for all that she'd lost.

Here, Amytis could smile to herself, laugh, cry as the memories rushed forward. She could savor them, lift and turn and set them down again. Amytis could review those memories of Khai – the sober young man who'd accompanied the fateful caravan intended for Mandane that became Amytis's... and Kara's instead; of Cassiya her first friend; Bushu, his birth, the singular pleasure of seeing him grow into a man, their own journey to Media... And so much more.

As the wheels of her carriage rumbled over the stone street, Amytis settled into the darkness. She could almost hear Kara – scolding, guiding. Let the others enjoy this moment with all its pomp. For her part - yes, Amytis thought – it was an uncommon relief to be absolved of attending.

CHAPTER 78

'Tossa turned to her brother. "Aren't you excited, By? Babylon! Proud and powerful for, like, two thousand years."

The small prince remained quiet.

"Or more. City of art and intellect, great even beyond its amazing buildings." 'Tossa sighed at the wonder of Babylon.

Cyrus glanced back and said, "An eye for an eye, a tooth for a tooth. The Babylonian king Hammurabi, over one thousand years ago, said that. Limit retaliation." Cyrus twisted and rose in his saddle. He looked up and over the carriages following until his eyes settled on the carriage at the end. Slowly, he sat back down again. "Justice. Presume innocence unless proven guilty." He looked over at 'Tossa. "Amytis told me that in Hammurabi's time, women served as creditors and lenders, led businesses, and kept their own books."

The crowd of citizens at the gate was growing, and the Persian forces were stretched to keep them out of the roadway.

* * *

When Cyrus rode through Babylon's luminous gate of the goddess of love and war, two weeks after the army had attacked, the very air spelled relief. It was late October and temperatures had dropped from sweltering summer to a soft warmth. Cyrus had commanded that the Persian troops desist from any violence in advance of his entry. The faithful couldn't help but believe that this great change in leadership would be for the good. After all, only the gods could have made an end of Babylonian kingship, ushering in a new line and a new rule with the handsome Persian who rode before them. Whispered rumors that Cyrus had not yet agreed to every detail of the citizenry's negotiations gave the day a suspenseful edge. But the relative quiet as Persian forces enabled regular temple rituals and protected the orchards, fields, and houses eased anxieties about the future.

Cyrus sat deep in the saddle, his shoulders relaxed, back straight as he held his trotting charger to the pace of a walk. Whatever sorrow and worries he bore, Cyrus let them go for the moment. He had attained the status of the greatest of men. This ancient city, he thought, with its storied history of world leadership by ingenuity, prosperity, and raw power would be the place where kings from all over the world would come to kiss his feet. Such a king. Yet clothed in his ordinary, partly-leather riding dress -- A belted tunic over leather trousers with half-boots, Cyrus might have been any Elamite recently arrived in Babylon's court.

'Tossa turned in the saddle and craned her head, trying to get a look at Amytis's carriage. She wished Amytis were with her now. Her aunt, who knew this city as both immigrant and queen had told 'Tossa that for centuries even before them, Babylon had been an ancient city of arts and letters, power and pride. 'Tossa turned back again.

"Did you know," she said to Cambyses, "that two hundred fifty years ago, the Assyrian king Sennacherib nearly destroyed Babylon, so enraged was he by its refusal to fall into step with his plan for the world. His successor and son was different. Inspired by a greatness that transcended the city's tiles and bricks, he worked swiftly to rebuild the city. Babylon was the pulsing heart and intellectual capital of the empire that followed. Amytis told me that Babylon is still great today in part because Nebuchadnezzar imported skilled residents from the lands he conquered. All over the world!"

As they neared the city, people lined the roadway, more and more. To 'Tossa they seemed as diverse as the world itself. She knew that they included not only native Babylonians and ordinary citizens but also the world's foremost craftsmen and intelligentsia -- exiles uprooted from lands that the Babylonian Empire had added to its own and their descendants. Amytis had told her. Among them were Phoenician architects, Syrians trained to fashion exquisite carvings in ivory, worldly scribes who copied the classic Gilgamesh epic already one thousand years old, and Jews who never forgot their scrubby land to the west and the devastated temple that they had loved where sacrifice and song united them under one, invisible God.

Ahead of 'Tossa, Cyrus seemed to ride with the satisfied ease of a man made great by his own design. She didn't know how hard was trying not to think about Cassandane's persistent illness, the accusation against Amytis, or to worry about Cambyses's fits. The excitement of the crowd and the controlled pomp of the moment infected Cyrus's impressive mount, throwing its head against the restraint of a bit bookended by golden disks. With each toss, the animal's neck rippled and set its feet to dancing. She thought that the strength and vitality so visibly coiled in the nimble beast under Cyrus and deftly controlled by him would be a striking representation to those who witnessed this moment of how Cyrus would proceed as king of a diverse and restive empire.

The crowd was thickest along the street called "Procession Way." That road, twenty-five meters wide as travelers approached the city gate, was paved smooth with limestone slabs. Horses clip-clapped over the words of the city's most famous builder, engraved on the slabs' unexposed sides: "Nebuchadnezzar of Babylon, son of Nabopolassar, king of Babylon, I am. In the street of Babylon used for the procession of the great lord Marduk I made the road smooth with limestone slabs. May Marduk, my lord, give a long-lasting life." Once on this road, built to run straight into (or away from) the city, there was only forward or back. The road was flanked by walls seven meters thick.

Cyrus's company rode forward, between those walls, inset at measured intervals with short turreted towers, where Otanes's archers stood, bows slung over shoulders unobtrusive but ready.

Along the length (about two hundred meters) of each wall, tawny-gold images of the goddess Ishtar's totem animal strode timeless in brilliant, glazed bricks, their bodies emerging from the flat background in bas relief. Against a field of aqua and royal blue, with muscles defined and mouths creased in a snarl, a single row of lions on either side of the roadway escorted travelers away from the city. Courses of white-petalled rosettes, also symbolic of the goddess and each the size of a lion's head, ran in panels directly above and below these imposing animals. They were bounded by the regulating order of geometric designs in fierce orange and black.

They rode slightly uphill against those lions, gleaming mouths at their horse's withers, toward the most symbolically profound of the city's arched entryways. Although eight gates cut through the miles of double wall that surrounded the inner city, only the Ishtar Gate and its grand Procession Way served the city's god, Marduk, at the most important annual holiday -- the Akitu New Year festival. Then, in spectacular ceremony, the divine assembly gathered in Babylon. Indeed Babylon, some people believed, was built for this -- for the annual convention of the gods, with Marduk presiding at its head. At the most profound moment during the ritual proceedings, god and king would walk together along Procession Way in crucial public renewal of their bond to each other and of their promise to people and place.

Named for the great Mesopotamian goddess of love and war identified with the morning-star planet, the Ishtar Gate was no simple, hinged matter. It was an elegant composite fortress that glinted with the many blues of tousled water on a cloudless summer day. Double towers twenty-five meters tall with crenellated tops of glazed mudbrick stood guard on either side of the outer, arched entrance into a passageway running forty-eight meters to the main gate in the city's inner wall. Nathan had told 'Tossa that Jews assimilating to life in Babylonia were already named their daughters Esther, a version of Ishtar.

Matching the lions along Procession Way, the walls of the towers and archway bore images of animals striding in ordered repetition across the same enchanting blue-green background. Marduk's lanky yellow dragons – composite creatures with serpentine forked tongues – alternated in rows with the god Adad's hefty horned bulls, the color of cream. All one hundred fifty or so of them, each about the size of a mastiff, were on the move, legs stretched in unhurried walk, some into and some out of the gate's opening. Together with the images along the gate's passageway, over five hundred animals populated the walls. Nebuchadnezzar had relished the challenge of getting the gate to be just right. Amytis said that he actually rebuilt it several times. At its entryway, copper bulls kept fierce guard and open-mouthed dragons confronted visitors.

* * *

'TOSSA KNEW THAT THE DISTINCTIVE, offset brick walls to their right hid behind them the Northern Palace, whose luxuries she'd only heard about -- reliefs with lapis lazuli colored glazes, real stone for floors, and objects passed down over the years from past kings throughout the empire collected as booty, tribute, or gifts. Nebuchadnezzar had built the Northern Palace immediately outside the inner city walls after battling dampness in the Southern Palace, which lay just inside the inner city. Yet even when water levels exceeded the norm, the Southern Palace was still serviceable, especially since Nebuchadnezzar had raised the floors.

That's where, Amytis said, her son Amel-Marduk established his friend, the former king of Judah, after Amel-Marduk released Jehoiachin from the Babylonian prison. Jehoiachin lived, then, as a friend of King Amel-Marduk in this palace... until Amel-Marduk was murdered. 'Tossa shivered. She knew that people expected Cyrus to continue to use the Southern Palace as his predecessors had, as a seat of governance for the empire as well as a place to house foreigner dignitaries... when he wasn't in Pasargad. At a size of 71,500 square meters, there was plenty of space.

They passed through the Ishtar Gate complex with its long passageway made colorful by the brilliant tiles, past the "Marduk Turned and Stood" shrine and past the little "Sublime House," temple of Belet-ili the mother goddess. 'Tossa could feel on her right the massive walls of that older palace like a great being. The Northern Palace complex, of a style like the great Assyrian residences, would be the place where the carriages would stop. Cyrus, with Prexaspes and Cambyses on either side of him and 'Tossa in attendance on her brother, would continue from here to another shrine where Cyrus would claim the scepter of kingship and assume the crown.

'Tossa could hardly wait to talk to Amytis. She had seen Amytis's carriage pull into the courtyard, but Cyrus and the others were already moving out. So, 'Tossa took one more look at the carriage - its curtains were still pulled tight – then turned forward again.

'Tossa urged her horse to catch up as people ducked into the grooves and niches and behind the slightly projecting pillars of the palace's outer wall to watch their new king pass.

They passed New Town now, on the left. What a hive of activity clustered in dizzying arrangements of houses and markets. And on her right, immediately beyond the Southern Palace was another neighborhood. This one Amytis had explained was called "Ka-dingirra," meaning the same as "Babylon," "Gate of the Gods," but in ancient Sumerian. Just beyond it was the Marduk temple complex, containing fourteen temples or shrines. They passed over the bridge composed of bronze-coated cedar and fir, laid three deep that spanned the "May It Bear Plenty" palm-lined canal bringing water from the Euphrates to fields east of the city.

Their first stop would be here, in the Ka-dingirra quarter. Nabu's temple sat modestly in the shadow of the walled courtyard of the Entemanki, the seven-tiered temple tower that seemed to reach to the heavens. Even though Nabu's house appeared to be no more significant than that of the many other gods with houses in Babylon, it was called "the Scepter House." For Nabu, son of Marduk, was Babylon's kingmaker. Babylonian kings added his name to their own – Nabonidus, Nebuchadnezzar, Nabopolassar.

Nabu, the god of wisdom and writing, who usually resided in his hometown of Borsippa, was in town because the king had brought him there. Whether because Nabonidus had moved the date of the New Year Festival with its annual gathering of the gods to conform to Sin's calendar, because he wanted to protect the statue from invaders, or because King Nabonidus had hoped that having Nabu in Babylon would protect the city itself, Nabu was in town. And Nabu's blessing was essential for Cyrus.

Dismounting, Cyrus instructed Prexaspes to remain at the door.

From atop his horse, her brother Cambyses whispered to 'Tossa, "Is this where the drinking ritual happens?"

For the thousandth time, 'Tossa wished Amytis were riding beside her. She nodded. "Yes," she said.

$\mathcal{W}$alking between the snake-dragons that guarded inside from out, Cyrus – after a brief if animated exchange with Prexaspes – went forward alone. Inside, the temple was cool and dark.

As his eyes adjusted, Cyrus saw Zeriya and other temple officials waiting at the far end. They had prepared the statue of Nabu and stood ready with the special goblets, empty as yet. Eunuchs next to them held the officials' assigned staffs.

It was quiet. Yet between him at the door and the officiants at the far end, Cyrus could make out a great number of people. They flanked the walls, leaving clear an aisle straight ahead. He knew he was expected to walk that, to stride forward and take the signs of kingship. But it was so quiet. This was why Prexaspes was so reluctant for Cyrus to go in alone.

Cyrus scanned the crowd. He knew that these were among Babylonia's most respected and illustrious citizens. Some he could recognize by their dress; others he guessed at, based on Amytis' explanations. He'd already met some of the palace officials including the chief baker, the superintendent, and chief of the sanctuaries. The portly, distinguished eunuch Cyrus guessed must be the overseer and scribe of the House of the Palace Women. He figured the eunuchs near him were probably the slave-women's overseers. He recognized the chief of police and merchant commander, and assumed the others included chiefs of livestock and head boatmen.

Toward the front, a group of men stood in the finest dress of Assyrian style. Long fringed robes hung from their shoulders. These they wore wrapped, loosely, and fastened with a belt. Short sleeves revealed sinewy forearms. Strips of gold hammered with rosette designs wound around their wrists. Their expressions were flat, their demeanor imposing. "Princes of the land," he'd been told, the most important and influential in all the empire.

Cyrus took a deep breath. He stepped forward. Immediately, there was a rush of sound. Shards of light flew. At the front of the room, the princes of the land raised their hands, fists clenched. Wary, Cyrus kept walking toward the god's cella and the officiants waiting there. As he approached, the men opened their hands in welcome blessing, some nodding. Some even smiled. Cyrus exhaled.

Then he noticed: among the group, standing at the back, stood three young men so similar in visage that they had to be related. Especially striking, though, were their heads. Where the others had long hair that dropped in ringlets down their backs and beards carefully kempt, these had only the dark shadow of stubble from hair recently shaved. Each stood stiffly, as if defying anyone to oust them. Cyrus thought he recognized one of them but couldn't quite place him.

He didn't have time to wonder.

"Within the assembly of the gods," the temple's high official cried out, "the highest god our Lord gave to Cyrus the ruling power. He shall be the king, the chief commander and caretaker of Babylonia!" He let the words echo in the chamber. Then he turned to Cyrus, "To you, Marduk says, 'With this standard I shall constantly conquer your enemies. I shall place your throne in Babylon." Then the chair-bearer took Cyrus's hand and officials solemnly set the standard on his head over and over again.

As the officiant led Cyrus to the throne and put the royal seal into his hand, a cheer went up. When it had died down again, the princes of the land approached the cella, and sat down as a group before Cyrus. With a great shout, they called "O lord, O king, may you live forever! May you conquer the land of your enemies! May the king of the gods, Marduk, rejoice in you, and may Nabu the scribe make your days long! May the warrior god Erra, make your sword quick and fatal and all gods lend you their character-istic strengths. May you always do justice in and for this great land."

An official filled the *haru*-vessels. Cyrus drank deeply. As he lowered the last of the cups, Zerija announced, "I present to you the King of the universe, mighty king, king of Babylon."

Even Amytis within the closed confines of her carriage outside could hear the cheering roar that concluded the requisite ceremony. With that ritual completed, Cyrus turned and walked out. The crowd had grown.

Cyrus stepped forward, a designated caller at his side. They stepped onto a wide plinth from which Cyrus could see the whole crowd. They quieted before him.

While the caller read aloud the speech that Cyrus had prepared for this occasion, it struck Cyrus again how diverse the peoples' dress. And to listen was to hear a veritable confusion of tongues. He hoped that each could understand at least one of the languages in which his message was delivered. For with it, Cyrus assured the people that he would strive for justice and the welfare of all, respect the deities of the peoples of the empire and ensure that its citizens were free. Cyrus did not mention those of foreign descent. Amytis had said that she had a plan, but that was before... he looked at the closed carriage that bore her. And he thought of Cassandane.

What was that that Nathan had said? – to be chosen was not to be excepted from suffering.

CHAPTER 80

$\mathcal{A}$s is the way sometimes, solitude morphed to loneliness. Whatever relief Amytis had experienced of having such radical privacy during their entry into Babylon, evaporated after a eunuch had deposited her in her rooms. She looked around. Some of the furnishings were different than she remembered, but much was the same. Amytis lay down on the bed. When she closed her eyes, she could imagine Kara on a pallet next to her, her old slave and closest companion so long ago. There was a knock on the door, then some skirmishing outside. Kara would have told her to get up, greet the visitor, take the news, stand up to whatever or whoever was to come. Amytis squeezed her eyes more tightly shut. Kara was gone – Amytis pulled the pillow around her ears – killed in these very halls the day that Amytis was absolved. Kara, her mother.

Muffled voices, and then it was silent again.

The irony of it all overcame her. Amytis had first come to Babylon, to these very rooms, as a teenage bride to King Nebuchadnezzar not only to fulfill an oath of nations but because the former queen had been accused of witchcraft... and died during the trial. Amytis had protected her sister from such charges. And now it was Amytis herself who sat here, accused. At least she didn't have another child to lose or to leave behind. Still, the bright face of 'Tossa shone in her mind. 'Tossa, who was so nearly Amytis's daughter – more to add to Cassandane's bitterness. Now, with Khai dead, too, Amytis almost hoped the trial would kill her as it had the woman she replaced years ago. Still, to leave Amel-Marduk without a legacy to speak of, and her mountain home without her vigilant care, and little 'Tossa... Amytis had to keep breathing.

CHAPTER 81

"So, where is he, our great general?" Cyrus asked. "The formalities are done; I've gotten all the acclaim. Now, where the man who accomplished it? Oh, and bring those golden rhytons of the local beer. Or wine, bowls of it – what's the best that's here?"

Prexaspes retrieved a veteran of the Babylonian palace staff. Chief of something, Cyrus couldn't remember. A young man shadowed him.

"He's Gutian, sir?" the man asked.

"Yes."

"King Nabo-" the man stumbled. "Former..." He recovered himself, straightened. "Nabonidus boasted some time ago that he'd gotten a lot of what he called 'beer of the mountains.' It's wine from that region."

"Perfect! A taste of home for Ugbaru. Bring that."

"And do you have a cupbearer, sir?... You know, a young man – very prestigious position, close." The man nudged the youth with him to step up.

Cyrus looked at Prexaspes, who shrugged.

"Aspacanah!" Cyrus said. "Prexaspes's boy."

Prexaspes's reaction was hard to read. Any other man would have straightened his back, thrust out his chest a little with the pride of it. Well, Prexaspes already stood with pride.

Looking at him, Cyrus said, "But for now, it'll be only us."

"You heard the king," the man looked at the youth, "Golden bowls and get wine from the palace storehouses. Belshazzar's former steward can direct you. Hurry, now."

As they walked, the lieutenant slowed his stride.

"He's not as well as he told me, is he?" Cyrus asked.

The man exhaled and picked up his pace. "He didn't want to affect your celebration with it. He's badly wounded."

"Tell me," Cyrus said.

"He was shot in the neck with an arrow. It's hard for him to talk, to drink, to eat. But a worse wound festers on his back from a dagger that must have punctured something inside. The gash isn't closing but leaks some foul-smelling stuff. There's been blood in his urine. Truth is," the lieutenant said as the approached the door to Ugbaru's room, "he's in good spirits. Remarkable, all that pain." The man shook his head. "And the doctors say that with these symptoms, 'he is at an acute stage of injury.'"

Cyrus stopped. "He'll die soon, won't he?"

"Yes, sir. That's what doctors say."

"Thank you for telling me."

When Cyrus gripped the lieutenant's shoulder, the man's eyes were wet.

The stench of rotting flesh and oozing infection nearly stopped Cyrus at the threshold. But he inhaled heartily and strode into the room. Ugbaru lay cushioned and propped by an assemblage of pillows and linens on a finely carved divan.

Seeing Cyrus, Ugbaru struggled to rise.

"Stay, man! Stay." Cyrus commanded. "I am coming to you."

"Sir," Ugbaru said, and bending his head, "My king."

"My friend," Cyrus replied.

Just then, the door swung open to the chief-of-whatever and his boy delivering the great libation vessels.

Ugbaru brightened and smiled.

"A drink! Cyrus said, "And I'll hear whatever you'll tell." He gestured for the wine to be brought and pointed to the boy. "You there will be my general's cupbearer for the afternoon." The boy grinned. "Step up!" Cyrus gestured the boy to Ugbaru's side and accepted the bowl extended to him. "I'll hold my own."

CHAPTER 82

When 'Tossa had first returned from the coronation, she had hurried to where Bagapates said that Amytis was staying. She wanted to tell Amytis everything about the day. She also wanted to know what Cassandane was hiding. The doctors had been very hush-hush, and Cassandane's eyes hadn't met hers when 'Tossa asked what they had said. 'Tossa felt sure that her mother was keeping something terrible from her and trusted that Amytis would know, or know how to figure it out.

Besides, she wanted to get away from Cambyses. Her brother had become so full of himself, crown prince of Babylon, indeed. He resented 'Tossa's presence. He hadn't had a fit for weeks and ignored her as well as he could. Well, let him humiliate himself in front of the Babylonian administrators and officials, for all she cared. She didn't particularly want to sit in on all the state business, anyway. Even if something interesting and important came along, no one asked her what she thought.

Amytis would understand. But as she turned away from Amytis's door, 'Tossa's head hung low. Now even 'Tossa's great aunt wouldn't see her. Still, the day's events had been grand, and her spirit wouldn't stay down for long.

* * *

ASPACANAH WAS WAITING outside Cassandane's rooms.

As 'Tossa, still glowing from the day's grand events, approached, he smiled.

"Tell me?" Aspacanah asked.

'Tossa shook her head. "Wonderful. So amazing." Then she nodded to the room. "How is she?"

Aspacanah's smile faded. He shrugged. "The doctors have been in there this whole time. I can't hear what they're saying."

'Tossa squeezed her eyes shut. Aspacanah stood very still as she slowly leaned her forehead against his shoulder. Aspacanah raised his arms to wrap around her, then stopped. He looked over her head at his father. Prexaspes glared at Aspacanah and shook his head fiercely. Aspacanah put his hands gently on 'Tossa's shoulders, eased her away from him, and said, "You should go in. She'll want to see you."

'Tossa wiped her eyes, nodded, and went in the door.

Aspacanah scowled at his father, then disappeared into a narrow hallway.

CHAPTER 83

*U*gbaru died a little over a week after Cyrus joined him in Babylon. Despite the natural grief of losing such a good man, ally, and friend, there was comfort in knowing that Ugbaru accomplished his purpose – to avenge Thaer's death. But apart from brief formal acknowledgment that Ugbaru died "on the night of the eleventh of the month of Arahsamnu" (November 6, 539 B.C.E.), Cyrus had little time to dwell on it. He was on his own. Amytis was all but gagged by the damning accusation that she had caused the illness ravaging Cassandane just when all Cyrus wanted to do was get those damned doctors to cure her. Patience, he told himself. They said it might take some time.

CHAPTER 84

*A*mytis stood before the royal judge – in the audience room of Cassandane's private suite.

Amytis had told only Nathan about the charge, Nathan who had so many years ago boldly – yet unsuccessfully – tried to defend her and Bushu from Nebuchadnezzar's punishing rage. That, too, had proven to be based on a false accusation. Yet this time there would be no crowd of support, no uprising to exonerate Amytis. This, even Nathan wasn't allowed to attend. And Amytis was too tired to protest.

Cyrus was present, and Cassandane, too. Cassandane's disease was no better for the all the incantations, bitter tinctures, and stinging salves that the Babylonian doctors prescribed. Amytis had done little to protest her innocence. So the trial went forward. But it was a small and private affair, as Cyrus had commanded that the accusation be kept from anyone except those directly involved until they had proof. Only one doctor was present, the most senior of those who had been involved in Cassandane's treatment.

"Have you seen such a condition before?" the judge asked the doctor.

"A few similar, only one close enough to compare. That one proved to be the doing of a particularly powerful witch."

"A foreigner?"

"No, a Babylonian."

"And how did you discern this?"

"The afflicted could show that the accused harbored a jealousy that led the witch to curse the victim in this way."

"Jealousy?"

"Of her husband and children, sir."

"And you think that's like this?"

"Perhaps. And in this case, there is additional motive – to be primary queen of a considerable empire."

Cassandane shifted on her chair. Amytis looked at her once, and then resumed gazing straight ahead at the judge, or through him.

Cyrus leaned forward. "What proof do you have?"

The judge looked at Cassandane. She shook her head. He looked at the doctor-priest.

"We were of the impression that the victim saw this woman," the doctor pointed to Amytis, "as the cause of her disease."

Cyrus looked at Cassandane, who stared straight ahead.

"Normally, we would subject the accused to a test, an ordeal," the doctor said.

A shiver shook Amytis's shoulders. She knew of them.

"But surely you must have more evidence to go forward with that," Cyrus said.

Suddenly 'Tossa, from the bedroom next door burst in, an attendant lurching after her. The woman got ahold of 'Tossa's arm and held it gently but firmly, stopping 'Tossa in her tracks. But she didn't stop the girl's mouth.

"What are you doing?!" 'Tossa shouted across the room. "Amytis!"

But Amytis turned her back to 'Tossa and stood still.

"What's going on?" 'Tossa demanded.

Cassandane's face was red as she began to rise. "It's nothing, Tossa. Go on now. We'll tell you everything later."

'Tossa looked at her parents on their chairs, the judge in front of a heavy desk, the recording scribe, and doctor... and Amytis, standing before them all.

"No!" 'Tossa cried, and with a violent twist, she wrenched free. 'Tossa ran to Amytis and grabbed her hand.

Amytis's shoulders dropped. Her face softened as she bent to the girl. She smoothed 'Tossa's hair back from her face. Amytis took a deep breath, looked up at the doctor, the judge, and back to 'Tossa. "They think that I have made your mother sick."

'Tossa dropped her hand. "You haven't, though, have you?"

"I'm not sure," Amytis said.

"You tried to help her! You even taught me: what herbs do what –"

"Be quiet, now," Amytis said, her tone a warning.

"How to clean a wound," 'Tossa ignored her, "and how ease to pain..."

The silence that fell seemed as loud as her voice had been.

"It's true," Cassandane said, her voice quiet but clear.

Amytis stood again, 'Tossa next to her.

"This woman, Amytis, has only helped. She has not hurt me. The hurt is my own." Cassandane looked at Amytis then. Her eyes were warm, soft. "You don't deserve this."

"Neither do you. The injury in your body," Amytis said. "It's not your fault."

"It's not hers, either," Cassandane said to the judge. Then, brusque, she added, "I have been praying to Gula..."

The Babylonians looked at one another in surprise.

"The goddess of healing, yes?" Cassandane didn't look at Amytis.

But Amytis almost laughed. So Sanda *had* been listening, when Amytis regaled 'Tossa with stories of Babylon.

"And Gula," Cassandane said, "has never indicated the involvement of a witch."

The judge looked at the doctor.

"Do you have any other evidence?"

"No sir."

The judge said to the recording scribe, "Then note that she is innocent."

CHAPTER 85

$\mathcal{N}$athan was in the hall when they walked out, hopping from one foot to the other. When he caught Amytis's eye, and she nodded, she let out a great breath and grinned. She slipped past him – 'Tossa had begged to see the palm orchards and "that Akitu house" – leaving it to Cyrus to explain what had happened.

When he was done, Cyrus hung his head. "They're out of answers. Anyone can see that." He laughed ruefully, "Not that it'll keep them from their rituals - prescribing or advising as dictated by their gods..." Cyrus stopped and studied Nathan.

"What about your god?" Before Nathan could answer, Cyrus launched into a description of Cassandane's condition growing more and more animated with hope. "This wasting disease... Can you or someone – maybe from that community near Sippar – heal her?"

Nathan took a deep breath. "I know this disease. I think."

"Well?!"

Cyrus's eager hope pained the old scribe. "It's taken some of our women, too." Nathan rested kind eyes on the young king. "I am sorry – for you, your children..."

"What?!" Cyrus exclaimed. "Nothing? No ritual to rid her of evil? No incantation or prayer?"

"Prayer, yes." Nathan said. "God is mysterious and may yet heal her. Nothing is beyond the maker of heaven and earth." The scribe's calm began to settle Cyrus again. He walked on, thoughtfully, Cyrus beside him. "Our god seems indeed to have chosen you," Nathan said. "But to be chosen is not to be immune to suffering and death." They stopped at the arch into the hanging gardens. "Meanwhile," Nathan said, "You – and she – have living to do."

"$\mathcal{I}$'m thinking of offering Gobryas a position – a good one," Cyrus said, "in my administration."

Amytis nodded. "If he's developed any of the aptitude he showed as a boy... and brightened that foul disposition..." She tilted her head. "Sounds good. Oh, but he's going to want to go to Pasargad... or anywhere else, for that matter."

"That's why I'm thinking Governor of Babylon."

Amytis raised her eyes. "That *is* a good position." She shrugged. "And he'll probably be good at it. He's definitely had opportunity to learn the inner workings of this place."

"Besides," Cyrus said, "it would honor the promise I made to Mardonius. And also in honor of Ugbaru."

Amytis grinned. "Same name."

So it was that over the coming weeks and months, Amytis and Gobryas helped Cyrus to understand what the Babylonians expected of a king, their customs, and beliefs – the kinds of things Babylonia's cadre of citizen-elders had mentioned when they met in Sippar.

Despite Amytis's prodding, Gobryas talked very little about his life in the Egibi household. After a while, she quit asking. She did notice, however, that he'd lost his churlish attitude and wondered what role Khai might have played in that. And he did say that he continued the tradition of telling his daughter every night that her mother and father loved her... and her grandfather, too.

That there was no end to the work proved a kind of blessing to Cyrus. There was nothing he could do for Cassandane except wait, hope, and pray for the moment when she could travel again. At the earliest opportunity, they'd return to Pasargad.

Meanwhile, among the first things and most important things that Cyrus did was return the gods to their respective home cities. These were the statues that Nabonidus had gathered into Babylon for the controversial festival of Nanna-Suen.

Then there were tasks of temple maintenance and renovations - a critical responsibility of the Babylonian king. There was always more to do. But other things demanded attention, as well.

"The economic and social situation –" Amytis said.

"Also divided," Cyrus gestured to a chair for Amytis to sit. "I know." Despite the gloom of winter, Cyrus was in a good mood – better, anyway. Cassandane had let 'Tossa bring her to Nebuchadnezzar's museum of treasures.

"When I first came here," Amytis said, "there were hundreds of other people new to this place. Nebuchadnezzar had taken them from distant lands, countries that he conquered. I came because it was the best hope to save my land (and reflexively to protect my sister, your mother). These people had been forced to come because Nebuchadnezzar had defeated them. He brought to Babylon the best and brightest, intellectuals and artisans, and put them to work here. At the time, there was plenty to go around, since he was such an ambitious emperor and energetic builder. The exiles added much, and the lower class, native non-citizens enjoyed new opportunities, too."

Cyrus nodded.

"But there has always been hostility and resentment among

some Babylonians toward the foreigners, even those who have now been here for generations. Ironically, many of the people they look down on or despise, such as Nathan and other Jews, want nothing more than to be able to return to their native lands, worship their own gods."

"This is the plan you mentioned." Cyrus nodded. "We send them back."

"That western frontier along the Great Sea... Nathan said it's really weak. Nebuchadnezzar's armies destroyed much of it. And it's never recovered."

"I see the value. We send them back with money, resources." Cyrus sat forward. "And in the process, we secure our borders *and* build goodwill among both the foreigners and the long-time Babylonians. *If* we allowed, but didn't force, the exiles to return home. And a place such as Nathan's... Judah...? It stands at a crucial location. If we gave them economic support and a mandate to rebuild... if we gave back their sacred objects..."

"They would see you as the greatest of liberators and be loyal to you and greater Persia long into the future."

Gobryas entered the room. He looked from Cyrus to Amytis, both looking so pleased. When they didn't explain, he shrugged.

"There's a stretch of the southern city wall where water deflected from the river's main course has worn it down to the foundation," Gobryas said. "We need to rebuild from the ground up."

"There it is!" Amytis grinned. "A good occasion for you to install a public declaration."

"Install?" Cyrus asked.

"It is common protocol for a king to place a document beneath the foundation of a building to elicit divine protection," Gobryas explained. "It gives the king an opportunity to spell out his accomplishments and intentions for the empire. Nathan can show - "

"Intentions, yes. I can make this announcement then!" Cyrus said.

Gobryas looked at Amytis.

"I'll explain later," she said. "Something else?"

You should also consider carrying some of the bricks or bitumen," Gobryas told Cyrus, "To demonstrate that you accept the responsibilities of Babylonian kingship. That's what's done."

"He's right," Amytis said. Her smile faded. "I'll miss Nathan."

"I'll just –" Gobryas motioned to the door. But again neither Amytis nor Cyrus seemed to notice him anymore, so Gobryas left.

"I'm not sure he wants to be among those who go back."

"Nathan's been talking about Jerusalem from the day I first met him," Amytis said. "So, you'll do a public reading on the occasion of the wall's dedication?"

"That's the plan. There's a scribe, Qishti-Marduk, who will cut it into a clay cylinder."

"Just like the old kings."

"Not exactly." Cyrus sobered. "I will be identified, first and foremost, as 'King of Anshan,' no matter how petty the old nobility here may find it to be." He stood.

"And as soon as Cassandane is well, we'll return. We'll finish the palace at Pasargad and never leave it again. I want to bring her home."

Amytis simply nodded.

* * *

WITH WINTER PASSING, the skies over Babylon brightened. The day was fair, the air mild and redolent with hints of spring when the people assembled to hear Cyrus's declaration. He'd requested that Cambyses stand beside him. The whole family there – even Cassandane, on a litter and pale.

A scribe read the king's statement aloud, rotating the clay

cylinder in his hands as he went. When the reader finished, the crowd barely moved. The only sound an occasional murmur as someone asked their neighbor was what they heard correct? The words were familiar, the sentiment traditional. But still. This far foreigner had accepted the terms. He would rule as a Babylonian king should. A slight breeze off the river might as well have been the crowd's collective sigh of relief.

Another moment, and Cyrus himself spoke. He looked long at Cassandane, smiling back at him with the same confident strength he'd noticed when he first saw her, the same warmth she'd shown that night she had joined him on the plateau in Pasargad and told him about growing up there, about the way the place had shaped her, how dear it was. Cyrus began, then, by speaking of home.

He told of his intention for those whom Nebuchadnezzar had taken into exile here – whoever among them was still alive – and whoever among their descendants wished to return, that Persia would provide for them to rebuild their houses, their cities, and their temples. Ripples of surprise worked through the crowd. He said that they should worship their gods in the places in which those gods dwelt... In the places that were home. And when he said that Babylonia would give back whatever sacred objects they had taken in conquest decades earlier, the murmurs rose to a cheer.

* * *

THERE WERE those among the Jews who wept when they saw the candelabrum, the vessels for sacrifice, and incense burners.

"It's all yours," Cyrus said, "Just as it had been. But it belongs in Jerusalem, not here. Go. Make lives back in Judah. Repopulate the cities and reclaim your land. May your god be pleased and make you prosper."

Nathan stopped at the private counsel room. He wore rugged

clothes – a travel robe – and the trousers that Amytis had introduced to him from Media. He carried a satchel.

"You are leaving indeed, then," Amytis said, her smile tinged with sadness.

"Yes. Just a small group. Others, we hope, will follow."

"You'll be gone before the new year, then," Cyrus said.

"You won't stay?" Amytis said despite herself.

"There's a saying circulating in Jewtown." Nathan set his satchel gently on the ground. "A prophet in my father's tradition..."

Amytis sat back, her eyes full of fondness and memories.

"He says that Yahweh our god has called him to 'Comfort, comfort my people. Speak tenderly to Jerusalem. Tell her that it's over. Her wrongs are forgiven.' God subjected her to twice the punishment that she was due." Nathan smiled. He lifted his satchel again. "We want to be back in time for our own new year." Nathan smiled. "This, conducted mostly with family at the dinner table celebrates the memory of liberation from captivity in Egypt. Our actual New Year we mark not with feasting but with a fast, repenting for past sins and praying that God be merciful toward us, forgiving and sustaining as we begin another year. Both liturgies end with our saying, 'Next year in Jerusalem!'"

"Perfect," Amytis said.

Nathan's eyes shone with happiness. "This will be a special year, a new liberation, a new exodus."

"The way back," Cyrus said. "It's a long and difficult road. Do you really think others will follow?"

"Already one of my colleagues is saying 'In the wilderness, prepare a way for Yahweh. Make straight in the desert a highway for our God.' There's a big push. And God gives strength to the weary, to those who attend Yahweh-God. Then, we can fly like eagles, run, walk and not grow faint."

"Godspeed," Amytis said. She stood and threw her arms around the old scribe. Nathan started in surprise then closed his eyes to Gobryas's gaping and hugged her back. When they let go of each other, both Amytis and Nathan laughed to see the tears in one another's eyes.

"You see," Nathan said. "The things once predicted have come. And now I foretell new things, announce to you ere they sprout up." He turned and as he walked out the door called, "Sing to Yahweh a new song, his praise from the ends of the earth!'

PART IV

538 B.C.E. —

CHAPTER 87

*S*pring came to Babylon with snow melt from the far northern mountains and a bustling trade in all sorts of goods, heightened with need for Akitu materials. Only a few weeks now until the Babylonian New Year, auspicious and suspenseful and this year permeated by joyful excitement. Despite Nabonidus's efforts, recent traditions had resumed and it was understood that Marduk had taken Cyrus's hand in defeating Nabonidus. Surely, then, King Cyrus himself would appear there on the greatest of the floats, holding Marduk's golden hand before the gods rendered their verdict for the year ahead. But the new king wasn't from Babylonia and hadn't pledged to every detail of the elders' expectations. So suspense was high.

And Cassandane's condition worsened. As the Tigris and Euphrates rivers rose with new life – abundant fish, fowl, and the capacity to irrigate Babylonia's thirsty soil, Cassandane seemed to dry up. She was in constant pain now and not only from the wound, which had grown and festered. Everything hurt now.

"But what can I *do*?!" Cyrus shouted at the doctors one day. "You name the problem but have no answer. Get out!" After that, only the women who tended for Cassandane's comfort were allowed.

Meanwhile, Cyrus included Cambyses in everything, which meant that 'Tossa did, too. Those were the only occasions that Amytis shared with her. And although they were many, they were busy and full of the company of others. When 'Tossa could be free, she was often with her mother. And Amytis was glad of it.

While the nurse changed Sanda's dressings, 'Tossa reported to her mother the strange things that flooded Babylon's markets like the river flooded the city's moats. They argued less now. Cassandane didn't have the energy for it. Together, mother and daughter composed a message for Vishtaspa's family, inviting them back to Pasargad, to rendezvous there when the fruit trees, the rosemary and thyme, indeed the whole green hills were in bloom. They'd return after this upcoming Babylonian festival.

FOR ALL HER stories about life in Babylon and the excitement of preparing for their first akitu, Atossa didn't tell Cassandane how much time she spent with Amytis. 'Tossa could see the grief it caused her mother, and with Cassandane barely able to move for the pain, 'Tossa bit her tongue rather than contribute more to it. But one day, while she sat - 'Tossa, bent over tangled embroidery – with her mother, Cassandane laid a bony hand over her daughter's. Startled, 'Tossa looked up. Cassandane tried to smile. She opened her mouth to speak, but coughed instead, wincing at the pain. 'Tossa leapt up.

"I'll get the nurse!"

But Cassandane held tight. She shook her head, tugged 'Tossa nearer.

'Tossa slipped to the floor and kneeling bent to her mother's mouth.

"What is it?"

"Get –" Cassandane winced again.

"Anything," 'Tossa popped up, then knelt again. "What do you want?"

Her voice barely above a whisper, Cassandane said, "Amytis."

'Tossa rocked back on her heels. She frowned, her young forehead creased with worry.

Cassandane shut her eyes. Her body tensed in a spasm of pain. Her neck tight, she said again, "Get Amytis."

'Tossa leapt up and ran.

CHAPTER 88

*T*he smell was its own wall. Despite the open window, its stench stopped Amytis at the door. It had been weeks since the trial, weeks since Amytis had seen Cassandane. What she saw now bore little resemblance to the proud woman Amytis had met, so easily a queen from Parsa's noblest tribe. This woman was dying.

'Tossa took Amytis's hand and started to lead her to the bed.

But Cassandane shook her head. It was clear to Amytis that the gesture itself pained her. Clear, too, its intent.

Gently, Amytis took her hand from 'Tossa's. "Off now. I'll speak with your mother alone."

'Tossa looked at Cassandane whose expression relaxed, then up at Amytis.

"Go on."

After 'Tossa had left, Cassandane looked away. Amytis crossed what was left of the space between them. Cassandane did not watch her come but stared at heavy beams in the ceiling. Amytis picked up a stool. Carved ivory – Phoenician? – stronger than it looked. She brought it to the side of Cassandane's bed.

"As I think 'Tossa's told you, Babylonia's greatest festival begins in a matter of days."

Cassandane winced.

"She and Cambyses have been a big part of its preparation. Cambyses has even let Gobryas teach him some things. Gobryas," Amytis began to fill the stale air with more news, the good news that Gobryas was easier to be around now, that the youths got along better now... But Cassandane squeezed her eyes shut. And Amytis felt silly for acting as though that was why Cassandane had summoned her. So instead, Amytis laid her hands in her lap, and simply sat.

Her eyes still closed, after a time, Cassandane seemed to relax. Each breath was so shallow it barely raised the linen sheet, woven of the finest lightest thread. A puff of soft spring air shifted the fabric, revealing heavy bandages and a strip of skin, mottled with bruising over a bony rib. Amytis reached out and gently laid the sheet back in place.

"I'm sorry," Cassandane said so quietly that Amytis questioned for a moment hearing anything. Amytis bent forward as a tear slipped from the corner of Cassandane's eye.

Amytis dabbed Cassandane's cheek. "So am I," she said.

"'Tossa..."

"Shall I get her?"

Cassandane shook her head.

Amytis waited. After a long pause, she said, "She's becoming a fine young woman."

Cassandane nearly smiled at this.

"She helps Cambyses still, though he hasn't seemed to need it lately."

Cassandane closed her eyes in a grimace. "'Tossa."

"Yes," Amytis said, and let the silence fall around them again.

A bird trilled from the gardens. Amytis could barely make out the shouts of barge men navigating the river somewhere along the quays below. The clang of a cymbal from the temple complex marked the midday offering to Marduk. Throngs of people busy below with so many tasks, worries, and joys.

Cassandane drew her hand out from under the sheet and let it fall next to the bed. In the hallway outside, someone dropped something, what sounded like a copper pate, clanging as it rocked and spun. Cassandane wriggled her fingers. Amytis took her hand and leaned in.

"Look after her," Cassandane said. "All of them," she wheezed.

Amytis heard herself inhale to protest, prepared to say that Cassandane would be better soon, that Amytis would return to Ecbatana superfluous and distant, that the children would grow in Babylon in Pasargad or wherever Cassandane and Cyrus determined they should be, that everything would be just fine... Those were the things that reflexively flooded her mind, sprang to Amytis's tongue. But she was older now. For good or bad, there was nothing to say. Only "I will."

Cassandane tightened her grip.

"I promise." Amytis swiped her free hand across her eyes, rubbed it dry against the fabric at her thigh and sniffed.

"Cyrus, too," Cassandane said.

"Cyrus, too." Amytis's said, her voice husky with emotion. "My sister's son."

"Thank you," Cassandane released Amytis's hand. Then, "Cyrus," she called.

And Amytis fled to find the king.

CHAPTER 89

*C*assandane died. And as would be told for centuries, all the people of Akkad mourned her death. They laid their heads bare and joined Cyrus for a full week of mourning. Cyrus was inconsolable.

"I promised her," he said. "I promised her Pasargad. Forever."

The period of mourning overlapped with the first three of the twelve days of *Akitu*. Even King Cyrus could not have stopped its inauguration. Not that he had the energy to try, if he wanted to. No, the festival would proceed as custom dictated. And as custom had it – a kindness of tradition – those first three days were sober ones.

So, on the first day of the month of Nisan, just as the sun was beginning to show its light, while the city still wore the somber cloak of grief, the head chef of Marduk's temple rose, took up the wooden key, and went to the temple courtyard. There, he opened the door of Exalted Gate and approached the cistern. Just as had happened every day from the beginning of time, as far as the people gathered were concerned, Marduk's head chef performed the water rites and prepared the precinct. The festival would proceed.

After the priest's customary bathing and prayers to Marduk "who crosses the heavens and heaps up the earth, who measures the waters of the sea and cultivates the fields,... Before the people of Babylon, let there be light!" and to Marduk's wife "whose garment is light... who saves the captives and grasps the hands of the fallen... Grant mercy to the slave who speaks good things of you. In difficulty and trouble, grasp his hand. Grant him life when he is in sickness and pain. Let him walk constantly in happiness and joy," were yet more prayers – sad and penitent.

And as it happened, the last official day of mourning for Cassandane marked a new beginning, the New Year. Marduk's *sheshgallu* kicked off the holiday to come. Because of the timing, on this year especially, it felt to the people as though the Akitu began not three days earlier but indeed on this, the New Year Day. On the fourth day, finally came the singing and dancing, launching the pomp and pageantry for which people had waited all year. On this day, in Marduk's Esagila, they would hear the great creation story.

But Cyrus wasn't present for the performance of recitation. Instead, it was expected that he went to Nabu's temple to take up the scepter of kingship, then on to Borsippa to retrieve the statue of the god from Nabu's home city. That he could spend the night in Borsippa while the rest of Babylon celebrated was a relief. Somehow he had to figure out how to get through the rest. The first next step – return to Babylon with this god, Marduk's son.

CHAPTER 90

*D*ays before, "It isn't without precedent," Amytis had said after they'd reviewed the order of service, the festival's schedule, and its expectations of the king.

They sat in the only room that Cyrus could bear – the throne room, so large and tiled with life-size images of trees that it could have been a suburban palm orchard. Cyrus had asked Amytis to think with him about charging Cambyses with the role of king, having the crown prince perform in the upcoming Akitu. Cassandane had died and there was nothing in the world Cyrus felt he could ever celebrate again.

"Nabonidus and Belshazzar got away with it," Amytis continued, "though with their defeat, you've heard how people judge them now." She ran her hands through her hair – she'd never resumed wearing the gold clips of Babylonian nobility. She sighed. "My son was reluctant to do so. Although he was crown prince at the time and Nebuchadnezzar unwell, it is the king's prerogative. But that's how Igliss got him – framed him with an impossible situation." She inhaled deeply. "Then again, if you – the king – make clear that it's your choice..." Amytis nodded. "That's different."

Cyrus bent forward, his head in his hands.

"What about his fits?" Amytis asked. "Would 'Tossa join him in this, too?" Amytis looked out the window. "I can't imagine how Babylon would respond if..." She didn't need to finish the sentence.

Actually, she *could* imagine. They both could. It would be catastrophic: If in that most public moment – atop the most decorated float carrying the highest of the gods and on the most auspicious of days, Cambyses took Marduk's hand and then fell into one of his uncontrollable fits...

"On the other hand," Amytis said, "I don't know of any other time when the king has conducted this ritual with another person beside him. It's a risk, but –" Amytis laid a hand on Cyrus's shoulder. "Whatever you decide, make it your own."

* * *

As per custom, Cyrus did go again to Nabu's temple. But he didn't go dressed in the manner expected of him. To the surprise of the crowd watching along the roadway, Cyrus appeared not in the regalia of a Babylonian king, but in the court dress of his homeland -- an Elamite king, "King of Anshan," as he persisted in identifying himself. His robe was of a fabric seldom if ever seen in Babylon – cotton – decorated with embroidery and bands of interlaced, geometric patterns. It shimmered with golden bracteates. Along fringes the length of the robe, from shoulder to ankle, ran a single elegant row of rosettes. Those simple flowers like the foods Cyrus would ceremoniously consume demonstrated a more rustic and simple life – the life he'd planned to have with Cassandane, a world away from Babylon.

Striding some lengths behind, Prexaspes smiled to hear the crowd's murmurs. When this was done, he would take Cyrus's Elamite robe to keep safely stored for every such monarchal display to come. The unconventional dress wasn't the only surprise Cyrus had for the crowd. Yes, he walked toward the scepter-house of Nabu as was expected. But he didn't go alone. For this auspicious show of kingship, Cambyses walked beside Cyrus. And when they arrived, Cambyses also went in. He didn't hesitate, and no one stopped him.

When they reappeared, blinking in the bright spring sunshine, Cyrus carried his weapons. It was Cambyses who bore the scepter of the land. The two strode on to Esagil, father and son, to drink in Marduk's grand temple with the high god. For the remainder of the festival, Cambyses would play the role of Babylon's king. And 'Tossa would attend – from a respectable distance.

With that, having turned the king's role in the festival over to Cambyses, Cyrus disappeared into the rooms he had shared with Cassandane. No one was permitted to enter.

CHAPTER 91

Cambyses got through the grand parade without a seizure. Without her. 'Tossa didn't have a chance even to talk to him until the spectacle was done. Eager to hear all about it, 'Toss caught her brother at the door to his quarters. She watched Cambyses approach, walking with a confidence that 'Tossa had never seen before. He would have walked right past her and Aspacanah, too, if 'Tossa hadn't stepped in the way. She grabbed his sleeve.

"How did it feel?" she asked. She'd seen it all – but from the side. That was different. "In your arm... the one that held Marduk's hand...?"

Cambyses snatched his sleeve free. "I've been told I should rest," he said, his tone scolding. "Though I feel full of energy." His eyes did burn with a peculiar heat. "It's a lot to bear, such proximity to the god." He adjusted the diadem along his brow. "You wouldn't know."

'Tossa stepped back. She clenched her teeth and her hands into fists.

"Come on," Aspacanah said. "It's right that your brother should rest."

'Tossa glared at Cambyses but let Aspacanah lead her aside so that Cambyses could pass. She watched her brother dismiss his attendants and step into his room. Alone. Guards pushed the wooden doors shut behind him.

'Tossa stared at the doors through slitted eyes. "I've been nothing next to him all my life." She pursed her lips as if to spit. "Eldest son, crown prince. I'm nothing more than his shadow. That's how everybody sees me, if at all."

"Not everybody," Aspacanah said quietly.

But 'Tossa wasn't listening. Her eyes grew wide and glazed, her feet rooted in place.

Aspacanah looked hard at her stony face. "It's happening, isn't it?" he said.

But 'Tossa was too far gone in the prescient trance.

One eye on her, Aspacanah called, "Guards, open up."

But the door guards had taken their orders from the crown prince. A thirteen-year-old courtier from Persia was not going to convince them otherwise.

"Now!" Aspacanah said.

But the men crossed their arms in front of their chests and frowned at him.

Aspacanah sputtered. What to do? No one was supposed to know Cambyses's weakness. 'Tossa had made that clear. She protected that secret like no one else even could. Aspacanah took 'Tossa's arm and shook it gently.

"Tossa, Tossa," he said, while straining to hear what might be happening inside Cambyses' quarters.

But the doors were thick, and the prince's rooms went back and back.

"You have to let us in," Aspacanah said. "The princess must see her brother."

But the guards simply stepped closer together in front of the door.

Aspacanah huffed.

Beside him, 'Tossa shook her head, recovered. "Serves him right," she said to Aspacanah. "I'm leaving. Leave me alone."

To his astonishment, Aspacanah watched her walk away. One last glance at the guards, and Aspacanah dashed away, too.

* * *

AMYTIS FOLLOWED the boy back to Cambyses's rooms. As they hurried along, Amytis noted how Aspacanah had grown. Despite his mother's fair complexion, and gentle demeanor, the boy looked more and more like his father, muscular and athletic.

To her knock and call, a faint voice responded. "Let them in."

Finally, the guards opened the doors.

Cambyses was in the second room, slumped across the remnants of chair. One of its arms lay in splinters on the floor. Blood dripped from where his crown had driven through the skin dripped over one eye. The prince groaned, twisted in the broken furniture.

Then, Amytis saw it - where a lamp had fallen, spilling its oil across the wool rug, fire. Flames licked the air as if tasting a feast to come.

"Your robe!" Amytis said as she rushed toward the prince.

Aspacanah yanked his robe from his shoulders and threw it over the fire. While Amytis ran toward the prince, Aspacanah stamped the fire out.

"Help me get him up," Amytis said.

Aspacanah draped one of Cambyses's arms over his shoulders.

"Careful," Amytis said as Aspacanah slowly stood, his arm around the prince's waist.

Cambyses's face was pale, sweat dripped from the hair that hung as limp as his head and mingled with the blood.

Amytis looked around the room. A table upended, another lamp – this one blessedly unlit – lay broken on the floor, a spray of blood across the stones, another rug stained with the rhyton of wine that Cambyses had ordered. "Take him in there," she said, gesturing to the bedroom abutting an inner courtyard. She tipped the table back up and began gathering the pieces of broken lamp.

Aspacanah walked awkwardly with his load. At the bed, he leaned Cambyses over and eased the prince onto the rich sheets. Cambyses groaned.

"Ma'am," Aspacanah called.

Amytis rushed in.

Cambyses opened his eyes, groaned, and shut his eyes again. His hands gathered the sheet into fists that he lifted and brought down hard. "Get 'Tossa," he said through clenched teeth.

* * *

ASPACANAH FOUND 'TOSSA in the gardens. She sat huddled under her favorite shrub, knees pulled up, arms hugging them tight. Her eyes were red and swollen with crying. Aspacanah sat on the bench nearby.

As far as Aspacanah knew, this was the first of Cambyses's episodes that she'd not helped with – alerting the adults, preparing the space to protect her brother until it was over and Cambyses came to again.

"He's okay now," Aspacanah said. "And he wants to see you."

"I'm not here," 'Tossa said, her voice muffled against her knees.

"He feels really bad."

"I said it serves him right."

"I think he feels bad about ignoring you."

'Tossa hugged her knees in her tighter. "What business is it of yours? Just go away."

Aspacanah inhaled sharply, exhaled again.

"Why are you still here? I said, Go!"

CHAPTER 92

"**W**here have you been?!" Prexaspes grabbed his son's shoulder and spun him around.

Aspacanah had left 'Tossa in the gardens, left only when he was certain that she really would go to Cambyses, that the prince would apologize to her, and things would find a new normal.

"I've been looking everywhere for you!" Prexaspes shouted.

"That's a first," Aspacanah muttered. He turned again to go.

Prexaspes seized his arm. Aspacanah started in surprise, though why he should be...

"Don't speak to me like that."

"What?" Aspacanah straightened under his father's grip. "Do you wish to speak to me?"

Prexaspes dropped the boy's arm as if it were suddenly poison.

"Don't answer that," Aspacanah said bitterly. "I already know."

Prexaspes cuffed him across the mouth.

Aspacanah slowly put a finger to his lip and drew it away. He studied it, blood on the tip. "Talk, then," he said, his voice level though his eyes were fierce.

They stood a moment like that – Prexaspes taken aback by Aspacanah's equanimity.

Then Prexaspes shrugged. "Cambyses had another fit."

Aspacanah didn't say, anything, merely ran a hand across his mouth.

"We're going to Pasargad, accompanying the king. We leave tomorrow."

Aspacanah glanced back at the palace.

"She's not coming."

"What? Who?" Aspacanah flushed.

"The girl."

"What girl?"

"You know exactly what girl. I see the way you look at her, as if she is light itself. Listen to me now. Atossa is not for you."

For a moment, father and son stood, fixed in a shared gaze.

For a moment, Aspacanah considered saying: Not for me, like Cyrus is not for you? For a moment, Prexaspes wondered if he would.

Instead, Aspacanah said, "Who said anything about it?"

"Don't argue with me." Prexaspes snapped. "No one has said anything. And I hope to the gods that I'm the only one who's noticed, but I doubt it."

"But why not?" Aspacanah asked, his tone now almost pleading. "Why couldn't 'Tossa have me? You're the king's oldest friend, and I am his cup-bearer… You could -"

Prexaspes grasped Aspacanah roughly by the arm, suddenly noticing that he no longer had the sinewy limbs of a little boy. What he grasped was strong and hard. "I can do nothing of the sort. That girl is princess of an empire whose boundaries increase by the year. We may be friends of the king's – thank the gods for that. But that's where it ends. Besides, Cambyses needs his sister. You know that. For the welfare of this empire, 'Tossa must remain at her brother's side, and she cannot do that if she's with you. So stop it right now. Your feelings are no more than a silly crush." He looked with disgust at Aspacanah's stricken face. "Cheer up. No king wants a dour-faced cupbearer."

Aspacanah glared at this father.

"And sometime, I'll find you a wife."

"I don't want a wife."

"You will."

CHAPTER 93

'Tossa was there beside Cambyses, she and Bardiya each holding the hand of their little sister, when Cyrus's small band left Babylon. Once – only once – Amytis had asked Cyrus if he wouldn't like to take the younger children, Bardiya and Irtashduna, with him to Pasargad. The look he gave her was uncomprehending, as if he had forgotten that he had children at all.

So, it was agreed that Cambyses would continue to function as the king's proxy, with 'Tossa beside him until Cyrus returned. Amytis would be available for counsel and guidance. Gobryas had proved to be a valuable administrator, and Otanes would stay, too. Zarin loved Babylon as did Phaideme, of course. Because of her, Otanes asked to stay, and Cyrus didn't say no.

They traveled lightly. The heaviest burden, for Cyrus at least, was the long box containing Cassandane's remains. Painted with the signature deep colors and geometric patterns of Pasargad, it would ride on a padded cart pulled by a pair of white horses from their own stock. Hundreds of times a day since Cassandane had died, Cyrus's red eyes had wandered east and stayed there unfocused until someone or something wrenched his attention back to Babylon.

When at last the caravan pulled out, only Aspacanah looked back. He had hardly spoken with 'Tossa since the incident with Cambyses and his father's reprimand. Prexaspes was right; 'Tossa was too good for him. Soon they'd be far too many miles apart, something to get used to. So, in the days before they left, Aspacanah had watched 'Tossa go to the places they frequented, but he hadn't followed. And when at dinner she spoke to him, in the quiet manner she used by way of apology, Aspacanah found reasons in his cup-bearing responsibilities to duck away.

Now, astride the horse that would take him away from Babylon and from her, Aspacanah turned back in the saddle. He couldn't take his eyes off the king's daughter, at almost thirteen already as tall as Cambyses. 'Tossa stood with her shoulders back – defiance, he recognized; he knew her so well – a hold on pride when confronted by hurt. Aspacanah's eyes smarted. 'Tossa didn't raise her hand or call out. She just stood with the others and watched him ride away. He wouldn't be there when she doubled over in private later. And he wouldn't be there when she gathered herself together again to attend to Cambyses or stride down to the quay, to reattempt the lyre playing that her instructors patiently demonstrated or to seek out the smith workers just to be near horses.

He would be gone, and he had no idea for how long. When 'Tossa said something to Cambyses, Aspacanah finally turned forward – facing, like his father, Cyrus, and the others in their band, toward Pasargad.

CHAPTER 94

*I*n honor of her pledge to Cassandane, Amytis would stay in Babylon long enough to ensure that the children were fine. It wouldn't be long. Cambyses, no child anymore at all, was an eager proxy regent. 'Tossa was as busy as he. The little ones couldn't have had more devoted nurses and were themselves – on balance – cheerful and willing. Indeed, it seemed that when Cyrus left so too did the troubled atmosphere, a chronic tension that Amytis hadn't noticed until it was gone. Unless some crisis arose – and she couldn't imagine what it would be – Amytis had only a few more things to do before she could leave – sensitive cases to adjudicate, ironically with the same judge Nadinu who had ruled in her case only a few weeks before.

This time, Amytis was the king's own representative. A capable scribe had briefed her. The trial, he'd explained, was against a wetnurse accused of starving her charge by secretly taking on another infant whom she suckled for double the pay. It was not unprecedented that such should happen, but Amytis was surprised when Qudashu entered the room.

Amytis caught her breath and straightened her back. She

tucked a stray strand of hair back into place and laid her hands carefully across the chair's wooden armrests. Qudashu was as stately now, perhaps more, Amytis thought, as when Amytis had met her so many years ago. Amytis knew that Iddina had been running the corporation for several years now. She had heard that each son received a portion of the estate; but Khai left the plum of the Egibi holdings to his wife Qudashu, who retained independent ownership of a field along New Canal. It had been his first really large purchase, so big that he had had to buy it in partnership with another businessman, going in on it fifty-fifty. Its value had increased over the years as the orchards matured and the grain crops planted around the trees yielded well. The small portion extending along the south bank of the canal contained 500 date palms alone.

Her sons would surely look after her. But also Qudashu's income, measured in dates, from the rental of that land, was substantial; and its location along the canal – a ready source of water and means for transport – would not depreciate. But that wasn't the cause of a twinge of jealousy... No, that was seeing again the dignified wife of the only man Amytis had ever truly loved.

CHAPTER 95

$\mathcal{I}$t was not until Cyrus wandered through the gardens and sat on the open dais of the half-finished palace, Cassandane's box laid out beside him, that he wept. During their whole long journey from Babylon to Pasargad, he had barely said a word, barely showed he was alive at all. Now, finally in Pasargad again, he wept. Prexaspes came to him, and gentle Aspacanah too, Nahhunte, Pharnaspes Cassandane's father. None could comfort him. The day passed into night. He dismissed them all. But the next day, at first light, he had wrung himself clean.

Cyrus stood then and with great ceremony carried the first of the bricks that would be a tower for his love, his queen. Its sides would be solid. No one, no thing would be able ever to desecrate Cassandane's remains. But for her, who he remembered looking far out into the hills of Pasargad that first evening they'd shared, she with a love for that place that he'd hoped she would one day see for him, he would fashion the shape of windows. Mid-way up the tower, he would set squares through which only the dead could see, that Cassandane might still and forever look out in all directions across the plain. And Cyrus, from nearly anywhere in Pasargad, could see where his wife lay.

Cyrus's own tomb was already under construction nearby that when he died they might forever be close. Forever in Pasargad.

CHAPTER 96

One day, a group of visitors arrived from the north - Vishtaspa and his family. They came as per the invitation Cassandane with 'Tossa had sent. They came though they knew that neither mother nor daughter would greet them there. They knew the magnitude of Cyrus's grief.

It was Aspacanah, who rode with his father Prexaspes to greet them. When they had arrived at the palace grounds and dismounted, Aspacanah noticed that the dark-haired Darius had grown, but Aspacanah was happy to find that he was still the taller. And where Darius was smooth in athletic limbs, Aspacanah was muscled and broader.

Nahhunte, seeing the boys together, smiled. Aspacanah had been so sullen and forlorn. "Why don't you show Darius their rooms?" the steward said to Aspacanah.

Aspacanah nodded but gritted his teeth. They'd never be friends.

"You can carry this," Darius said, extending the heavy satchel of his personal things.

Aspacanah frowned but took the bag. "It's this way."

Darius looked around as they walked.

"So, the others aren't here? Cyrus's children?"

"No."

"No, they're not here?"

"That's right. They're not here."

"Oh." Darius resumed appraising the details of the palace. "Nice what he's doing here, Cyrus, the king."

"Sure."

"So how is the girl? – Atossa, named after my mother, as I recall."

"Fine."

"Must have been something, the New Year festival and all for her." Darius looked at Aspacanah, trudging along, and snorted, laughing a little.

"I suppose."

"I mean, lying in the temple tower all night like that."

Aspacanah stopped. "What are *you* talking about?"

"When the daughter of the king has to lie on a bed at the top of the temple. They say that the god comes and ravishes her, though I've always suspected it's some priest dressed up as Marduk and more than happy to oblige."

Aspacanah gaped at Darius.

"Well, she is a virgin, isn't she?"

Aspacanah's face flushed. He dropped Darius's bag, and before Darius could speak again, Aspacanah punched him in the stomach.

Darius bent over, gasping. When he recovered, he stood. He looked at Aspacanah with a steady gaze. "So it's true?"

Aspacanah drew back again, but seeing how much his anger pleased Darius, Aspacanah lowed his hand again and simply said, "That's a stupid story. She was with me the whole time."

Darius turned the corners of his mouth down and nodded slowly. He reached for his bag. But Aspacanah snatched it up, his eyes angry slits, and walked on.

* * *

AMYTIS, now home in the shadow of Mount Alvand again, among the wild things of her native mountains and woodlands, Amytis hoped that Cyrus had found some peace. There'd been trouble to the east, in the far high plains – Scythians, she'd heard. No great surprise – they were a fierce people, resistant to anything that smacked of rule. Still, Amytis told Cyrus of it. And with her message, added the solace of wild places, and good wishes that he'd found in Pasargad some of the same.

* * *

CYRUS DID INDEED FIND some comfort in the presence of these dear friends. He asked them about the traders, the people from the steppes –these Scythians. Yes, they were still a fierce people, resistant to anything that smacked of rule, but with the Parthians got along well enough. Still, rumor had it that their warring had cost them nearly all the men. But their women were no less fierce, and formidable warriors themselves. Cyrus asked Vishtaspa about the sage they had talked about before – Zarathustra. Yes, the man remained with them in Parthia, still pondering deep mysteries and contemplating the universe, seen and unseen.

Cyrus found some comfort in his friends' visit. But as he'd reported to Amytis, having finished the tower, laid Cassandane's remains within, and sealed it tight, he'd only grown more restless, more dis-eased with a kind of desperation that made him want to climb out of his skin itself. Even with his friends nearby, serenity had evaporated from Pasargad.

"I can't shake it, Vishtaspa," Cyrus said to his friend one day, when Vishtaspa found Cyrus sitting overlooking the plain from a garden pavilion.

"I feel both exhausted and on fire all the time. I can't stop thinking about Cassandane, millions of tiny details and hundreds of regrets. At the same time, and almost worse, I'm beginning to forget exactly what she looked like. I feel guilty about that and other things, too. I don't know how I can get to another day. I want her beside me. I want her to see this place, how it's come along. All those things we planted, the vision... I want to ask her what she thinks of the guardian at the gate – its wings, the crown. I want her to tell Cook how to make the tea she brought the day I asked her father to marry her. I want her. I want to stop missing her."

Vishtaspa was silent – breathed in, breathed out.

"I don't know what to do," Cyrus said.

After a moment, Vishtaspa said, "I hear there's a sage... a magi of sorts, but different too, far to the east."

"What of him?"

Vishtaspa looked into the haunted eyes of his friend and king. "Born of great wealth and privilege," Vishtaspa said, "he renounced everything for a quest." Vishtaspa smiled gently. "They say that he's found a cure for suffering."

CHAPTER 97

"*W*hy do you keep ignoring me?" 'Tossa asked Amytis.

Amytis put her arm around 'Tossa. "I don't mean to. I am distracted, maybe sad."

"Why?"

Amytis measured the girl in front of her. 'Tossa, as lean as her mother and on track to be equally tall, was nevertheless filling out in the hips. Often, Amytis had caught Aspacanah darting his eyes away from 'Tossa's chest, flushing as he looked instead at the girl's mouth and eyes. She sighed. It was probably just as well he'd left with Cyrus.

"A woman came today," Amytis said, "that I knew a long time ago. Qudashu, the widow of Khai Egibi, the man Gobryas used to work for. I hadn't seen her for a very long time." Amytis gathered 'Tossa to her. "Her daughter-in-law had a baby, Qudashu's grandson. The baby died because the nurse they had hired was dishonest."

"And the baby died?" 'Tossa pulled back in surprise.

"Yes, the nurse was also taking money from another family to nurse a different baby. Qudashu's grandson died because he didn't get enough milk."

"What did they do?"

Amytis pursed her lips.

"The judge sentenced the nurse."

'Tossa's eyes were wide. "What was her punishment?"

"They amputated one of her breasts."

'Tossa's arms flew to her tiny chest. She lowered them slowly. "Will she live?"

"I don't know."

* * *

WHEN THE MESSAGE ARRIVED, that Cyrus was going to go, to "go east," he'd said, Amytis wasn't sure which it was that drove him. Of the Scythians, Cyrus said Vishtaspa had confirmed the same. It was welcome news – "formidable warriors," refusing rule. Cyrus wanted to move, to fight, and to move again. He would expand Persia, bring the Scythians to heel. And, in his message he asked – did she know of their chief, a woman Tomyris? Amytis could almost hear the hunger, his fierce desire to meet such a warrior, to be such a warrior... Tomyris of the Massagetae. Had she heard, he asked, so determined were they to draw the bow in a clean close line that the Greeks called these Scythians *a-mazos*, "without breast." They had shorn them clear away.

Amytis lowered the message, lifted her eyes to the north, eager to return to the snowy peaks of Mount Alvand and home. She knew that Cyrus would fight his way to the east. But she hoped, too, that Cyrus would find that man Vishtaspa told him about. ... And tell her what he learns. After all, she thought, who among us doesn't need a cure for suffering?

THE END

CAST OF CHARACTERS

A few things to note: Even for historical characters, there may be some question or disagreement regarding specific details – see "Author's Note." I do not provide here dates of death or other details that don't transpire during the course of this particular narrative. With the exception of Iddina, nicknames are my own. An asterisk (*) denotes non-historical characters, i.e. people that I've totally made up.

Adad-guppi: Aramean (from the defeated Harran); attendant in the Babylonian courts of Nebuchadnezzar and Amel-Marduk; mother of Nabonidus, grandmother of Belshazzar.

Amel-Marduk (Bushu), born Nabu-shuma-ukin: son of Amytis and Nebuchadnezzar II; succeedes Nebuchadnezzar as king of Babylon 562 B.C.E. until his assassination in 560 B.C.E. In the Bible, his name appears as Evil-Merodach.

Amytis: daughter of Astyages, king of Media; twin sister of Mandane; wife of Nebuchadnezzar, king of Babylon; mother of Amel-Marduk; aunt of Cyrus II.

Aspacanah: son of Prexaspes.

Astyages: son of Cyaxares; king of Media; father of Amytis and Mandane; grandfather of Cyrus II.

Atossa (named for Hutaosa): daughter of Cyrus and Cassandane; sister of Cambyses II.

Bagapates: eunuch in Cyrus's household.

Bardiya: son of Cyrus and Cassandane; younger brother of Cambyses and Atossa; older brother of Irtashduna.

Belshazzar: son of Nabonidus and Nitocris and so the (illegitimate, I imagine) grandson of Nebuchadnezzar.

Cambyses I (King Cam): King of Anshan (Parsa); husband of Mandane; father of Cyrus II.

Cassandane (Sanda): of the Pasargadae, Achaemenid clan; daughter of Pharnaspes; sister of Otanes; wife of Cyrus II, mother of Cambyses (II), Atossa, Bardiya, and Irtashduna.

Cassiya/Kassiya: daughter of Nebuchadnezzar; wife of Neriglissar; mother of Labashi-Marduk; (half-, I imagine) sister of Nitocris and Eanna-sharra-utsur (sharing the father Nebuchadnezzar).

Croesus: king of Lydia from 585–547/546 B.C.E.

Cyrus II: son of Cambyses I and Mandane; niece of Amytis; grandson of Astyages; raised by Median slaves Spaco and *Mit(hradates) who called him Bartatua until he was ten years old, then returned to Parsa; husband of Cassandane; father of Cambyses (II), Atossa, Bardiya, and Irtashduna; succeeds his father Cambyses (I) as king of Anshan (Parsa); becomes king also of the former Median empire, Lydia, and the Babylonian empire.

***Davcina**: Babylonian daughter of Qudashu and Khai; sister of Iddina; wife of Gobryas; mother of a daughter (with Gobryas).

Eanna-šarra-utsur (Ean): son (I imagine eldest) of Nebuchadnezzar with his first wife (unnamed); in 587 B.C.E. receives rations in a sick-house in Uruk (historical). I imagine he suffers schizophrenia and kills himself.

Egibi: family name of Babylonian entrepreneurial family that becomes a powerful corporation beginning with **Nabu-ahhe-iddin (Khai)** and endures for several generations.

Gobryas: from Susa; club-footed son of Mardonius; as a boy, becomes Cyrus's and Cassandane's ward after Mardonius is killed.

Harpagus: palace steward to King Astyages.

Hutaosa: from Susa; wife of Vishtaspa/Hystaspes; mother of Darius (I).

Irtashduna/Artystone: daughter of Cyrus and Cassandane; sister of Cambyses (II), Atossa, and Bardiya.

Itti-Marduk-balatu (Iddina -- this nickname is historical): eldest son of Nabu-ahhe-iddin (Khai) and Qudashu; heir to the Egibi estate.

Labashi-Marduk: son of Cassiya and Neriglissar; becomes king of Babylonia after Neriglissar; assassinated within months of taking the throne (556 B.C.E.).

*Mithradates (Mit): Shepherd slave to Astyages's palace who with his wife Spaco raised Cyrus II (whom they called Bartatua) from infancy until Cyrus was ten years old.

Mandane: (legitimate) daughter of Astyages, hence princess of Media; half-sister of Amytis; wife of Cambyses I; mother of Cyrus II; I imagine that she commits suicide upon being told of her newborn's (Cyrus's) death.

Mardonius: army veteran who served in the Elamite palace in Susa; father of club-footed Gobryas.

Nabonidus: Aramean from defeated Harran; son of Adad-guppi; courtier in the Babylonian court; husband of Nitocris; father of Belshazzar; becomes king of Babylonia after Labashi-Marduk is assassinated.

Nabu-ahhe-iddin (Khai): son of Babylonian farmer Shula Egibi; scribe, entrepreneur; husband of Qudashu; father of Itti-Marduk-balatu (Iddina); founder of the Egibi family corporation.

*Nahhunte: head of the palace in Anshan.

*Nathan: from Nippur, Jewish scribe for Nebuchadnezzar; son of *Rabbi Yakov ben-Isaiah and *Michal; moves with Amytis to Media.

Nebuchadnezzar II: son of Nabopolassar; king of Babylon/Babylonia from 605 B.C.E. until his death in 5462 B.C.E.; father of Nitocris (illegit, I imagine), Eanna-sharra-utsur (Ean), and Cassiya by an Ishtar temple slave from Uruk (I made up this unnamed earlier woman/wife); husband of Amytis; father of Amel-Marduk by Amytis.

Neriglissar (Igliss): probably served with Nebuchadnezzar on campaign against Jerusalem in 587 B.C.; husband of Cassiya (so, Nebuchadnezzar's son-in-law); father of Labashi-Marduk; king of Babylonia after Amel-Marduk; reigned from 560 B.C.E. until his death in 556 B.C.E.

Nitocris: daughter of Nebuchadnezzar; wife of Nabonidus; mother of Belshazzar; high priestess of the goddess Ishtar at the Eanna temple in Uruk.

Nupta: of the Babylonian Nur-Sin family; wife of Iddina.

Otanes: Achaemenid; son of Pharnaspes; younger brother of Cassandane; brother-in-law of Cyrus; husband of Zarin; father of Phaideme.

Phaideme: daughter of Otanes and Zarin.

Pharnaspes: Achaemenid; father of Otanes and Cassandane; father-in-law of Cyrus

Prexaspes: son of the chief (zapanitu) of the Pasargadae; father of Aspacanah

Spaco (probably itself a nickname; means simply "Dog"): Shepherd slave to Astyages's palace who with her husband *Mit(hradates) raised Cyrus II (whom they called Bartatua) from infancy until Cyrus was ten years old.

Ennigaldi-Nanna (born *Susanni): daughter of Nabonidus and Nitocris; becomes high priestess of the Babylonian god Nann-Suen's temple in Ur.

Thaer: son of the Gutian chief, Ugbaru.

Tigran: chief of the Urartians.

Ugbaru: chief of the Gutians; father of Thaer; general of the Persian army that took Babylon.

Vishtaspa/Hystaspes: from Susa; joins Cyrus's army; husband of Hutaosa; father of Darius (I).

Zarin: of the Pasargadae; wife of Otanes; mother of Phaideme.

SOURCES FOR QUOTES

(see also the list "Some of my sources for information")

p. 2 "'Amputation,' the judge said..." Affluent families hired women to nurse and/or look after their children. They could be paid quite well, but the stakes were high. One inscrip tells that the consequence should a baby die under the care of a wet nurse found guilty of taking on another baby(s) without the primary parents' consent is that her breast be cut off. (*Diagnoses in Assyrian and Babylonian Medicine* Translated with commentary by Joann Scurlock and Burton R. Andersen 2005, Illinois, 409).

p. 14 "He'd already been rewriting – merely editing, really – the inscriptions..." From Paul-Alain Beaulieu, *Legal and Administrative Texts from the Reign of Nabonidus*, 2000, Yale, 240-241: "A newly discovered fragment (3) concerning rebuilding the Elhulhul in Harran elevates Marduk in a way consistent with inscriptions from the time of Belshazzar's regency. ("Among the monumental inscriptions of Nabonidus, only those written during Belshazzar's regency fully acknowledge Marduk as supreme god with a befitting array of titles and epithets, while relegating Sin to a subordinate position" p. 240). "The position of

Marduk in fragment 3 is compatible only with the 'orthodox inscriptions' written under Belshazzar's auspices during his father's stay in Teima." It's possible either that "rebuilding the temple was entirely Belshazzar's responsibility and was completed while the king was still in Teima, or it was initiated by Belshazzar but completed by Nabonidus after his return to Babylon. The second alternative has the advantage of harmonizing the contradictory data of the Elhulhul inscriptions in that it explains how Nabonidus could claim in inscription 13 to have restored Elhulhul after he left Teima, while at the same time the funerary stela of Ada-guppi could insist that she witnessed the rebuilding before her death in the middle of Belshazzar's regency."

p. 18 "The timber is unparalleled. Like us they breed excellent horses..." This description is informed by Seton Lloyd, *Ancient Turkey: A Traveller's History* 25th ed., 2013, California.

p. 20 "With the reverence which Nanna-Suen has placed... long life." Based on the stele of Adad-guppi from Harran. See Amélie Kuhrt, *The Ancient Near East, c. 3000-330 BC*, 2 vols., 1997, Routledge, 608; James B. Pritchard, ed. *Ancient Near Eastern Texts Relating to the Old Testament*, 561-562; see also Frauke Weiershäuser and Jamie Novotny, *The Royal Inscriptions of Amēl-Marduk (561–560 BC), Neriglissar (559–556 BC), and Nabonidus (555–539 BC), Kings of Babylon*, 2020, Eisenbrauns.

p. 65 " Nanna-Suen, god of the gods who dwell in the highest heaven... firm forever." Based on a prayer of Nabonidus's quoted by Ronald H. Sack, *Images of Nebuchadnezzar: The Emergence of a Legend*, 2004, Susquehanna, 91.

p. 68 " I branded my two little boys... may eat." From a historical document (*YOS* VI: 154) cited in Paul-Alain Beaulieu, *The Reign of Nabonidus, King of Babylon, 556-539 BC*, 1989, Yale, 202.

p. 90 " The gods dip and bow, sway and rock... rescue you." The passage in the Bible, Isaiah chapter 46 is likely a reaction of Jews to witnessing the Akitu in Babylon.

p. 90 "May Nabu and Marduk bless my brothers! ... on the Euphrates." This is a real letter. See *YOS* III: 145, cited by Paul-Alain Beaulieu, *The Reign of Nabonidus, King of Babylon, 556-539 BC*, 1989, Yale, 220-221.

p. 98 "Clothed in splendor,... brilliantly." J. Bidmead, *The Akitu Festival: Religious Continuity and Royal Legitimation in Mesopotamia*, 2004, Gorgias, 98; quoting M. B. Dick, *Born in Heaven, Made on Earth: The Making of the Cult Image in the Ancient Near East*, 1999, Eisenbrauns, 98.

p. 117 "That I be allowed to kill Belshazzar..." This is my extrapolation on Xenophon's *Cyropaedia* IV, vi. 1-10. It is further informed by the murderous anger of Artaxerxes after Megabyzus killed a lion that had attacked the king. According to Ctesias (parag. 40), Artaxerxes had Megabyzus decapitated. As Briant explains, "Megabyzus had not just violated the rules of protocol... Megabyzus had cast doubt on Artaxerxes' abilities as a hunter and thus also his qualification to be king" (Pierre Briant, *From Cyrus to Alexander: A History of the Persian Empire*, translated by Peter T. Daniels; 2002, Eisenbrauns, 231).

p. 119 "When it was time, Cyrus himself carried..." The geography of the feast, its purpose and participants divine and human are informed by Wouter Henkelmann's "Parnakka's Feast: Sip in Parsa and Elam," in *Elam and Persia*, 2011, Eisenbrauns, 89-166.

p. 130 "Still, some of the gods,... did not come to Babylon." From Nabonidus's chronicle for year 17, lines 11-12 (cited by Paul-Alain Beaulieu, *The Reign of Nabonidus, King of Babylon, 556-539 BC*, 1989, Yale, 220). It does not specify why these gods didn't come.

p. 130 "The Telmun dates... not available here." This is based on lines 17-23 of a tablet presently in the collection of the Oriental Institute (Univ. Chicago), nos. A 5345 + A 536, and cited by Beaulieu, "An Episode in the Fall of Babylon to the Persians," *Journal of Near Eastern* Studies, 1993: 52: 241-261.

p. 142 "From the east, our God has summoned..." See the Bible, Isaiah 46:11-13.

p. 147 "**Fetch that scholar, dan-El**" See the Bible, Daniel 5:10-12.

p. 147 "**Your kingdom is divided,... Persians.**" See the Bible, Daniel 5:1-30.

p. 151 "They're saying 'Yahweh loves Cyrus... prosper in his way." See the Bible, Isaiah 48:14-15.

p. 157 "**Mighty One, Mighty One, who renders our judgment...her own self.**" The text is from the *maqlû* ritual, cited and explained in Daniel Schwemer, "Empowering the Patient," *Pax Hethitica*, 2010, 311-312.

p. 160 "**The god Ishum called it 'a gemstone seal on the neck of the sky.'**" From the Erra-epic See Benjamin R. Foster, *Before the Muses: An Anthology of Akkadian Literature*, 3rd ed. 2005, CDL.

p. 166 "Cyrus scanned the crowd... head boatmen." These details come from a list of Nebuchadnezzar's court officials. I also consulted info from Neo-Bab Sippar temple texts (A. Bongenaar, *The Neo-Babylonian Ebabbar Temple at Sippar: Its administration and Its* Prosopography, 1997 Peeters.)

p. 166 "**Eunuchs next to them held the officials' assigned staffs...**" Details of the coronation ceremony (except list of attendees) are based in part on a fragmentary epic poem concerning Nabopolassar. See Amélie Kuhrt, *The Ancient Near East, c. 3000-330 BC*, 2 vols., 1997, Routledge, 604, following A. K. Grayson, *Babylonian Historical-Literary Texts*, 1975, Toronto, 84-5.

p. 167 "**I present to you the King of the universe, mighty king, king of Babylon.**" From the Cyrus Cylinder 1. 20.

p. 169 "**What he called 'beer of the mountains.'**" W. Röllig, "Erwägungen zu neuen Stelen König Nabonids" in *Zeitschrift für Assyriologie und Vorderasiatische Archäologie* 1964, Walter de Gruyter, 258; cited by Powell, "Wine and the Vine in Ancient Mesopotamia," in *The Origins and Ancient History of Wine*, 1995, Routledge, 102.

p. 178 "**Already one of my colleagues is saying... not grow faint.**" See the Bible, Isaiah chapter 40.

p. 179 "**The things once predicted have come... ends of the earth.**" See the Bible, Isaiah 41: 6-10.

p. 185 "**who crosses the heavens and heaps up the earth... in happiness and joy.**" Tablets in the Daily Telegraph Collection of the British Museum 15 (lines 240-241, 249, 254, 261, 268-271) quoted in J. Bidmead, *The Akitu Festival: Religious Continuity and Royal Legitimation in Mesopotamia*, 2004, Gorgias, 60-62.

p. 186 "**Cyrus appeared not in the regalia...**" See Javier Álvarez-Món, "Notes on the 'Elamite' Garment of Cyrus the Great," in *Antiquaries* 2009, 89:24.

p. 193 "**She had heard that each son... 500 date palms alone.**" These details are historical. See C. Wunsch, "The Egibi Family's real estate in Babylon (6th Century BC)," in *Urbanization and Land Ownership in the Ancient Near East*, 1999, 391–419.

The information about a class of citizenry meeting with the conquering king and establishing terms is thanks to Amélie Kuhrt's presentation at Freer and Sackler Gallery in DC, April 27 2013.

A few of the resources I leaned on for details about the looks and layout of ancient Babylon include Andrew R. George, "A Tour of Nebuchadnezzar's Babylon," in *Babylon: Myth and Reality*, 2008, British Museum, 54-59; Joachim Marzhan, "Koldeway's Babylon," in *Babylon*, 2009, Oxford, 46-53; and Marc Mierhoop, "Reading Babylon," in *The American Journal of Archaeology*, 2003, 107:257-275. The following description of the Akitu festival is heavily dependent on J. Bidmead, *The Akitu Festival: Religious Continuity and Royal Legitimation in Mesopotamia*, 2004, Gorgias.

SOME OF MY SOURCES FOR INFORMATION

I am tremendously grateful to those scholars of ancient Near Eastern history and literature who have made troves of information available and keep adding to what we know and how we think about the people, the places, and times that these narratives so lightly brush. I'm deeply sorry not to provide exhaustive documentation for all the research that informs these books. In lieu of even a bibliography, here is a list (itself incomplete) of some of the hundreds of scholars, past and present, whose work informed the story I tell.

Abraham, Kathleen
   Abusch, Tzvi
   Ackerman, Susan
   Ackroyd, Peter
   Adams, Robert McCormick
   Ahn, J. J.
   Aiken Littauer, M.
   Albenda, Pauline
   Albertz, Rainer
   Albright, William F.

Alexander, Robert L.
Algaze, Guillermo
Allen, Lindsay
Al-Rawi, F. N. H.
Álvarez-Mon, Javier
Amiet, P.
Aminzadeh, B.
Anthony, David W.
Ataç, M. A.
Austin, M. M.
Avigad, N.
Axworthy, Michael
Bahrami, B.
Bahrani, Zainab
Baker, H. D.
Balcer, Jack Martin
Bandstra, Andrew J.
Barkworth, P. R.
Barnett, R. D.
Barr, James
Basham, A. L.
Basirov, Oric
Beach, Eleanor F.
Beaulieu, Paul-Alain
Beckwith, Christopher I.
Bedford, Peter Ross
Berman, Joshua
Betlyon, John W.
Bidmead, J.
Bivar, A. D. H.
Black, Jeremy A.
Boardman, John
Boda, Mark J.
Bodi, Daniel

Bongenaar, A.

Bottéro, J.

Boucharlat, Remy

Boyce, Mary

Pierre Briant

Brosius, Maria

Browne, Edward Granville

Calmeyer, P.

Cameron, G. G.

Carter, C. E.

Castle, W. E.

Chalmers, C.

Choksy, Jamsheed K.

Cohen, Andrew C.

Crowell, Bradley L.

Curtis, John

Curtis, Vesta Sarkhosh

Dalley, Stephanie

Dandamaev, M. A.

Davies, Malcolm

Davies, W. D.

de Miroschedji, Pierre

De Souza, Philip

Dever, William

Dick, Michael B.

Dillery, John

Dougherty, Raymond P.

Draycott, Catherine M.

Drews, Robert

Dubberstein, Waldo H.

Dusinberre, Elspeth R. M.

Dvornik, Francis

Eilers, W.

Elgood, C.

Errington, Elizabeth
Eshel, Esther
Eskenazi, Tamara Cohn
Farazmand, Ali
Farrokh, Kaveh
Finkel, Irving L.
Flattery, David Stophlet
Fleming, D. E.
Foltz, Richard
Forsyth, Neil
Foster, Benjamin R.
Foster, Karen Polinger
Fried, Lisbeth S.
Frye, Richard N.
Fuchs, Esther
Gabrielli, Marcel
Galil, Gershon
Garrison, Mark B.
George, A. R.
Gese, Hartmut
Gopnik, Hilary
Goulder, M.
Grabbe, Lester L.
Gray, Louis H.
Grayson, Albert Kirk
Green, Anthony
Green, Jack
Griffiths, A.
Guliaev, Valeri I.
Gurney, O. R.
Hallo, William W.
Handley, Morrison
Harmatta, J.
Harris, Rivka

Harrison, Thomas
Harvey, D.
Head, Duncan
Hedrick, Larry
Henkelman, Wouter
Hirsch, Steven W.
Hoglund, Kenneth G.
Holtz, Shalom E.
Horsley, Richard A.
Houston, Mary G.
Huff, Dietrich
Ibrāmī, Hūshang
Ivantchik, Askold I.
Jackson, A. V. Williams
Jacobs, Bruno
Japhet, Sara
Jawad, Laith A.
Jennings, Justin
Joannes, F.
Jong, Albert de
Jordana, Xavier
Jursa, M.
Kaptan, D.
Katz, Steven T.
Katzenstein, H. Jacob
Kawami, Trudy S.
Kessler, K.
Kessler, John
Killick, R. G.
Kleber, Kristin
Knapton, Peter
Knoppers, Gary N
Knowles, Melody D.
Kratz, Reinhard

Kriwaczek, Paul
Kuhrt, Amélie
Lacocque, André
Lambert, W. G.
Landes, David S.
Lang, Mabel L.
Langdon, S.
Lavī, Ḥabīb
Leach, E. R.
Leiden, W. H. C.
Leloux, Kevin
Lemaire, André
Lerner, G.
Lincoln, Bruce
Linssen, M. J. H.
Lipiński, Edward
Littman, Robert J.
Liverani, Mario
Lloyd, Alan B.
Lloyd, Seton
Lucas, C. J.
Luckenbill, Daniel David
Lukonin, Vladimir G.
MacGinnis, John
Machinist, Peter
Malandra, William W.
Malbran-Labat, F.
Marzhan, Joachim
Master, Daniel M.
Matsushima, E.
Mattila, R.
McGovern, Patrick E.
Meier, S. A.
Middlemas, Jill

Miller, M. C.
Mills, Lawrence Heyworth
Mierhoop,
Miroschedji, P.
Moorey, P. R. S.
Muscarella, O. W.
Mukherjee, Siddhartha
Nashef, Khaled
Nefiodkin, Alexander K.
Nejad, Hadi
Nesbitt, M.
Neumann, C.
Neusner, Jacob
Newman, Judith H.
Nodet, Etienne
Noll, K. L.
Novotny, Jamie
Nylan, M.
Nylander, Carl
Ogden, Graham S.
Olson, J. S.
Oppenheim, A. L.
Page, Hugh R., Jr
Pallis, Svend Aage
Parpola, Simo
Parker, Richard A.
Panaino, Antonio
Paspalas, Stavros A.
Pearce, Laurie E.
Pedersen, O.
Pelikan, Jaroslav
Peradotto, John
Pettinato, Giovanni
Pham, Xuan Huong Thi

Pinches, T. G.
Poebel, A.
Polosmak, Natalya
Pongratz-Leisten, B.
Potts, Daniel T.
Powell, Marvin A.
Pritchard, James B.
Oeming, Manfred
Rainey, A. F.
Reiner, Erica
Rolle, Renate
Röllig, W.
Rollinger, Robert
Root, Margaret Cool
Roth, Martha T.
Sack, Ronald H.
Salonen, A.
Sancisi-Weerdenburg, Heleen
Sanders-Goebel, P.
Sandison, AT
Sarraf, M. R.
Sarshar, Houman
Sasson, J. M.
Schaudig, Hanspeter
Schauensee, D.E.
Schmid, H.
Schmidt, H. P.
Schwartz, Martin
Schwemer, Daniel
Scurlock, Joann
Seymour, M. J.
Shahgolzari, SM
Shea, William H.
Shiff, L. B.

Simpson, St John

Skjærvø, P. O.

Soudavar, A.

Stadter, P. A.

Stausberg, Michael

Stein, Gil J.

Stevens, Marty E.

Stol, Martin

Stolper, Matthew W.

Stott, Katherine

Stronach, David B.

Sumner, William M.

Suter, David W.

Tavernier, J.

Thomas, D. R. A.

Thureau-Dangin, F.

Trotter, James M.

Tuplin, Christopher

Ulansey, David

Ungnad, A.

Vallat, F.

Van de Mieroop, Marc

Van Driel, G.

Vargyas, P.

Vaughn, Andrew G.

Veen, J. E. van der

Vogelsang, W. J.

Waerzeggers, C.

Waters, Matthew W.

Watts, James W.

Weiershauser, Frauke

Weinfeld, M.

Weisberg, David B.

Weiss, L.

Weitzman, Steven
Widengren, G.
Wiesehöfer, J.
Wiggermann, F. A. M.
Williamson, H. G. M.
Winter, Irene J.
Wiseman, D. J.
Wunsch, C.
Yamauchi, E.
Yavari, A.
Younger, K. Lawson
Zaccagnini, Carlo
Zadok, Ran
Zawadzki, S.
Zevit, Z.
Zimansky, Paul E.
Zimmern, H.

AUTHOR'S NOTE

Siddhartha Mukherjee begins his Pulitzer-prize-winning *Emperor of All Maladies: A Biography of Cancer* with Atossa. He suggests that Cyrus's daughter is the first person recorded as having had a mastectomy (and survived). When I read this, I was already deep into my research on Cyrus and intrigued by the women in his life. This added to the intrigue. There's debate about the precise nature of the ailment that Herodotus writes so alarmed the young wife of Darius that she approached the king's esteemed physician, a captive Greek, to help her. I don't know whether or not Cassandane died from breast cancer. But I imagine (as you've seen in this book) that Atossa had witnessed both death from such a condition and the survival of women with amputated breasts. (The crime and its punishment that opens this book is historical.)

I began this project over fifteen years ago, putting it down and picking it back up over and over again. The degree of research that I've poured into it exceeds even the intensity of research and writing that I dedicated to my doctoral dissertation or even working toward the whole daggone Ph.D. And still, these four volumes don't represent all the stories the research has generated for me. One reflects the roles that Amytis of Media and Cyrus's restless nature played at an inflection point in the development of several of the world's enduring religions. Siddartha Gautama (the Buddha) is barely a rumor here. Another lacuna is Atossa's story, namely the breast pathology – cancer or mastitis – that might have, depending on how you interpret the ancient sources, launched the Greco-Persian wars. (Related, the final era of Cyrus's rule and the drama of his succession from Cambyses II, the intrigue of Bardiya, and the question of Darius's own rise to power). Maybe one day I'll return to all that. But these books each stand on their own with plenty of drama sufficient to each. And the person – Cyrus the Great – who first beckoned me into the kaleidoscope of characters and drama, continues to prove both cipher and source of the stories herein.

Without Cyrus, we may never have had a Bible. And without Amytis, we may never have had such a Cyrus. But few people have heard of Cyrus much less of Amytis. And the role of Babylon in biblical development remains largely the purview of scholars and academics. I excuse our collective ignorance in part because the relevant facts are few, hard to come by, and riddled with uncertainties. That doesn't mean, however, that they can't make for a good story.

This book – and the others in what has become a multi-volume (and could be many more) saga – happened because I started making things up. I had intended to write a nonfiction tome about a momentous period in human history (the transition from Babylonian to Persian rule) and the figure who stands at its center (Cyrus II, a.k.a. Cyrus the Great). But the more I learned, the more intriguing the women became. And the more I learned, the more I was forced to accept what all the experts say: we know very little... concretely, that is. But oh, so much was possible.

I threw myself into the research. At some point, what I was learning reached a critical mass and slipped its academic bonds. Turns out, the research had been seducing my imagination all along. Finally, I had to face it: they'd eloped. I found myself filling in the long blanks between certainties with imagining what might have been. Ancient characters had become real people. Events and places began to take the shape of a novel. Also, I have a terrible memory. In all that research, I was finding associations and connections that no one seemed to have made before, and I didn't want to forget them. My best vehicle for keeping track was story.

I agonized. My agent at the time pointed out the cold truth. We simply could not sell a book of nonfiction with, er, fictional elements no matter how extensive the disclaimers. So, I ordered the facts back into their house, and tried to send my imagination packing. Alas, the two would not be parted. Finally, a friend of mine who had herself recently made a shift from nonfiction to historical fiction confronted me. "Why are clinging to nonfiction?!" she said. "Accept it. It's a novel."

Once I did, the project became pure delight... and a full-blown series with Amytis, my tree-hugging bastard princess, their through-line. That said, this particular book stands (or falls) on its own.

How much of the book is true? I understand the question, I do. And my best short answer is: all of it and none of it. This is a work of fiction. I made it up. That said, it is entirely based on huge amounts of hard-core research undertaken over the many years that this particular project has demanded and over decades before that as a student of the history and literature of the ancient Near East (what today we call the Middle East), earning a Ph.D. on the topic and a tenured appointment as a professor of it.

The question deserves a longer answer. First, a warning: the information here is best read *after* the novel itself for a couple of reasons. Most obviously, it will spoil the suspense. Equally serious, your brain might break. There are so many odd names and potentially unfamiliar references below that without having a story to hang them on... well, consider yourself warned.

Second, a quick note about sources. This story takes place 2500 years ago. Many relevant records, such as they ever were, are long gone. But many remain. Sources for modern researchers are wildly diverse, some primary and many derivative. They range from ancient histories to modern archaeological excavation reports, from the list of wages due to workers in a Babylonian temple to the Bible's Psalm 137, from an ancient world map drawn on clay (now housed in the British Museum) to a palace gate in stunningly beautiful tile (now housed in Berlin).

No one knows it all. Much about the period and its people is still in question. Hints and rumors abound. Ancient histories followed different rules than what we might wish. For such as Herodotus, one of our most important sources, reporting absolute fact was not always as important as telling a good story. And not all of the sources, ancient and otherwise, agree with each other.

Take Cyrus himself. Of Cyrus's birth and even lineage, we cannot be sure. We don't know the date of his birth, whether he came from royal or peasant parentage, or even what the name Cyrus means. As to the latter, I follow the logic represented in the novel – that it is Elamite and connotes protection. Concerning his parentage, I follow Herodotus and others in naming Mandane as his mother and Cambyses I as his father. Both Cambyses I and Cyrus II called themselves kings by the Elamite title "king of Anshan" not "of Persia." I understand Anshan to have been a city (the modern archaeological site of Tel el-Malyan) within what was a relatively small and loosely confederated country of Parsa, itself arguably within the greater control of Media (and so of Astyages). In this fiction series, I follow Herodotus's dramatic and gruesome tale of Cyrus's birth and rise. (Indeed much – including those episodes involving Croesus and the battle at the Halys River – follows Herodotus's *The Histories*, which incidentally is a ripping-good read.) Cyrus has a reputation for taking Babylon without any resistance, that the Babylonians welcomed him with open arms. Yes, and no. It seems there *was* bloodshed; but maybe Cyrus wasn't directly complicit in it. Rather, as per this telling, Cyrus entered Babylon in "a carefully orchestrated, ceremonial welcome by the capital... engineered by his general" (Amélie Kuhrt, "Nabonidus and the Babylonian Priesthood," in *Nabonidus, King of Babylonia*, 1990 Cornell, 135).

And consider Amytis, one of this book's primary characters. That she is historical we can agree. But exactly who she was, not so much. Even her lineage is in question. Was she the daughter of Cyaxares or of Astyages? The (very few) records differ, and her mother is consistently nameless. That she is remembered as marrying Nebuchadnezzar II to satisfy the treaty established by Cyaxares and (Nebuchadnezzar's father) Nabopolassar allows me (almost) to have it both ways: I represent her as the daughter of Astyages, married to Nebuchadnezzar only because Cyaxares did not have any daughters. (I don't know if the historical Cyaxares did or didn't have daughters.) There is no record of Amytis being a bastard.

As daughter of Astyages, Amytis would have been sister to Mandane, Cyrus's mother. Herodotus tells the story hinted at here about Astyages's paranoia leading him first to get Mandane married off to Cambyses of Parsa and then of attempting to kill Mandane's infant son (the newborn Cyrus). I made up Mandane's subsequent suicide.

Herodotus tells that Nebuchadnezzar built the Hanging Gardens of Babylon for Amytis, homesick for the forested mountains of her beloved home, Media. There is reason to believe that such Hanging Gardens never existed, or if they did that they refer to gardens far north of Babylon built by an earlier monarch. But the legend was enough for me, and enough to imagine a young woman committed to protecting (by virtue of Nebuchadnezzar's honoring the historical treaty) her native land from Babylonian development.

Ancient Media (in modern Iran) was indeed a wild, biodiverse, naturally rich and beautiful place, even more so than I could describe in the novel. And ancient Babylonia (in modern Iraq), especially under Nebuchadnezzar had a reputation even greater than I show for destroying places in the course of conquest and building like mad. It is hardly a stretch to imagine the clash between what we now call environmental preservation and "development."

Another great conflict in the novel, Babylonian discomfort with a foreign presence, is likewise timeless and human (anti-immigration, xenophobia...). We know that Nebuchadnezzar's policy in war was to take from conquered nations the best and brightest, to bring them back to Babylonia and put their smarts and skills to work. Babylonian exiles such as those from the defeated nation of Judah were given positions throughout the empire, including the palace, as important tradespeople and intellectuals. Nebuchadnezzar's court was cosmopolitan, and not all Babylonians were happy about that. Some native Babylonians, especially of the higher classes and with a stake in the nation's face and future would have had issues with such integration. What's more, the descendants of many of those "exiles" came to identify more as Babylonian than with their predecessors' nations of origin. That a foreign woman might bear the crown prince, as in this story, may have been intolerable for some people.

We don't know for certain that Amytis was the mother of the historical Amel-Marduk (my Bushu). But among other things (timing, e.g.), it appears that after the historical Amel-Marduk succeeded his father, Nebuchadnezzar, to the throne of Babylon, there was a wave of Median immigrants. Many Babylonians didn't like it. Some of this bears on (and could spoil) the sequel's drama and suspense; relevant here is evidence that Amel-Marduk was sympathetic to these Medians, which supports the possibility that he was (half) Median himself.

I follow the scholar Irving Finkel in believing that a document recovered from this time, "The Lament of Nabu-shuma-ukin," is Amel-Marduk's. (Some of that historical text is in this novel.) Its composer, a finely trained poet, calls himself the son of Nebuchadnezzar and says he was wrongfully imprisoned. He promises to devote himself to the god Marduk, if the god would only secure his release. Hence, the name-change to Amel-Marduk, "servant of Marduk." In ancient Hebrew (transliterated), Amel-Marduk is Evil-Merodach and shows up in the Bible as the Babylonian king who released the Jewish king from prison and accorded him an honorable place "at the king's table." (Because of how easily English-speaking readers might confuse the English "evil" with the Hebrew "Evil," the transliteration [not to be confused with translation] of a name meaning "servant of," I chose to spell it differently [erroneously] as Evel.) This Evil-Merodach, nee Nabu-shuma-ukin, may well have met the Jewish king in prison.

Jewish legend also lands Amel-Marduk in prison (and furious with Nebuchadnezzar ever after). We do not know why the prince was imprisoned, but the most likely reason would be an attempt to usurp the throne. Sleeping with the king's women would have demonstrated such an effort. I made up the love story that supports it.

I also made up the love story between Amytis and Khai. But I didn't make up Khai and admit that I fell a little in love with the historical man myself. As I note in the character list, Khai is based on a Babylonian by the name of Nabu-ahhe-iddin, from the family Egibi. Nebuchadnezzar's near manic building – walls, temples, palace, quays – surely created a lot of work and opportunity. Babylonian society was stratified, with "citizens" (from among which politically powerful elders came) at the top. But for industrious, intelligent, and entrepreneurial people, advancement was possible.

The historical Nabu-ahhe-iddin (my Khai) was such a person.

We have a remarkably large repository of records from his businesses spanning generations and including some family information. From humble beginnings with a small family farm, this man developed a full-blown corporation with holdings in transportation, real estate (including rentals), banking, and of course farming. We know that he served for a time as a palace scribe and may well have had close dealings with Amytis during the course of a long and dynamic career.

The family of Adad-guppi, Nabonidus, and Belshazzar is historical. I found the historical Adad-guppi to be so intriguing and her name not too difficult that I decided not to call her anything else. No one but a handful of scholars knows about Adad-guppi, so I wanted to give her a chance out in the wider world. Adad-guppi is sometimes called a priestess. Indeed the historical record of her devotion to the moon god of her native place, Harran, is striking. Also, we know that she secured and maintained an important position in the Babylonian court lasting through several kings. Adad-guppi had been taken by the Babylonians along with her son, Nabonidus, from Harran, when the Babylonians and Medes together brought the Assyrian empire to its knees. It does seem to be the case that Adad-guppi lived, according to an inscription that we still have, in good health until the ripe old age of 104 years old.

Incidentally, those familiar with the biblical narratives might recognize the place name of Harran and maybe even link it with Ur. A whole lot of the greater biblical story begins in those sites. Abraham (then Abram) departs from Ur with his family, including father Terah, wife Sarah, and nephew Lot and settles in Harran, where Abraham is said to have heard God's call to "Go... to the land that I will show you." Ur and Harran were the two cities of the moon god. I'm not sure what to make of these connections, but there's yet another story in there somewhere. Oh, and Abraham's leaving Ur and then Harran appears in the

Bible right after the Tower of Babel story. (Babel/Babylon – not a coincidence. See below.)

When I first began this project, I was ill-inclined toward Nabonidus, having accepted the ancient propaganda against him. With a whole lot more learning under my cap, Nabonidus has become admirable and even dear to me. Ultimately, his story (only a tiny bit of which appears here) strikes me as a classic tragedy. Historically, he was the king of Babylonia whom Cyrus defeated. But I'm getting ahead of myself. The historical Nabonidus relevant for this book was indeed a person of Nebuchadnezzar's court and the father of Belshazzar.

The biblical book of Daniel, set during the period of the Babylonian exile but dating from centuries later, occasionally conflates or switches Nebuchadnezzar and Nabonidus. (Notice "switches" not "confuses," because it could have been intentional.) The Bible is a great resource for information about the ancient world, including the history of the ancient Near East. But it does not report things exactly as they happened, and we mistreat its narratives when we expect them to report facts like modern journalists should do. This does not make the Bible "wrong," but rather our reading of it. And we miss what may be of most interest and value in the biblical texts by requiring them to conform to our expectations. Stepping off my soapbox... The biblical book of Daniel portrays Nebuchadnezzar as enduring a period of madness from which God heals him. That's too delicious to ignore.

Many scholars, myself included, believe that the decade that *Nabonidus* (Babylonia's king at the time) spent apart from Babylon lies behind that story, at least in part. I nod to the fact that the Bible chooses to tell the crazy-guy story as Nebuchadnezzar's madness. There certainly was plenty about Nebuchadnezzar that could justify such a representation in the eyes of the people responsible for Daniel-the-Book's final form.

That Belshazzar is sometimes wrongly called Nebuchadnezzar's son makes more sense if they were otherwise related. I make the historical Nitocris the mother of Belshazzar (and so Belshazzar is grandson of Nebuchadnezzar). This is not historical but not impossible, either. Contrary to popular (Bible-based) belief, Belshazzar was never the king of Babylonia. He did however, perform kingly duties (and I suspect would have been delighted to be confused as king for real) when his father Nabonidus, then king of Babylonia, was absent from Babylon for those ten years mentioned above.

The conflict that I portray between father and son, king and prince – Nabonidus and Belshazzar – seems highly likely and for the kinds of reasons I dramatize in these stories. That conflict, simmering through all four novels, comes to a head in the moment I narrate here. After all, it's hard to imagine that it's mere coincidence that the historical date of Cyrus's army so successfully marching against Babylon is the same as the date when King Nabonidus's controversial religious reform would have been most keenly felt. And then there's the juicy story of Belshazzar's feast, narrated in the biblical book of Daniel.

The Jews. Next to Amytis, my favorite part of this whole story. Some background in super-brief: The nation of Israel, which gained international attention during Solomon's reign in the tenth century B.C.E. when the temple in Jerusalem was built, fractured into two after Solomon's death. The northern kingdom, confusingly also called Israel, was defeated by the Assyrians toward the end of the eighth century B.C.E. Many of those Israelites were removed to places within the Median empire, hence my reference to Jews in the capital, Ecbatana.

Judah, the former Israel's southern kingdom, with its capital of Jerusalem endured. But it was subject to the vicissitudes of politics to the east. Ultimately Babylonia's rise made Judah a vassal state. In 597 B.C.E., Nebuchadnezzar took issue with Judah's Egyptian alliance, laid siege to Jerusalem, and removed Judah's king of only three months, Jehoiachin/Coniah (the guy in this novel) and some of Jerusalem's best and brightest, including the prophet Ezekiel, and took them to Babylon. Ten years later (587 B.C.E.), Judah's effort to rebel was met with devastating punishment. Nebuchadnezzar's Babylonian troops, including the historical [Neriglissar/Igliss] utterly defeated the nation, destroyed the Jerusalem temple, brutalized its king, and took another wave of people to Babylon. It is possible that the "suffering servant" of Isa 52:13-53:12 was composed with Jehoiachin/Coniah in mind.

I think that the single most important event in the Bible's development is the Babylonian exile. It's important in two ways: for how it affected the theology and literature already circulating, and because it served as the catalyst to assemble and collect as well as compose what would become biblical texts. There was no "Bible" before this time. For all intents and purposes, there was no Judaism, either. That is, the religion recognizable to us today as Judaism largely grew out of the land-less, temple-less condition of exile. It was a painful and a fruitful time.

Among many biblical texts, some of which I cite in the novel, the biblical story of the Tower of Babel was probably written or informed by Jews living in Babylon who had occasion to observe the many and grand building projects undertaken by Nebuchadnezzar. One of those projects was a huge and seemingly endless renovation of the temple of Marduk in the center of the city. People from many different nations, no doubt speaking diverse languages, worked in Nebuchadnezzar's Babylon. (Hence the biblical story's "confusion of tongues" and what Jews saw as an arrogant effort to reach the heavens.) Nebuchadnezzar's policy concerning conquered peoples was to take advantage of their skills and learning, putting such to use wherever they served him best.

It cannot be understated – the enduring effect of efforts to make sense of the chaos and destruction of Babylonian control and the nature of God and God's relationship to people that the exile generated among the intelligent, devout, and literate Jews taken into Babylon. Those efforts and the diversity of their answers permeate the Hebrew Bible and shaped a multi-faceted theology that many centuries later could (not necessarily but by interpretation) identify a Jew, Jesus, as the redeeming incarnation of a fiercely loyal and loving God.

I have tried to show a little of that here. Judean exiles, whom I call simply (and not quite accurately) Jews, permeated Babylonian society. We know of Bariki-ili, the slave desperate for freedom; and we know that Ezekiel exercised a liberty to preach and gather with Jewish elders in Babylonian exile. We know that a community of Jews lived and worked at literary pursuits in a district of the town of Nippur; and we know that many of the exiles from Judah and their descendants ultimately adopted and integrated into Babylonian society.

The Babylonian pantheon was multi-faceted, with gods and goddesses gathering in Babylon once a year from their respective cities in the biggest annual festival, the Akitu. I chose to use the archaic Sumerian name "Nanna-Suen" for the moon god of Harran/Ur rather than the Akkadian "Sin" lest English readers misunderstand the name as some modern moral judgment. The gods and goddesses so named in the novel and many more besides were part of a complex pantheon. The massage ritual is real, as is the practice of reading divine messages in animal organs. The prayers I cite are based on extant documents of the time, and the biblical texts (not yet biblical of course) may have circulated or been composed under circumstances such as I depict.

Back to Amytis for a sec, specifically my observation that without her, we might never have had a Bible. My reason for saying so lies not least in the facts (if we're to follow the ancient sources) that she was Median (not Babylonian), married to Nebuchadnezzar, the mother of the next king of Babylonia, and was married to Cyrus when he conquered Babylonia. That is, not only did she know the city of Babylon inside and out as well as its power structure and even players, she also knew from firsthand observation (if not experience) the longing many of the people of foreign origins such as the Judahites (Jews) had for their native land and ways. She might well have encouraged the repatriation of exiles and the revitalization of religious traditions.

In earlier versions of these novels, I included footnotes citing sources, adding more information, and sometimes recording my own thinking about what I was learning. I did it mainly to help myself remember what led me to make the narrative decisions I'd made – from details about food and clothing and particular items such as the seal that Cyrus inherits (extant, discovered with the Persepolis Fortification Tablets), the Elamite bow, and intricate equestrian paraphernalia, to Nabonidus's religiosity and Cyrus's apparent devotion to Cassandane's Pasargad. I've had illusions of making those footnotes available to readers. But they're terribly unwieldy (in the hundreds), and the research keeps coming. Honestly, I've hesitated publishing these stories at all in part because of I've despaired at not being able to cite every source and explain every decision (and do anything else with my life). Ugh. But onward.

So, apart from the few direct citations that I listed above and the names of sources that I list below, I return simply to what drove me in the first place: to create a story-vehicle to keep track of a possible history, a drama of love and place and religion and ambition. And I admit to the same truth, which is both exhilarating and exasperating: there's always more to the story.

ACKNOWLEDGMENTS

I'm guessing that any project that spans more than a decade from inception to completion represents the support, goodwill, and contributions of all kinds from more people than a book's "Acknowledgments" can cover, no matter its author's efforts to be exhaustive. That's certainly true here. My apologies to those I've missed. Thank you.

And thank you, each and every named below. I've had illusions of providing detail to describe the nature of the contributions each person or group (libraries! my students! professional organizations!). But just as I bailed on providing an exhaustive list of specific sources and a more exhaustive Author's Note, finally I provide only the barest list here. Its notice – meager – is inverse to my gratitude – great. Thank you.

Finally, a special thanks to my dad, Richard Swenson, and my (late) mom, L. Cecile Swenson whose support of my work has been so unqualified that I might almost take it for granted. I don't. And to my husband, Craig L. Slingluff, Jr., a huge thanks for being so ceaseless a cheerleader of this project. I'm not sure I ever would have sent these books out into the world without your unflagging enthusiasm for the saga and the needling to publish it, such as only a person sharing one's life, day in and day out, can do.

Thank you sincerely also to the following, in order simply by alphabet: Richard Abate, Khooshe Aiken, Lindsay Allen, Hanadi Al-Samman, Gigi Amateau, American Academy of Religion, American Schools of Oriental Research, Willis Barnstone, Bennington Book Club, Biographers International Organization,

Bodleian Libraries of Oxford University, Christiana Brenin, Laura Browder, Ellen Brown, McKenna Brown, Theo Calderara, Bethany Carlson, Jamsheed Choksy, Susann Cokal, Meredith Cole, Jonathan Coleman, Michael Cordell, Rob Crawford, the cadre of Cville Women Writers, Stephanie Dalley, Cliff Edwards, Robin Farmer, Louise Finger, Greg Fontana, Jeannie Fontana, Donna Freitas, Shirley French, Kathleen Gacek, Brad Graff, Martien Halvorson-Taylor, Kate Hamilton, Sandy Hausman, Stacy Hawkins, Paul Hilding, Stephani Hilding, Historical Novel Society, Doug Hoffman, Denise Honeycutt, Kate Hunter, Molly Ill, James River Writers, Eric Jarrard, Gretchen Kainz, Andrew King, Dean King, Chris Park, Eva-Marie King, Amelie Kuhrt, John Kutsko, (late) "Boots" Mead, Meg Medina, Manny Mendez, Alex Nagel, Jen Pearson, Stephanie Pearson, The Porches (Trudy Hale), Debby Prum, Ginny Pye, Emilie Raymond, Dianna Rostad, Charles Shields, Guadalupe Shields, Society of Biblical Literature, Maya Smart, Patty Smith, Jack Spiro, Devon Sproule, Beth Stefanik, Matthew Stolper, Jon Swenson Tellekson, Linnea Swenson Tellekson, Deb Swenson, Nigel Tallis, Sandra Treadway, University of Virginia library, Rachel Unkefer, Virginia Commonwealth University library, Virginia (Foundation for the) Humanities, Claire Wachtel, Pat Watkins, Jon Waybright, Anne Westrick, Vera Wilde, Mark Wood, Women's International Study Center, Writer House, and Irene Ziegler.

MAP

This is a map of the Median Empire, Egypt, Lydian Empire and Neo-Babylonian Empire in the 6th century BC (1024 px; there are other sizes available).

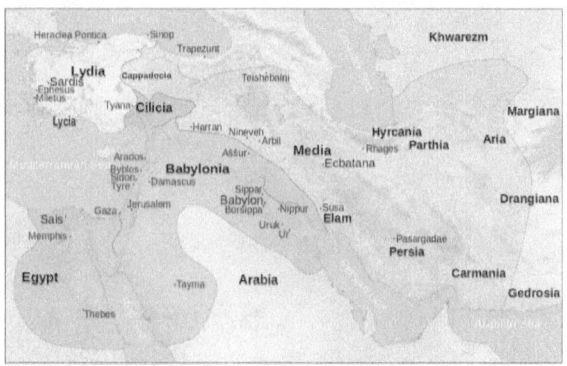

Date: 30 April 2013.
Source: File:Median Empire-hu.svg
ETOPO1 topographic data from NGDC (http://www.ngdc. noaa.gov/mgg/global/global.html).
Author: Original: User:Szajci; English: User:WillemBK

ABOUT THE AUTHOR

Kristin Swenson, Ph.D. writes across genres. Tenured professor of religious studies with speciality in the history and literature of ancient Israel (Hebrew Bible), she is passionate about the natural world and loves a good story. All the better if a story connects the disparate threads of women and lesser known persons with what history we have. In addition to her writing, Swenson has developed an eco-grief practice to help people continue to advocate for the wild with equanimity and joy. She also maintains a website celebrating (and advising for) the eco-friendly kitchen. Swenson lives and works in Charlottesville, Virginia and Duluth, Minnesota.

ALSO BY KRISTIN SWENSON

FICTION

In the Kitchen with Gracie May (PGB)

Let It Out at the Seams (PGB)

Genie of Pasargad (a Babylon/Persia novel; PGB)

Beat the Kettledrum (a Babylon/Persia novel; PGB)

A Falcon Takes Flight (a Babylon/Persia novel; PGB)

Howl of the Golden Jackal (a Babylon/Persia novel; PGB)

NONFICTION

A Most Peculiar Book: The Inherent Strangeness of the Bible (Oxford University)

God of Earth: Discovering a Radically Ecological Christianity (Westminster John Knox)

Bible Babel: Making Sense of the Most Talked About Book of All Time (Harper)

Living through Pain: Psalms and the Search for Wholeness (Baylor University)

What is Religious Studies?: A Journey of Inquiry (with Esther R. Nelson, Kendall Hunt)

POETRY

Haiku 365 at www.kristinswenson.com